BEFORE THE FALL

Also by Rachel Terry

<u>The Guardians Duology</u>

Lightbringer

Flameseeker

<u>Atlas Sea</u>

The Phoenix and the Crown

A Tale of Two Sisters

<u>Empire of Engines</u>

Beyond the Throne

Before the Fall

BEFORE
THE
FALL

RACHEL TERRY

PHARUS PRESS

ISBN: 978-1-960519-16-0

10 9 8 7 6 5 4 3 2 1

To those who never give in, no matter the odds.

THE AKKADIAN EMPIRE
SOUL STONE MINES
SHEMAR
RIVER CHARNEL
THE BADLANDS

THE CAPITOL

THE WORKHOUSES

VALDERAN
RAINFOREST

ELATH

ANARSHA

PART I:
THE RISE OF AN EMPIRE

I

"Shemar has fallen!"

The shout, so loud in the relative silence, seemed as though it came from just below the window. Chandra startled, the mold in her hands jerking with the sudden movement.

"Saints," she swore, as the delicate candle she'd been trying to extricate cracked.

Molds were never easy to work with in the best of circumstances, and these particular candles were more important than most. The grayish-green bayberries, found on the edge of the forest, produced a wax that not only burned cleanly, but smelled pleasant—sweet, even. So unlike those made of tallow.

The problem, for there always had to be one, was the low yield. She needed an immense amount of berries to produce even a single pound of wax. She couldn't afford for them to break, after everything.

Chandra sighed, staring down at the ruined candle as it tumbled out of the mold. All that hard work for nothing. She'd spent hours earlier that day, venturing out of the city to the edge of the forest, where the berries grew, collecting enough that she could finally attempt to make another batch. She'd boiled them into a wax, then heated them in a melting pot, before pouring the hot wax into her bronze mold. Then she'd had to wait for them to cool.

Perhaps Callum was right and she should just stick to tallow. Given the low yield, the bayberry candles would likely have been prohibitively expensive, out of the reach of many of her customers. But tallow stank so badly, it was a regular occurrence for the neighbors to complain whenever she made a batch. Never mind the fact that it was *her* candles that kept their homes lit when night fell.

She was tired of smelling of animal fat at the end of the day. And if she were honest with herself, she worried that the kingdom might outlaw the process altogether, should the right—or wrong—person complain.

Shaking her head, Chandra set aside the now-empty molds and removed the apron she'd thrown over her clothes to protect them from any hot wax. The voice that had startled her had moved on down the street; she could still hear him, further off now.

A glance out the window revealed that it was quite late. The sunlight was leaching from the sky and she would need to join Callum and their grandmother inside the house for dinner, providing she wasn't already tardy.

She stepped outside, inhaling a deep lungful of fresh air. Tilting her head, she listened to the cry repeated up and down the street, the words clearer now, despite the distance, without any walls to block them.

"Shemar has fallen!"

Chandra felt a chill bolt through her, sharp and instant. In the workshop, she'd heard the loudness of the voice, but the words hadn't registered.

Not like they did now.

Shemar had fallen. The Empire had won.

It hadn't been all that long ago—and yet it seemed like all Chandra could remember—that the kingdom of

Akkadia tired of being a mere kingdom. With aspirations of building an empire, they had launched a campaign to conquer the neighboring kingdoms around them.

Elath had fallen first, likely targeted for its rich mines and abundant fishing industry. Akkadia had then turned its sights on Shemar, who had held out longer than Elath.

But they, too, had fallen, and just like that, Anarsha was the only free kingdom left. *So fast,* Chandra thought. *How could this have happened so fast?*

Some had said the Empire would never succeed, that first Elath and then Shemar—after the first kingdom proved to be a disappointment—would put an end to their machinations. But Akkadia had technology that none of the other kingdoms could claim—not even Anarsha—and they'd proven victorious in the end.

So that's it, then, Chandra mused. Anarsha now found herself the last free kingdom, the only one left standing in the way of a conquered, unified empire.

Maybe they won't come here. Maybe Elath and Shemar would be enough to satisfy Akkadia's greed. But even as the thought crossed her mind, she knew it wasn't true. Anarsha, the furthest kingdom from Akkadia's Capitol, would find herself the Empire's next target.

The final, glittering jewel in an incomplete crown.

Chandra sucked in a breath. The idea of war, once such a far-off concept, now loomed on their doorstep. What would that mean for them? Chandra glanced over her shoulder at the door of her workshop, the failed batch of candles suddenly no longer so important.

She raced for the house, just across the yard, her red hair streaming behind her. It was a small dwelling, originally intended for just her grandparents. But then, of course, children had come along, and now it was just Chandra, her cousin, Callum, and their grandmother. Of all the members of their family that had once lived within those walls, they were the only ones left.

Chandra shoved the heavy wooden door open, bursting into the kitchen, immediately greeted with the smell of stew simmering over the fire. Lamb, she knew.

Callum stood over it, stirring occasionally. Her grandmother sat in a worn chair nearby, her gnarled fingers working at her current knitting project. Chandra frowned; she knew knitting irritated her grandmother's arthritis, but there was no talking her out of it.

"Make sure you save the fat," Chandra said, turning her gaze back to her cousin.

They always saved animal fat in this household. She could use it to make more tallow candles later on.

"I know," Callum said, a hint of exasperation in his tone. "You tell me every time."

Her cousin wasn't prone to forgetfulness, but Chandra took no chances. Any amount of fat they could save, no matter how small, was less she'd have to beg from one of the neighbors or the local butcher.

She stepped fully into the room. "Have you heard the news?"

"You mean the town crier who just passed by?" Callum remarked. He looked up. His green eyes, so similar to her own, were worried. "Do you think it's true?"

Chandra hadn't stopped to consider the veracity of the claim. She'd just assumed that Shemar had indeed fallen.

She shrugged. "Why wouldn't it be?"

Callum's shoulders slumped. "I suppose you're right. What chance did they have, anyway?"

"All right, you lot," their grandmother said, rising to her feet. "If we're going to have such lousy conversation, let's at least eat while we're at it."

Chandra joined Callum at the stove, helping to ladle the stew into three bowls while he withdrew a freshly baked loaf from the stove. She breathed in the warm scent of it greedily. She might have had the gift of carrying on the candle-making business, but Callum was the cook of the family.

"It smells delicious. As always."

He made a face. "I couldn't find any parsley, but it'll have to do."

She swatted him on the arm. "I'm sure it's fine."

Never comfortable with praise, her cousin always seemed to err on the negative side, at least when it came to his own accomplishments.

The three of them gathered around the table, Chandra waiting impatiently while their grandmother prayed to the saints. It always made Chandra slightly uncomfortable. She wasn't certain whether she believed they'd ever been real or not. Certainly, there hadn't been any saints in a long, long time.

Or any demons, either.

Near the end of the prayer, their grandmother tacked on a remark about the Empire, asking the saints to watch over Anarsha, bringing Chandra's thoughts back to the news.

Did they need protecting? Just how bad were things likely to get?

She picked up her spoon. A few hours ago, she still lived in a world where the Empire's eye wasn't turned toward Anarsha.

"What does it all mean? What happens now that Shemar has fallen?"

"It means I'll have to go away to war," Callum said.

His tone was light enough, but she could see the shadow that crossed over his face, and she realized how much more heavily the news weighed on her cousin.

War. Her cousin, Callum, going away to war?

It seemed unthinkable. Anarsha had never been to war in her lifetime and she didn't know anyone who had gone off to fight in one.

"Maybe it won't come to that," she said, trying to cheer him up.

"Of course it will," their grandmother said.

Chandra looked up at her in surprise. She'd never been one to sugarcoat things and she knew that lying to Callum would be of no help. Better to face things as they were.

But still…

"What?" her grandmother added, seeing her expression. "Do you think the Empire will stop now? Do you think it will be somehow sated?" She shook her head. "No, war is coming, whether we like it or not. We can only hope that we'll be prepared."

"We will be," Callum said firmly.

Chandra swallowed hard, the spoonful of stew going down with some resistance, as though it had congealed. None of the other kingdoms had been prepared, at least not enough to win. But then, Anarsha was different. She had always been different. And they had a weapon not even the Empire possessed.

She summoned up a watery smile, about to compliment Callum again on the stew, if only to change the subject, when he beat her to it.

"So, how did the latest batch of candles turn out?"

She sighed. Earlier, she'd dreaded being asked about it, certain her frustration would bleed through and she'd take it out on the two of them, never mind that she didn't mean to. She never did. But now, she was relieved to talk about something as mundane as a failed batch of candles.

It was part of her everyday life, but suddenly, the simple act of candle-making seemed bizarrely out of place amid everything else.

She told them both about the bayberry candles as dinner carried on. There was nothing that evening for dessert, but Chandra didn't mind. Nothing more was said about Shemar or the Akkadian Empire.

But the rest of that night, as she helped clean up the remains of dinner, all the way up until the moment she blew out the last candle and retreated to bed, the Empire lurked in Chandra's mind. As she lay in the darkness, fear for Callum coiled around her chest, cinching tight.

If he went away to war, he could die. He might never come back. That's what happened to people who went away to war, sometimes. They didn't come back. Limited though her knowledge of war might be, Chandra knew that much.

It won't happen. It won't come to that.

And even if war did come, Anarsha wasn't defenseless. There was a reason they hadn't involved themselves in the conflict, even when Elath and Shemar both appealed to them for aid. Anarsha had believed that the Empire would leave them be, so long as they stayed out of Akkadia's way. They were a larger, more powerful opponent than both Elath and Shemar, and they believed that Akkadia wouldn't dare touch them, for more than one reason.

The most convincing of those reasons being the weapon that no other kingdom could claim. If anything could stand up to the Empire's machines of war, it was the army of Anarsha.

For Anarsha had dragons and if Callum were to be conscripted, he wouldn't go into battle alone, but on the back of one of those mighty beasts.

Chandra felt a small thrill go through her at the thought. What must it be like, to ride a dragon? She desperately wished she knew, but she wouldn't like to join the army in order to find out.

But she could use her imagination and she imagined the sensation would make one feel like the most powerful person on earth, if only for a little while.

Some of her excitement faded as her thoughts returned, once more, to her cousin going off to war. He'd be all right, she assured herself, with such powerful allies at his side.

Even so, as she drifted off to sleep, Chandra sent up a silent prayer to the saints. If any of them were listening, she figured it couldn't hurt to ask.

II

Desmond jolted awake as the train rocked beneath him, wincing as his temple tapped against the window. With the return to consciousness came the awareness of pain. His forehead, newly added to the list. His legs ached from so long spent seated. His shoulder was the worst, the pain sharper rather than dull.

He shifted it slightly, felt the muscles pull against the stitches, and promptly stopped. He stared glumly down at the sling. There was nothing wrong with his arm, but the shoulder would be out of commission for some time yet.

For a moment, his dreams had taken him back to Shemar, the city of spires. Saints, had he only just left earlier that morning? It felt like a lifetime ago and yet not nearly long enough.

He could still hear the medic's instructions, echoing in his ears. "Try not to move it and *don't* lift anything. The muscles need time to knit themselves back together." And then, "You're lucky it missed the brachial artery. If it hadn't, you wouldn't be here."

Desmond didn't feel particularly lucky. He hadn't from the moment he'd been forced to climb out of his mech. The damn thing had run out of coal, which it burned in that infernal engine, powered by the steam.

At least Shemar had more mines. That would be good for production. Effective though the war machines were, they were also ravenous, consuming vast amounts of coal and iron ore. Desmond was immensely grateful that the campaign was over. He didn't know how much longer they could have held out—not that he'd ever say such things. Bad for morale.

But with his mech running out of fuel, it had gone from fierce fighting machine to useless husk of metal, and he'd been forced to abandon it. He was never exactly thrilled to climb inside one at the start of battle, but at least they offered some protection to the pilots inside. The life expectancy of a mech pilot wasn't high, but it was a damn sight better than that of an infantryman.

Desmond learned why shortly after climbing free of the inert machine. The arrow had seemed to come from nowhere—he still didn't know who had fired it or from what direction—but it had struck him in the shoulder, the force nearly knocking him to the ground.

One last defiant act, before Shemar was finally theirs. The surrender came shortly after, the fighting done, allowing Desmond to be seen to.

After the medic had patched him up, with barely anything to numb the pain, he'd handed Desmond some paperwork, which he'd taken to his superior officer's tent. The man had taken one look at it, stamped it decisively, and congratulated Desmond on earning himself some medical leave.

No, Desmond didn't feel lucky at all. Perhaps it would have been better if the arrow had nicked his brachial artery. Death, even at the hands of some cowardly Shemaran archer, seemed preferable to what awaited him in the Capitol.

He only hoped the news about the mines would make his father happy. The man already owned an ungodly amount and sought even more. Elath had proven quite the windfall for him. Only time would tell how profitable Shemar would be.

He hadn't written to tell his family that he was coming—there'd been no time—and so there was no one waiting for him at the station when the train pulled in. The trip hadn't taken nearly long enough for his liking, but Desmond was grateful for the trains nonetheless. A recent addition, connecting the kingdoms, though none connected the Capitol with Anarsha. *Yet.*

Briefly, he debated hailing a cab to take him to his home, all the way up in District IX, but then thought better of it. His legs could use the exercise. Besides, a Renault would rather be caught dead than travel by humble cart.

Sighing to himself, he started climbing, mounting the lowered platforms that connected the districts. In theory, they could be raised in case of assault, though that never happened and wasn't likely to, by the way things were going.

He walked briskly through the lower levels, not wanting to dwell, past houses crammed together, walls made of dark stone. Their sloping roofs were dusted with soot, the air heavy with smoke and steam.

It was a long walk, his family's mansion on the highest level there was, barring District X, which housed the palace. It was as high as one could go, socially at least, but Desmond had never felt so low as when he raised his good arm and knocked.

The door was answered by the butler, who was too well-trained to show any emotion at Desmond's sudden appearance. He was ushered inside and informed that his father and mother would be told of his arrival.

The reunion was tedious, but thankfully short-lived. Using the long trip and his injury as an excuse to slip away, Desmond retired to his old room, which he had rarely seen since leaving for the army.

His parents had inquired briefly about the extent of his injury and how he'd come by it. Was it just his imagination or had his father seemed slightly put out when Desmond told them it had been some archer's lucky shot?

Still, the news of the victory cheered them. Shemar had fallen and would join Elath as a vassal state of the Empire, now under their occupation. Mention of the mines didn't hurt any either.

Dinner was a more trying affair. Apparently, his parents had planned a dinner party and invited some of the other District IX families, some of them friends, some of them not. His father would have called them political allies—or at the very least, someone to keep an eye on.

No doubt they hadn't planned on Desmond being present for the event, but it was too late to cancel any plans now. His mother tried to reassure him that he could remain in his room for the evening and rest. No one would be any the wiser that he was there at all.

But Desmond knew that was no guarantee. Gossip spread like wildfire, especially among the upper classes. Someone might have seen him walking home earlier that day, a servant out on errands or a maid cleaning a room who happened to glance out the window and recognize the younger Renault son returned from the front. And with the sling indicating his obvious injury, the news of his sudden return became all the more interesting.

Desmond would have liked nothing more than to catch up on sleep. He felt exhausted down to his marrow. But though his mother had made the offer, he knew she would be disappointed if he took it. Showing weakness or taking the easy way out was not acceptable.

So he declined, put on a brave face, and said he would be present. And he was, dressed in an evening suit, which fit a bit snugly after his time in the army. No one was likely to notice, not with his sling. He would have had a devil of a time getting into the blasted thing, were it not for the assistance of the servants.

He raked a hand through his dark hair, cropped short, and hoped that he looked presentable. He'd just come from the frontlines, after all. Surely no one could expect much of him.

Much as he disliked such events, he was no stranger to them, and he was able to slip into his expected role with little effort. The guests arrived and he greeted them, engaging them in conversation if they approached him. He answered their questions with vague, simple responses, knowing they weren't looking for anything deeper when they asked about the war.

It was disappointing, but that was just the way people were. Shallow, most of them. Always skimming along on the surface, never desiring to sink deeper. It was one of the reasons why Desmond found he didn't much like other people. They were vain. Vapid. And disappointingly unintelligent, with no desire to change anything about themselves.

Oh, well. He didn't have to like them. He just had to entertain them.

But his dispassionate mood vanished the moment the next guest arrived, fashionably late—no doubt on purpose. His elder brother, Alaric Renault, had come directly from the Minister's office, for he still wore his gray silk robes. They were, apparently, appropriate attire for a dinner party.

Something sour curdled in Desmond's stomach at the sight of Alaric. His brother saw him at about the same time and headed his way.

"Brother!" he exclaimed—too loud, Desmond thought, but no one else ever seemed to think so. "Fancy seeing you here. My, my, whatever have you done to yourself?"

"Arrow," Desmond said curtly. "It'll mend."

"I daresay it will. You always were tough and hard to get along with. And the campaign coming to an end will help, I'm sure."

Desmond expected the other guests to swarm Alaric. The work he did for the Minister of Defense was important, after all, keeping the Empire safe from threats within and without, as he was only too keen to remind everyone. No official announcement had been made, but it was almost certain that Alaric would succeed the Minister when he stepped down.

Important, indeed.

Desmond was just a soldier, one of many, a grunt in the army, hardly better than an infantryman. What was that compared to the Minister of Defense's heir apparent?

But to his surprise, more people approached him than Alaric, though he would have been content to let his brother have all the attention. Usually, if people noticed him, it was for the wrong reasons. No one ever noticed the lowly second son.

How many nights had Desmond lain awake, yearning for a younger brother. A third son, who would be even lower, and a bigger disappointment, than him. What would have been expected of such a brother? Probably the cloth. Though Akkadians weren't very religious—not like the Anarshans.

Eager for a firsthand account of the campaign and the state of Shemar, the guests flocked to Desmond's side.

They asked after his injury as well. It seemed to lend him credence, that he'd been there, he had fought, he had *seen*.

Desmond quickly got over his initial surprise, basking in the unexpected attention and praise. Now he didn't bother holding back; he'd give them the deeper details if they asked for it. More than one woman fawned over him, saying how frightening it all sounded and that he must have been so brave.

Desmond knew he ought to be sickened by the artifice of it all, and yet now that he had their attention, he craved it. Out of the corner of his eye, he caught Alaric glaring at him with undisguised envy at being usurped. Desmond felt a rush of satisfaction.

His father soon caught wind of the conversation and joined him, telling the others how proud he was to have a son who was doing such dangerous, important work for the Empire.

That surprised Desmond most of all, though he knew better than to show it. His father was rarely pleased with *anything*, always managing to find some fault. The only thing he parted with less frequently than praise was money.

The pleasure he felt didn't last long, replaced by something hard and cold. As he listened to his father talk, he suspected that it would have been better, in the eyes of his family, if he hadn't been injured. That wasn't a good look.

It would have been better yet, he suspected, if he had died on the battlefield. A hero's death. A martyr. His mood darkened at the thought of how far his family could have run with that. Oh, he could only imagine how smug his family would have been at the outpouring of sympathy from mourners. Their son, a war hero, giving his life valiantly for his country.

Perhaps he was worth more to them dead than alive. After all, they were wealthy enough that they could have bought him an officer's commission. There was no need for him to spend the war crammed into a metal husk that was more like a furnace, risking his life alongside the sons of cobblers and bakers.

But they hadn't purchased him a commission and so he was left to conclude that perhaps they would rather he risk his life, knowing full well that he could die. Perhaps they secretly hoped for that.

Desmond felt a flash of resentment for how little they seemingly valued his life. If Alaric had gone off to war, they would have spared no expense for him, of that Desmond was certain. But Alaric was the heir and he was not.

Returning home, seeing his parents again, always dredged up a complicated mixture of emotions. The one that inevitably rose above all others, amid the disappointment and the anger and the hurt, was yearning. A yearning to be accepted as he was. A desire that always went unfulfilled.

And yet, tonight, he was finally getting a taste of the life he'd always wished for. Was this how Alaric felt? The center of attention, never doubting his place in society or that he belonged, being praised for his accomplishments— even though he hadn't really done anything and Desmond was the one who had gone off to war.

By playing along, being obedient, doing what they wanted, Desmond finally had what he'd longed for— approval. Acceptance. And even favoritism over Alaric, if only for a moment.

Desmond sighed softly to himself. If this was to be the way of things, then so be it. If they wanted him to be a good soldier, a good soldier he would be. He would strive to become the best soldier in all of Akkadia, for them, if that was what it took.

That was how he could bring honor to his family and to his Empire. And he was good at what he did, there was no denying it, even if it wasn't the path he had chosen for himself. He was a mech pilot who was still alive, after all. This was his only major injury and it was more of a nuisance than anything.

He would recover and return to the front. And he would fight again, of that he had no doubt. Perhaps he might even come to enjoy it.

As soon as he was able, Desmond resolved to return to Shemar. None of the barracks or the makeshift tents there would ever compare to the plush four poster bed he knew awaited him here. And things were bound to be difficult and uncomfortable for a while.

The transition period would be rough, as it always was. There would be unrest, those who would not submit to the Empire's rule. But even knowing that, he wanted to go back, more than he wanted to stay.

It wasn't the path he would have chosen, but that life had become his world. He belonged there, in a way he did not here, amid all these richly dressed wolves, circling, teeth behind their smiles, waiting to pounce.

Desmond smiled and carried on conversation as though nothing were amiss. As though there wasn't a storm of turmoil within him. Pretending was another thing he was good at.

He answered the question that everyone seemed to want to know. Alaric, being so close to the Minister of Defense, would be better placed to know, but they chose to ask him instead, and Desmond allowed himself a small smirk at that.

Now that Shemar had fallen, did he think the Empire would turn its attention to the kingdom to the south?

Anarsha.

Oh, yes, Desmond assured them. Anarsha would be the next target and it would fall, as surely as Shemar and Elath. They seemed pleased by that answer, pleased to be on the winning side of the war. Pleased, no doubt, by the swaths of land they would acquire, and the natural resources like the various mines Desmond's father had snatched up.

Such was the way of war, Desmond reflected as someone pressed a wine glass into his good hand. His father had dipped into his cellars, bringing out some of his best vintage to toast to Akkadia's victory.

All around him, glasses were raised, smiles were bright. A feeling of inevitability hung in the air, the Empire's continued victory nearly a foregone conclusion.

Desmond knocked his drink back. To the victor go the spoils.

Anarsha would be next. It was ready to fall. And Desmond would help bring it about.

III

"Is there any improvement?"

Roman listened to his father's voice, muffled behind the room divider, as he finished shrugging on his tunic. The healer had made their examination and left to give their report, giving him a brief moment of privacy.

As he did up the many buttons of his tunic, only half listening to the conversation, his eyes traced the gilded adornments that branched up the walls and over the ceiling. Soft, muted sunlight filtered through the tall, thin window to his left. The bed beneath him was low to the floor, making it all the easier to climb up into. An ornate chandelier hung in the center of the room, visible over the top of the room divider, its candles currently unlit.

None of that could distract from the reason they were all gathered there. Roman already knew what his father did not—that such report would be the same as it always was. Or perhaps his father did know and simply refused to admit it. Roman wasn't sure which was worse.

"There's no change, my lord," the healer murmured, his voice regretful.

Roman pitied him. The prince had lost count of how many healers his father had brought before him, putting

Anarsha's medical skills to the test. It must be a daunting prospect, no matter how skilled or confident the physician, to be brought to the palace and instructed to try and heal the prince when no one, not even Roman himself, knew what was wrong.

He didn't blame the healers, of course. They had done every imaginable test and were no closer to an answer. They examined his skin for blemishes, measured his pulse, felt for his temperature, peered into his eyes and down his throat. They even took some of his blood, for all the good any of it did.

Roman remained thin, weak, his form wasting away no matter how voracious his appetite might be. He knew, as they all did, that he would eventually wither away to nothing entirely if something wasn't done. But what? No amount of herbal remedies or suggestions made his body any stronger. Some of them had even made things worse.

Roman didn't hear whatever else might have passed between his father and the healer, but he did hear Ulric sigh. And then the healer departed, leaving them alone.

Slowly, his limbs feeling as though they were made of stone instead of flesh, Roman pushed himself up off the edge of the bed. He stepped around the corner and into the room where his father stood. The king seemed not to have noticed his presence, his shoulders slumped in defeat.

Roman sniffed, inhaling loud enough to announce that he was there and immediately, Ulric straightened.

"Never mind," he said, somewhat brightly. "I've already sent for another healer and we'll see what he has to say. I've got a good feeling about this one."

Roman sighed. He'd been dreading this conversation for weeks, ever since he'd first felt its approach. He'd hoped it wouldn't be necessary, but it seemed he wasn't to be so lucky.

"Father, perhaps it's time we face facts."

"Give up, you mean?"

Roman was surprised his father even gave voice to the idea. It sounded so bleak when put like that, but it was essentially what he was suggesting.

"I won't hear of it," Ulric went on, before Roman could respond. "Your case is a challenging one, to be sure, but there's no reason why we can't find a healer who will know what to do. Ours is a large kingdom and we haven't even begun to scratch the surface."

But the king didn't meet his eyes as he spoke, turning away absently, his gaze on the window, but not seeing it or anything beyond. His dark hair, just beginning to streak with gray, was disheveled, and his eyes were puffy and tired.

"I'm not saying we shouldn't try," Roman pressed. "But we've done nothing but. I just want to live my life, for however long I have left, and not be kept locked away."

Ulric shook his head. "There's nothing worth venturing out there for."

Roman closed his eyes. He'd known what his father's answer would be and yet he'd insisted on trying to change his mind anyway. *It seems neither of us is willing to accept what's right in front of us.*

The king, fearful for his son's life and anything that might shorten it, would never allow it. Roman doubted there was anything beyond the palace walls that would truly do him any harm—at least not any more than he was already suffering.

Perhaps he'd been a fool to push his luck. Now wasn't the time anyway, with the fall of Shemar and the looming threat of the Akkadian Empire. Roman had heard the news, though he knew his father tried to keep such things from him, not wanting to worry him or add to his burdens.

Instead, the king shouldered such weight himself, and Roman could see the toll it was taking.

No, Ulric had enough on his mind at the moment without Roman adding to it.

"It'll be all right, you know," he said softly. "We are more powerful than our neighbors, after all. Akkadia may have its war machines, but they do not have our dragons."

Ulric glanced up, startled by the sudden shift in conversation, but he summoned a small smile. "You're right, of course."

But the smile did not reach his eyes and Roman knew he had done little to assuage his father's fear. He felt a flash of regret that he himself could only add to that fear.

How strange it felt, he mused, to be a child comforting a parent, rather than the other way around.

But other than the Akkadians, which was a threat to the entire kingdom, Roman found he had little to fear. He had no doubt, despite his father's assurances, that he was going to die. Everyone did, sooner or later, and his time just happened to be sooner.

It didn't really bother him so much—the dying part at least. It was how little he got to do with the time that remained to him, how little he got to experience, how little he would get to see.

It was hard to be content with a life so lived.

He felt sorry for his father, far more than he felt for himself. Roman's mother, the queen, was long gone, which left only Ulric and himself. There were no other children.

No other heirs.

What would happen to the kingdom, to the line of succession, after Roman died, he had no idea. But that was a problem for the future, far less pressing than the Akkadians.

Roman crossed the room, going over to the long, narrow windows his father had been staring out. With the ease of long practice, he unlatched them and pushed them outward, allowing fresh air to stream into the room. Poking his head out of the opening, he looked down upon the kingdom from a dizzying height.

The city of stone sprawled out before him, much of it too small and far away to make out clearly, aside from the Great Wall. From beyond the city, only the tallest towers and furthest spires were visible over its peak.

Suddenly, he was seized with an image of the approaching Akkadian army, the Great Wall the only thing standing between them. He didn't know what their war machines looked like, never having seen one himself, and so he was left to imagine.

If he squinted, Roman could make out camps and tent cities that had sprung up, gathered around the wall, as though afraid to venture any further. Refugees, first from Elath and now flooding in from Shemar—those that were lucky enough to escape.

Roman wondered what they had seen. Just what, specifically, they were fleeing from. He would have liked to speak with them, to ask them himself, but such things were not for him to know.

They must be desperate indeed to abandon the only home they'd ever known and seek shelter in the last free kingdom.

Free for how much longer? Roman couldn't help but wonder, as he turned away from the window.

IV

Despite the dire announcement of Shemar's fall, the fear of an imminent invasion did not come to pass. The following days passed by much the same as they always had, and if she tried, Chandra found she could simply pretend that nothing had happened. Nothing had changed at all. The neighboring kingdom remained, locked in a struggle with the Akkadian Empire, and neither side had yet proven victorious.

She continued to hope that the information they'd received had been wrong. There was always the possibility that a rumor had simply gotten out of hand, but she knew better than to believe it. They needed to prepare in case it was true, whatever such preparations would look like.

Luckily, Chandra saw no obvious change in her daily life. People still needed candles, after all, the same as they would whether Anarsha went to war or not. Dark homes had to be lit.

Despite their poor showing, she returned to the edge of the forest in search of more bayberries, determined this time to make it work. Her grandmother hadn't wanted her to go, as though setting foot beyond Anarsha's Great Wall would bring Chandra face to face with the marauding Akkadians.

She promised her grandmother that she would be careful and set out, encountering no Akkadians or their machines of war. Silently, Chandra set her basket down and began plucking the berries, admiring their color among the sun-dappled leaves. The round fruit was somewhere between a plum and magenta, no two exactly alike.

She breathed in deeply. There was something so peaceful about being in the forest, away from the cramped bustling streets of Anarsha. Plucking the berries gave her hands something to do, for which she was grateful.

Through the trees, a slight breeze reached her, the fresh air so different from the smells of smoke, animals and the sheer mass of humanity within Anarsha's walls. Here, the air smelled like trees, of earth and loam, and something vaguely floral.

Chandra had never been afraid of venturing outside the city walls, and she'd never been afraid while inside the city either. But her grandmother's words had rattled her, more than she cared to admit. It was the acknowledgement of their situation, which hung precariously over their heads, never far away. Chandra would rather have forgotten it all, for a little while, and picking the berries gave her the opportunity to do that.

Turning, she made her way back toward the Great Wall. She paused as a shadow fell over her, far too large to be a bird. Shielding her eyes with one hand, she peered up to see the silhouette of a dragon pass overhead, its body momentarily blotting out the sun. It moved with a fluid grace, uncanny for such a large creature, and Chandra held her breath as she watched it, the sun glinting off its blue scales.

Surely not even the Empire's machines stood a chance against such magnificent beasts.

Shaking herself out of her reverie, Chandra hurried on her way. She still had to collect the leftover fat from the houses along her street and the local butcher's before she could return home.

It had been years since she'd walked up and down their street, asking the neighbors if they would be willing to save the unused trimmings from the meat they bought, in exchange for a generous discount on any of the candles she made. Most had readily agreed and she knew which houses to stop at and which to pass by.

The butcher, a large man who insisted that everyone call him Peter, looked up at her arrival. "Back so soon?"

Chandra shivered, glancing at the rows of meat hanging behind the counter, and the cut that graced the table that Peter had been working on before she walked in. It was always slightly cool in the butcher shop.

"Had some trouble with the bayberries," Chandra admitted, pushing a stray strand of hair out of her face.

"Haven't given up, though, from the looks of things," he said, glancing at her basket.

"No," Chandra replied. "I don't like to give up."

Especially when she *knew* she could do something. She knew she could coax the bayberry candles out of their mold, if she was careful and patient enough. Of course, if a screaming town crier didn't happen to pass by at that exact moment, it wouldn't hurt.

The butcher grunted. "Well, you be sure to bring one of those candles by, when you're done with them."

He handed over the bundle she'd come to collect and Chandra saw with a flash of pleasure that it was larger than last time. More people must have brought their animals in to be butchered.

"I will," she promised, accepting the tallow. "Anything for you, Peter."

He grunted again, but she could tell he was pleased. "Away with you, then."

If her bayberry candles worked, she wouldn't need so much of the animal fat from Peter, but if he was offended by that, he gave no sign. No doubt he would prefer a sweeter smelling candle, just like the majority of people. Chandra certainly would prefer not to spend her days in a workshop filled with the suffocating stench that never seemed to come out of her hair or clothes.

She'd become so used to it now that she scarcely noticed it outside of the workshop and often worried that other people would.

With her errands at last completed, Chandra turned and made for home, struggling to balance the collected tallow and her basket of berries. She should have thought to bring Callum along, but it was too late for that now.

Sweating profusely by the time she reached her front door, Chandra swore as she tried to open it, balancing the basket on one knee.

Seeing—or perhaps hearing—her struggle, Callum came around the corner. "Here, let me help you with those."

"Thanks," Chandra gasped, finally stepping into the shade of the house.

"Well," her cousin remarked, "if the bayberries don't work again, at least you've got plenty of tallow."

She swatted him lightly on the arm. "They *will* work."

"I don't doubt it." The playful, teasing light faded from his gaze and he suddenly looked a lot more serious.

Chandra's stomach plummeted. "What?"

"There's something you should know."

What could have possibly happened since she'd ventured out that morning?

With mounting dread, she followed him into the kitchen, where their grandmother sat at the table, her gnarled hands clasped in front of her. It was always hard to tell what the crotchety old woman was thinking, but Chandra thought her expression looked particularly bleak.

"What is it?" Chandra demanded. "Who died?" Though she could think of no one they knew who might have passed on.

"No one," Callum answered.

He reached out, picking up a folded piece of parchment from where it had been lying on the table. Chandra glimpsed the broken wax seal, the imperial symbol of a dragon, and she knew before he even spoke again.

"I've received my recruitment notice. I'm to report to the barracks at first light."

The peace that Chandra had felt just a short time ago in the forest was such a distant memory, she wasn't sure it had ever been real. While she had been gone, galivanting through the woods and collecting berries to make frivolous candles, her cousin had been called up to join the army.

How was that possible? How could both things, both realities, exist at the same time?

"You can't go," she said stupidly, her voice sounding like it was coming from far away.

Without really intending to, she reached out and clasped the back of the chair nearest to her. Nothing felt real. Solid. It felt as though she'd given up control over her own body. Her movements were not her own, nor her thoughts, of which there was only one.

Not my cousin. They can't take Callum.

"I have to go," Callum said, "It's a royal summons, of a sort. I can't just ignore them."

"Or what?" Chandra demanded. "They'll arrest you? Better that than dying."

She flinched. She hadn't meant to say the last bit, but the fear slipped out, too big and real to be contained.

"I'm not going to die, Chan," Callum said gently, which somehow only made things worse. "It's just a precaution. We're not even at war yet."

Suddenly, it felt like her lungs had constricted and she couldn't get in enough air.

Yet. They weren't at war yet. But it was only a matter of time until they were and what then? Callum was no soldier. He liked to cook, and he was damned good at it. He occasionally helped her in the shop, when there were big orders to fulfill, usually in the autumn and winter, when there was fewer daylight to rely on.

He was not a soldier and if it came down to war, what chance did he have?

"You're not a soldier, Cal," she whispered.

"Stop it," their grandmother snapped. "Do you think this is going to help? Your worries won't make what he has to do any easier."

"And I do have to do it," Callum added, with a wry smile that wasn't really a smile at all. "Even if none of us like it. Don't worry, Chan." He stepped closer until he was right in front of her, wrapping his long arms around her. "No one starts out knowing how to be a soldier. They'll train me."

Chandra stiffened. She wasn't short, but she suddenly felt so *small*, so vulnerable, in her cousin's arms. He was so much taller than her, her head pressing against his chest, and she leaned into him, returning the embrace, as if she could somehow stop him from leaving and keep him right there, if she only held on tight enough.

He smelled of flour and cinnamon, and she knew he'd been baking bread. Her favorite cinnamon twist loaves.

She had to choke back a laugh at that. Had he known and baked her favorite treat in order to cheer her up?

It was ludicrous. She should have been comforting him, not the other way around. It was his life being derailed. He was the one going off to war, not her.

With an effort, Chandra pulled herself together and stepped back. No, she could do this. She would be strong, for him, for both of them.

"I should get to work," she murmured, gesturing to the supplies she had gone to collect that morning.

"I'll help you carry them out to the workshop," Callum offered.

"No," Chandra said quickly. Too quickly, perhaps. "I can manage."

What she really wanted, now that the news had been delivered, was to be alone for a bit. To lose herself in the work and mull over what must be done now. Callum understood that and he stepped back without argument.

Without his help, it took Chandra two trips to transport everything to the workshop. She could have tried to carry it all in one go, but she knew better than to get too greedy. The last thing she needed was to drop something and spill it all over the yard. Having to chase down all those purple bayberries might be just the thing to break her.

Once that was done and the door shut carefully behind her, Chandra allowed herself one small moment, slumping against the door and breathing deeply, in through the nose and out through the mouth.

She pushed away from the door and tied her hair out of the way. The only thing she could do now was simply get on with it. That's what they had always done, through every trial that was thrown their way. Get on with things.

She started with the bayberries, happy to have a challenge to distract her. She melted the berries down into wax, heated over the melting pot, which she then transferred to the molds. The wicks were carefully suspended above the molds, from horizontal rods.

While the bayberry candles cooled, Chandra moved on to the tallow. She would have preferred to work with bayberries or beeswax all the time, tricky as they were, but they were too expensive and she hadn't gone to the trouble of collecting all this tallow for nothing.

She cracked open the windows, to help with both the heat and the smell, but the workshop soon became sweltering from the fires used to heat and boil the wax. Sweat rolled down the back of Chandra's neck, clinging to her hairline. The thick stench of tallow filled the air, but Chandra savored it for once. It was a familiar smell, that represented that which was certain in her life, when it suddenly felt anything but.

Some of her earlier emotion threatened to make a reappearance and Chandra brushed any tears away angrily. She didn't have the time and she needed to focus.

She hardly dared to breathe when it came time to free the delicate bayberry candles from their molds. She moved slowly, with infinite care, as though she had all the time in the world. As though her world didn't feel like it was ending.

Chandra shook her head at that, telling herself not to be so melodramatic, but she couldn't help the way she felt.

In the end, left uninterrupted, her patience was rewarded. The berries had produced only a handful of candles, but not a single one had cracked or broken. Chandra regarded them, her sense of triumph bittersweet.

The sun had long since vanished from the sky, the air cooler in its absence. Chandra left the windows cracked open to air the place out, stepping outside and making her way across the lawn to the house. She could see flickering light from within, courtesy of some of her candles.

It was long past dinnertime, and though no one had come to get her, they had probably waited for her all the same, to see if she would venture out on her own. Chandra felt a flicker of guilt at that.

But as she stepped inside, she was greeted by the smells of seared meat and roasted vegetables, the table laid with a hearty spread.

"Got a late start," Callum explained, as though they hadn't been waiting for her after all.

Of course, she thought. This would be their last dinner together as a family, before he went off in the morning. Of course they would have waited for her. *You fool.*

"Sorry I took so long," she said, pulling out a chair.

"Was it a success?"

She nodded.

"Then that's all that matters."

Chandra's stomach rumbled. Locked away in her workshop, she hadn't stopped to notice how hungry she was, having eaten nothing since breakfast early that morning. She would have liked nothing more than to dig in at once, but their grandmother had to perform the customary prayer first.

This time, when she invoked the saints and asked for their protection, Chandra found she didn't mind so much.

The meal was delicious, as always, the meat seared to perfection, the vegetables buttery and flavorful, the dinner rolls soft and liberally slathered with honey.

But none of them could completely ignore the reality of their new circumstances, though Callum valiantly tried to engage them in conversation, and soon an awkward, stilted atmosphere descended upon the little gathering. The food, despite its richness, suddenly tasted like ash in Chandra's mouth and she struggled to swallow.

Who would do the cooking when Callum was gone? Her grandmother? Surely not. She'd had a taste of the old woman's cooking when they were younger, before Callum had learned, and though the memories were fuzzy, it wasn't something she was eager to return to.

It would have to fall to her, then, among all the rest of her responsibilities and duties. *When will I find the time?* That was something that Chandra had always disliked about cooking. It took so much time and effort, far more time to prepare a meal than it took to eat it. She supposed she could understand the simple joy of creating something for someone else, so that it might bring them joy. But while Callum got that from cooking, she experienced it through candle making.

And Callum knew Peter, the butcher, even better than she did, to say nothing of the local greengrocers. He knew who to buy the best vegetables from, the ripest fruit, what the best cuts of meat were. All Chandra knew how to do was render animal fat into suitable wax.

Her musings were interrupted as Callum pushed back from the table, returning with the cinnamon twists she'd smelled earlier, placing them in the center of the table.

Chandra stared at them with a wistful sort of longing. This would likely be the last time she tasted it until Callum returned.

If he returns. Chandra shoved the intrusive thought away. *When. When he returns.*

It might take a long time, years from now. She didn't know how long wars lasted, if it ever came to a war at all. But it couldn't last forever, that much she knew, and any amount of time spent waiting would be worth it in the end, if it meant he got to come back to them.

She could feel Callum's eyes on her, waiting for a reaction.

"You shouldn't have," she said, summoning a smile that felt surprisingly convincing. Cinnamon wasn't the cheapest or easiest of spices to get ahold of.

"I thought you might appreciate it," he said, picking up the serrated bread knife to saw off a piece.

Chandra was struck by a sudden idea, staring at the knife as it cut through the bread. What if Callum were to become injured? Would they still make him go? Would they still make him fight? He might still have to report to the barracks and help out with the war effort in some other way, but he wouldn't be a soldier, surely. Why would they want a soldier who was injured and couldn't fight?

But what sort of injury would be sufficient enough to prevent him from fighting? It would have to be something somewhat serious, not a mere cut, and Chandra winced at the thought. Part of her brain was already screaming at her to take the thought back, but it was too late.

She didn't like the idea of Callum being injured, but injured was better than dead, and she would help him with this if it meant he didn't have to go. If he could stay.

She vowed to bring it up to him later, after their grandmother had retired for the night. In the meantime, she smiled as Callum offered her the first piece.

By the time the meal had drawn to an end, it was quite late. Their grandmother lingered, torn between heading to bed or offering to help clean up, but Callum told her to go on, that he and Chandra would finish up in the kitchen.

She hesitated. "Don't stay up too late," she said finally. "You have to be up early tomorrow."

"I know," Callum assured her.

The two of them watched their grandmother's shuffling form disappear around the corner.

"As if I could sleep anyway," he muttered, shoulders deflating slightly.

Despite her own exhaustion, Chandra wasn't eager to climb the stairs to her bedroom, where she would simply lay awake, staring into the dark, and all the fears and worries she had tried so hard to keep at bay throughout the day would finally swarm her.

This is it, she thought, gripping the towel she held as Callum turned his attention back to the dishes that were soaking in the sink. This was her chance to bring up the idea she'd had to Callum, though she was no closer to figuring out what sort of injury would be sufficient.

She didn't want to maim him or permanently impact his life. But even worse than going too far would be not going far enough. The idea of deliberately harming her cousin was bad enough, but if it turned out that whatever she did was all in vain and he would have to go anyway...

Chandra squeezed her eyes shut. She had to try.

"Cal?"

"Hmm?" He didn't take his eyes off of his work, scrubbing away at the plates they'd used.

Chandra opened her mouth and suddenly, she was overcome by the desire to forget it all and simply say that she would finish up here. He shouldn't have to spend his last night with them doing the dishes, especially not when he had already done so much.

That was the smart, considerate thing to say. But it was also a way out, an excuse to not even try, and Chandra saw it for what it was. She would not be a coward, even though in that moment she felt like a ball of nerves, made of nothing but fear.

"What is it?"

Chandra started as he turned to face her. Her silence had stretched on too long.

"I was just thinking, maybe…" *Oh, hang it all.* "What if you didn't have to go?"

His brow furrowed. "What do you mean?"

"I mean, what would it take for you not to go?" Saints, she was going to have to spell it out. "I mean, what if you were injured? Nothing too serious." *Probably. Maybe.* "Just enough that you wouldn't have to go."

"But I'm not injured," Callum started to say, then understanding dawned and his features hardened. "You mean deliberately wound myself." He turned away, back to the dishes. "The coward's way out."

"It's not cowardly!" Chandra cried. "It isn't fair for them to ask you to go. You're needed here."

"Maybe," he conceded. "Maybe they don't need me yet. But what about when they do? How can I sit back while everyone else is doing their part?"

Chandra was silent for a moment, not knowing what to say. Then, quietly, she ventured, "So you won't even consider it?"

"What's to consider?" he asked, his jaw tight.

"But you could die!" she protested.

"Do you really have so little faith in me?"

His voice was so quiet, Chandra knew she ought to leave it. She'd angered him, questioned his capabilities and wounded his pride. But in that moment, she couldn't care less about men and their pride.

How could she make him understand? It wasn't that she didn't think him tough, or manly enough. It wasn't that she didn't think he could be a soldier. It wasn't him she had no faith in, it was those he would be fighting beside. The commanders, giving orders from afar, while they sat back and observed their soldiers carrying out their chosen commands like pieces on a game board.

The Akkadian Empire she trusted least of all. It didn't matter how much Callum meant to her, or that he was so very young. She herself had barely seen twenty summers and he a handful of years older than her.

How short a life…

"It doesn't matter what I think, Cal. People die in war all the time, and that's all there is to it."

He stiffened and she knew something she'd said had struck a nerve. "You can finish up here, can't you? There's not much left."

In truth, they'd barely started, and there were more dishes than usual, with all the effort he'd gone to for that night's meal. But Chandra merely murmured her consent and watched as he stalked off, leaving the warmth of the kitchen behind and vanishing into the darkness.

Her stomach felt like it was trying to twist itself into knots. *Idiot.* She'd been a fool to believe that Callum would ever take her up on such an idea. He had too much honor for that, an overinflated sense of right and wrong. *Damn him.* For once in her life, she wished he would be just a little bit selfish.

It had been a mistake to bring it up and now they would have spent their last evening together angry with each other. Chandra finished the dishes and trudged up to her room. She didn't even bother to undress, sinking down onto her mattress with a heavy sigh, knowing she would have only a short window of opportunity in the morning to make things right.

She was certain that sleep would elude her, but she rose the next morning knowing she must have dreamed at some point, though the finer details escaped her. She was up with the first weak rays of dawn, slipping through the still-quiet house to her workshop. Chandra picked up one of her bayberry candles, wrapping it in the special paper she usually reserved for more expensive orders.

Both her grandmother and Callum were up by the time she returned, holding the little bundle close to her chest. Callum had a satchel draped over one shoulder, already packed and ready to go.

He glanced at her as she stepped inside and then turned back to their grandmother. "I'll make you proud."

"I know you will," the old woman said gruffly, reaching out to lay a hand on his shoulder. Then she lifted it higher, cupping his cheek and taking a good, long look at him, as though memorizing his features. *As though afraid she might never see him again.* "You already have."

Chandra scolded herself for such thoughts. If she kept at it, she was likely to make them come true. Some sort of self-fulfilling prophecy.

When at last their grandmother released him and stepped back, Chandra thought she saw tears on her cheeks, but she turned away before she could be sure.

Callum turned to her.

"About last night—" Chandra ventured.

"Forget it," Callum interrupted. "Never happened."

She gave him a grateful look and held out the wrapped candle.

"What's this?"

"One of the bayberry candles. Has a much nicer scent than tallow. At least your bunkmates won't hate you if you want a bit of light to read by."

"Or write by."

"Yes," Chandra agreed. "Make sure you write. Every day."

"Every day?" The corner of Callum's mouth quirked up in a smile. "I can't imagine the army's all that interesting."

"I want to know everything. What the food is like, who your new comrades are. And the dragons. Make sure you tell me everything about the dragons."

"I will," he promised. "By the time I'm done, you'll know so much, it will be like you're in the army yourself."

"Perish the thought. They wouldn't know what to do with me."

"I suspect you're right."

Their playful banter trailed off, the conversation seemingly at an end. Chandra felt a stab of panic. She wasn't ready for it to be over yet. She wasn't ready to say goodbye.

She nodded to the candle. "Think of me every time you light it."

"I will," he promised again.

And then Chandra was squeezing him as hard as she could, the way they had when they were little, as though the mere force of her grip could keep him there with them, where he would be safe.

She stepped back, sniffing hard to keep the tears at bay. "Try not to piss off any of the dragons. It would be embarrassing if you were eaten before you ever saw action."

Callum laughed. "Little chance of that. I'm quite charming."

"And annoying."

"Not as annoying as you."

"I can't help it I'm the best at everything."

He shook his head. "I really do have to go, Chan. I don't know what happens if you're late, but I'd rather not find out."

"Just use some of that charm," she retorted, following him to the door. "I'm sure you could weasel your way out of any punishment."

"If I'm late, I'll tell them it's your fault."

"Oh, sure, blame me."

They might have stood there, bickering good-naturedly until one or the other finally failed to come up with a good retort. But Callum had stepped out onto the cobbles, glancing over his shoulder.

"What? I thought you were the best at everything. That includes making me late."

"Hurry up, then!" she said, waving him on.

He turned and went on his way, waving as he went.

"Be careful!" she called after him.

And then at last, all too soon, he was swallowed up by the crowd. Chandra swallowed, the levity she had felt, conjured by the moment, gone. She couldn't recall ever feeling so alone.

The sensible thing to do, she knew, would be to lose herself in her workshop. There were always more orders to fill, after all, and that didn't stop just because Callum was no longer there to help. She and her grandmother would have to feed themselves somehow.

Instead, she found herself stepping out into the street after him, her feet taking her in the opposite direction. The streets were busy despite the early hour, market stalls already assembled, eagerly awaiting their first customers. Maids and housewives alike perused their wares, trying to snatch the best bargains before they were all picked over.

None of that interested Chandra today. A few other families were bidding tearful goodbyes of their own, standing in the doorways of some of the houses she passed, and she couldn't help but wonder how many other families had received such summons. How many more were experiencing the same sense of resigned loss?

Chandra quickened her pace, her destination already in sight at the end of the road. The temple loomed before her, carved lovingly out of marble and stone. She climbed the stairs—ten of them exactly—and passed beneath the massive pillars supporting the ceiling, the colorful banners snapping in the breeze.

Inside, it was instantly quieter, the sound muffled by the thick stone. It was cooler, too, at the edges of the room, furthest away from the central brazier, always kept lit.

Chandra slowed. The temple was a single room and she could see at once that she was alone. She hadn't often come here, not nearly as much as her grandmother, but the place never seemed to change. It was a shrine to the past.

With the exception of the entrance, every wall was covered in stained-glass, each panel representing one of the saints, portraying the moment of their greatest triumph.

Chandra walked around the perimeter slowly, her footsteps echoing in the large space. Most of the saints had a dragon beside them.

The old beliefs claimed that the world was once filled with demons, who had populated the realm before the arrival of humans. Obviously, demons and humans were a combination that could not co-exist, and so a group of brave heroes rose to the occasion, trapping the demons within soul stones, gems that were harder than iron and indestructible, save for one vulnerability.

Dragonfire.

The central brazier was rumored to have been lit from dragonfire, kept eternally burning, but Chandra didn't know if she believed that. She didn't know if she believed any of it. It was all so long ago. There was no proof that the saints had ever existed, aside from historical record, which was more often than not little more than myth and legend.

The last of the demons, if they had ever existed at all, were long gone, and no one alive had ever seen one or met a saint. The soul stones, though, were real enough.

Or at least one was.

A single blue soul stone lay atop the altar at the far end of the room, beneath the stained-glass mural of Sonera, the last saint. It lay, innocuous enough, atop a silk cloth, the light blue facets reflecting the firelight.

Chandra raised her eyes to the saint above. Sonera, her blonde hair spread around her head like a halo, stood with her faithful blue dragon behind her. History hadn't bothered, it seemed, to remember the dragon's name.

They were never praised or venerated the way the saints were, which struck Chandra as wrong. The dragons were just as important. True, they couldn't seal demons away like the saints could, but without them, the demons would remain trapped in the stones, contained but never banished.

Still, it was the saints, not the dragons, that had drawn Chandra there, Sonera in particular. She was associated with good luck, fortune, and general good outcomes, since she had been the final saint and hadn't suffered a horrible death.

The saints always seemed to come to a bad end, of one sort or another. They were never killed by the demons they sealed. They were instead targeted and hunted down by other demons after the fact, who came to view them as a threat.

Sonera, though, had been the last. After her, there had been no more demons to seal, humankind at last free of them. Or so the stories said.

Chandra could think of no better saint to appeal to. Callum needed all the good fortune possible sent his way.

And even though she wasn't sure whether she truly believed or not, it couldn't hurt to try.

Displayed before her, etched in stained-glass, was some of Anarsha's history, the origin of their long-standing relationship with the dragons. They had joined together with the saints long ago to seal and banish the demons and now they would fight alongside Anarshans once more, this time against a different kind of threat.

Chandra knelt before the altar and prayed that Callum, and Anarsha as a whole, would be protected. She felt a little foolish and not a little bit helpless, but it was all she could do. All she could offer her cousin.

She would gladly come to the temple every day and pray for hours if it meant keeping Callum safe.

V

The army barracks were situated deep in the heart of Anarsha, near the palace. The ground sloped gradually upward as one approached and Callum's calves ached by the time the massive gated entrance came into view. Sweat prickled across his forehead; the sun was high overhead and the day was warm.

The compound loomed before him, its walls and towers, parapets and spires all made of stone. He imagined, perched at the top of one of those towers one would be able to see over even the Great Wall itself—which, he reflected, was likely the point.

As he approached, a group of dragons flew overhead, swooping low as they cleared the walls. A unit, coming back from patrol or a training exercise. His throat tightened slightly at the idea of riding one of the beasts. He wasn't particularly fond of heights—or placing such trust in an animal that could so easily kill him. He need not wait for the Akkadians at all.

Callum shook his head and mounted the last of the stairs, on even footing now with the gates. A pair of guards, each dressed in glittering mail and holding halberds addressed him, demanding identification.

Callum produced his recruitment papers and was ushered through, informed that he was late and that his commanding officer would be waiting for him. He swore under his breath, knowing that his prolonged farewell with Chandra would cost him, but he'd done it anyway. He hoped the punishment for tardiness wasn't too severe—kitchen duty, perhaps, or mucking out the dragons' stalls. Did they have stalls? The sheer scope of his ignorance threatened to overwhelm him.

So long as he wasn't flogged, surely it wouldn't be too bad.

Before he could find his commanding officer, realizing he had no idea who that was or what they looked like, Callum was stopped at various checkpoints along the way. They took copies of his fingerprints, painting them with ink and then pressing them down in a thick ledger. They also took a bit of his blood and he wondered what on earth that could possibly be for.

He was given a uniform in his size and informed that he would be provided with leathers once he'd been assigned to a dragon. Only then was he told where to go and to whom to report.

His commanding officer, a man called Khan, was an imposing figure of insignificant height. He was well-muscled, though, with a thick neck and a wide jaw, his golden hair cut in sharp, precise lines.

That jaw tightened as he took Callum in. Before Khan, standing at attention in neat, orderly lines were other recruits. Though none of them turned to face him, Callum could feel the weight of their attention.

"You're late," Khan said.

"Apologies, sir—"

"Fall in," the man snapped.

Callum clamped his mouth shut and fell into line as Khan led them around the compound. He had a quick stride for such a short man and Callum was panting with the effort of keeping up by the time their group arrived at one of the outbuildings.

He listened as Khan explained that these were to be their new quarters. They were given a brief moment to put their belongings inside and change into the uniforms they were given.

Ducking inside the shadowed, unlit building, Callum located the first bunk that appeared unoccupied, plunked his pack down on the thin mattress, and changed into his uniform. It fit a little loosely, but he wasn't going to complain.

Outside, Khan was waiting for them, with a sour expression on his face as though they had taken hours, when in truth, it had likely been less than five minutes.

"Right," he barked. "Follow me and try to keep up. You won't spend much time in there," he added, jerking his head back at the quarters. "You'll have most evenings to yourselves, and of course, that's where you'll sleep, but it will be unoccupied during the day. Now, I'll assign you each a dragon and then you can meet up with the other members of your units. If things seem a bit hectic, we've had a rush of new recruits and finding a place to put them all is easier said than done."

Callum thought it best to refrain from comment, but the compound didn't look disorganized to him. Then again, he didn't know what it usually looked like, never having been there. But to him, it seemed to function like a well-oiled, if large, machine.

As they walked, Khan pointed out the various parts of the complex, including the various training grounds. There seemed to be people everywhere Callum looked. He was used to encountering large numbers of strangers out on the street, but nothing like this. Here, everyone clearly belonged and had a common purpose, dressed in their identical uniforms. They passed several organized groups of people—units, he supposed—walking briskly, intent on being somewhere.

Khan led them all the way up to one of the highest levels, onto a long stretch of open platform, where several dragons waited. Callum's pulse, already quick from the walk, spiked faster as he drew near. He'd never seen a dragon so close and he had to remind himself that they were on the same side. He wasn't coming here to be sacrificed and eaten—though he supposed that would have been a particularly gruesome punishment for being late.

Callum waited as Khan went down the line, assigning recruits and dragons in pairs, until at last, it was his turn.

Khan stopped before one of the dragons, nodding between the two of them. "This is K'Sante."

And just like that, Callum had a dragon.

When the last recruit had been paired off, Khan addressed the group, his raised voice carrying easily. "I'll give you all a minute to settle in. Report down there when you're done." He pointed to one of the lower levels.

A brief glance revealed some sort of targets down below, but Callum turned back to the dragon before he could ascertain what they were for.

And then Khan had turned, making his way back down the stairs, leaving Callum and the others in the presence of the beasts.

What had he called the dragon? K'Sante. Not an Anarshan name.

Callum's eyes roamed over the creature, taking in every detail. The dragon wasn't as large as he'd been expecting, only a little more than double his own height. K'Sante had brilliant vermillion scales, a line of black spines trailing down his back. His claws, long and wicked, were silver, as were the two horns protruding from his head. There were frills behind his jaw and he regarded Callum with bright green eyes.

"I'm Callum," he said, flushing almost immediately. How did one introduce oneself to a dragon? He couldn't very well offer to shake hands.

The dragon dipped his head. "K'Sante."

Callum knew that dragons could speak, from the stories of when they'd fought alongside the saints, but he was surprised at how human K'Sante's voice sounded. It was deep, but not at all gravelly the way he'd expected. How could a creature, with such a large maw and sharp teeth, be so capable of human speech?

He swallowed. "So, looks like we're in this together."

"So it would seem." K'Sante inclined his head in the direction Khan had disappeared. "We should join the others."

Callum followed his gaze and for a moment, his eyes strayed over the walls of the compound, to the city beyond, stretching out below them. It was only then that he realized just how high they were, his stomach bottoming out at the sight.

He gladly started down the stairs, eager to return to the lower levels, the dragon falling into step beside him. "Have you had a rider before?"

The dragon shook his head.

"Honestly, I'm a little nervous about the whole thing," Callum admitted and then instantly wondered why he had done such a thing. A dragon didn't strike him as the kind of beast who would tolerate displays of weakness or vulnerability.

K'Sante turned his large head to face him. "So am I."

"Really?" Callum said, surprised. "I didn't know dragons could be nervous."

The dragon snorted. "We are not like animals, who feel emotion but do not reason why."

Callum nodded. "Right. I'll keep that in mind."

He had noticed it at once, that this was not some mere animal. This was a sentient being, capable of rational thought. With each passing moment, K'Sante, though still intimidating and impressive, seemed more and more human. Little wonder they had fought alongside the saints, united against a common enemy. *Just as we are now.*

"Do you think the Akkadian Empire will strike?" he asked, wanting to know his new partner's opinion and whether or not all of this was necessary.

The dragon made a low sound in his throat. "Sooner or later. Their curiosity will get the better of them. And they will see Anarsha's continued freedom as an insult."

Dread settled in Callum's stomach. He didn't feel ready to face such a challenge. The day had already proven overwhelming and it wasn't even half over yet.

The two of them arrived at the large training ground Khan had indicated. The targets, Callum now saw, were for archery. Already some other recruits were lined up, each with a bow in hand, taking turns firing at the targets and moving back at ever-increasing intervals.

Callum stiffened. He'd never used a bow in his life. There was no need to go out hunting for meat when one could find everything they needed at the markets. He felt woefully out of his depth, but for some reason, he found K'Sante's quiet presence reassuring.

He had a dragon at his side. Surely that meant he could do anything.

Once again, Khan took the lead, dividing the group into their respective units, introducing new recruits to already established soldiers.

He steered Callum over to some of the others, barking out, "Anake, Victor!"

A young man and woman, about Callum's own age, lowered their bows and came over to join them, their dragons trailing behind.

Khan introduced the members of Callum's new unit and their dragons, Vitanni and Bane.

Anake was a tall woman and Callum had only to look at her to see that she was a fighter. Her skin was brown, her black hair cut short and shaved entirely on one side. She regarded him with open hostility. Her dragon, Vitanni, was viper-green, with yellow eyes.

Victor, too, had a soldier's physique, his dark hair swept back from his forehead. His dragon, Bane, was visibly larger than K'Sante and Vitanni both, his limbs thickly muscled beneath the black and orange scales.

Anake crossed her arms. "So where are you from, then?"

When Callum told them the name of his street, Victor snorted. "And what is it that you do? Fishmonger?"

Anake shot Victor a nasty look that he chose to ignore.

"No, I—my family makes candles."

"A chandler!" Victor exclaimed. "The Empire doesn't stand a chance."

Apparently having exhausted what little interest he had in Callum, Victor turned and walked away, his dragon following.

"Are all units so small?" Callum asked, not expecting Anake, who clearly didn't like him much either, to answer.

But she surprised him. "For now. They haven't brought in that many recruits yet, but I expect that will change."

With one last hard look, she followed after Victor.

This is my unit? How could a unit be so small, and comprised of people who didn't seem to like each other very much?

But Callum didn't have time to dwell on any of it. Khan was soon barking out orders, instructing them to line up in formation. Callum found a bow thrust into his hands and he stared at it as though it were a foreign object, while K'Sante went to stand over to one side, with the other dragons, only able to observe for this part.

It was a disaster. Callum didn't think of himself as weak, but when he notched his first arrow and attempted to draw the bow back, it refused to fully extend.

"Never seen a bow before, chandler?" Victor called, smirking.

Saints, I hate him, Callum thought, surprised by his own vitriol.

Khan ordered a different bow found for Callum, with a lower weight draw, until one was located that he could draw all the way back. Even then, his aim was terrible, face burning at the humiliation of being singled out.

What did you expect, that you would be good at something you've never done before?

He hadn't been good at making candles when he'd first started out and neither had Chandra. *And yet, look at how good she is now.*

Callum gritted his teeth and persisted, drawing and then firing when ordered to, even when his arms began to tremble and the muscles in his back screamed in agony. He hadn't realized archery required the use of so many different muscles. He'd never thought about it. He'd never had to.

It was the longest day of his life and he was relieved when they were dismissed. He would have rather stood over a boiling-hot melting pot for hours on end, making one batch of tallow candles after another, than endure another moment of this.

But this was his life now. He was expected to be a good soldier, to follow orders, to bond with his dragon, and to know how to wield weapons.

I may have to kill someone with this, he thought, as he returned the bow to its rack.

The thought was not a pleasant one and his mood only soured further when he turned and found Anake and Victor waiting for him.

"Of course, the new recruit they assign to our unit doesn't know how to use a longbow. Is there anything you *do* know how to do, chandler? Do you know how to fight?"

"I can learn," Callum said stiffly, hoping Anake might come to his rescue, but she simply watched, impassively.

Victor sniffed. "If the Empire could see the state of our army right now, they'd laugh at us. Let's hope they don't invade any time soon. Still, you'd make good fodder, I suppose."

"We're on the same side, here," Callum protested weakly.

"That may be true, but make no mistake, chandler. We are nothing alike."

Callum watched the two of them stalk away, trying to resist the urge to bury an arrow in Victor's back. But he knew better than to try. Not only would that *definitely* result in some sort of punishment, he'd only miss anyway. He couldn't hit the broadside of a barn.

"He's not worth it, you know," K'Sante said softly, coming up beside him.

Callum shook his head. He had no idea what he'd done to deserve their scorn, having just met them, and he told K'Sante as much.

The dragon sighed. "Sometimes, I think humans are crueler than even dragons."

Silently, Callum agreed. The day had been miserable, and he looked forward to the reprieve of returning to quarters, but such hopes were quickly dashed. As he had feared, there was a punishment for reporting in late, and Callum found himself on kitchen duty, scrubbing floors and washing dishes until well into the night.

When he finally retired back to the barracks, every muscle in his body seemed to cry out in protest. His feet dragged, as though they were made of lead, and he wanted nothing more than to curl up on his bunk and sleep for a week. But he knew he would be expected to rise early in the morning and get back to training with everyone else.

He sighed, sinking down onto his bunk. This was his life now. He'd better make the most of it. Tired as he was, he couldn't forget his promise to write to Chandra. The rest of the barracks were quiet, the others asleep, and he knew he might not get a better chance to put his thoughts down on paper.

He withdrew the bayberry candle Chandra had given him, hating to light it, because then it would just be gone that much faster. But that was foolish, he knew. The purpose of such things was to be used, otherwise they would never be enjoyed at all.

A slightly sweet, pleasant smell wafted into the air as he sat back, admiring it. Chandra had really outdone herself with these, so much nicer than tallow. He was sure if he'd lit one of those, the tell-tale stench would have woken the others and then he would have gotten an earful.

Callum snorted to himself, amused at the idea of annoying Victor with a tallow candle.

By the light of Chandra's candle, he began to compose his first letter to her and their grandmother. He didn't want her to worry, but he knew better than to be anything less than honest. She would know, even through writing, that he was holding back, that something was wrong.

And so he told her that things were more difficult than he'd expected—although in truth, he wasn't sure what he had anticipated. He told her about K'Sante and Anake and Victor and how the new members of his unit didn't seem to care for him very much.

At last, when all his thoughts had been exorcised onto the page, Callum felt a fresh wave of exhaustion wash over him. He folded up the letter, tucked it beneath his pillow and extinguished the candle, wanting to save it. Tomorrow, he would find out where to post the letter.

His days at the training compound continued much the same, leaving him sore and tired at the end of each day. It was monotonous work, for the most part, though there was something to be said for having a schedule.

Neither Anake nor Victor warmed up to him and he did his best to ignore them. Gradually, he became better at archery, able to draw back bows of increasingly higher draw strength. The uniform, which had been too loose when he'd first arrived, soon fit snugly, as his form filled out.

But Khan never let them get too comfortable. As soon as Callum began to feel confident in one skill, a new test was introduced. So, he could finally hit a target in archery? Could he do it from the back of a dragon in flight?

Flying was the most daunting part by far, but Callum loved it, soaring above the complex walls on K'Sante's back, peering down at the stone streets and homes below. He felt free and even, for a time, happy.

They spent countless hours practicing archery from the air, running through drills where the dragons raked designated targets with fire, and occasionally the dragons even sparred with each other, in case they were ever downed in combat and found themselves face to face with Akkadia's war machines.

Callum had gathered that the mechs were based off the living dragons, only slower, less agile, and unable to fly or access the dragons' most powerful weapon—fire. Still, they were more advanced weaponry than any of the other kingdoms possessed and had delivered both Elath and Shemar into the Empire's hands.

"You," Khan liked to remind them, "and your dragons are the only thing standing in the Empire's way."

It still felt wrong to think of K'Sante as *his* dragon. K'Sante was a sentient being, and while they certainly worked together, the dragon belonged to no one and could do as he wished.

Khan impressed upon them, day after day, of the importance of their bond with their dragon. They needed to forge a bond that would see them through combat, should the need arise, and deliver both of them safely back at the battle's end.

The idea of actually seeing action made Callum feel physically ill, even though he knew that was why he was at the barracks in the first place. Despite his improving skills, he didn't know how efficient he would be in an actual fight. He didn't know if he could bring himself to kill another human being.

But the idea of going into battle with K'Sante alleviated some of those fears. The dragon was more powerful and dangerous than he would ever be. And whenever he climbed up into the saddle, specifically made to fit the dragon, he felt powerful, too.

Still, he couldn't help but confide some of his worries to his dragon. He didn't want to show weakness, but he also thought sharing such vulnerabilities might strengthen their bond, and he thought back to the first day they'd met, when both of them had admitted to nerves.

Despite being so much stronger than him, K'Sante never seemed to mock him for his human weakness, contrary to how Callum had expected dragons to view his kind.

"Killing isn't something to be taken lightly," the dragon replied, one evening while they were alone.

It was stuffy inside the barracks and Callum had retreated outside to compose his letter to Chandra. Receiving her replies was always the highlight of his day, but he sometimes struggled to find something interesting to put in his letters. Life at the complex was monotonous and he didn't want to sound repetitive—or worse, boring.

K'Sante lay stretched out on the grass, Callum beside him, leaning against the dragon's flank. The sun was setting behind them and Callum knew he needed to hurry before he lost the last of the light.

"Do you think it's hard for the Akkadians?" he asked suddenly. "Killing, I mean?"

The thought had never occurred to him before, but now it was all he could think of. Did the Akkadian soldiers also find it difficult to kill? Surely at least some of them must. Killing wasn't something that came easily or naturally.

"No," a firm voice said and Callum turned to see Anake, standing in the doorway to the nearest quarters, apparently having overheard part of the conversation. "It's not hard for them."

"How do you know?"

Her jaw tightened. "Because I watched them slaughter their way through Elath. Akkadian soldiers barely think of themselves as human. Their lives mean little. They are but a cog, one of many, in the efficient machine that is the Empire. That is their purpose—to serve, to bring glory to

Akkadia—nothing more. So, if they are barely human and their own lives mean so little, what are the lives of their enemies compared to that?"

Her voice softened for a moment, her eyes somewhere far away. "When you view your enemy as less than human, there's no limit to the things you'll do."

Then her gaze hardened again. She shot him one last look and stalked away, her hands balled into fists. Callum watched her go, wondering where she was off to.

"She saw the Empire attack Elath?" he murmured.

K'Sante made a rumbling sound behind him. "That confirms what I heard. I spoke to Vitanni and Bane. Anake is an Elathan refugee. That's why she doesn't like you. Well, not you personally. She doesn't seem to think too highly of Anarshans in general, since Anarsha never came to Elath's aid."

"If she's not fond of Anarshans, what's she doing fighting alongside us?"

"Isn't it obvious?" K'Sante snorted. "Because she hates the Empire more."

VI

Two years passed much the same way, with no closer sign as to why Callum had been summoned to the barracks in the first place. The Akkadian Empire, if they intended to march on Anarsha, showed no sign of it. But there was a danger to complacency. The moment you let your guard down was the moment disaster struck, swooping down from where it had been waiting in the rafters. Anarsha remained vigilant, despite the lack of threat, and their vigilance was rewarded.

Despite spending two years training beside them, Callum felt he was no closer to getting to know the other members of his unit—or their dragons, not that he associated with them much. They all seemed to avoid each other where possible, which filled Callum with a sort of dread. What kind of unit were they, if they wouldn't even speak to each other? How could they be expected to work together cohesively, should the threat they'd all been preparing for finally arrive?

He told himself not to worry and simply got on with things, training with K'Sante, strengthening their bond, and improving his skills.

His thoughts strayed often to home, wondering how Chandra was faring, if there were things she wasn't putting in her letters, and how much of a difference two years had made on both of their appearances. The sharp loss of home had turned to a dull ache and Callum almost found himself wishing that the Akkadians would attack, if only so they could be repelled and sent back where they came, allowing him to finally return to his family. With Anarsha safe, his services would no longer be needed.

One day, his wish came true.

Training was interrupted, murmurs drifting through the crowds of recruits as the news spread that a scouting party had spotted an advancing column of Akkadians, approaching the city.

Callum's heart leapt into his throat. They had done it. They had really done it. He hadn't thought they would actually go through with it. At last, the Akkadians were coming for them.

Training sessions were immediately suspended, Khan and the other officers barking out orders. Not wanting to engage with the Akkadians in the Valderan rainforest, where the dragons would be at a disadvantage with all the trees, they would wait until the advancing army broke clear of the tree line. Though they weren't moving out, everyone was instructed to be on high alert and prepare to mount up at a moment's notice.

The rest of the army, those who would be on horses or on foot, were mobilized and departed the barracks, moving to the city's Great Wall in preparation for the engagement.

Callum could focus on nothing for the rest of the day, expecting at any moment to be summoned by the horns, the call to mount up and move out. But no such announcement came.

Time seemed to pass at an agonizing crawl, but soon enough it was evening and there was still no word, leaving Callum a nervous ball of energy with nowhere to turn.

He had already chewed his nails down to the quick by the time dinner was over and he'd returned to quarters, staring off at the Great Wall, as though he could somehow hope to see past it and glimpse the approaching army.

He reminded himself that the Akkadians weren't just right outside the city walls, waiting to rush past their defenses and flood into the streets. If they made a move or appeared at all, the scouts would send word and they would know of it.

But even so, he couldn't recall ever having been so nervous in his entire life, on the precipice of his first real battle, the thing he had been preparing for and yet felt not at all prepared for. *That's what you get for wishing for some excitement, you idiot.*

"I'd try to get some sleep if I were you," Anake said, appearing by his side, her gaze also on the wall. "I doubt they'll make their move before morning."

"What if they're just waiting for nightfall?" Callum asked.

Suddenly, he was certain that was precisely what the Akkadians were doing, the better to disguise their approach.

Anake shrugged. "If they do, then the alarm will go up and we'll be summoned. No use staying up all night worrying about it. The Akkadians will attack when they're ready."

He turned to her. "How are you so calm?"

Her lips twisted. "I've seen battle before. You haven't. I know better what to expect." She shrugged again, in that way she had. "I trust my dragon. I trust those I'll be fighting beside. But more than that, I watched the Empire slaughter my countrymen. I'm eager for a chance to return the favor."

For Anake, the fight was personal. She was fighting for a chance to strike back for what she had lost. Callum hadn't lost anything yet. He was fighting to keep it that way.

Only if they failed and Anarsha was lost, there would be no retreating to another kingdom, no joining up with another army as a refugee, the way Anake had. Anarsha was the last free kingdom. If they fell, there was nowhere left to run.

They made their stand here.

Something else she'd said struck Callum, about trusting the people she fought beside. While also applicable to the Anarshan army as a whole, he thought she specifically meant him and Victor.

Strangely, he was touched by her faith in him. She'd said scarcely more than a handful of words each time they'd spoken, and she hadn't seemed impressed with him when he'd first arrived, though she'd never been as openly hostile as Victor. His hard work must have paid off, enough to gain her approval.

Callum debated what to say, to acknowledge her faith in him and let her know that he appreciated the sentiment.

Anake looked at him. "Trust your dragon. He'll see you through."

And then she was gone, ducking into the barracks, leaving Callum to stare at the distant wall, lit by the dying sun.

True to her word, the Akkadians did not make a move that night. Callum reluctantly retired to his bunk, certain sleep would elude him. His nerves were wound too tightly.

The next thing he knew, his eyes were flying open, woken by the great tolling of a bell, summoning the riders to the wall. The Akkadians had been spotted.

Callum leapt up, quickly changing into the leathers he'd been given. They offered a little protection from fire, but would do nothing against a direct hit. Nor would they be able to withstand one of the Empire's mechs, should he be so unfortunate. But they were lightweight and presented no additional burden to the dragons.

As they suited up, he glanced across the room and caught Anake's eyes. She nodded to him mutely.

Then they were off to the armory. Each rider was equipped with a short sword, at their belt, a dagger in each boot, a quiver full of arrows, and a longbow. The dragons, of course, would be the main weapons, but they could use the bows to pick off any infantry.

K'Sante landed beside him, far too graceful for such a large creature. Callum's hair stirred in the wind kicked up from the dragon's wings, but he barely heard him land.

The dragon knelt down and Callum climbed up into the saddle, slotting his boots into the stirrups and connecting the straps to his flight leathers. The dragon could dive and wheel through the air as he pleased with no fear of Callum being unseated.

K'Sante spread his wings and launched into the air, flying over the city until he came to perch along the Great Wall with the rest of the assembled riders. He stood with Vitanni and Anake on one side, Victor and Bane on the other.

Now that there were no more motions to go through, no more preparation to be done, there was nothing to distract Callum from the enormity of what they were about to face. He felt a lump rise in his throat as he gazed across the span of ground that stretched out before them.

There were a few trees, small patches of forest, but for the most part, the land that separated the wall from the forest itself was sparse. Great rocky outcroppings sprung up from the ground here and there, the earth covered with gorse and scraggly bushes, but not much else.

The Badlands.

The relatively open plain offered a clear view of the approaching Akkadian army, their pace unhurried. Callum sucked in a breath as the early morning light glinted off the bronze mechs. They looked small, but Callum knew the distance to be deceiving. He could barely make out the infantry soldiers, but he could tell they looked tiny beside the mechs.

And even from a distance, he could *hear* them, the metallic clanking ringing out over the plain.

The wind ruffled Callum's hair and he shivered, glancing along the line as they stared down the Akkadians from the height of the Great Wall. It was an impressive array, his fellow dragon riders stretching as far as he could make out, interspersed with archers who would remain on the wall.

But there were so many mechs and as Callum watched, their numbers just kept coming. They made no attempt at stealth, marching straight toward the Great Wall.

Such a bold tactic made Callum nervous. Were they that confident that they would win, that they made no attempt to conceal their approach? The clanking noise would likely have defeated the point anyway, but still… Perhaps they thought their sheer numbers would overwhelm the Anarshans.

He recalled what Anake had told him, about Empire soldiers believing their lives to be of little value, their only purpose to serve the Empire. Perhaps they didn't care how many of them died in the attempt, so long as Anarsha belonged to the Empire by the end.

That won't happen, Callum thought, tightening his grip on the longbow. There were no reins to hold onto; riders needed to be free to use their bows and dragons were not horses, to be led where one wished.

Sensing the movement, K'Sante turned his head slightly, to glance back at Callum with one bright green eye.

"Don't worry," the dragon murmured. "Just stick close to me. I'll protect you."

Strapped in as he was, Callum thought it unlikely he was going anywhere, but he was touched by the dragon's words all the same.

A horn rang out, the long note soon joined by others down the line until the sound drowned out even the clanking of the approaching mechs. And then, as one, the riders took to the air.

K'Sante sprang from the edge of the wall, his powerful wings snapping downward. Callum felt the familiar sensation, which he always experienced when taking to the air, of his stomach trying to sink down to his legs. Below them, the ground seemed to pass by alarmingly fast.

Callum reached over his shoulder, plucking an arrow from his quiver and nocking it. The Akkadian army loomed before them, growing larger with each beat of K'Sante's wings.

Already it was horribly hot inside the mech and Desmond was looking forward to ending the battle as quickly as possible. It had been a long, hot march, navigating the mechs through the seemingly endless Valderan rainforest. He'd been relieved when they'd finally arrived at the edge of the woods, at last able to climb out of the cramped container and stretch his legs.

But come morning, rising before dawn, he'd had to duck back inside. He could feel sweat slick on his skin, dampening his hair and running down his neck, beneath the collar of his uniform.

Pilots did not wear armor; there was no more room inside the mechs to spare and with the added heat, they would quickly succumb. Even without armor it was possible and Desmond had heard tell of more than one pilot who had died of heat stroke.

He sat crouched in the dragon's belly, his knees practically up to his ears, and found himself thankful, not for the first time, that he was only average height. The rear of the mech radiated heat, burning the coal that powered it, with the pilots nestled at the opposite end, in the chest cavity.

The mechs could not yet breathe fire, a flaw that he knew the engineers were eager to remedy, but for now, Desmond would make do without the added power. If there had been any more fire kindling in the thing's metal husk, he would certainly overheat.

Desmond felt the mech's body shift beneath and around him as he worked the pedals and levers that powered its limbs. It was a heavy machine, lumbering and slow, but it could put on a burst of speed if needed, at the risk of burning through his remaining fuel.

Akkadia had never attempted to conquer a target as remote as Anarsha and extra coal reserves had been brought along, fueling the mechs during the lengthy journey. Desmond only hoped that his fuel would last for the duration of the fight. Battles were chaotic; there was no telling what he would be forced to do. The more demanding he was of his mech, the more demands he placed upon the fuel reserves. A pilot who ran out of fuel and was forced to abandon their mech was usually a dead man.

He sighed, wishing that there was some kind of gauge to let him know how much coal he was burning and how much he had left. But there wasn't. The engineers hadn't managed to figure out that bit of technology yet either.

At least they had improved the sightlines. There had been talk, he knew, of some kind of visor with sensors or even a screen through which he could view his surroundings. Either would have helped immensely, but no such option existed.

In the meantime, he made do with what he had. The eyes of the mechs were open holes, slotted with iron bars. If he lowered the mech's head, the creature's neck stretched straight forward on an even level with his own, he could peer through either the eyes or its open mouth. By far the most useful, and the one he relied on the most, were the grilles set into the beast's chest, closest as they were to his own eye level.

Still, despite improvements, the Empire's war machines felt little more than iron coffins, the walls closing in, constricting. Desmond took a deep breath of hot, damp air. He would either live to see the end of this battle, or he wouldn't. The same risks and chances as always. Neither really mattered to him.

Of course, he didn't want to die, but if he did, at least he would be free of his family's expectations, which sometimes felt even more suffocating than the mech's interior—which he would also be free of. And if he succeeded, well…he'd be giving them exactly what they wanted.

Desmond reached out with one gloved hand, shifting the lever that controlled the mech's head, raising it. Through the grille in its chest, he could just make out the opposing forces. The Anarshans had leapt off the city's Great Wall and were closing in fast. He stiffened, preparing to engage.

With the mechs too heavy to fly, they were of little use against real dragons. He'd been warned about the Anarshans, how they had a long history of fighting beside the winged beasts. He'd hardly dared to believe it—much of what was said of Anarsha was a confusing jumble of myth and legend—but he knew better than to discount the rumors entirely.

Now, here he was, seeing the proof with his own eyes. Both Elath and Shemar had relied on human soldiers, both on foot and horseback, and the typical weaponry. Bows, swords, war hammers, shields, and the occasional siege weapon, only the latter posing a real threat to the mechs. They had never faced a challenge like this.

But the Empire had anticipated such a threat, as it had all others laid before it. Turning his mech slightly to the side, Desmond saw the siege weaponry that had accompanied them, now in position. There were catapults and trebuchets far back behind the line, ready to be brought forward once the Anarshan force had been taken care of.

That Great Wall, if Akkadia had her way, would not stand much longer.

And as for the dragons, Desmond was eager to see how they would fare against the ballistae the Empire had waiting for them, each already fitted with a long bolt.

He heard the unmistakable sound of the first ballista firing and turned back to face the front. Limited though his view of the battlefield was, he could still hear it well enough, raging around him.

Unnatural shrieks and roars rang out, which could only mean some of the ballistae had struck true. Desmond smiled grimly to himself.

To his left, the first dragons had arrived, swooping down low to strafe the line of mechs with fire. He watched as their jaws parted, a blast of orange flame shooting forth. Desmond could see the nearest rider, astride the beast's back, drawing back the longbow they carried. He heard it strike the side of his mech, but the metal didn't so much as dent.

And then the heat rolled toward him. Desmond's pulse kicked into a gallop, his earlier feeling of satisfaction fleeing in the face of fear—not a sensation he was used to feeling while inside a mech.

But if the flames reached him, it would roll over his mech in an unstoppable wave, forcing him to either abandon it or burn to death, trapped inside. Given how hot the flames already were, without having yet reached him, he doubted he would have time to extricate himself.

He grabbed one of the levers and shoved it forward as far as it would go. The mech responded, leaping forward, its long metallic limbs extending as it accelerated into a run.

Never a smooth ride at the best of times, Desmond was jostled painfully within the mech's interior, straps digging into him as his body strained against them. But he had escaped the flames.

He could feel the power in the metallic beast as it charged forward, joints hissing with expelled steam. He pulled back the throttle, slowing the creature, the reminder to conserve fuel forever lurking in the back of his mind.

Desmond moved his hands to other levers, his feet constantly pumping the pedals, as he brought the mech about. They resisted him slightly; one needed to be somewhat strong to operate such a heavy machine. Gazing through the grille, he took in the scene around him.

Some of the dragons must have been driven from the air by ballistae, because one of the riders stood just ahead of Desmond, shaking his head and looking around in a daze, eyes widening as he took in the mech.

Desmond thrust the throttle forward again and the mech responded. The man didn't even have time to run before the machine was upon him, Desmond already pushing the button that opened the mech's jaws, clamping them shut on the Anarshan.

Tossing the man aside as though he weighed nothing, Desmond turned back to face the direction he'd come, expecting to see a line of mechs behind him. He froze, hands stilling on the levers.

There was a line, sure enough, but it was one of fire, the crumpled, warped forms of the mechs lying motionless. The dragons had easily strafed them, destroying the Empire's most powerful weapons before they could fully be brought to bear. The ballistae might have been capable of bringing a dragon down, but there were simply too many of them, and not enough siege weapons.

Already the Akkadian line was scattered, disorganized, thrown into a panic. As he watched, the closest ballista vanished, consumed in an explosion of angry red flames.

He needed to get out of here. They all did. They were too exposed, out in the open plain, and with the dragons able to take to the air, they could easily fly out of view of his sightlines. One could be hovering just over his mech even now and he wouldn't know it until it was too late.

Panic threatening to constrict his lungs, Desmond flung the throttle forward, convinced a wall of fire was even now hurtling down toward him. The mech lurched forward. He could see the tree line ahead. If they could just duck beneath the cover of the forest, it would conceal them from the dragon's view.

The mech had taken perhaps a dozen steps when a wave of heat washed over it. Desmond cried out, the air searing his lungs. The walls of the mech seemed to glow orange for a moment and then the machine stumbled, pitching forward.

Through the grille, Desmond watched as it fell, face-first, its metal snout gouging into the ground as it slid to a stop. He was thrown forward, the straps arresting his momentum, digging into his shoulders.

He gasped, frantically jerking the levers. The heat was still there, licking at his heels. He could smell smoke, the air within the mech's chamber too thin. It felt as though his skin might melt away at any moment, but somehow, he wasn't dead yet.

The mech did not respond to his commands. A hiss of steam escaped the mech's gaping mouth, sounding to Desmond like a dying breath. He let go of the levers, turning his fumbling fingers to the straps that held him in. He was moments away from burning to death, trapped within his own downed mech.

The straps came undone in his hands and Desmond pushed out of the seat, pressing against the side panel that would allow him out, hoping the mechanism hadn't been damaged.

The mech's side slid open and Desmond staggered free of it. He coughed as smoke rolled over him and then he was clear of it, breathing deeply, the awful heat behind him.

He slowed to a stop, the early morning sunlight on his face as he stared up into the sky. There was nothing to block his vision now and he watched, with a mixture of horror and wonder, as dragons swooped above.

It was a rout.

Callum's fear had remained, threatening to choke him, right up until the moment the two advancing sides had collided. And then there was no time to think. He had loosed his first arrow, trying to watch and see if it hit, but they were moving too fast. And then K'Sante was strafing the nearest line of Akkadians, the heat of his flames washing harmlessly over Callum.

The Empire's mechs, fearsome though they undoubtedly were, had been rendered useless. Stuck on the ground, slower than their living counterparts, they were sitting ducks, easily destroyed before they could be used.

The siege weapons were an unexpected twist. One bolt from a ballista narrowly missed K'Sante's wing. Callum heard it as it soared past, stirring the air in its wake. He drew another arrow and sent it flying toward the man operating the machine. Callum felt a surge of satisfaction as the man went down.

"Did you see that?" he called.

He hadn't missed.

"Nice shot," K'Sante replied.

The dragon let out a roar, the sound reverberating through Callum's chest, and turned his attention to the other siege weapons. The Empire hadn't been foolish enough to lump them all together, but unlike the mechs—which were clumsy and slow enough as it was—the ballistae couldn't get out of the way in time to avoid the fire.

Callum continued to fire at any Akkadians unfortunate enough to be on foot. He didn't see if any of his other shots landed, but he felt confident that at least a few had.

K'Sante was far more effective, his fire carving large swaths of destruction. Briefly, Callum glimpsed Anake atop Vitanni, the dragon's green scales glittering in the sun. He thought he saw Bane, swooping low over the Akkadians. It was risky, getting so close, but from such a distance, he could hardly miss, large wings spread wide.

Callum felt a rush of pride for his unit—and their force as a whole. They had trained for this. They were ready. The Empire would not find them so easily conquered as they had Shemar and Elath.

He had thought killing would be difficult, and perhaps the weight of it would catch up with him later. He had loosed the arrow as though it were nothing, the motions familiar from the countless hours spent training. He had been too high to make out the Akkadian's face, too far away to hear any cry of pain he might have made, or see any blood. He was just another nameless, faceless enemy, one who would not think twice about doing the same to Callum—or any other Anarshan.

No, in the moment, all Callum felt was a savage sort of exhilaration. He was riding atop a dragon and they were *winning*.

Below, he could see the Akkadian line breaking. Those that remained scrambled to get away, falling back instead of pressing forward. Somehow, the order to retreat must have been given.

We've done it. We've won.

He wanted nothing more than to chase after the retreating Akkadians, snapping at their heels. Instead, he settled for laughing aloud. He had been so worried about his first battle, expecting it to be difficult, when in reality, it had been anything but.

Too easy, he might have said, suspecting a trap, if he hadn't just seen the Akkadian force decimated.

How was this the mighty Akkadian Empire he had heard so much about? The one that had marched across the land, conquering first Elath and then Shemar, with little resistance from either kingdom.

The Empire had simply shaken off the other kingdoms' efforts as though they were nothing, a minor irritation, the way a horse might shake off biting gnats.

And yet, here was the Empire, throwing themselves at the Anarshans, their advance breaking like a wave upon the rocks.

Behind him, Callum could hear cheers going up. Victory was theirs, the last of the Akkadian line falling back toward the forest. A few stragglers remained, as though reluctant to give up the fight, but they could be dealt with easily enough.

Callum laid a hand against K'Sante's scales, burnished bright red in the sunlight. "We did it!"

The dragon turned, as though to say something. Instead, he bellowed in pain, shuddering beneath Callum.

For a moment, Callum simply stared in shock, unable to comprehend what had happened. Then he saw the ballista bolt protruding from the dragon's chest, puncturing straight through the scales, burrowing deep.

His stomach plummeted and he reached out toward the bolt, helplessly, though he could neither reach it nor hope to pull it out. K'Sante's wings beat frantically, managing to keep them aloft for a few more seconds, and then they were falling, rapidly losing height.

The wind whipped at Callum's hair, at his clothes, stinging his eyes, until his vision blurred. He reached out to touch K'Sante once more, calling out to the dragon, trying to encourage him, assure him that it would be all right.

The dragon struggled, trying to slow their descent and regain some semblance of control, but it was no use, his efforts already weakening. He gazed back at Callum with something like regret until even that was gone, fading along with the light.

Callum fumbled for a moment with his harness, the straps securing him to the saddle, but he couldn't get them to disconnect. He sat back. What good would it do? Without the straps holding him down, he would likely be blown out of the saddle and the end result would be the same.

He hadn't thought they were so high, their fall dizzying as the ground rushed up at an alarming rate. Callum blinked back tears. They had been so close…

His thoughts turned to Chandra and their grandmother, waiting back home. *I'm sorry.*

Anarsha remained free, safe from the Empire, at least. Their efforts had not been in vain.

He closed his eyes, not wanting to see the moment the ground rose up to meet him.

Perhaps he had been right to be afraid.

VII

By nightfall, news of Anarsha's victory had spread throughout the city, tales of how the mighty Empire had been routed and forced to flee without ever coming close to breaching the Great Wall. A feast was prepared at the palace, the best wines brought up from the cellars, as the rest of the city celebrated in their own way.

Ulric, it seemed, had no intention of joining the feast. Roman found his father still seated in the throne room, where he had received the news earlier in the day, the generals and commanding officers arriving to personally inform him of Anarsha's victory.

Now, the light in the long, narrow room was slanted, the setting sun pouring in through the thin windows. Ulric sat on his throne, chin resting on one hand, the picture of a man deep in thought.

In the doorway, Roman sighed and made his way painstakingly forward, leaning heavily on his cane. He was rarely able to get around without it. Two more years gone, bringing with them a litany of healers, each one at a loss just as much as the last.

Roman resented the cane, but could not deny its necessity, his muscles wasting away as though he never used them at all.

Much as he hated needing the cane, he was grateful that he still had some way of getting around and maintaining his independence. He feared the day when not even the cane would be enough.

Ulric glanced up at the sound of his son's uneven footsteps.

"They'll miss you at the feast," Roman said, coming to a stop. "The king should be seen to celebrate."

"There's nothing worth celebrating," the king replied, turning to stare out one of the windows, the city beyond just visible, red stone in the sunlight.

Roman frowned, not liking his father's tone. "What do you mean? We won, didn't we?"

"For now. The Empire will be back. It's only a matter of time."

"Do you really think they'll try again, after how soundly they were beaten?"

"It will only strengthen their resolve. Besides, we suffered losses of our own. Too many."

Roman said nothing. The battle had been swift and decisive. The Anarshans had lost soldiers, it was true, but nothing like the losses suffered by the Empire. The ground beyond the Great Wall was still littered with the corpses of their fallen war machines.

Ulric shook his head. "They weren't trained enough. They didn't have enough time. The dragons may be more than a match for the mechs, but the humans riding upon them are not so."

"So what do we do?" Roman asked. He tightened his grip on his cane, dreading the answer.

"We must increase recruitment efforts and intensify their training." The king stood. "Make no mistake. The Empire will be back and you can be sure they will have learned their own lessons from this battle. We must be ready."

Ulric strode past his son, heading for the doorway. Roman watched him go and then sank down onto the vacated throne with a sigh, his legs no longer able to support him.

He had come here for nothing and would have to find the strength to rise again and make his laborious way back to his quarters.

As he sat there, watching the last of the sun bleed through the windows, he couldn't help but wonder if Anarsha was fighting a hopeless battle, refusing to admit it, the same way he was.

Hadrian, the first self-proclaimed emperor of the burgeoning Akkadian Empire, tapped a single finger on the arm of his throne, listening to the report being given by both his general and the Minister of Defense.

The throne room was a chamber of marble and glass and the two men's voices echoed softly as they spoke. Hadrian listened with growing impatience. The battle had gone poorly and he did not like being thwarted.

No, worse than poorly. It had been a disaster from the very beginning, the greatest and most humiliating defeat the Empire had yet suffered since they'd first gone on campaign. It was an embarrassment and that was yet another thing Hadrian did not like. He would not be mocked, especially not by some southern pagans who still believed in demons and worshipped long-dead saints.

He didn't bother keeping his facial expressions in check. There was no need beneath the mask he wore, which covered his entire face from forehead to chin. He could see through the eyes, but none could see him.

Usually, he did not wear it in the presence of his most trusted advisors. They already knew what he looked like and the purpose of the masks was to disguise his appearance. But he found it useful when dealing with difficult conversations. It was tiring, always keeping one's emotions under control, especially when one had been cursed with as mercurial a temperament as he.

Three other men stood off to one side, motionless. They could have been carved from stone, hardly seeming to breathe at all. They were dressed in silk robes, identical to the one Hadrian wore, and each wore a mask, hiding their own features. But for the throne he sat on, they could have been him, and that was precisely the point.

His Masks, his bodyguards and body doubles. Each had sworn an oath of loyalty to him, forsaking their former lives and selves, becoming nothing more than his shadow.

There was no need for them now, no need for them to be in the room at all, privy to this conversation. But they would hardly tell anyone and Hadrian found them useful to keep around, much like his own mask. Other people found them unsettling, the blank masks forever staring and Hadrian found it useful to make petitioners and supplicants feel uncomfortable.

"So," the emperor said, leaning forward when at last the report had been concluded, "what can we do to make sure this does not happen again?"

The Empire had never faced a challenge such as this. As powerful as their mechs were, it seemed the Anarshans had a version that was far superior. Hadrian tapped his finger more rapidly against his throne. This was a problem.

What if the southern kingdom decided that chasing the Akkadians from their borders wasn't enough and came marching for *their* door? Hadrian didn't think it likely. He doubted the southern kingdom had the hunger for conquest. They were too soft, they thought too small, content to remain isolated, clinging to their outdated myths.

Hadrian sniffed. One of his greatest accomplishments, he thought, was to all but banish religion, the practice so discouraged it was practically abandoned. The Empire was his subjects' god. Their protector, their provider, the one who deserved their obedience and devotion. Certainly not some saints!

No, the saints would not save Anarsha. They couldn't even save themselves. This was but a temporary setback, annoying though it was. He would not be thwarted by a kingdom of ignorant heathens.

Neither the Minister nor the general had yet given him an answer, so Hadrian continued.

"Flight is out of the question. The mechs are too heavy and always will be. Their armor plating is what makes them such strong weapons."

"Some would argue that armor plating is a vulnerability, not a strength, when it comes to the dragons," the general said, his lips thin.

"Regardless, flight is impossible." Hadrian waved a hand. "What else is there? What would even the playing field? The mechs must be able to breathe fire if they are to stand a chance against real dragons." He turned his head, just enough to let the Minister know he was looking at him from behind the mask. "I want your best engineers working on it."

He nodded. "It will be done, my lord."

"Our ballistae are vulnerable, but effective. I want more siege weaponry brought to bear. We must force those beasts from the air. If we can ground them, I'm confident our mechs will prove more than a match."

"I will see it done, my liege."

Hadrian ceased his tapping. "And one more thing—it does not matter how well-trained the Anarshans may be. They are no match for our machines. The dragons are the only real threat. It does not matter to me how long it takes to thin out their numbers, but thin them out we will. Dragons do not hatch and mature overnight, but our mechs can. I want production doubled. Day and night. Do not cease until the work is done."

The Minister bowed. "As you wish, my lord."

Hadrian dismissed them to carry out his orders. Much as he loathed it, he could be patient. He knew the cost of rushing, of pushing too hard, too fast.

Elath and Shemar had been too easy, offering up little in the way of resistance. He had been spoiled with those two campaigns, but here…here was a real challenge.

If this was to be a war of attrition, so be it. He was confident he had more soldiers to throw at Anarsha's Great Wall than the southern kingdom had to defend it, dragons or not.

And once the dragons' numbers were thinned, there would be nothing standing in his way. His mechs would march into the city, mowing down all who opposed them. The last kingdom would be his and his Empire would be complete.

Behind his mask, Hadrian smirked. It might be best if the southern kingdom were to develop a taste for blood, striking now while Akkadia was weakened, licking her wounds. But he knew they wouldn't. They were too weak, just like all the others. Akkadia was the one who had dared to take the first step, to be the kingdom that rose above all else, to lead them all. That was what most people didn't seem to grasp. Most people in the world were like sheep, desperate for someone to lead them.

Hadrian was only too eager to provide.

PART II: THE MADNESS OF WAR

VIII

Two years. Two years and Callum had so little to show for it.

Chandra eagerly devoured each of his letters, hearing his voice echoing in her mind as though he were reading aloud to her. But it wasn't the same as seeing him in person and she wondered when she would finally get to lay eyes on him again.

She had been aware of the impending battle, as had likely every person in Anarsha. She had heard the bells and horns, she had seen the dragon riders fly overhead, gathering at the Great Wall. She had even heard snatches of the battle taking place beyond the city walls. And of course she'd heard news of Anarsha's victory, spreading swift and wide.

She told herself to be patient when Callum's letter did not arrive. The post could be slow, having no consideration for her pulse whenever a missive from her cousin failed to arrive on time. He was likely too busy in the aftermath of the battle to write.

But some part of her knew, the part where dread resided, coiled and waiting.

No letter from Callum arrived. Instead, a letter from his commanding officer, impersonal and hurriedly dashed off, regretfully informing her of her cousin's death. The letter did not specify how he had died, only that he had fallen in defense of his kingdom, that she should be proud of him for that, and to take what solace she could from the knowledge that he did not suffer.

Not knowing how he died, Chandra doubted that. He had died in battle and such deaths were rarely peaceful ones. It wasn't a question of whether suffering was involved, only how much.

Along with the letter came a box, pathetically small, of Callum's personal effects, which Chandra could scarcely bring herself to look at. She set it, all that Callum had left behind, along with the letter, on the kitchen table and stepped back, numb, as her grandmother wordlessly sorted through it.

She had seen more of life and perhaps took a more pragmatic view. Callum was gone and denying it wouldn't change or solve anything. Something had to be done with the box; it couldn't rest forever on the kitchen table, untouched.

Two years in the army. An entire life lived besides and this was all that remained to show for it.

There was a uniform, neatly folded, along with a pair of civilian clothes that Callum had worn the day he left. Chandra tried to picture him in her mind's eye on that last day, when he'd said goodbye, but she couldn't have said what he'd been wearing—not with any certainty.

There was some stationary, mostly unused, along with writing utensils, though one note had a few attempted lines of writing, haphazardly scratched out. Callum had never gotten around to finishing it, if he'd ever intended to, and now Chandra would never know what he'd meant to say or to whom.

And then there was a bundle of letters, neatly tied with twine so as not to be lost. Every letter she had sent him, he had kept. She wondered whether he had ever gone over them more than once, in the long, lonely hours of the night, as she had, reading them in each other's voices.

The only other item of interest in the box was the stub of a bayberry wax candle, burned down to nearly nothing, but not quite. Chandra blinked back sudden tears. It was the same candle she had made and insisted he take with him, all those days and months ago.

He had savored it, in that way he'd had, of wanting to be careful, to cherish things, knowing that one day they would be gone. She'd tried to tell him time and time again that that was the purpose of candles. To be used, but that hadn't stopped him from savoring this one.

Chandra turned away then, ducking out the back door and seeking the shelter of her workshop. She could stay there for as long as she wished, in solitude, missing as many meals as she could stand, and still her grandmother would not set foot in there. She never did.

She wondered how the old woman could stand it, losing so many family members. Both Chandra's own parents and Callum's were gone, which was why they had come to live with their grandmother in the first place. How did someone lose so many people and still keep going?

Chandra had been too young to remember her parents. She felt their loss only distantly, the knowledge that she had lost something, something that was precious to most people, but it didn't touch her personally. It was the knowledge that something had been lost, rather than the *feeling* of its absence.

She felt Callum's loss keenly. On the surface, it was no different from any other day. A week ago, he would still have been gone, staying at the barracks, and she still wouldn't know when to expect him back. It was hard to believe, to accept, after not seeing him for two years, that he was actually gone and would never come back.

There was no body, no funeral, nothing to prove he was really gone. No closure, nothing to mourn over.

Chandra huddled in her workshop and welcomed whatever feelings may come. It wasn't bloody fair! The very first battle—a rout by all accounts—and still it had to take her cousin from her. Her cousin, who was more like a brother, who couldn't even survive his first battle.

Where was the fairness in that?

She let the tears come, cursing the Akkadians until she could think of no more hateful words to spew at them.

The time for dinner came and went, Chandra's stomach knotted with hunger, but she ignored it. It only added to her pain and somehow, she deserved it.

Only after darkness fell and all lights were extinguished within the house did she emerge. She ducked into her room and withdrew the small box that contained every letter Callum had sent to her over the last two years.

With the bundle of her own letters returned to her, she could read them, one after the other, each one carefully dated, and recreate the events of the past years. But she read only his, by the weak light of one of her bayberry candles. They were the last words he would ever speak to her, little had she known it at the time.

Callum told her much about his time in the army, every little detail that leapt into his mind, that he thought she might find interesting. He'd told her about his dragon, K'Sante. Briefly, she wondered if he had also perished along with her cousin. From what Callum had written of their bond, she thought it likely. K'Sante hadn't seemed the type to abandon his rider.

Once again, she wondered how they had died. She would likely never know. She tried to convince herself that it didn't matter, that it was better not to know, but she didn't quite believe that.

Callum had also written of the two members of his unit, an Elathan refugee named Anake and an arrogant man called Victor. Everything that Callum had known about them, so did she, and in that moment, she hated them for failing to keep her cousin safe. Wasn't that what a squad was supposed to do?

She read the letters until the candle burned out completely, the first gray hint of morning slipping through the curtains. Only then did she go to bed.

Pragmatically, Chandra knew that life still had to go on, even without Callum in it. There were still orders waiting for her in the workshop, that needed to be fulfilled. But she couldn't bring herself to care. It was as though Anarsha had lost after all. They had failed, there was nothing left to hope for, simply waiting for the end.

How long she would have been content to carry on like that, Chandra would never know. It could have been weeks or only a handful of days—time had lost all meaning—but soon enough, her own recruitment notice arrived.

For a moment, she stared at the hateful letter, many different thoughts racing through her mind, quick as lightning.

She debated hurling the notice into the fire and watching it burn, ignoring the summons altogether. They could come drag her away from hearth and home. She would go without a fuss, but not a moment before. What did any of it matter anymore?

Her grandmother shuffled into the room, her knobby hands wrapped around the head of her cane as she regarded the piece of paper.

"You'll be off, then," she said simply.

"I thought we defeated the Empire," Chandra said, her voice sounding flat. *We drove them back. What use, what need is there in recruiting more soldiers? Surely, it's over.*

It had better be over. How much more would be asked—no, demanded—of her? How much more would she be expected to give?

Her grandmother shook her head. "They'll be back. You'd best begin packing."

"I can pack later," Chandra said, folding the letter tightly along the creases. "There's something I have to do first."

Much as she had the day Callum had left, Chandra made her way to the temple. It, at least, hadn't changed in the past two years. The sky was overcast; it had rained the night before, the cobblestone streets still glittering with moisture, though it seemed to be done for now.

Unlike her last visit, Chandra did not find the temple empty when she mounted the stone steps and she fought down a wave of annoyance. The saints belonged to everyone, not just her, though it seemed that they did not belong to her at all.

She glared at the stained-glass mural of Sonera, the saint she had begged to protect her cousin, suddenly unsure of what had brought her there. To ask for protection for herself? The idea was laughable.

The saints had failed to keep Callum safe, despite her prayers and in spite of her grandmother's daily pleas. Why would they treat her any differently?

Suddenly, Chandra didn't want to pray. She doubted she would have been able to anyway, but what was the point? It wouldn't change what would ultimately happen. Her prayers had done nothing to change Callum's fate.

Whatever was meant to happen would, and no amount of pleading would change that.

Chandra's hands curled into fists, her fingernails biting into her palms. And now it was her turn, called up to take her cousin's place.

But she would not die at the hands of the Akkadians. She would do everything in her power to send as many Akkadians to the afterlife as possible. They could burn in hell and she would happily send them there.

They would not take her. They would not take her kingdom.

She could not bring Callum back. But she could avenge him with every drop of Akkadian blood spilled.

I will do this for you, Callum, she vowed, lifting her gaze to once again stare down the saint Sonera. *I swear it.*

She left the temple without uttering a single prayer. All she had offered the saints was her oath of vengeance, committed in their presence.

Back home, the only thing left to do was gather the few possessions she was allowed to bring with her. She couldn't help but wonder, as she filled her pack, whether another little box would be sent back to her grandmother, filled with the items she now packed.

Her grandmother was waiting for her in the kitchen and Chandra felt a stab of guilt, her anger melting away. She had thought of nothing but her own grief and desire for revenge, she hadn't stopped to consider what would happen to her grandmother with her away.

Now there would be no one to fulfill the orders. With Chandra gone and no more candles being made, how would her grandmother provide for herself?

Chandra swallowed. "I'll send money."

Callum had done the same, sending his army salary back to the two of them and she wanted to assure her grandmother that she intended to do the same. There would be less money without the candle orders to supplement their income, but if she was frugal—

Her grandmother waved a hand. "Don't worry about any of that."

"I'll do it," Chandra insisted.

They'd received some money from the throne shortly after Callum had died, a paltry sum in the grand scheme of things, but better than nothing. It felt strange—wrong—to put a price on a human life. To know that Callum was worth so very little.

But Chandra knew it wasn't enough for her grandmother to live on and it wouldn't last.

"I'll write, too," she added, remembering the promise she'd asked of Callum. "Every day."

Though saints knew what she would write about. She didn't have Callum's way with words.

To her surprise, the old woman shuffled forward and wrapped her arms around her only remaining grandchild. Her arms were thin and birdlike, but her grip was strong.

"Be careful," she whispered.

"Always," Chandra whispered back.

"The Akkadians will try to take Anarsha, no matter how many times we beat them back."

Chandra swallowed, remembering her vow. "Then we'll destroy them. Every last one."

Chandra thought she knew what to expect as she mounted the stairs to the military complex. Callum had written of his experiences and surroundings in such detail that she could nearly picture it herself. Of course, reality always differed from the imagination, no matter how vivid the description, but she knew where to go and what to expect.

She was far from the only new recruit. People seemed to be everywhere, some shuffling along, reluctant, and others in a hurry to reach their destinations. Once she was inside the complex, Chandra found herself funneled forward, the other recruits pressed tightly around her.

Quickly, they were taken to be assigned a dragon and then told to report to the training area. Chandra had thought that this moment would involve more pomp and circumstance. She was to be assigned a *dragon*. The creature she would be training and fighting alongside, and with whom she was supposed to forge a bond that would see them both safely through battle.

Briefly, she couldn't help but wonder if Callum's bond with K'Sante had been weak and that was why they had both fallen. That wasn't the impression she'd had from his letters, but how could one truly know until such a bond was put to the test?

Whatever had happened that day, Callum hadn't survived his first and only battle.

She swallowed, staring up at the dragon the officer named Khan had led her to. It was all happening too fast, but she supposed there was no time to waste after the last battle. Akkadia could strike again and they had to be ready. Anarsha had responded by shoring up her ranks.

She was a soldier now, one of many in a great army. She was no one special and would receive no more time or consideration than anyone else.

The dragon stared down at her with hard green eyes. Her scales were black as midnight, but they seemed to shift color in the sunlight as she moved, Chandra catching glimpses of blue and green hues.

Her front feet closely resembled human hands, with four fingers and a thumb, each tipped with deadly curved claws. Her face was long and narrow, her snout slightly more pointed than round. Large, thick scales like armor plating covered her from neck to tail tip. Frills ran down her back, beginning in the middle of her forehead and ending just before her tail.

Her bright green eyes were surrounded by slightly darker outlines, as though to help with glare. It made them stand out all the more starkly.

Sheboleth was her name and the two fell into step beside each other as they made their way to the training compound.

"Have you had a rider before?" Chandra asked, wondering if her previous partner had been killed in the battle and she was now being reassigned.

"No," Sheboleth replied. "I was asked to step in after the last battle, same as you, I expect." She glanced sidelong at Chandra.

"Yes."

Chandra had wanted to ask the dragon if she'd known either Callum or K'Sante, but she was a new recruit like Chandra herself and so likely wouldn't have known either of them.

Once the new recruits had gathered with their dragons, they were assigned units. Chandra was led over to a young man and woman. She knew who they were before their names were even spoken, recognizing them from her cousin's writing.

There was Anake, with her dark hair and muscled arms, which she crossed as she regarded Chandra. And Victor, an irritating smirk on his lips that Chandra already wanted to slap off his face.

She tensed, bracing herself for the comments that were sure to come. Victor had made no secret of his dislike for Callum and there was no reason to think he'd like her any better. That suited her just fine; she already disliked the both of them, for failing to keep Callum safe.

Of course, she'd be assigned to her cousin's old squad.

Victor watched as she approached. "And who might you be?"

"Chandra. No need to introduce yourselves. I already know who you are."

Victor grinned. "Hear that, Anake? Our reputations precede us."

"I don't think that's the reason, you pompous ass," Anake snorted, though there was no real rancor behind her words. "She said her name was Chandra. Callum's cousin?"

"Ah," Victor said flatly, his eyes still on Chandra. "No doubt he told you all about us?"

"And from what I'm gathering," Sheboleth added, her green eyes cutting to Victor, "you didn't exactly make a great impression."

Chandra felt a rush of warmth toward her new companion, already sticking up for her against these two, making her feel less alone.

Victor frowned. "How do you know who she is?" he demanded, turning to Anake and ignoring the dragon.

"Because Callum talked to me more than he did you— though I can't imagine why. He told me things, occasionally, and I listened, whether I really wanted to or not. Knowledge can be useful—you should try it sometime, Victor."

If Anake's razzing irritated Victor, he didn't show it. Instead, he grinned as he took Chandra in with new eyes.

"The candle maker. I can't believe I didn't see it before. I can smell the stench of tallow from here." He turned to

Anake. "I don't know what all the fuss is about. We're obviously going to win the war. Why, with an army made of candle makers, bakers' sons, and fishmongers, how could we lose?"

"Yes," Sheboleth drawled, gazing around. "They needn't have brought in so many new recruits. From the sound of things, you could win the war all on your own."

At that, Victor's face darkened. "Well, at least your dragon's tongue is sharp. Whether the same can be said for her claws, we'll have to wait and see."

"We don't have to wait," Sheboleth retorted. "We can find out, right here and now." She flexed her claws against the stone they stood upon.

Chandra thought they looked plenty sharp to her, but she was spared having to find out whatever happened next.

"Excuse me," a new voice piped up. "Sorry I'm late."

Sheboleth moved to the side, revealing a young man—who looked more like a boy, really—mounting the stairs, his dragon right behind him.

He was thin and on the shorter side, his thick head of gold curls only adding to his youthful appearance. At least, Chandra assumed he was old enough to enlist. Surely Anarsha hadn't resorted to recruiting children just yet.

"Oh, saints," Victor muttered. "Another one."

"I'm Gideon," the newcomer announced, holding out his hand to no one in particular, his eyes darting awkwardly between the three of them.

He let his arm slowly fall, coming to rest at his side like a dead thing. He cleared his throat, gesturing to his dragon. "This is Mael."

The dragon was a far more impressive specimen. Her scales were a beautiful mix of yellow, green, and brown, like the skin of a pineapple. Her multiple sets of horns and spikes lent her a dangerous air.

Since no one seemed keen to make introductions, Chandra did, taking pity on him.

There was, thankfully, no more time to talk. Orders were being shouted down the line. Chandra took a deep breath. This was it, time for her first training session. Thanks to Callum, she had a pretty good idea of what to expect there as well.

"I'll find you later," Sheboleth said, turning away with a curt nod.

Chandra picked up a bow, testing its weight in her hands. She had no idea how to use it, but that didn't matter. Callum hadn't either, when he'd first come here. She could learn.

She *would* learn. She would not be like him, falling in her very first battle. She had come here to avenge him, to kill Akkadians, and this bow was how she would do it.

Gideon, standing beside her, looked terrified, staring at the bow in his hands as if it were a snake that might strike him. On her other side, just past Anake, Chandra saw Victor roll his eyes.

She clenched her jaw. "Just stick by me," she whispered to Gideon. "We'll figure it out together."

The look he gave her was one of such genuine gratitude that she was momentarily taken aback. And then warmth replaced the shock.

She had found at least one friend in this hostile place and Sheboleth seemed promising, too. That would have to be enough. After all, she hadn't come here to make friends. She had come here to spill Akkadian blood, and despite what Victor thought of her, she intended to do just that.

IX

The day ended much too quickly for Chandra's liking. She would have been content to remain on the training grounds, practicing long into the night. Even though her muscles cried out in protest, used in ways they had never been tested before, she was reluctant to call it a day and retreat to the mess hall and barracks.

She savored the pain, uncomfortable as it was. With each draw of the bowstring, she became a little stronger. A little more accurate. A little more confident, all qualities she would need to bring down the Akkadians.

She tried to console herself, as she made her way to the mess hall for dinner, that the Akkadians were not on their doorstep. They were not, so far as they knew, even on their way. She had time. She could afford to be a little patient, but saints knew it was hard.

Chandra's eyes widened at the tray she was handed, filled to the brim with more food than she would have normally expected at home. There was a helping of boiled vegetables, seared chicken, a mixed variety of fruit, and a roll of bread. It seemed Anarsha wanted its soldiers well-fed.

She turned, debating where to sit. This was an opportunity, she knew, to get to know the members of her squad. Anake sat at the same table as Victor, but on the edge, as though relegated to the outskirts, by force or by choice, Chandra didn't know. Victor appeared to be holding court, a group of sycophants gathered around, clinging to his every word. Occasionally, Anake shot him a dark look and Chandra snorted to herself, wondering why the Elathan put up with him.

Instead, she found herself drawn to Gideon, seated alone. He picked at his food, looking even more boyish and frightened without his fearsome dragon, Mael. He brightened as she sat across from him.

"Mind if I join you?" she asked, feeling it rude to simply assume.

"Not at all."

"Not hungry?" She nodded to his tray.

He shook his head. "My stomach can be…sensitive sometimes."

Chandra nodded. No doubt he'd never been away from home before and the anxiety of the situation wasn't helping his nerves any. She had never been away from home before either and she swallowed hard as the realization struck her, the piece of bread she'd been chewing going down with difficulty.

"What did you think of training?" he asked.

Chandra shot him a look of surprise, not expecting him to be the chatty type, but she found she didn't mind his questions.

She considered for a moment how best to answer. She wanted to be truthful, to be honest with at least one person here.

"I'm…behind," she said at last.

Anake and Victor had both been soldiers for much longer and it showed.

Gideon grimaced. "Not as much as me."

It was true that her experience had gone much better than his. She was behind, unskilled, and certainly nowhere near ready for battle—a fact that Victor had been keen to point out. But Gideon was an easier target for his taunting and criticism, and like all bullies, he went for the easy prey like a hound scenting blood.

"I can help you," Chandra offered, though she wasn't sure how much use she would be, still learning herself. It wouldn't be as useful as someone like Anake offering to assist him, but surely it had to be better than nothing.

His eyes brightened. "You will?"

Chandra shrugged. "Why not?"

In truth, she had a more selfish reason for wanting to improve—for wanting both of them to improve. She would have to work twice as hard in order to catch up, to be ready. And so she would. She would not be thought of as weak. She would not be the weak link that held others back.

Gideon grinned at her. Chandra ate her food while he happily prattled on, telling her about his family and where he grew up. His circumstances were not dissimilar to her own. He'd come from one of the poorer sections of the city, rising early and retiring late in order to help in his father's bakery.

Chandra looked at his hands, which he moved animatedly as he spoke. She could spot calluses and small scars here and there, where he'd been burned or cut himself. He wasn't a stranger to hard work, but archery and hand to hand combat were something else entirely.

There was something soft about this boy, something that was better suited to making pies and pastries than the madness of war. Victor had already noted it, pointing it out in his cruel way, but Chandra saw it too.

It was a shame that Gideon could not remain in his old life, bringing joy to other people, brightening their day with his homemade bread and desserts, the same way she did with her candles. But the world was cruel, war did not discriminate, and their kingdom needed them now.

Unlike her, Gideon did not have any other siblings or relatives that had been called up before him. He had been spared the first round of recruitment on account of him being an only child.

Briefly, Chandra wondered what would happen to his family if he were lost, a pit of dread settling in her stomach.

"I always wanted a sibling," Gideon sighed. "Apparently, I did have a brother, for a short time. He died as an infant and I was too small to remember him." He looked up. "Do you have any siblings?"

"No. I had a cousin, Callum. He was more like a brother to me, though." *Or what I imagine a brother to be like.*

Her chest tightened at the mention of her cousin and suddenly it was harder to breathe than a mere moment ago. She pushed the feeling aside, searching for the rage, or anything else, to bury it beneath.

"Do you think he's worried about you being here?" Gideon asked. Apparently, he'd missed her usage of past tense.

"He would be, if he knew. He died, in the last battle."

Gideon's face crumpled. "I'm sorry. I shouldn't have pressed. My aunt's always saying that I talk too much..."

Ah, there it was. The rage she had been searching for. Chandra grabbed for it, holding it close. He did talk too much, but her anger wasn't directed at him.

"That's why I'm here," she said. "Not just to take his place. It's why I want to train, to get better. To be the best that I can be. I want to make the Empire pay for what they did."

I want to make them suffer.

Gideon had not lost anyone to the Empire and so he didn't understand the fury that drove her. But there was someone who might.

She caught up with Anake as they were leaving the mess hall, preparing to return to their quarters or enjoy what little free time remained. Chandra wasn't sure what she would do with such spare time. She felt restless, the urge to *do* something threatening to overwhelm her. But there was nothing she could do. At least for now.

She called out to Anake and the Elathan stopped, turning.

Chandra swallowed. This was it. The moment she dreaded, unsure if she really wanted to know, but knowing she couldn't go on unless she did.

"You knew Callum," she said, recalling Anake's earlier remark that her cousin had sometimes spoken to her, and that she had listened.

Chandra raised her chin. "I want to know how he died."

Anake sighed. "It won't bring him back. Believe me, you're better off not knowing. Let it go."

"I can't," Chandra insisted, knowing that she really meant *I won't.*

"Fine. If that's what you want."

Before she could continue, Victor interrupted. Chandra hadn't noticed him before and she frowned, suspecting he'd eavesdropped before sauntering over.

"Your cousin died because the rage of war didn't suit him. He didn't have the stomach for it. He was weak, scared, and he died like the coward he was. Couldn't even survive his first battle. We don't need deadweights like that, unable to defend themselves, always putting others at risk." His eyes flashed between Chandra and Gideon, standing a short distance behind her, as though he saw more of the same when he looked at him.

"Victor—" Anake hissed.

He ignored her, drawing himself up, disdain in his every movement. "He probably pissed himself at the first sight of a mech."

The rage that Chandra had felt earlier surged to the surface.

"Take that back," she growled.

Her sore muscles trembled; her skin aflame.

"Truth hurts, doesn't it?"

Without stopping to think, Chandra reared her arm back—her thumb tucked on the outside, the way Callum had shown her—and slammed her fist into Victor's jaw.

She heard Gideon gasp behind her. To Chandra's chagrin, Victor barely flinched from the blow, while pain radiated through her knuckles. She'd never punched anyone before—even if she knew, in theory, how it was done—and she was surprised by how much it *hurt*. Wasn't it supposed to be more painful for the person being punched?

Gideon called out to her, but before she could react, Victor slapped her across the face, the force of it sending her stumbling down onto one knee. It hurt even more than her bruised knuckles, the pain searing across her face.

But more than anything, it was humiliating, and that was worse than any pain.

A shadow fell over them and a moment later, Sheboleth swooped down to tower over Chandra's kneeling form, Gideon hastily scrambling out of the way. The dragon made no attempt at a soft landing, bringing the force of her weight to bear.

She bared her teeth at Victor. "Enough."

He scoffed. "Too scared to face me without hiding behind your dragon? You really are Callum's cousin."

The rage coursing through Chandra's veins chased away all other thought. She didn't pause to consider how much larger he was than her, or the wisdom of what she was about to do.

She pushed to her feet and advanced toward him, but Victor simply shoved her back down again, as though she weighed nothing at all.

"I don't think I gave you permission to get up."

Sheboleth let out a snarl and lunged. Large Victor may have been, but he was just as helpless against a dragon as Chandra was against him.

The dragon slammed her hand into his chest, pinning him to the ground, her claws splayed.

"How does it feel?" she hissed. "To be small?"

Victor squirmed, but the weight of the dragon was too much.

He let out a frustrated huff, turning to Chandra. "Call off your beast. We both know she's not going to do anything, so let's leave off the dramatics."

"You wanna bet?" the dragon challenged. "I am not a dog that heeds its master."

Her lips peeled back from her teeth and she leered close, hot saliva growing heavy and dripping onto his face. Chandra even glimpsed flames beginning to gather at the back of the dragon's throat as she watched Victor thrash, his façade cracking, panic taking hold.

Suddenly, Victor's dragon, Bane, was there, launching himself at Sheboleth with a snarl. Chandra scrambled back on all fours, still on the ground where Victor had shoved her, as the two dragons scuffled for a moment before drawing apart.

Gideon reached out, helping Chandra to her feet, but she brusquely shoved him off, mentally scolding herself. None of this was his fault. He only wanted to help. But the fury hadn't quite left her.

Victor was glaring at her, part of his hair still damp with drool. His gaze promised that this was far from over, but Anake stood between them now, pushing him back.

"Your hand," Gideon murmured, looking down at Chandra's knuckles.

She glanced down. The skin had split open, already darkening with a bruise. Slowly, she flexed her fingers, wincing at the pain.

"We'd better go to the infirmary," Gideon added. "Make sure nothing's broken."

Sheboleth stared after Victor's retreating form, breathing heavily after her struggle with Bane. She trailed behind them as they made their way across the complex to the infirmary.

"I'll take things from here," Sheboleth told Gideon, once they'd arrived.

He ducked his head, scurrying away. Chandra sighed, wondering if she'd managed to scare off the one friend she'd made.

She watched him go. "It seems Victor isn't the only one nervous after your little display."

Sheboleth snorted. "My little display? The hell do you call all that back there?" She jerked her head in the direction they'd come. She ducked, following Chandra inside the building.

Her knuckles weren't broken, thankfully, though she was informed that they would be quite tender for some time. She remained seated, gazing down at her bandaged knuckles, even after the medic had moved on.

"You're quite the little spitfire, aren't you?" Sheboleth remarked.

Chandra looked up. It was hard to believe that she'd only arrived that morning. She and Sheboleth hadn't even known each other for a full day. She considered how little the dragon knew of her thus far—how little either of them knew the other—and wondered what she must think.

She sighed again. Not even a full day and already, she was picking fights. But Sheboleth had backed her up, in dramatic fashion, when they still barely knew each other.

Perhaps that boded well, a sign of how they would fare in battles to come.

"You know," Sheboleth went on, "if the two of you saved your animosity for the real enemy, we might actually get somewhere."

"Tell that to Victor," Chandra retorted.

"Oh, I already did."

Yes, she most certainly had.

"Thanks," Chandra murmured. "For backing me up."

The dragon snorted. Chandra was quickly coming to understand that she had different snorts to express derision, dismissiveness, and amusement. This one sounded dismissive.

"You're my person, foolish creature that you are. Clearly, you'd never make it without me."

There was amusement in Sheboleth's tone now, along with what Chandra realized was a sort of brusque affection.

She looked back down at her bandaged knuckles to hide her smile.

X

Gideon sought her out the next morning. "How's the hand?"

"Bruised, nothing broken."

He nodded. "I hope it doesn't interfere with your training."

Chandra flexed her knuckles experimentally. They were still sore and had stiffened up quite a bit. Her stomach clenched at the thought. She was already so behind; she didn't need any more setbacks—and this one of her own making.

In the end, it did hurt more than the day before, though that was likely due to the fact that *all* of her ached that morning. Training was hard. It was meant to test them, to push them to their limits, and Chandra reveled in it. She pushed herself, ignoring the pain at times and at others, letting it fuel her, with a single-minded determination that bordered on masochism.

She'd felt Victor's eyes on her when she'd first arrived and she brazenly met his gaze, refusing to look away. She expected some sort of punishment for what she had done—and braced herself for more confrontation to follow. But none came. He kept his distance and neither of them spoke to the other.

Gideon followed her gaze as they left the training compound for the day, Victor having gone on ahead. "I wonder why he doesn't like me," he murmured, almost as though speaking to himself.

"I don't think he likes anyone," Chandra replied.

"He'd like to think he's better than everyone else," Anake remarked as she passed them on the stairs. "But he isn't and he knows it."

In his letters, Callum had written that Victor was the son of one of the commanding officers, though he'd never specified which one. Chandra thought that would explain why Victor looked down on those less skilled—and from a humbler lineage—than himself.

"How can you stand him?" Chandra asked.

Anake looked thoughtful. "He tolerates me," she said finally, "because I'm a decent fighter. I tolerate him for the same reason. I don't care if he's an ass. If he can help us beat the Akkadians, that's all that matters to me."

Chandra cocked her head. She had no argument for that.

Gideon paled at the mention of the Akkadians. "Do you think they'll come back?"

"Don't you?" Anake countered. "Why do you think you're here?"

"Well…we've already beaten them once."

"That won't teach them. They won't stop until we make them. Until we pound them into the dirt so hard, they won't ever think about getting back up again." She shook her head. "No, they won't give up. They've come too far to quit now. Anarsha is the last free kingdom, the last one standing in their way. That makes us even more appealing to them."

Chandra watched as Gideon went on ahead, Anake's dark eyes flashing to her. "About your little fight…"

Chandra bristled slightly at Anake's tone, the way she reduced the confrontation down to nothing more than a spat. As if it wasn't Callum's honor that had been blackened.

She would never admit as much, but Chandra didn't think that Callum would be too concerned over any perceived insults to his honor. She was the hotheaded one, where he had always been the more even-tempered. She suspected she'd merely wanted to hit something, to lash out, and Victor had stepped in her way.

She shrugged. "What of it?"

Anake shrugged back, mimicking her movements. "Some would say it was a bold choice."

"And what would you say?"

"Bold is not the word I would use."

In spite of herself, Chandra grinned, some of her earlier anger melting away. It felt strange to be smiling, after everything that had happened. It felt wrong.

Anake grinned back and Chandra found she had a grudging admiration for the Elathan. She and Sheboleth would get along well, she thought.

"I expected there to be repercussions by now," she admitted, "given Victor's station."

"What do you mean?"

Chandra frowned. "I thought he was the son of a commanding officer." Could Callum have been wrong?

Anake grunted. "He is. Don't ask me which one, though, because I don't know. I doubt Victor knows either."

Chandra looked at the other woman in some surprise.

"He's the son of an officer, but whoever his father is, he never claimed Victor. I don't know if he joined the army to try and earn his father's approval, or at least acknowledgement, or if he came here for another reason.

Maybe he had nowhere else to go. There's a rumor that his mother never wanted him and sent him away the first chance she got. Either way, he's a bastard—literally. Whatever the truth, it doesn't matter to me." Anake's voice grew quiet as she looked over the stairs at the city sprawled out below. "I know what it is to not belong."

Chandra considered her, the refugee from Elath who had no place left to call home, joining the ranks of an unfamiliar—and slightly unfriendly—kingdom. Little wonder she felt some kinship with Victor. His father may have held a coveted and respected rank within the military, but that did Victor little good if the man refused to acknowledge his own son.

"That doesn't excuse him being bloody," Anake added, her voice firm once again. "But it does explain why he didn't report you. It won't win him any points in his favor if he goes crying to a father who wants nothing to do with him, instead of being a man and resolving the issue on his own. That, and I think he respects you."

"*What?*" Chandra exclaimed, certain she'd heard wrong.

"In his own way," Anake clarified. "Like I said, some would say what you did was bold. Regardless, not many would have done it."

She walked on, leaving Chandra to ponder her words.

Ulric's words haunted Roman.

That this wasn't over. That they hadn't seen the last of the Akkadians. That they had merely been granted a reprieve, not a pardon, and that the Empire would march again. How long could they be expected to hold out? How many times would they be asked to stand against the Empire of Engines?

He wished he knew. If they were doomed to eventually lose the war, at last worn down by the Empire's persistence, he wanted to know, to get it over with. Anything was better than the endless agony of waiting.

It was a feeling he was all too familiar with. Each day felt like an eternity, waiting, wondering when his body would eventually give out and he would die.

Yesterday had been a bad day. He'd lacked the strength to even rise from his bed. Roman hated those days the most, lying there, his own body refusing to obey him. His father was busy and though the servants would stay with him if he wished, they were not his friends and could not provide the companionship he longed for in those endless hours of solitude.

Roman sighed as he sat on the edge of the bed, waiting for that morning's healer to finish their ministrations. They could do little aside from monitor his vital signs and give him herbal concoctions to drink, each one more unpleasant than the last.

The last healer had even tried placing spirit shards over his body, the red gems cool against his skin. Though they could not contain a soul like a soul stone supposedly could, they were said to have some power of their own. Perhaps the healers hoped to stave off his demise, by tethering his spirit to his weakening body.

He had seen no obvious effect, despite the healer stretching his hands out, over Roman's body, beseeching the saints for healing. Roman believed in the saints and the stories that surrounded them, but they were all dead now and he doubted they would come to his aid.

The saints were gone and with them, Anarsha's golden age of healing. There were tales of soul stones and the power of harnessing the souls trapped within. The stories suggested that there was almost nothing the soul stones could not heal, but the stones were all but gone now, and no demons left to trap within them.

Briefly, Roman wondered if his soul could be trapped within one of the stones. If his soul could live on in the mortal world, encased in a soul stone for a thousand years. There were rumors of other types of souls, other than that of demons, being sealed in soul stones, but nothing that had ever been proven.

If it were possible, would his father resort to that? If it allowed him to stay, in some capacity, would Ulric be tempted? Would Roman even agree to such a thing?

Roman shook the bizarre thought away. It wouldn't happen; it wouldn't come to that.

But no matter what the healers did to him, what cures they recommended, or what dietary changes they suggested, Roman's body continued to weaken, his limbs small and weak, the muscles wasting away.

His father was terrified of losing him, of him physically dying, but Roman felt as though he were already dying, wasting away, cooped up in the palace, smothered by his father's caution. The same routine, day in, day out, with nothing to live for.

When the healer had blessedly finished, Roman hefted his cane and set out to find Ulric. His steps were slow, but at least he didn't have to stop and rest or reach out to hold onto something, like he sometimes did.

His father was in a meeting with his advisors and Roman waited outside. He looked up as the door opened and the men streamed out, garbed in their robes and jewels. They eyed him as they passed, catching a rare glimpse of the prince, and Roman saw flashes of pity in the eyes of some.

He didn't care whether they pitied him or not. It wouldn't make what was to come any easier, regardless.

He rose when the last advisor had trailed out and then stepped inside himself. The room was surprisingly small, devoid of any decoration so as to eliminate distraction. The only exception were the tall marble pillars on either side of the room, to Roman's left and right.

A large circular table dominated the center of the room, draped with a white sheet, stone chairs surrounding it. The one directly across from Roman was the largest, intended for the monarch, and Ulric stood behind it, gripping the back, his head bowed.

He looked up at the sound of Roman's shuffling footsteps, his cane ringing out across the austere chamber.

"You should have sent a servant to fetch me," Ulric chided, coming forward a few steps and then stopping short. "There was no need for you to come all this way."

His hands twitched at his sides, slightly outstretched, as though he wanted to reach out to Roman, but feared to touch him. As if he might break. Roman suppressed a sigh; the whole thing was so wearying.

He straightened, knowing that he needed to present a strong front if his request were to be honored. He needed his father to think he felt better than he truly did. And really, what harm would it be to pretend, if only for a little while? To help ease some of the weight that bowed his father's shoulders. He had enough to worry about, without Roman adding to the mix.

"Actually, I wanted to take a walk. I'm feeling much better this morning."

Ulric's face brightened, tinged with wariness. A fragile, cautious hope that had been too often crushed. "The new treatment—it is working?"

"Too soon to tell for sure, but I think so."

Roman didn't bother pointing out that he felt much improved from the day before because he'd spent all day in bed, recovering his strength. No doubt he would have to return to it once he'd overexerted himself.

"Good," his father breathed. "Saints be praised."

"In that light, there's something I want to speak to you about."

Ulric's expression shuttered, becoming guarded once again, but he didn't want to dampen what little joy he believed they'd been granted.

"In regards to what?"

Roman tightened his grip on the head of his cane. This was it.

"You increased recruitment for our soldiers, intensified their training. I would like to visit the barracks. Maybe stay there for a while. It might be good for morale. It would certainly be good for me."

Something passed over his father's face and that was when Roman knew. Ulric hadn't wanted to keep him in the palace solely for his own safety. There was some part of him that was ashamed, embarrassed to have a son—his only heir—so sickly. He did not want the people of Anarsha to see him, to know the truth.

The knowledge settled in Roman's stomach like a stone, bitter and difficult to swallow.

"I won't get involved," he hastened to add. "Just to observe."

Perhaps if he thinks I won't be seen, he'll agree. And then, once there, I can decide for myself.

For as much as he yearned for his life before the illness, before his body had turned on him, Roman was not ashamed to be seen. The illness was something that had happened to him. It was something he had to deal with. But it did not—would not—define him.

"Yes…" Ulric said slowly. "Perhaps for a few days. The fresh air might do you good. Provided you don't overdo it and you continue with your treatments."

Roman nodded, fighting to keep his relief from showing. "Thank you, Father."

He knew the spirit shards had been a waste of time, but all that mattered right now was that his father believed in them. He would let the healers place as many of the stones on his body as they liked, so long as it meant obtaining a small sliver of freedom.

"I'll go pack my things," he said, then turned and walked away before his father could change his mind.

It took every ounce of his strength to keep his back straight and walk without trembling, but he managed it until he was out of his father's sight, where he no longer had to pretend.

The hiss of steam and the clanking of gears filled the air around Desmond, so loud it was deafening. It drowned out all other sound, even that of his racing heart. But he could feel it well enough, pulsing in his throat, his temples, and even the tips of his fingers, as he reached for the lever. There was also a new sound, the thrumming of an engine, sounding almost like a growl.

It was no less hot inside the cockpit of the mech. In fact, it almost seemed worse than ever—or was that just his imagination? Sweat rolled down the back of his neck. He couldn't remember what it felt like to be cold and was certain he'd never feel it again.

He'd been in the Capitol since returning from the failed assault on Anarsha. He could have gone home, for a time, if he wished, but more often than not, he spent his nights at the barracks, not far from the warehouses that stored the mechs, surrounded by his fellow soldiers, strangers all. He did not know them and they owed him nothing. Perhaps it was better that way. At least then, they couldn't fail to provide that which they should have.

Desmond shook all thoughts of his family from his mind, returning to the task at hand. It was at one such warehouse he found himself now, crammed in the cockpit of a mech to test out the newest model.

The new design was sleeker, heavier, and used more materials to make, but was also more armored. The engine was more powerful, yet more efficient. It required less coal to power its body, while also having room to store more fuel—all of which was a step in the right direction, as far as Desmond was concerned.

But there was another feature, one that rumbled in the beast's chest, waiting to be summoned, that had him hesitating, his hand shaking as he reached for the lever.

This is madness, he thought, lunging forward in frustration and clamping his hand around the lever. He squeezed it, feeling the mechanism slide back against his applied pressure.

Peering straight ahead, through the grilles in the beast's chest, he watched as the bottom jaw lowered. A moment later, a torrent of flame burst forth.

He jerked back in his seat, startled by the force of it, feeling the heat roll over him through the open grilles. He released the lever and the flames cut out at once.

Desmond stared, breathing hard. The mechs were one step closer to the real thing. They still could not fly and he doubted they would ever be capable of such a feat. But it seemed the engineers had taken the emperor's directive to heart. Desmond had heard rumors that the man had not been pleased, to say the least, that they had been defeated—and so soundly!

Whether these new improvements would be enough, Desmond couldn't say. Thankfully, it wasn't his job to know or make such decisions. He simply had to pilot the monsters. He slid the cockpit hatch aside and stepped out, tugging off his gloves, the cooler air kissing his skin.

"What do you think?" a voice called.

He turned to see his brother, Alaric, striding toward him, dressed in his uniform, arms spread wide, grinning like he'd designed the mechs himself.

Desmond frowned, his eyes raking over the coat of Alaric's uniform. It wasn't as grand as the gray robes of a Minister, but the pips on his epaulettes already declared, for all to see, that he outranked him. Desmond could already picture Alaric in a Minister's robes, the position he'd been groomed for.

"Magnificent, aren't they?" Alaric said, coming to a stop before him, gazing up at the mech. It let out a hiss of steam as it began to power down.

"Certainly an improvement," Desmond acknowledged.

Alaric nodded. "The emperor will be most pleased."

That familiar envy flickered through Desmond at the reminder of his brother's proximity to the emperor. Right now, it was the Minister that Alaric worked for that had the emperor's ear, but if his brother was indeed the Minister's heir, it would be him one day. While Desmond would always be nothing but a soldier.

"The emperor will be pleased when we deliver him victory," Desmond retorted. "Do you think it will be enough?" With one hand, he gestured to the mech behind him.

The improvements were just that—improvements— but the Anarshans had defeated them easily enough. Surely, it would take more than the ability to breathe fire to change that.

Alaric didn't look the least bit concerned. He continued to gaze adoringly at the mech, though he spoke to Desmond. "Oh, yes. One way or another, it will be enough."

His cryptic answer further annoyed Desmond. How easy for Alaric to say, when he had never set foot on a battlefield himself. He had never witnessed the chaos, the unforeseen and unaccountable variables that could change on a whim. He had never seen a real dragon before. Desmond had, and they were even more terrifying than the mechanized beast behind him.

Suddenly, he found himself conflicted. He could not fulfill his own role and win his family's approval if Akkadia lost the battle—but it would reflect badly on Alaric and the Minister if they failed. If their implemented improvements weren't enough.

Even knowing the cost to himself, the selfish part of him wanted Alaric to fail, to see him brought low, lessened in the eyes of their parents, the Minister, the emperor himself.

What difference would it make anyway? Failure would be far less of a blow to him than it would Alaric.

His previous discontent, never far away, crept once more to the forefront of his mind. His family might approve of him now, but what would happen when the war was over? When Anarsha was conquered? When the last free kingdom fell, free no longer? The Empire would cease to have a use for him, and so would his family.

Either way, his days were numbered.

Perversely, Desmond almost didn't want the war to end. But it would, one way or another, in victory or failure.

He had to find some way of keeping himself relevant. Useful. Important. He would not be discarded like an outdated mech when this was all over, regardless of how it ended. He must find a way to make his mark, to make himself indispensable.

Desmond turned and considered the mech he had climbed out of: new, shiny, without any battle scars on it.

"Yes," he murmured, at last replying to Alaric's question, though he'd likely not expected one. "They are rather magnificent, aren't they?"

When he climbed inside, uncomfortable though it could be, he became more than himself, more than he could ever be on his own.

He was powerful, unstoppable, his limbs longer, his body heavier, stronger. Fire itself was his to command now. The power of a dragon lay at his fingertips, his to control as he wished.

They were a means to an end, these mechs. Perhaps they could be the means to *his* ends, too.

<h1 style="text-align:center">XI</h1>

Chandra fell into a routine, familiar if not comfortable. Each day at the barracks seemed to take an eternity, but weeks slipped by in an instant. She threw herself into her training, holding nothing back. Her only goal was to improve, and there was plenty of opportunity to do so.

In the evenings, she sparred with Anake, practicing her hand-to-hand combat, which she then tried to teach Gideon. He was unsure of himself and she often found herself repeating the same instructions as she had the day or week before, as though he had forgotten.

This irritated Sheboleth, who sometimes watched their sessions, getting up and leaving with a huff when she could take no more. Part of Chandra felt frustrated with Gideon; she wanted him to succeed against the Empire, too. The other half couldn't help but feel sorry for him, extending him the same grace he was so often denied by others. This was not a life he was suited to, that much had been clear from the beginning. Victor may have berated Callum for being soft, for not having the stomach for battle, but those accusations were more accurately laid at Gideon's door.

"I can't do it," Gideon gasped, doubling over to try and catch his breath during one of their training sessions. "I'm not like you."

Like me? Chandra thought. *What am I like?*

They had come from similar backgrounds. Neither of them had possessed any military training at all before coming to the barracks. But she didn't question him. She wasn't sure she wanted to know what he saw in her.

Her favorite training sessions, and the ones she looked forward to the most, were the ones where she got to work with Sheboleth. The first time she had climbed up into the saddle, the dragon had been forced to lean down, allowing Chandra to reach the stirrups.

Sheboleth rose to her full height before Chandra had been completely settled and she felt her stomach clench. She could feel the power of the creature beneath her. She had never ridden a horse, much less a beast of this size, and she gazed down at the ground below. It wasn't really that far and yet it seemed impossibly high.

There were no reins to hold onto, so Chandra was forced to rely on the straps that attached her leathers to the saddle, gripping with her thighs.

The first few times they simply flew over Anarsha, to get used to the sensation of flight. Having to carry a bow and then wield it would come later. But they needed to familiarize themselves with being up in the air, the way their dragon would move.

Sheboleth shifted beneath Chandra, testing her weight. "Do you trust me?" she asked, a note of amusement in her tone.

"I'm strapped in," Chandra replied. "You can hardly drop me."

The dragon snorted. "Such faith! I'm wounded."

"I've never exactly done this before," Chandra pointed out, thinking it best to be honest.

Their bond would be tested in the rage and madness of battle. It needed to be strong enough to survive whatever might be thrown at them and Chandra didn't think Sheboleth would appreciate bravado.

"You're not going to fall off. Though I might not duck low enough beneath one of those arches…"

Chandra followed the dragon's gaze, toward the Great Wall in the distance and the stone towers that stood sentinel nearby. Their peaks were crowned with open windows, capped by arched roofs. If a dragon swooped through one of the openings and misjudged the distance, their rider could be scraped against the ceiling of the roof.

"Not funny," Chandra growled. She knew the dragon was teasing, but didn't always find her particular blend of humor amusing.

"You won't fall," Sheboleth said, her tone conciliatory.

Rarely ever did she sound so gentle that Chandra knew she was being deadly serious.

She took a deep breath. She wasn't a child; she didn't need to be coddled. She was a soldier, a fighter, deadly and quick. She knew where to strike a man to ensure death, whether swift or slow. She could do this.

But what if the straps don't hold? What if you do *fall?*

Chandra tried to shove the thoughts away, hoping Sheboleth couldn't sense her unease.

Sheboleth unfurled her wings, stretching them wide. Chandra marveled at their breadth, the delicate bones similar to those in a human hand, the fingers infinitely longer, the leathery material of her wings stretched taut.

She raised them high. Chandra felt the dragon's muscles gathering beneath her and then Sheboleth sprang upward, snapping her wings down, displacing the air.

Chandra's heart lurched into her throat, but it all happened so fast, she barely had time to register the fear. And then they were off, the city falling away below them.

With nowhere else to put them, Chandra's hands gripped the horn of her saddle. Sheboleth's powerful wings beat the air on either side of her, lifting them higher and higher, until they rose above even the Great Wall.

The wind whipped through Chandra's hair, tangling it. The air stung her eyes slightly, making them water, but she blinked it away, staring at the world around her as Sheboleth's ascent leveled off. Her wings stilled and they drifted over the city, soaring.

Anarsha lay sprawling below them. It looked at once similar from such a height, and utterly alien. Chandra had expected to recognize the landmarks or even streets. To know exactly where she was in the city that had been her home the entirety of her life. But nothing looked familiar from up in the air. If not for the Great Wall, she could have been peering down upon any city in the world.

Chandra glanced over her shoulder, half expecting to be able to make out the Capitol in the distance. But no. There was the Badlands, that separated Anarsha from the Valderan rainforest, filled with its rocky outcroppings and gorse. Beyond that, there lay only trees, thick and verdant, for as far as the eye could see. Not even Shemar or Elath were visible.

Suddenly, Chandra wondered how far away they really were. What did those cities look like, the two kingdoms she'd heard so much about, but never seen?

"Well?" Sheboleth called, her voice rising above the wind and cutting through Chandra's thoughts. "What do you think?"

Any fear she had felt had melted away, leaving behind an unfamiliar, but not unwelcome, sensation.

"Free," Chandra replied. "I feel free."

She couldn't remember the last time she had felt so weightless, so unburdened. The anger that she carried within her had momentarily dropped away, as though it weighed too much to leave the ground with them.

She didn't resent the anger. It was a useful tool and a good reminder. But it felt nice to leave it behind, if only for a little while.

Chandra blinked, not realizing she'd been grinning until she felt the pain in her cheeks. It felt wrong, feeling so happy and carefree while Callum rotted away in some military graveyard. There had been no body for her and their grandmother to bury. None had been returned to them.

But in that moment, up in the air, on top of the world, not even that knowledge could bring her down. Chandra let out a whooping laugh. She was riding a dragon. She was powerful, meant to be feared. The two of them could do anything, go anywhere, and no one could stop them.

"Having fun?"

Chandra turned to see Anake, rising to their level. She perched on Vitanni's back, perfectly at ease, the dragon's green scales glinting in the sun like emeralds.

Where Gideon and Victor were, Chandra didn't know. They had all taken off around the same time, but she didn't care to look for them now.

Anake smirked. "Savor it. You only feel this for the first time once."

It was a little sad knowing she would never feel this exact way again, but that only made the experience sweeter.

"If you want to know what real flight feels like," Anake offered, "I'll race you."

Chandra's pulse thrummed, quickening in anticipation rather than fear. She laid a hand against Sheboleth's side. "Your call."

Sheboleth eyed the green dragon soaring beside her. "You're on."

Anake grinned. Vitanni folded her wings and plummeted. Chandra let out an involuntary yelp as Sheboleth did the same, her wings tucked close, her body angled as they pitched forward, rapidly losing height and gaining speed. They cut through the air like an arrow, Chandra's stomach hollowing out.

The wind stung her eyes and tears leaked from the corners, but she didn't care. Head start aside, Vitanni had already drawn further away from them. Chandra held her breath, her heart seeming to race faster than the city hurtled toward them.

Never had she felt such speed. Never had she done something so reckless. If Sheboleth lost control, if she failed to pull up in time, there would be no coming back from it. And yet, Chandra wasn't afraid. *Faster,* she urged Sheboleth silently, as though the dragon could sense her will. *Faster.* She loved every moment of it and didn't want it to ever end.

But there was only so far they could go. Vitanni unfurled her wings, leveling out, and Sheboleth followed suit a moment later. Her wings snapped out, halting their fall, jolting Chandra in the saddle.

Just ahead of them loomed one of the towers. Chandra swallowed a shriek as Sheboleth flew right for it. The dragon tucked her wings back in, darting through the opening, extending them once more on the other side. One of her wings dipped down, her body tilting, and then they were rolling together through the air. Chandra felt the straps stretch taut, catching her as she began to slip from the saddle, gravity tugging at her, and then releasing her as they drew level again.

Rapidly beating her wings to slow them, Sheboleth alighted on the Great Wall. Chandra was breathing hard, but the dragon seemed barely winded. She straightened in the saddle, pushing hair out of her face. Already she could feel the tangles, catching against her fingers. Next time, she would have to braid it.

"Nice try," Anake called from further down the wall.

Vitanni had avoided the tower, flying straight over it, rather than ducking through, but Chandra suspected Sheboleth had merely wanted to show off.

"We lost," she said, though not the least bit upset about it.

"We were always going to lose," Sheboleth replied, eyeing Vitanni. "Her wings are more angular than mine, meant for diving and speed. I'm more suited to endurance."

"What's the furthest you've ever flown?" Chandra asked.

The dragon considered for a moment. "I don't really know."

"Do you think you could fly all the way to the Capitol?"

It was the furthest distance Chandra could think of.

"I bet I could."

Chandra didn't doubt it.

Later, Chandra learned that Gideon had barely gotten off the ground, Mael snorting and tossing her head in displeasure, sensing his fear. Heights, it seemed, bothered him, which was no minor disadvantage when it came to dragon riders. One of the officers advised he find some way of getting over his fear sooner rather than later.

When she spoke to Sheboleth about it, the dragon rolled her eyes.

"He's not afraid of heights, he's afraid of falling."

It seemed like a perfectly reasonable fear to Chandra, but she didn't know what Gideon's dragon was like. She was lucky to have Sheboleth as a partner, but not everyone was so fortunate.

"She lost her previous rider," Gideon confided, when he told Chandra what had happened. "I don't know how; she refuses to talk about it."

But whatever their difficulties, Gideon and Mael would have to overcome them. As training advanced, they spent more time with their dragons. Flight training occurred almost daily, including scouting parties.

Groups of paired dragons and their riders would take turns, one group tasked with being the scouts and the others playing the role of enemy, attempting to sneak as close to the city wall as they could, using the cover of the forest.

Sometimes, the scouting parties were allowed to fly out. Others, they were instructed to remain perched along the Great Wall, using only their senses to spot any movement. Sheboleth's eyes were sharp and keener than Chandra's, but neither of them had much trouble finding Bane or Vitanni among the foliage. Vitanni's scales were too bright a green to truly blend in and Bane's few orange scales all but begged to be noticed.

Mael was far trickier, her mottled green, yellow, and brown scales blending in. Though none seemed as adept as sticking to the shadows as Sheboleth, who clearly knew the forest well.

There was a large circular aerie at the uppermost level of the compound, where the dragons could retire for the night if they wished to remain in the city, but most preferred to return to the forest. Chandra marveled at the trust Anarsha placed in these wild beasts, who truly owed loyalty to no one. And yet, they always returned at the start of each day, regardless of where they had spent the night, for they knew, all too well, what was at stake.

As easy as Vitanni and Bane were to spot, it seemed to make no difference for Gideon. He peered, squinting, into the forest, his brow furrowed as he sat on Mael's back beside Sheboleth and Chandra.

Chandra had already located Bane's hulking form, her eyes tracking him silently. Occasionally, she cut a glance at Gideon, half expecting him to look to her for guidance, to try and see where it was she looked. But if he thought to use her knowledge for his own ends, he did not act on it.

She felt Sheboleth shift beneath her, the dragon's impatience rising, but she held her tongue.

At last, Gideon sucked in a breath, pointing, "There!"

He turned to Chandra, grinning, pleased that he had found their squad mate on his own. Chandra didn't have the heart to tell him that she had found Victor's dragon long before he had—or point out how long he had taken.

It was hardly a unique incident. Scouting from the air presented its own set of challenges, mainly that anything could be lurking beneath the thick forest canopy, forcing them to fly lower than they'd like.

The ground rushed by in a blur. There was but a split second to detect movement, to truly see anything, before it was passed—and it was harder to see such movement when you were moving yourself.

On one such occasion, Chandra leaned low over Sheboleth's neck as the dragon wheeled high overhead, the treetops just above them. Her large wings made it difficult to fly in some sections of the forest, where the tree trunks gathered close. Vitanni, able to turn on a dime, was more suited to such a task, but they all needed to learn and what Sheboleth lacked in maneuverability, she made up for with her sharp eyesight.

Just ahead of them, Mael flew with Gideon, the wind tousling his blond hair. How small he looked on the back of such a beast. Chandra tore her gaze away from him, returning to the task at hand. Today was a competition. She and Gideon had been tasked with finding Anake and Victor.

Victor and Anake had already had their turn trying to find Chandra and Gideon. They'd done a good job hiding; Chandra had heard Victor expressing frustration to Bane as the two of them had flown overhead, just missing their hiding spot.

They had found Victor and now only Anake remained, but time was running out. If they didn't find her soon, their time would be longer than the other team's had been. And they would lose. Chandra hated losing—especially against Victor.

Come on, she thought. *Where are you?*

She and Sheboleth saw it at the same time: a flash of too-bright green. The dragon angled her wings sharply, slowing, but Mael continued on, as though neither she nor Gideon had seen anything.

Sheboleth hissed, turning and backtracking to where they had seen Vitanni. It took Gideon several more seconds to realize they were no longer behind him and only then did he and Mael catch up.

Sheboleth refrained from comment, even though Chandra could practically feel her vibrating with agitation. It was only after they had returned to the city, and were informed that they had lost, that the dragon could no longer hold back. They hadn't lost by much, but it was enough. Victor and Anake had the better time.

Sheboleth rounded on Gideon as he dismounted. "Didn't you see her? You flew right over her!"

Gideon shook his head. "I didn't see anything."

"Just like you didn't notice we had stopped, hmm? She was right there!"

He flushed, ducking his head. "I'm sorry."

"Sorry?" Sheboleth barked. "I don't want your apologies. I want you to *pay attention*. What we did today might have been a friendly competition, but this isn't a game. If you're unobservant on the battlefield, you die— or you get someone else killed, saints forbid."

Chandra held out a hand toward her dragon. "Give him a chance."

Sheboleth snorted and turned, walking away with Mael.

"She's right," Gideon muttered. "I suck."

"You'll get better," Chandra said, nudging him with one elbow. "You can only improve from here, right?"

But he didn't smile as she wanted him to. Logically, anyone's skills should improve with enough practice, but Chandra had to admit that she was worried about Gideon. He was the slowest of them to pick up on a new skill and more was being asked of them all the time.

He sighed and followed after his dragon. Chandra watched him go. Gideon's lack of ability should have irritated her. If they were going to defeat the Akkadians, they needed to be the best soldiers they could be. The last battle may have been a rout, but she doubted the next would go so easily and regardless, the Akkadians would show no mercy.

Gideon was nowhere near the kind of soldier he needed to be. And yet, that didn't irk Chandra at all. If anything, she felt sorry for him, a bit protective of him, and she knew that, in her own gruff way, Sheboleth did too.

She was hard on him because she cared. There was no place for coddling. But no amount of criticism or encouragement seemed to have any noticeable effect.

Archery was by far the worst. Gideon was a passable archer, so long as his feet stayed firmly on the ground. Once they took to the air, it was a disaster, and the more they trained, the less time they devoted to normal archery. In battle, they would be shooting from the backs of their dragons, as Khan liked to remind them.

"You will not be a member of the infantry," he called, pacing up and down the line they had formed. "If you are separated from your dragon, you are dead. You need to be able to hit a target, stationary or not, from a dragon in flight. I doubt I need remind you that this is incredibly difficult, so you will practice it again and again, until you can do it in your sleep."

And they did.

Chandra's muscles ached at the end of each day. When she looked at herself in the washroom mirror, she barely recognized herself, the muscles of her back and forearms more developed than they had ever been. She went through the motions of drawing back a bow so many times throughout the day that her arms trembled at night, wanting to continue emulating the movement long after training had ended.

Even in sleep there was no escape. In her dreams, she rode a dragon, firing again and again at targets that did not exist, with quivers full of arrows that never ran out.

Any progress she thought she'd made with archery had been wiped out, firing from the back of a dragon infinitely more difficult. Each time she missed, she clenched her jaw, holding the curses between her teeth, and tried again, determined to master it.

Victor, of course, was already proficient at such a skill. Anake wasn't bad; her aim could improve, but she moved through the air with a fluid grace, completely in tune with her dragon.

The same could not be said for Gideon. He was out of sync with Mael, their movements off where they should have been simultaneous. It was clumsy and painful to watch.

Khan had had enough and he ordered Gideon to stay behind after training, accusing him of being undisciplined and ordering him to run laps around the complex.

"That'll take him all night," Sheboleth murmured as she and Chandra departed, trailing after the others.

Chandra glanced back at Gideon, her heart swelling with pity, but she dared not linger, fearful that Khan would include her in the punishment for being too soft.

"I wish I could help," she said. "But I don't even know what's wrong."

She couldn't magically gift Gideon the skill he needed.

"He needs confidence," Sheboleth replied. "He needs to stop doubting and believe in himself. I spoke to Mael—what little I could get out of her anyway. She can feel his anxiety, his doubt, and it affects her. It's distracting."

"But what is he anxious about?" Chandra asked, not really expecting an answer. She would have to try and talk to Gideon herself, but every time she brought it up, he seemed to withdraw, shrinking into himself and mumbling that he didn't want to talk about it.

"It happens every time he climbs into the saddle, from what Mael said. He sort of just…freezes. Locks up. He's afraid of flying. He doesn't trust her and, well, how can she trust someone who doesn't have any faith in her?" Sheboleth moved her wings in a semblance of a shrug. "It's a recipe for disaster. How can they ever work as a team if neither trusts the other?"

Chandra glanced over at her. "I'm glad I can trust you."

"Of course you can. But *why* do you?"

Because you've been there from the start. Because you've never belittled me or made me feel small. Because you encourage me, reminding me that I'm never alone, that we'll face whatever comes together.

All of that seemed too vulnerable to speak out loud.

"Because you don't just say things. You mean them," Chandra answered instead, and it was just as true as any other reason. "The day we first flew together, I was nervous, at first. You told me I wouldn't fall and I didn't."

Sheboleth nodded. "They need the chance to just trust one another, with no one else around. Just let go and be free."

Chandra thought of how she had felt that first day and how she still felt glimpses of that freedom each time they took to the air. If Gideon could feel that, she didn't see how he could fail to love flying. He would hunger for it. There was simply nothing else like it and Chandra almost loathed being forced to return to the ground.

"Of course, it's always possible that they're ill-matched," Sheboleth added. "You know, the dragon used to pick the saint, not the other way around."

"Really?" Chandra asked with some surprise. "Is all of that true, then?"

"All of what?"

She waved a hand vaguely in the air. "What they say about the saints."

"Bit before my time. But in my experience, there's not much truth to be found in what *they* say."

Chandra waited for Gideon to return to the barracks. It was late, full dark, and most of the others had already retired for the night. The deadline for curfew had already come and gone, and all the lights were extinguished, leaving a clear view of the stars. She sat outside their quarters, having told Sheboleth of her plan. The dragon was skeptical, but willing to take the chance.

The idea, once formed, refused to leave Chandra. How could anyone fear flying, once they'd had a taste of the freedom it provided? If only she could help Gideon see the beauty of it, she was certain he would no longer be afraid, or at least more confident in himself and his abilities.

She looked up as he came trudging down the path, shoulders slumped, head bowed. He walked unevenly, as though his muscles were sore—and they probably were after what Khan had put him through.

Chandra stood and Gideon glanced up sharply, startled by the sudden movement, not expecting anyone to be there.

"What are you doing out here?" he asked.

"Waiting for you."

"You waited up for me?" He shook his head. "There was no need."

She shrugged, as though what she was about to suggest was of no importance. "I wanted to ask you to go on a flight with me and Sheboleth. Well, you'll bring Mael, too, obviously."

"Why?"

"Just for fun."

"Chandra, it's curfew. We can't leave."

"We can if no one catches us."

He shook his head again and she could tell she was on the verge of losing him.

"We could all be dead tomorrow, you know. None of us know when the Akkadians might come back." She almost mentioned that one of them could just as easily have a nasty accident during training, but she was trying to build his trust in his dragon and thought better of it.

"When do we ever get the chance to just do something for the hell of it, huh? Live a little. I'll be right there with you. No one will ever see us and we won't get caught. Nothing will happen."

Still, he hesitated, glancing at the door to the barracks. No doubt he longed for his bed.

"It's your call. But I'm going either way. Just thought you might like to come along."

She started to turn away, but Gideon stopped her.

"Wait!" He sighed. "If you're going regardless, then I guess I'd better go with you."

"It'll be fine," Chandra assured him, leading him to where Sheboleth and Mael had agreed to wait for them.

The moon was out, though not quite full, and the braziers that had been lit along the ramparts gave off an orange glow. Guards patrolled along the walls, but the complex was large. No one expected to see two new recruits sneaking about after curfew, meeting up with their dragons, and so no one did.

Moving in the darkness, Chandra climbed up onto Sheboleth's back. There was no saddle—there had been no time—and Gideon balked, hesitation etched in every line of his body.

"I don't know about this…"

Chandra let out a sigh. "We're already here…" Part of her felt bad for using his guilt against him, knowing how eager he was to please. "Just follow my lead. Trust your dragon. Trust me. We won't let anything happen."

She did not take for granted how much faith Gideon was placing in her as she watched him scramble up onto Mael's back, a more difficult endeavor without a saddle.

"What do I hold onto?" he asked, staring helplessly down at his hands.

"Like this," Chandra said, demonstrating as she gripped the frills that ran along Sheboleth's back.

Mael had spines instead of frills, but they were spaced far enough apart to accommodate a rider and Gideon wrapped his hand around the one just in front of him, holding on for dear life.

"All right," Chandra murmured. "Here goes nothing…"

"I hope this plan of yours works," Sheboleth hissed. "If he falls, he'll scream all the way down."

"Don't say that!" Chandra admonished, glancing back to see if Gideon had heard, but it appeared not.

If he can pull this off without a saddle, he'll have no problem riding in one from here on out. If not, well…Sheboleth is probably right.

"Just follow our lead," she called to Gideon again as Sheboleth spread her wings.

Suddenly, she wondered if perhaps she was thrusting Gideon too quickly into the deep end. Maybe the whole idea was more ill-advised than she had stopped to consider. But it was too late now.

Sheboleth leapt off the rampart, falling through the air before snapping out her wings, using the height to effortlessly become airborne. Instinctively, Chandra tightened her grip, clenching her thighs against Sheboleth's sides, feeling the heat of her scales through her trousers. As they fell, her stomach gave a familiar lurch and a grin spread across her lips.

Behind her, she heard Gideon give a muffled cry, but when she turned back, Mael had taken to the air just behind them, her rider having thrown his arms around her neck.

Chandra laughed as they soared over the rooftops below. "Relax, Gideon!"

The city of stone sprawled below them, illuminated by the silvery moonlight. Chandra gazed down at the lit windows below, wondering what the occupants were doing at such a late hour—and if any of them were burning her candles.

Her chest tightened at the thought. It had been months since she'd last made a batch of candles. She almost feared if she were to try now, she wouldn't remember how. Utter foolishness. She'd been trained in how to make candles as soon as she was old enough. She'd been a candle maker for more of her life than not.

The Great Wall came into view, the mighty bastion looming before them. No doubt some of the guards could see their silhouettes as they flew overhead, but there was nothing that would identify them specifically. Perhaps they would even assume them to be out on patrol.

A moment later, Sheboleth alighted on the roof of the highest tower, large enough for four dragons to perch upon. Mael joined them, her movements as fluid as Chandra had ever seen, and she landed with barely a sound.

"Well, what do you think?" Chandra asked, spreading her arms to encapsulate the view that surrounded them on all sides.

"It is impressive," Gideon admitted. He'd straightened on Mael's back, no longer clinging to her desperately. He made no move to dismount.

"Did you ever think you'd see the city from up here?"

"Of course not. Did you?"

"No," Chandra replied. *And would that I never had.*

The thought came suddenly, like a blow to the chest. If the Akkadian Empire had never come, Callum would never have been recruited. He would never have died in battle and she never would have been recruited to take his place. She would never have been paired with Sheboleth, never known what it was to fly, to soar above the earth, looking down upon it as the saints must.

Oh, why did such joy come on the heels of sorrow?

She hadn't known what she'd been missing, of course. Hadn't known that she needed such an experience in her life. *But at what cost?* If she'd never known such freedom, her cousin would still be alive.

She knew such a connection wasn't fair to make. Her love of flying had nothing to do with Callum's death. She hadn't caused it or brought it about. But it was true that without one, the other would never have come to be.

"What is it?" Gideon asked. "You've gone quiet."

For a moment, Chandra debated telling the truth. To say that she'd been thinking of Callum. But that was a door that must be kept safely locked and even to speak his name would be to turn the key.

"Nothing." Chandra turned back to him, summoning a smile. It felt frighteningly real. She had become too adept at faking, at concealing her true feelings.

Except for anger, never far away. That, she could never truly conceal and it scared her.

"Do you think they're out there?" Gideon asked, staring off into the forest.

"Who? The Akkadians?"

He nodded.

Chandra shrugged. "They're out there somewhere. Probably still holed up in the Capitol, licking their wounds."

"Funny, I almost thought I'd be able to see it from up here," he said, echoing her earlier thought. "Have you ever seen it?"

"Saints, no! And I don't care to." *Unless it's on fire.*

"Me neither."

She turned, glancing over her shoulder, back toward the city. The moon had lowered in the sky. In the morning, another day of arduous training awaited them. It wasn't fair of her to ask Gideon to accompany her, forsaking the sleep he desperately longed for after the punishment he'd been given. They needed to return if either of them were going to get any rest.

"We should head back." *Much as I don't want to.*

She wanted to linger in this moment forever, a moment of peace, of what-ifs. In this moment, the Empire's next attack was yet a far-off possibility. And Chandra knew, regardless of what happened in the coming days or months, she would look back to this moment with fondness.

Mael shook herself slightly. Gideon glanced at his dragon, something unseen passing between them, and then at Chandra.

"You go on ahead. We'll catch up."

A flicker of hope lit in Chandra's chest. Perhaps this hadn't been a bad idea at all.

"Of course," she said as Sheboleth launched off the top of the tower, wings snapping taut, wheeling lazily around, back toward the barracks.

Chandra leaned forward and closed her eyes, the wind brushing past her cheeks. Her thoughts strayed back to their conversation, of what Gideon had said of not having seen the Capitol, and was reminded that she didn't know what most of the burgeoning Empire looked like. She had never been to Shemar or Elath when they'd been free kingdoms, and it was too late now.

Whatever else they might once have been, now they were little more than vassal states, under the control of the Empire.

She clenched her teeth. If she had her way, there would not be an Empire.

XII

The stone keep that comprised the training complex and barracks was massive. Roman began to regret his decision as soon as he arrived, faced with the daunting prospect of mounting the stairs. He suppressed a sigh, hefted his cane, and began.

More than once, he threatened to lose his balance and he had to stop several times to catch his breath, refusing to sit down. Silently, he cursed his weak body that seemed to thwart and limit him at every turn.

But the sun felt good on his skin and he breathed the fresh air deep into his lungs. He was no longer confined to the palace and that was worth any hardship.

His father's agreement to the idea still surprised him, but as with anything, such acquiescence did not come without a caveat. Roman couldn't go alone; guards would have to accompany him, chaperones ensuring he did not get into any trouble.

Roman snorted at that. How much trouble could a crippled prince get into? But even so, no chances would be taken with his safety. He was only one man and would hardly be able to defend himself should the need arise, especially against hardened soldiers.

What did his father think? That the Akkadians had spies among their own army and that one would take the opportunity to assassinate the prince? They would probably be doing him a favor, putting him out of his misery. He'd hardly live to inherit the throne, after all—not that the Akkadians knew it.

Most Anarshans didn't even know and Roman suspected his father would like to keep it that way. It was a miracle he'd consented to the visit at all. Roman had claimed that such a visit might help boost morale, but discovering that the crown prince—and heir to the throne—likely would never live to see the throne, was hardly encouraging.

Yet Roman wasn't miserable, despite his circumstances. His body ached and complained with every step by the time he reached the top of the stairs, but he felt lighter than he had in a long time. Happy, even.

In this moment, he was free. Or as free as he could be. He still had his father's chaperone to contend with, but that, too, wasn't as bad as it could have been. He'd been kept away in the palace for so long, it was unlikely that anyone outside would recognize him. He hadn't made many public appearances since his illness began and he looked utterly different now, his muscles and limbs wasted away by the disease.

A contingent of guards following him around at every turn would only attract attention and invite unwanted questions. Roman didn't intend for his visit to be common knowledge. He'd merely wanted out of the palace, to observe as unobtrusively as possible. How, then, to ensure his safety?

Ulric's answer had been simple—and rather smart, if Roman were honest. He would be accompanied by a dragon, one of Ulric's councilors, of sorts.

The dragon, Koal, was an ambassador between the Anarshan leadership and the dragons they fought beside. The dragons had no leader as such, from what Roman had learned, but someone did have to speak for them and keep both sides apprised of the situation.

Koal, it seemed, had been appointed for the task and now he found himself playing babysitter to the king's son. Roman doubted such a powerful beast was all too pleased with that, but if so, Koal gave no sign of it.

His scales were a rich blue color, the armor plating that protected him from neck to the tip of his tail a darker hue. Two sets of horns protruded from the back of his head and thick, black hair ran down his back instead of spines or frills. His black claws clicked on the stone as they walked.

A dragon guardian would blend in perfectly and invite no questions at all. If anything, the soldiers would think him a new recruit, arrived with a dragon they would have seen around only occasionally, if at all. Or at least, they might have thought him a new recruit if not for his cane.

Roman paused, tilting his head as a group of riders flew overhead, running through drills with their dragons. The riders held longbows in their hands and as he watched, they fired at a line of targets far below.

Suddenly, it was no longer enough to simply be out of the palace, taking in the sun and fresh air. Roman wanted to be up there, on a dragon of his own. How must it feel to be so free?

But as soon as the fantasy came, it withered and died, reality setting in. The moment his father heard of such a thing, Roman would be ordered back to the palace and never allowed out again. And Roman doubted Koal would consent to it, if Roman were to ask him.

He frowned, remembering why the dragons and riders were here in the first place. This wasn't all fun and games.

They were there, in this position, out of necessity and nothing more.

"Are you all right?" Koal asked, his deep voice quiet. "Do you need to lean on me?"

"I'm fine," Roman replied and kept on walking.

He was moving at a decent pace today, though he leaned heavily on his cane. One of the officers gave him a nod of acknowledgement as he passed. No doubt his father had informed the leadership that his son would be coming. They were the only ones here who knew who he was and likely knew better than to draw attention to it.

Koal followed him toward the training complex, where rows of archers were lined up on the ground, firing at the distant targets. Roman paused, grateful for a moment to rest, as he watched them, both hands resting on his cane.

There was a dark-haired man, tall and broad of shoulder, who hit the target dead-center nearly every time. On his other side stood a smaller man, his hair golden, who occasionally struggled to even nock his bow—and very rarely hit the target. The dark-haired man let out a snort of disgust, but if this bothered the smaller man, he made no sign.

The golden-haired man wasn't pulling the bowstring back far enough, which shortened his range. He was also relying on his arms too much, neglecting the other muscles that went into drawing a bow.

But it was the woman, beside the smaller man, who snared Roman's attention. Her hair was a flaming red. It was early in the afternoon, already hot, and she wore a sleeveless black tunic that exposed her defined biceps. Roman eyed them appreciatively. She had good form, the muscles in her back flexing, as she drew back the bow.

A smattering of freckles dotted across her shoulders and down her arms. She wasn't as fast at firing or reloading as the dark-haired man, but her movements had a precise sort of intention about them. She was deliberate, taking her time, not releasing too early, like the blond man had done.

Her aim was slightly off though, and looking at her, Roman could instantly see why. Leaving Koal standing silently behind him, Roman shifted his weight and made his way forward.

"Excuse me," he said after the red-haired woman had completed her shot.

She turned. Her eyes were a bright green and Roman instantly thought of the emerald ring one of his father's advisors always wore. Freckles splashed across her cheeks, which were red from exertion. Sweat beaded along her hairline, glistened along her collarbone.

She looked him up and down. His clothing could hide the wasted muscles, though not his smaller frame. Roman had purposely worn his plainest clothes, not wanting to draw attention to himself, though there was no denying the cut and quality of the fabric, if one looked closely.

He didn't look like a soldier—that much was inescapable—and her eyes lingered overlong on the cane.

"Do I know you?" she asked, though they both knew she didn't.

"No. I just arrived today." He nodded over his shoulder at Koal, as though to vouch for the legitimacy of him being there.

"Is that your dragon?" she asked, following his gaze.

"Yes—for now."

If she thought his response odd, she said nothing, waiting expectantly to see why he had interrupted her.

"Forgive me—it's forward, I know—but I couldn't help but notice your form just now."

Her brow furrowed. "My form?"

"Yes. You turn your hips slightly too far when you draw back. I can show you, if you like."

For a moment, he thought she would refuse, to spurn the advice of a stranger, who was being rather forward indeed. Roman felt out of practice, conversing with other people. Lately, the most people he'd interacted with had been his own father and whatever healers he'd brought in for the day.

But instead of refusing, she shrugged, the movement careless, easy, without a hint of offense. "All right."

Roman nodded. "Go ahead and draw again, but don't fire."

She did as instructed, reaching to pull an arrow from her quiver and nocking it, all without having to look. She placed her fingers on the string, one above the fletching of the arrow and the rest below, pulling the bowstring all the way back to the edge of her mouth, sighting down the arrow. As she did so, her body rotated slightly too far, through the hips, so that her aim was off.

Roman stepped forward, holding one hand out. "May I touch you?"

Wordlessly, she nodded.

Hooking his cane over one arm for a moment, Roman reached out and gently touched her waist, rotating her body back to where it should have been. He could feel the heat of her through her tunic. There was muscle there, too, but he was always surprised by how soft the human body felt.

"There." He stepped back, letting go.

She released her hold on the string. It snapped forward with a twang, the arrow whistling through the air for the briefest moment until it embedded itself deep into the center of the target.

Suddenly, Roman was reminded of the feel of the bowstring between his fingers, running them along the arrow's fletching. It had once been as familiar to him as breathing and he hadn't been aware of what he'd lost until now.

Out of the corner of his eye, Roman saw the dark-haired man watching the two of them, his expression unreadable.

The red-haired woman turned to Roman with a grin. "I'd say that's one dead Akkadian."

"Indeed."

"Impressive that you managed to point out the flaw in my aim before any of the instructors."

"I'm sure they would have addressed the issue soon enough. They have many recruits to watch and keep track of." *While I was watching only you.*

The unspoken thought brought a flush to Roman's cheeks. He hoped she would attribute it to the heat.

"I'm sure," she replied, still eyeing him, an expectant look about her gaze. "You know what you're talking about, I'll give you that. Want to have a go? Show me how it's really done?"

She held out the bow, offering it to him.

Roman looked down at it. There was no way to tell by sight alone how much weight the draw had to it. His fingers twitched atop his cane, itching to reach out and touch it. He was sure his body would remember what to do, even though it had been years, but memory and ability were not the same.

As much as he wanted nothing more than to reach out and take it, he knew he would not be able to draw it back, no matter how light the weight. His body would simply not do as he wished.

For a second, he wondered if she were mocking him, but the look in her eyes was sincere enough. No doubt the cane gave her pause, but she probably thought him another soldier, just like her. He'd given her no reason to think otherwise, showing off his knowledge of archery as he had, and showing up accompanied by a dragon. Despite the cane, what else was she to think? On the back of a dragon, he had no need to walk, after all.

"No, thank you. I'm afraid I'm rather rusty." It pained him to admit it. Just when Roman thought he had no pride left to be wounded, he proved himself wrong.

But you're right. I did know, once, what to do.

She shrugged again, as though nothing truly bothered her. "Suit yourself." Roman liked that about her, he decided.

"I'm Roman, by the way," he said, offering her a hand.

He regretted it instantly. It wasn't the hand of a soldier and would only further expose him. There were no calluses or scars. His skin was perfectly smooth, the nails neatly trimmed, not a speck of dirt or blood to be found. But it was too late to take it back now.

"Chandra." She reached out to clasp his hand. Her grip was firm, confident but not crushing. Her hand was rough, fingers callused from the bowstring.

She let go, stepping back. "You must be new, if you just arrived today. I'd have remembered seeing you around."

Roman had just opened his mouth to reply when a cry rang out. He turned to see the smaller man with the gold hair doubled over in pain, clutching his left arm. The bowstring had slapped it when he'd released, another sensation Roman knew all too well. The skin hadn't broken, but it was already turning an angry red.

"That'll leave a nasty bruise," Roman said. "But otherwise, you should still be able to shoot."

"You're fine," the dark-haired man snapped. "Now man up and keep shooting, unless you want Khan to see you slacking off and make you run around the entire complex again."

The blond man shot him a dark look, but straightened. "I'm all right," he murmured, likely embarrassed by all the fuss now that the pain was beginning to subside.

"Try not to overextend your elbow when you're getting ready to release," Roman added. That was another thing he'd noticed about the man's form.

"You're just full of advice today, aren't you?" the dark-haired man called. "And who are you, again?"

"Don't mind Victor," Chandra hissed. "He's just mad someone knows more about archery than he does."

Roman ducked his head. "Well, I've distracted you all long enough. I should take my leave."

He tore his gaze away from her and returned to Koal's side, refusing to allow himself to look back.

"Are you sure this is wise?" the dragon asked as they walked away.

Roman would have to find somewhere to rest soon. He'd been on his feet too long and his legs were starting to protest. The last thing he needed was for any of them to see his legs fail him entirely, giving out from under him.

"What do you mean?" he asked, a note of irritation creeping into his tone.

He wasn't annoyed at Koal, but the pain had a way of wearing at his nerves—and his patience.

"What if they find out who you are?" Koal clarified.

"Would that be the worst thing?" Roman challenged.

The irrational urge to confide in Chandra had come over him as he spoke with her. To tell her who he really was, why he was there. It suddenly felt like he was deceiving her, even though that wasn't his intention. And that was why he needed to leave, to walk away.

He truly was out of practice, interacting with others. He was out of his depth and he didn't belong here, that much was obvious.

Was he really so grateful that someone had looked at him and didn't see only his disability, the way his father always did, that he suddenly wanted to tell them everything? *How pathetic.*

He sighed before Koal could answer, about to suggest they find some shade, when the clanging of bells rang out. Roman glanced around, trying to discern the source.

"There," Koal called, nodding toward the distant towers.

"What does it mean?" Roman asked, his stomach clenching with dread. All activity in the complex seemed to have ground to an abrupt halt. He turned, eyes once more meeting Chandra's.

Her green eyes were wide, frightened, her skin pale in the afternoon sun. And Roman knew.

Then orders were being shouted, though Roman couldn't make out the words. The soldiers scrambled to get into position, the keep going from orderly to chaotic in the blink of an eye.

Without thinking, he reached out to stop Chandra as she made to move past him, still gripping her bow in one hand.

"What's going on?" he asked. "What's happening?"

"I'm not sure, but the last time those bells rang—"

We were under attack.

She trailed off, her gaze far away. Then she blinked as another young woman bounded up the stairs toward them. She had dark hair, shaved on one side, her skin bronze in the sun.

"Anake!" Chandra called. "Do you know what's going on?"

The other woman frowned. "Scouts have reported Akkadian forces on the move. They're coming this way."

"Saints," Chandra breathed.

And then she was gone, rushing after the other woman. Roman watched helplessly. There was nothing he could do to help and he certainly couldn't keep up with them.

"Do you want to return to the palace?" Koal asked, hovering at his shoulder.

"No, I'll stay here." He might not be able to fight, but he would see this through. He hoped Chandra would survive whatever battle was coming. He hoped his archery tips would help, if only a little.

"Let's find some shade," he said at last.

If there was nothing he could do, he might as well stay out of the way and try to make himself comfortable. Who knew what the next few hours might bring?

The fear clawing in Chandra's chest threatened to undo her. If she stopped moving, for only a moment, she would freeze. But the keep had become a flurry of activity. There were positions to be manned, preparations to be made, and more than enough work to lose herself in.

It helped keep the fear at bay, but she worried what would happen when darkness fell. When vision began to fail and fear crept to the surface.

The Akkadians were coming—and so soon! It hadn't been all that long since their last attack, or so it felt. The last battle had been a rout, a complete disaster for the Akkadians by all accounts. How had they recovered so quickly?

Dread curdled in her stomach. Perhaps the Empire truly viewed its citizens as nothing but cogs in their machine, willing to throw them into the fray again and again, to break against the Anarshan wall.

The suddenness of it frightened her and that made her angry. *This is what you wanted, isn't it?* Here was her chance to avenge Callum, brought to her doorstep.

And yet, she did not feel ready.

War camps were erected outside the city walls. If the Akkadian army left the cover of the forest behind, they would know of it and be able to leap into action at a moment's notice, engaging the enemy before they could draw near the wall.

Chandra felt horribly exposed, despite the sheer number of soldiers and dragons milling around her. They had set up camp in the Badlands, the area between the city and the Valderan rainforest, covered with its rocky outcroppings and gorse bushes.

As far as the eye could see, tents stretched in every direction, hastily assembled, their canvas flapping in the wind. There was no protection from the elements out here.

Distantly, she heard the grinding noise of a blade being sharpened on a whetstone. Smoke drifted through the air from the campfires and she could smell meat roasting somewhere. It smelled delicious, but she had no appetite. She doubted she could have forced any food past the knot in her stomach anyway.

The work had run out all too quickly as the sky darkened and Chandra paced, casting anxious glances at the forest, waiting for their enemy to appear.

For all that she dreamed of battle, this would be her first. She was not naïve enough to think that the sheer force of her rage alone would shield her from harm. People died in battle, sometimes their first battle, no matter how badly it had ultimately gone for the other side. Callum was proof enough of that.

Instinctively, she pushed all thoughts of him aside. That would not be her fate. She reached deep inside herself, searching for the familiar anger and hate, but it had been swallowed up by the fear.

She was not prepared for this, even though it was what she wanted, craved, the most. She hadn't had enough training. She was a soldier, yes, and certainly a far better one than she had been when she arrived, but it wasn't enough.

And war waits for no one.

It hadn't waited for Callum to be ready and it wouldn't wait for her.

"You should eat something."

She turned to see Sheboleth behind her. She'd been so caught up in her own thoughts, she hadn't heard the dragon approach.

"I'm not hungry."

"You'll need it," Sheboleth pointed out. "Besides, approaching army or no, I wouldn't let them deprive me of a good meal."

Chandra swallowed, pushing down her pride. It wouldn't help her and there was no place for it here. "I'm scared, Sheboleth."

The dragon grunted. "You'd be a fool if you weren't."

Chandra knew Sheboleth was right, but she forced herself to shrug anyway, in that careless way she had, when really, she cared far too much.

"I hope we don't have to wait much longer. I'm eager to finally spill some Akkadian blood."

To see if they bleed red and can be killed like anyone else.

But as sunset gave way to dusk, there was still no sign of the approaching army. Either they were farther away than expected or they were taking their time. Perhaps they intended to bed down for the night, before attacking fresh and rested in the morning. Did mechs need rest?

"Any action yet?"

Chandra looked up from where she'd been sitting by one of the fires, composing a letter. It was supposed to be for her grandmother. This might be the last time she had a chance to write to her and she felt the pressure more than usual. It had never been as easy as writing to Callum and she felt the weight of every word, wanting to get them just right.

It had devolved into mostly nonsensical rambling by the time she'd given up. She'd already thrown several pieces of parchment into the fire, watching as the crumpled balls blackened. She couldn't afford to waste paper and, in the end, she'd resorted to pretending to write to Callum instead, the words instantly flowing freely.

It was more of a one-sided conversation than anything, Chandra asking him the questions she wished she could have asked in person, but would always be robbed of an answer. She asked him how he had felt before the battle, if he had been afraid, then teasingly insisting that of course he hadn't been.

Her pen had stilled, even as she wrote the words. *Had* her cousin been afraid? Was he afraid in his last moments, realizing he was going to die, with no one there to comfort him?

The thought made her sad and she immediately turned away from that line of questioning. Sadness wasn't allowed, especially not on the eve of her own battle.

She was grateful for the interruption, glancing up to see Roman standing before her, leaning heavily on his cane.

"No," she answered. "Nothing yet."

She couldn't help but study him, wondering why he was there. Did he intend to fight? *Could* he fight? Clearly, he had some knowledge of archery, but he looked even less like a soldier than Gideon.

Chandra's chest gave a small lurch of guilt as she thought of her friend, wondering how he had taken the news. In the chaos, she hadn't seen him, but she felt bad that she hadn't thought to seek him out now that things had calmed down. She'd been too absorbed in her own mess.

But Roman was here now and it would be rude to run off and leave him. He had a thin, narrow face, his features handsome but sharp. There were dark shadows beneath his cheekbones and the flickering firelight only made him look more ghostly. He had a thick head of hair, dark brown streaked with lighter strands, and he apprised her with pale blue eyes.

"Where's your dragon?" she asked, glancing about for the blue dragon that had accompanied him earlier, but there was no sign of it.

"Oh, he's around somewhere. Sulking, probably. He doesn't approve of my being here."

She cocked an eyebrow at that. "Really? You mean you're not forced to be here like the rest of us?"

His brow furrowed. "Not exactly, no."

"So you're not a soldier, then." It wasn't a question. "Are you an officer of some kind?"

He looked slightly surprised. "Technically, I suppose I would be." He shifted his weight and his expression tightened. "Do you mind if I sit?"

Chandra gestured for him to go ahead and he sank down, somewhat awkwardly, with a sigh.

"I'm sorry. My legs…"

"You don't owe me an explanation."

He looked at her. "No, I think I do. You're right. I'm not a soldier. I'm the prince." He held up a hand and carried on quickly. "But please, keep that between you and me. I'd rather not the entire war camp know I'm here."

Chandra tilted her head, studying him anew. "I knew there was something different about you."

Perhaps, given enough time, she would have put two and two together. She knew the crown prince was named Roman, though she'd never laid eyes on him before—or at least, not that she recalled.

His lips twisted in a wry smile. "The cane give it away, did it?"

"It was the accent, actually."

Had she known that the prince used a cane? Chandra didn't think so. She wanted to ask about it, but it didn't seem right, and she'd meant what she said. He didn't have to explain anything to her.

"So why are you here?" she asked instead.

"My father is allowing me to observe. Boost morale, perhaps, though I somehow doubt it," he said, self-deprecatingly. "I think it best if I maintain as low a profile as possible. That's why I'd appreciate it if you don't tell anyone."

"You don't have to worry about that. But why tell me at all?"

"It's nice to tell someone."

And that someone is me?

Chandra felt a pleasant rush of warmth. The prince had chosen to confide in *her*, a lowly candle maker. It would irk Victor to no end, if he knew.

"Who are you writing to?" Roman asked.

Her satisfaction faded as she remembered where they were and why.

"No one."

The prince had confided his true identity to her, but she couldn't bring herself to say that she was writing to her dead cousin. A cousin who had died in the war, killed by the Empire that now lurked somewhere beyond the tree line.

"I see," Roman said, though it was clear he didn't see at all.

"Do you think we'll win this war?" Chandra asked bluntly.

She wanted to know the prince's opinion on it and whether she was about to risk her life for nothing.

He was silent for a long moment and when he finally spoke, it was not the answer Chandra had been hoping for.

"If fate is kind, and the saints are watching out for us, I believe so."

But Chandra could have told him that fate was not kind, nor were the saints watching out for them.

XIII

By morning, the Akkadians had not appeared. Morning turned to afternoon and still there was no sign. The camp functioned as an extension of the training complex back in the city. There were still tasks that needed to be done, training that waited for no one. The latter could have waited, Roman supposed, until they were back in the city, but what would be the point? Who wanted to sit around, waiting?

Chandra clearly didn't. He sat off to one side, watching as she sparred with the young woman called Anake. He'd said something to upset her last night. That much had been obvious by the way she'd brought the conversation to an abrupt end, bidding him a goodnight.

He had no idea what he'd said to upset her, but whatever the cause, she'd kept her promise not to reveal his identity.

There was an anger to her now that hadn't been there before—or perhaps he simply hadn't noticed. It was there, in the lines of her body, tensed as she stood across from Anake, her body angled, fists raised. It was there in her green eyes, glittering with deadly fury.

There was nothing for them to do but wait and even less than most for Roman, so he watched the sparring, offering no tips or advice this time. He knew nothing about this particular set of skills. No one expected a prince to be versed in hand-to-hand combat.

He had debated throughout the previous day whether to tell Chandra the truth. He knew the smart thing to do would be to keep his identity a secret. And despite whatever he'd told his father, no one's morale was likely to be boosted by the sight of their crippled prince.

Roman had worried what Chandra would think of him—which was ridiculous. He was here of his own free will and he could leave at any time, should he no longer find his visit pleasant. She was a stranger to him and her opinion should not matter. And yet, it did. He was even more out of practice with people than he thought.

Would she resent him for not being a soldier, like her? For not putting it all on the line, as she was being asked to do? Perhaps that was the source of her anger, but he didn't think so. She hadn't seemed the least bit displeased when he'd confided in her. The anger had come later.

The man with the golden hair, Gideon, stood off to one side, also watching the proceedings.

He stared off across the camp, brow furrowed, before returning his attention to the match. "What if they're not coming?"

Anake grunted as she dodged a swing from Chandra. "If the scouts say they're coming, then they are. They're just making us wait, that's all."

Gideon frowned. "For how much longer?"

"Saints, Gideon, do I look like a seer? I don't know any more than you do."

At that, Gideon flushed slightly, embarrassed by his own question.

"At least when they do get here, we'll be sure to see them," Anake added, somewhat conciliatory. "There'll be no element of surprise to their approach."

Chandra snorted. "Not very imaginative, are they?"

Roman shrugged, chiming in. "They've never met this kind of resistance before. But in any case, I don't suppose you've much need for tactics when you have overwhelming numbers."

Chandra hissed as Anake landed a blow, her concentration slipping. She cursed under her breath and turned to Roman.

"Do they? Have overwhelming numbers?"

He offered a vague, unhelpful gesture. He didn't truly know. "The Empire's soldiers are barely human. They're trained not to think of themselves as individuals, but rather parts of a machine, an efficient whole. So…they may not value their own lives the way you or I would."

"So I've been told," Chandra muttered.

Roman grunted. The Empire's mindset was hardly a secret. They weren't called the Empire of Engines solely for the mechs they commanded.

He returned his attention to the sparring. Chandra was light on her feet, but Anake was patient, baiting her out, waiting until Chandra's own impatience got the better of her.

Still, she absorbed more hits than Roman would have put up with before she finally surrendered.

"I still can't beat you," she panted, doubled over, hands braced on her knees. "You're too good."

Anake grinned, rubbing her wrapped knuckles. "You just need more patience."

Chandra straightened, a glint in her eyes as she turned to Roman. "What do you think? Want to spar with me?"

Roman blinked, surprised by her request. It felt strange, asking it of him when she knew him to be the prince. But perhaps he didn't feel like a prince to her. At least, not in the way one would expect a prince to be. After all, instead of residing in the palace with the best luxuries life could offer, he had chosen to spend his days here, in a war camp of all places.

She knew of the cane, too, but perhaps she didn't realize the full extent of his limitations. His loose clothing helped hide how frail his frame really was. Roman had made no mention of the healer who had come to see him, ducking into his tent early enough that he hoped the visit would go unnoticed.

No matter what he had already confided in her, he could say none of that.

He smiled ruefully. "I'm afraid I have to decline, tempting as the offer is."

How much better that sounded than admitting the dreaded words *I can't.*

"Afraid I'll thrash you?" Chandra challenged.

He was pleased to see some of the anger was gone, seemingly no longer directed at him. She was teasing him and he found that he rather liked it.

"You would thrash me," Roman replied, trying to make light of it.

But the words were no less true.

Chandra couldn't figure him out. There was something about Roman that intrigued her, to say nothing of why he was there. For a brief, stupid moment, she considered that perhaps his cane was all an act, part of his cover to prevent him from having to join in combat—should the need ever finally arrive.

But she'd seen the way he leaned on it, his limp too convincing to be an act. And she'd seen the lines of pain show on his face when he thought no one was watching.

She shook her head. Roman was a mystery she could puzzle out another time. By midafternoon, she and Sheboleth had been called to join the hunting patrols. The army had to be fed.

"Is this a good idea?" Chandra asked as she climbed up into the saddle. "The Akkadians could be out there."

By now, the camp was rife with rumor. Some were saying that the Akkadians weren't coming, that the whole thing was nothing but an elaborate ruse. To hear others talk, the Empire was practically on their doorstep, just beyond the tree line.

Chandra wasn't sure which she believed and there was no point trying to get any sense out of them. But the lack of news troubled her.

Sheboleth snorted. "I thought you were eager to spill Akkadian blood."

"I am," Chandra retorted. "But I'd rather not encounter their entire invading force alone."

"You're not alone. You have me."

"True," she acknowledged, unexpectedly touched by the gesture. "Still, some of the other dragons are going hunting on their own. It's safer that way. And I'm sure you're a better hunter than I am." *So why do we both have to go?*

"The practice will be good for you. Have you ever killed a living thing before?" The dragon asked the question as though it had just occurred to her.

"Kind of hard to kill something that isn't living, isn't it?"

"All right, smart ass," Sheboleth muttered, unfurling her wings. "You know what I mean. And don't tell me you've killed a wasp that wandered into your house. That doesn't count."

Chandra hesitated, having opened her mouth to do just that.

"I don't see that there's much difference," she said defensively, once they'd risen into the air, "between an Akkadian and a wasp."

"On paper, there shouldn't be," Sheboleth replied. "You're going to have to approach the coming battle with the same amount of mercy for the Akkadians as you would have for that wasp."

"That shouldn't be too hard," Chandra muttered, thinking the dragon wouldn't hear her over the wind.

She was wrong. "You'd think so, but I think you'll find that it's easier said than done. Harder than you think not to hesitate when the moment comes to take a life."

Chandra's hands clenched on her bow as her thoughts strayed back to Callum and the underlying anger that drove her. It was so hard not to think of her cousin, to dwell on what she'd lost. Impossible, too, to think of him without conjuring the fury.

It colored everything she did.

"I won't hesitate."

Hesitate to kill a wasp and you risked being stung. Hesitate in battle and you could suffer a far worse fate.

"Good. You can practice on that deer down there."

Chandra had been so preoccupied with her own thoughts that she hadn't noticed the deer, its brown coat stark against the leaves. Its head was lowered, grazing, oblivious to the danger that soared just overhead.

"We do need the meat," Sheboleth reminded her, "in case your moral compass needs some guidance."

Chandra didn't deign to respond. She nocked an arrow and drew. Sheboleth's wings stilled, making barely a sound, holding them steady. Chandra inhaled deeply, held, and fired.

She watched the arrow zip downward, losing sight of it among the branches. The deer flinched, though whether from being struck or startled, Chandra didn't know. It bolted into the undergrowth.

"You hit it," Sheboleth called, able to see what she could not.

The dragon darted after the deer, trailing it far more efficiently than a hunter on foot ever could. There was no need to look for a blood trail when they could track its progress from the air.

Despite having hit it, the deer ran a fair distance. Chandra nocked another arrow, debating whether she should try and shoot it again. But it was running now, no longer standing still, and she didn't trust her aim.

It was agonizing, waiting for the deer to finally weaken and slow. Chandra didn't like how far they'd gone, having to chase it. She glanced around as Sheboleth began to descend, searching the trees for any sign or sound of the iron mechs. But the forest was quiet, aside from birdsong and that seemed like a good sign.

Chandra dismounted, sliding to the ground, her bow still nocked. The deer had collapsed, sides heaving, and she could hear its labored breath as she approached.

She had hit it—she could see the arrow protruding from its body—but it hadn't been a clean, killing blow, and the animal lingered, suffering.

"Let me," Sheboleth took a step forward.

"I can do it," Chandra said quickly. *She still thinks I'm too weak.*

The dragon looked at her levelly. "I know you can, but it will be quicker this way."

It's already suffered enough. Sheboleth didn't say the words, but Chandra knew they must both be thinking it. *And it's my fault.*

Wordlessly, she nodded, removing the arrow from her bowstring. She felt like she owed it to the deer to watch, having done this to it, even though she wanted nothing more than to look away.

The deer's legs flailed weakly as Sheboleth reached it, but it had the strength to neither fight back or flee. With one long, black claw, Sheboleth sliced into its neck, severing the artery there.

Within moments, it was over, the deer at last falling still.

Chandra couldn't help but feel a twinge of regret. She tried to bury it. The feeling was a weakness, of no use to anyone.

"Come on," Sheboleth called. "We should get back and see if the Akkadians have arrived yet."

Chandra wasn't surprised to learn that they were still waiting on the Empire's arrival. There had been no further word. They had spent nearly a full day in camp and unless something changed, it looked as though they would spend another day more.

To distract herself, Chandra helped butcher the deer they had brought back, one of several successful hunts. She tried not to think too hard about what she was doing, but the fact that the animal was now dead seemed to make it easier.

That evening, she gathered around the fires, leaning back against Sheboleth's side, the air filled with the pleasant smell of meals being prepared. If the Empire could see their fires from wherever it was they waited, no one seemed too concerned.

Good, Chandra thought, turning the meat every now and then over the fire, not wanting it to burn. *Let them know we're here, ready for them. Maybe they'll think better of the whole thing and turn back.*

Her stomach growled, displeased at being made to wait and Sheboleth looked up. "What's taking so long?"

"The meat has to cook. It's not done yet."

The dragon tilted her head to one side. "Why?"

"You didn't know that humans cooked their food?"

She was the first rider Sheboleth had been assigned, but the dragon had been around people long enough that she ought to have known.

"Of course I knew, but I don't understand why. Seems unnecessary to me. Does it improve the flavor?"

"Sometimes."

"Can't you just eat it raw?"

"We could," Chandra acknowledged. "But it can be dangerous. If you don't cook it at the right temperature, it can make you sick."

Sheboleth sighed. "You humans are so fragile."

"You don't know the half of it," Chandra said, at last removing the meat from the fire. Its exterior had darkened nicely and it smelled so good, it made her mouth water. Or maybe she was just that hungry.

She'd never been much of a cook. Callum had always done that. He'd enjoyed it, where she had not, and he'd done it well.

Chandra froze, blinking back sudden tears, telling herself that it was just smoke from the fire making her eyes water. *Why must every thought come back to him?*

She supposed it wasn't unreasonable, given that she wouldn't even be there if not for him. But it was an unwelcome intrusion, no matter why or when it happened, stealing her happiness, if there was any to take. Stealing her peace. She just wanted to eat her meal.

Suddenly, she felt very tired, but it was a mental, or perhaps spiritual, sort of tiredness, not physical. Too quickly, she tore off a chunk of meat, gasping and huffing as it burned the roof of her mouth.

Gideon came over to join her, but once the meal was over, he moved on, leaving her alone with her thoughts. Chandra sighed. If she was going to be in a pensive mood, she might as well try to finish the letter she had meant to send to her grandmother. She had never completed it; hardly even started it. And certainly hadn't picked it back up since she'd decided to write her thoughts to Callum instead.

Sheboleth was a solid presence at her back, her side warm. Chandra tried to relax, propping her legs in front of her, bent at the knees, bracing her letter against her lap.

This time, thankfully, the words did not fight her.

With Callum, for the most part, his letters had tried to remain upbeat. Regardless of what might be happening or how he might really feel, he'd hesitated to put anything negative in his missives home, likely not wanting her to worry—even though she'd worry regardless and knew well enough how to read between the lines of what he did and didn't say.

With her grandmother, though, Chandra didn't think the old woman would appreciate being lied to, even with the best of intentions. She would want Chandra to be honest, to hold nothing back. She would want to know precisely what was going on, what they faced, and what Chandra felt. The woman had always been pragmatic, facing things as they were, not as she would like them to be.

"You should get some sleep."

Once again, Chandra looked up to see Roman standing before her. She blinked, glancing around. The camp had quieted around her, most of the others bedding down for the night. It was never completely silent; there were always sentries on duty and those who simply could not or did not wish to sleep.

Behind her, Sheboleth's breathing had slowed and deepened, a slight rumble in her chest, like purring—or an engine rumbling. The dragon was either asleep or pretending to be. Either way, Chandra didn't really care if she overheard the conversation.

"I will," she replied to Roman. "Once I'm done."

Now that the words had decided to flow, she didn't want to quit. And the same reminder lurked in the back of her mind that this might be the last chance she would have to write to her grandmother. One just never knew.

"Then I'll keep you company," he said, lowering himself to the ground.

"Aren't you tired?"

"No."

A lie. The fire had died down, but its waning light was more than enough to reveal his expression, drawn with pain, the shadows beneath his eyes. The past few days had not been easy for him and she wondered again why he was here.

"Who are you writing to this time?" he wondered. "Or am I not allowed to ask?"

"No one said you weren't allowed to ask. You just might not get an answer."

"Oh, I see how it is." He grinned. "You have a lover waiting for you back in the city."

Chandra looked up sharply, wondering why he wanted to know. Was it mere idle curiosity, making polite, small conversation, or was there something more to it than that?

No, surely not. They'd only just met, though her traitorous thoughts couldn't' resist straying back to the memory of his hands on her body, adjusting her form during archery practice.

Even in the light of the fire, which could be unforgiving, he was undeniably handsome, in a severe, sharp sort of way.

She flushed in spite of herself. "Sorry to disappoint, but I'm writing to my grandmother. She's all the family I have left."

The admission slipped out before she thought better of it, but once spoken, words couldn't be taken back.

His grin faded. "I'm sorry."

She waved his sympathy away. "I hardly remember my parents."

She would not speak of Callum. Not to anyone and especially not to him, the prince of the kingdom that had demanded Callum's loyalty and later, his life.

Chandra looked at Roman then and thought that perhaps she should hate him, being the heir to the throne that had demanded and taken so much. But she couldn't.

She understood the desire for revenge and she had become well acquainted with fury, but she did not understand placing blame anywhere other than where it truly lay. And the blame for Callum's death lay with the Empire. If they had never attacked, none of this would have happened. It wasn't unreasonable for Anarsha to ask for soldiers to rise up and defend it.

"Neither do I," Roman said, surprising her. "My mother, at least. She died during childbirth and the baby followed her not long after."

"I'm sorry," Chandra said, repeating the same helpless words he had spoken because what else did one say in the face of something so horrible?

"It was much harder on my father than it was on me. Just like that, I was to be his only son. The one heir."

His mouth twisted briefly with what looked like bitterness and she thought for a moment that he would go on, but he said nothing more.

"I can see how that would be hard on him."

Roman shook his head. "Nothing's been easy on him for a long time. I worry about him, actually. The stress of war, the fear of being conquered—" He clamped his mouth shut. "I'm sorry. I shouldn't say such things."

"But if you meant it," Chandra protested. "If it was true…"

"It could be…demoralizing ahead of the coming battle."

Chandra looked down at her letter, filled with truths of her own, and plenty of information that could be considered demoralizing. She folded it carefully. There was nothing more to be said. She would have it sent in the morning, if she were provided with the opportunity.

She rose to her feet, the weariness that had been held at bay at last flooding in. "You should never apologize for telling the truth."

XIV

It rained during the night. Chandra woke to the sound of it pattering on the roof of her tent, but it tapered off by morning, leaving behind a heavy fog. It seemed to roll out from the forest, across the Badlands, toward their camp. Chandra eyed it distrustfully. Anything could be lurking behind its cover.

With the sky overcast and the thick mist, it was hard to tell what time it was. The sun hadn't yet risen high enough to burn through the fog—if it would at all.

She first heard it as she was standing in line at one of the cookfires, waiting to spoon some of the overcooked oatmeal into her bowl. The camp collectively froze around her, coming to a standstill at the unmistakable clanking, a telltale sign that the mechs had arrived. It was horribly loud, almost as if the Akkadians were already on top of them.

At once, the camp leapt into a frenzy of motion. Fires were doused and riders scrambled to collect their weapons and find their dragons.

Chandra tossed her bowl aside, breakfast forgotten, turning to look for Sheboleth, but the dragon had already found her.

"They're here," she gasped as Sheboleth trotted up to her.

"I know."

It seemed to take an eternity to collect her quiver and bow and then attach the saddle to Sheboleth's back. Chandra's movements were too slow, her fingers shaking too much, her body filled with a frenetic energy that had nowhere to go.

The fear that she had felt, briefly, at the news that the Akkadians were once more on the march surged back, threatening to drown her. Her first battle, finally upon her. Waiting had made her complacent. It really hadn't been that long since the news had first come, and yet, she had doubted that this moment would ever arrive. And now, it was here.

Chandra swung up into the saddle and fumbled to strap herself in as Sheboleth moved to get into formation with the others. They stood, facing the fog that continued to roll out of the forest. A few had been ordered to take to the air in the hope that it would provide better visibility, but that was quickly dashed. The mist concealed all.

Chandra shivered. The air was cool and damp. It felt as though beads of moisture clung to her skin, turning the ends of her hair frizzy. She'd hastily tied it back, but she had missed one strand that now hung in her face.

Where are you? She scanned the fog, searching for where the tree line must be hidden, for any sign of movement. The clanking continued to grow louder, the sound distorted by the mist, causing it to echo strangely. The approaching army should have been visible by now and Chandra wondered if they were nowhere near as close as they sounded. She tensed, running her fingers over the fletching of her nocked arrow.

She couldn't see Roman anywhere, which was for the best. She hadn't seen him since last night. Hopefully, he had made himself scarce in the camp, far enough back that the fighting wouldn't reach him.

Still, the clanking continued, the mist rolling implacably forward until it was nearly upon them. Below her, Sheboleth shifted her weight—though whether from impatience or nerves, Chandra couldn't say.

"Hold!" a voice shouted—Khan, she thought.

They weren't the only ones being affected. Surely something had to give. The clanking would either cut out entirely, the Akkadians would burst free of the mist right in front of the Anarshan forces, or one of them would break ranks and charge headlong into the approaching fog. Just when Chandra thought she couldn't take it anymore, something did happen—though not anything she had expected.

Sheboleth tensed at the first sign of movement within the mist, shapes coalescing into something solid as the figures burst free, charging onward.

Chandra sucked in a surprised breath. She had expected mechs—she could still hear them marching—but instead, infantry soldiers burst clear. They wore very little armor, if any, and carried bows or swords and shields.

Facing down a line of dragons, they charged, too far away to see if any of them were terrified by the prospect.

At last, the Anarshan line sprang into action, taking to the air before any of the infantry could reach them. Sheboleth rose up through the fog, Chandra blinking as drops of moisture struck her in the face, dampening her skin.

Below, she could see nothing of the forest through the fog, but the camp was laid out neatly beneath her, and the line of soldiers advancing on foot. Some had stopped, looking around bewildered, perhaps wondering what they were supposed to do now that the enemy had taken to the skies. Others charged onward, heedlessly, toward the camp.

They couldn't be allowed to reach it. And they wouldn't, Chandra knew. These soldiers had never stood a chance.

Some of the other dragons were already raking their lines with fire, the orange flames shockingly bright against the gray dawn. Sheboleth's jaws parted and she sent forth a torrent of flame. Chandra watched with a sort of savage satisfaction as the soldiers vanished beneath a wall of heat.

More infantry surged forward, but they were all mowed down as soon as they appeared. But beneath her glee at seeing her enemies fall, lurked a sense of unease. Something was wrong.

Where were the mechs? Chandra could no longer hear them over the roar of the flames, the air rushing past her ears, the screams of dying men, and the frantic pulse of her own heart. She hadn't imagined hearing them before, so where were they now?

"Chandra!"

She turned, twisting in the saddle to see Mael come up beside Sheboleth, a decent distance kept between them so that the two dragons' wings would not collide.

Gideon sat perched in the saddle, his golden hair windblown, one fist clenched around his bow. "Where are the mechs?" he called, echoing her own thoughts. "Have you seen any?"

Chandra shook her head.

Sheboleth wheeled about in midair, beating her wings feverishly to stay in place as she scanned their surroundings, searching for any sign of the elusive machines.

But there was no sign of them, only the last few infantrymen who had broken ranks and were fleeing, stumbling in their haste, back toward the safety of the mist and the forest beyond.

Gideon grinned as he watched them, the expression resembling nothing like the boy who had been scared to fly, who had put no faith in his dragon.

Chandra felt a small rush of warmth to look at the two of them now, hovering high above the battlefield without a trace of fear despite the distance. They looked as synchronized as any dragon and rider could.

"Look at them run," Gideon said, reaching out a hand to touch the side of Mael's neck. "What do you say? Should we finish them off?"

Mael let out a snort and dove eagerly downward, toward the fleeing soldiers.

"Gideon, wait!" Chandra cried, but her words were lost, vanishing into thin air.

The warmth she had felt had vanished, overwhelming dread rising in its place, swallowing it whole. Something was *very* wrong. Where were the mechs?

Gideon wasn't the only one eager to finish off the foot soldiers. Other dragons had leapt eagerly forward, scenting blood.

Sheboleth snorted and folded her wings slightly, her snout pointing down as they began to dive after Gideon.

Above the din of battle, a new sound rose, one Chandra had never heard before, but it chilled her blood all the same. It was a mechanical sound, like something being released. She had no idea what it could be, but she didn't have to wait long to find out.

"Ballistae!" Sheboleth cried, throwing her wings wide as a massive bolt shot through the air, directly where they would have been had she not reacted.

Chandra yelped, ducking in the saddle, as the bolt whistled past, stirring the air in its wake, entirely too close.

Below, cries rang out as the dragons who had chased after the fleeing infantry were struck. Other bolts, too many to count, flew through the air, many finding their marks, judging by the cries.

Chandra watched in horror as one dragon, its body hanging limp, plummeted from the sky. She couldn't tell if its rider was still alive, but there was no surviving the bone-shattering impact.

Her stomach roiled. Was that how Callum had died? Plunging to his death on the back of a dead dragon? Was that why there had been no body? Because there hadn't been much of a body to send back? His every bone shattered into a thousand pieces, his body crushed against the earth like a bug smashed beneath one's finger?

With an effort, Chandra managed to swallow the bile that had risen in her throat, instead of hurling over the side. Now was not the time to be scared. She reached for the familiar anger, summoning it like one would a loyal dog. And like such a companion, it came when called, rising to the surface until everything—her fear, her disgust, her horror—were blotted out and only fury remained.

"Fall back!" a voice was shouting. Again, she thought it was Khan.

Very clever of the Akkadians to use the infantry to bait them out. The foot soldiers had been too easy of a target, simply too good to pass up, and then, once they were within range of the hidden siege weaponry, they opened fire. The mist shielded the siege weapons, preventing the Anarshans from targeting them. Wherever they were concealed within the forest, they must have had better lines of vision than the Anarshans did.

Or perhaps they just got lucky.

Sheboleth began to turn, to put more distance between them and the edge of the forest, when a roar of pain rang out. Chandra peered over the side and saw Mael. She had been forced to the ground, one of her wings hanging awkwardly.

At the edge of the mist, the first mechs stepped clear, revealing themselves.

"Were they always so big?" Chandra asked, watching their massive heads sweep back and forth, surveying the field.

"Hard to tell from up here," Sheboleth replied. "But I don't think so."

To Chandra, they seemed massive, their tread heavy, steam hissing from their joints with each step. She imagined the ground must shake beneath their feet as they lumbered forward, jaws wide.

No sooner had the first line of mechs appeared than other dragons were swooping down toward them, eager to rake them with dragonfire, their one true weakness.

"No!" Chandra cried, but of course they couldn't hear her.

Drawing the dragon riders closer, within range, was precisely what the Akkadians wanted. Ballistae shots rang out, carving through the Anarshans.

"Fools," Sheboleth murmured.

What do we do?

The battlefield was chaos, smoke and fog still obscuring most of it. Without knowing where the siege weapons were located, they had no idea how far they could safely venture without coming into range. But neither could they allow the mechs to advance unchallenged.

Were battles always so disorganized? It was a wonder anyone managed to survive them. There was simply too much going on, too much that demanded your attention, when death could fly out at you without warning.

"Look!" Sheboleth called.

Chandra's eyes returned to Gideon and Mael and she let out a curse. The mechs were closing in on them.

Where were the other members of her squad? Where was Anake? Or even Victor? Annoying as he was, Chandra found she wouldn't mind having him by her side now.

Desperately, she searched for any sign of them. Bane's black and orange coloring, the viper-green of Vitanni, but she couldn't spot them in the madness and her eyes kept flicking back to Mael.

She squinted. It looked like Gideon was fumbling with the straps that were hooked onto his leathers, connecting him to the saddle. *Don't, you fool. Stay with Mael.*

Being forced to the ground was bad enough, but a rider separated from their dragon stood almost no chance against the advancing mechs. Chandra still didn't know where Anake or Victor were, but she didn't have time to wait for them. No help was coming.

Gideon had freed himself from the saddle, his bow drawn, as he stood beside his downed dragon. Around them, the mechs closed in.

Mael shot fire at them, beating back the first two, but they kept coming. As one mech drew too close, she launched herself at it, biting and clawing at the iron plating, to little avail.

"Sheboleth!" Chandra cried. "We have to help them!"

Sheboleth let out a hiss of displeasure, but she had already folded her wings tight against her body. They dropped, speeding toward their friend and ally.

Sheboleth can get Gideon out of there, Chandra thought, blinking rapidly as the wind stung her face. Mael, though, they could likely do nothing for. With a damaged wing, she would have to make a run for it on foot, if she could.

They were going too fast, the mechs rapidly growing in size as they suddenly loomed before them. Sheboleth wouldn't be able to stop in time and they would slam right into one of the machines.

But even as she thought it, Chandra also knew they weren't going nearly fast enough. They would not reach Gideon in time. All the rage in the world couldn't stop what was about to happen and she could do nothing but watch, helpless, as one of the mechs opened its mouth.

A torrent of flame issued forth. Gideon and Mael both vanished from view.

Chandra screamed something, unsure quite what, her voice inaudible to her own ears.

Fire. The mech had breathed fire. Last she heard, they hadn't been able to do that. Someone had changed the rules.

Sheboleth thew her wings wide, attempting to slow her descent, but it was too late, as Chandra had known it would be. The dragon slammed into the mech, knocking it back a few feet, its metallic claws gouging the earth. But it absorbed the blow, never in the slightest danger of losing its balance or toppling over.

Sheboleth was not so lucky. Her body rolled over the seemingly immoveable mech. She tucked her wings close to her body to shield them as she tumbled to the ground. Chandra cried out as the dragon rolled from the forward momentum, her leg pinned, for a moment, between the dragon's side and the ground beneath.

And then the pressure was gone and they were upright again, the straps yanking and tugging Chandra every which way. But they held and she remained in the saddle.

Sheboleth's sides heaved. "Are you hurt?"

Chandra's leg ached and she feared it might have been broken, but that was a problem for another time. A problem for a future that only existed if they survived.

"I'm fine."

The mech turned toward them, its body slow and lumbering. Sheboleth never gave it a chance to fire at them the way it had Gideon. Snapping out her wings, she rose to the air and, angling her neck downward, engulfed the mech in flames.

Sheboleth kept the fire going longer than was strictly necessary, to be sure the threat had passed. When the flames finally cut out, the iron had warped from the barrage of heat, melting like candle wax.

Chandra patted the dragon's neck to get her attention. "We have to go back down there!"

She could see Mael slumped on the ground, unmoving, possibly lifeless. She could see no sign of Gideon and she hoped that he hadn't simply been reduced to ash.

"There's nothing you can do," Sheboleth warned. "And it's probably not something you want to see."

"I don't care!" Chandra shouted recklessly, knowing that the dragon was likely right. Whatever horrific sight awaited her was not one she would forget. But she had to know. She couldn't turn away.

With a quick glance to make sure it was safe to land, Sheboleth settled back to the ground, hurrying over to where Mael lay.

"Gideon!" Chandra clawed at her own straps, but her hands were slick, from the mist or sweat, and couldn't seem to get a grip.

One of Mael's eyes opened. She was still alive, but only just, each breath an agonized wheeze.

"Gideon?"

Mael moved one of her legs and the wing that had fallen over her side, revealing what lay concealed beneath. Chandra turned away sharply, but it was too late.

Mael had tried to save her rider, shielding him with her body, but the heat had been too much. Sheboleth turned away, leaping back into the air. The rage that Chandra had reached for had failed her, leaving behind an empty hollowness.

It felt as though she hovered over her own shoulder, watching herself wrench in ragged breaths, as though the whole thing were happening to someone else. As though none of this were truly happening at all.

"Come on," Sheboleth called. "This battle's not over yet."

Dimly, Chandra knew she should try to pull herself together. They were still in danger and Sheboleth needed her. But she couldn't bring herself to care. The dragon would have to manage on her own.

Desmond urged the lever of his mech forward, feeling the beast respond beneath him. With the upgraded design, he wasn't as concerned about running out of fuel, but he *was* impatient, never a good trait in battle.

They had arrived later than expected and the wait had worn on his nerves. The assault should have begun a day earlier, but dark clouds had been spotted through the forest canopy, promising rain. Fighting in such conditions was anything but ideal.

The dragons were free to take to the air, but the mechs, trapped on the ground, would have to contend with treacherous footing. And a mech that slipped might not be able to get back up again, with the newer, heavier design.

The rain had also come with an unexpected but welcome advantage, changing their strategy once again. The heavy fog cover had helped conceal their approach perfectly, shielding their siege weapons and hiding their infantry's charge until the last possible moment.

That fog was starting to dissipate now though, and Desmond knew they needed to press their advantage. The moment the siege weapons were visible, they would become targets and Desmond wasn't confident that they had taken enough of the dragons out. Many had fallen, that much was true, but a quick glance up into the sky revealed many more. Too many for his liking.

Just one of those creatures could take out an untold number of mechs with one passing sweep and this battle would devolve just like the first.

Directly ahead of him lay a downed dragon. One wing hung limp and useless. He could see the gaping hole that a ballista bolt had ripped through it, rendering flight impossible. There was no sign of the dragon's rider, the saddle empty.

He would have to be careful of the fire, but he found that he wasn't afraid. He was still impatient and eager to fully test the limits of these new mechs in battle. Perhaps too eager. But there was only so much one could learn and experience from training scenarios.

Desmond thrust the lever forward and the mech charged, its stride long, joints absorbing the impact smoothly.

As expected, the dragon breathed fire at him, the mech's exterior engulfed by it. The temperature in the cockpit rose instantly, uncomfortable but not yet unbearable. The mech would reach the dragon before that happened.

The two bodies collided, one made of steel, the other flesh and all-too-breakable bone. The real dragon was bowled over by the impact, claws scraping ineffectually against the iron plating. With the thicker armor, the dragon's claws could no more puncture the mech than it could stone, but it was welcome to try.

Desmond's mouth twisted into a smirk. There was something so satisfying about having such a powerful creature completely at one's mercy. If only his parents could see him now. Hardly the weak and unimpressive son they believed him to be.

The dragon heaved against the mech, to no avail. With the hollow bones that granted them the gift of flight, the dragon had no hope of moving a mech against its will.

With the push of a button and a few careful adjustments of the levers, the mech's jaws parted, its neck bending, head striking downward like a viper. The metallic jaws closed around the dragon's neck, a hiss of steam the only hint of the crushing force being exerted.

Desmond pushed the button to release the mech's hold, but nothing happened. Annoyed, he pressed it again, harder this time, but still the mech did not respond.

He cursed. The new dial wasn't displaying that he was out of fuel, though perhaps it was faulty. Broken dial or not, he'd still let it get dangerously close, consuming more fuel than he'd meant to. Perhaps the dragon, in its death-throes, had managed to do more damage to the mech than he'd thought.

Whatever the case, the mech refused to respond, as though every joint had locked up. Desmond huffed. How vexing.

Though the mech offered him some protection, he knew better than to remain within the body of one that had broken down. All it would take was one dragon passing by to set the whole thing aflame and he would be trapped inside, left to burn to death in an iron coffin.

Desmond shuddered. It was the fate he feared the most.

Much as he loathed leaving the mech and what little safety it provided behind, it was simply a chance he couldn't afford to take. A disabled mech was a target too good to pass up.

He unstrapped himself from the seat, the panel in the side of the mech sliding clear, and Desmond stepped out. There was little in the way of grass out in this barren terrain, but at least the ground had soaked up the rainfall. He wouldn't have to worry about losing his footing in the mud.

There also wasn't anywhere to hide, but it was too late to worry about that. He unsheathed the sword at his side, the only weapon available to him now.

Against a live dragon, he could do nothing, except avoid them and hope they didn't see him. But plenty of riders had been downed along with their mounts and if the fall hadn't killed them, he could at least finish the job.

As satisfying as it was to pilot a mech, there was something even more pleasing about this. Now, he was wielding the weapon, not merely hiding inside of one.

Just ahead, Desmond could already spy some of the downed riders and he stalked forward, the wind cool against his face, bringing with it the scent of smoke and iron. His blade sang as it cut through the air, crying out for blood.

It got its wish, soon covered in it. As was the way with blood, it went everywhere, spattering against Desmond's uniform, warm but quickly cooling.

A few of the riders were not so badly injured and were able to put up some semblance of a fight. But few of them were armed with swords and a depleted quiver was no match for a blade. He had to be careful of any archers, but Desmond charged ahead, heedless of the danger to himself.

His pulse roared in his ears, his own blood singing. Each swing of his sword an extension of his own arm. He was a soldier and more than that, he was good at it. With each slash, with every stab, he cut down one more of the Empire's enemies. He would see the Empire bathed in glory. He would be its sword arm, carrying out its will.

Suddenly, the din of the battlefield fell away. He no longer saw Anarshans before him, standing in his way, but enemies of another kind. The soldiers before him took on the shape of his father, his mother. Alaric. The Minister of Defense. And even, treasonous as it was, the emperor.

It didn't matter who was placed before him; Desmond cut them down the same. With every enemy he struck down, there was one less obstacle standing in his way. No longer would they stand in judgement of him. No more would he be beholden to them.

He carved a bloody path ever nearer to the camp, so consumed in his work that he barely heard the order to retreat.

He slowed, lowering his sword, and stared around, blinking, in the Anarshan Badlands once more. The mechs were turning back. He could only make out a handful of foot soldiers, pilots like himself who had been forced, for whatever reason, to abandon their mechs.

Retreat?

At last, the word finally penetrated his mind, but it didn't make any sense. Not when they were on the cusp of victory, of pushing the Anarshans back and reaching their city walls.

His feet yearned to carry onward, his sword not yet heavy in his hands. Out on the battlefield, alone, matching his skills and wits against that of another soldier—Desmond had never felt so alive. Never more powerful, whether he was within a mech or not. Never more *in control.*

The path of a soldier was not one he would have chosen for himself—*had* not chosen for himself—and perhaps he would have preferred not to risk his own life, but he couldn't deny that he liked the feeling it gave him. Power over others, instead of the other way around, and control over his own life, over what he chose to do next, even if only for too brief a moment.

No, they could not retreat! Their work here wasn't finished.

But the mist had cleared fully, exposing their ballistae, which had already been decimated. His earlier fear about the remaining dragons being more than a match for the ground-stuck mechs proved true.

As the mechs fell back, their lumbering forms darting for the safety of the forest, there were dragon riders even now who swooped after them, giving chase. One of them would soon notice him, as far forward as he had come, if he didn't hurry and join his comrades.

Desmond hissed and set out for the forest at a run. Another failed attempt, another battle lost. Yet more men and supplies thrown at the Anarshans only for them to absorb the blow.

It was true that the Empire had recovered from their last attempt far more quickly than Desmond had expected, but it was still another setback. And how much longer would this latest one take?

He could almost hear his father's disappointment. But he had survived, regardless of what his family would think of that, and Desmond couldn't bring himself to be upset with such an outcome.

A roar sounded overhead and he ducked instinctively, as if that would help. The forest was just ahead, his view of the tree line jolting erratically with each step. His pace was beginning to flag, his strides shortening, the muscles in his legs protesting each step over the uneven ground. His lungs burned, matched only by the searing pain in his side.

Desmond glanced up, over his shoulder, and his heart leapt to his throat. A dragon hovered overhead, too close for comfort. There was nothing to stop it from swooping down and taking him in its claws, rending his body apart—

Desmond put his head down and ran.

Chandra came back to herself as the battle was ending, with little recollection of how they had arrived there. But the Akkadians were retreating, darting back into the forest from where they'd come.

Through the trees, she could see the smoking remains of the siege weapons that had decimated their initial assault. The mist had provided wonderful cover, but it couldn't last. The Anarshans had held out long enough. Still, Chandra shuddered to think what might have happened if the mist had lingered. How many more would they have lost to the ballistae's cruel aim?

She watched the small figures fleeing below her, scattering like rats, craven, one and all.

Anger smoldered in her stomach, until she felt as though she could breathe fire herself. They weren't allowed to come here and wreak such havoc and destruction and then walk away from it all.

They would be so easy to pick off. Sheboleth could reach them in moments.

"Chase after them," she said, tapping a hand against the dragon's side, as though to urge her onward.

She expected the dragon to dive after them at once, raining hellfire down upon them, but she shook her head.

"No. Let them go. There are injured that must be seen to."

Injured? For a moment, Chandra couldn't believe it. Surely anyone down on that battlefield who was not already dead was well on their way. How had anyone survived?

Gideon certainly hadn't.

Her rage grew, until it felt like a physical presence beside her, a hand on her throat, choking. Better to give in to its smothering embrace than whatever had come over her earlier.

She stared down at the fleeing Akkadian soldiers, drawing ever nearer to the forest. With each second that slipped by, so did their chance.

Those bastards had come here, to her home, and killed at least one of her friends. She had never managed to find Anake or Victor, though she'd hardly call the latter a friend. Either one of them might be down there, dead or dying.

And they were just going to let them walk away. No number of slain Akkadians could ever make up for even one dead Anarshan.

"But Gideon—"

"Is beyond our help," Sheboleth said, her voice flat and too factual. "We must think of the living now."

Gideon's dead. Just like Callum.

There were moments when her cousin's death still didn't feel real. It was still hard to believe he was really gone. Chandra yet expected to run into him, somewhere in the training complex. Or he would be back at home, with their grandmother, waiting for her. Perhaps if she had sent that letter she'd composed to him, when the words had otherwise refused to come, he would write back.

It was only his absence that confirmed his death. If he still lived, he would have found some way of coming to her and the fact that he didn't was proof enough. Only death would keep Callum away.

But even *knowing* that, without a body, without any kind of closure, Chandra knew it was only a matter of time before that feeling came creeping back.

She'd thought that her first battle, her chance to finally strike back at the Akkadians, would bring some of that closure that she so desperately craved. But sitting atop Sheboleth's back as the dragon angled for the ground, she felt little different than she had before.

No, that wasn't true. She felt worse.

Gideon's dead. And I couldn't save him.

She had watched him vanish beneath a wall of fire and caught a glimpse—though she wished she hadn't—of what remained. Unlike Callum, she had watched Gideon die, the very moment it had happened. She had witnessed the instant his life was snuffed out, as easily as one of her candles.

There was no denying that he was gone, no sense of the uncertainty that surrounded her cousin's demise. But that didn't make it any easier.

The rage still smoldered inside Chandra's chest, compressing her lungs, threatening to steal her breath. It hadn't diminished. It felt hungrier, if anything. The Akkadian blood that had been spilled that day had done nothing to sate it.

It wanted more.

As Sheboleth alighted gently on the ground, Chandra no longer wondered what or how much would ever be enough.

She was starting to believe there was no such thing.

XV

The stream of injured seemed endless, though most of the bodies littering the battlefield were beyond help by the time Chandra and Sheboleth reached them. She was exhausted when she finally slid from the saddle. The war camp remained the same, untouched. The enemy hadn't reached it. The sun had already begun to sink toward the horizon and the commanders saw no reason to order everything packed up and relocated to the city just yet.

The soldiers were too tired, the injured needed to rest, the Akkadians would not be coming back that night, or any night soon. The daunting task of packing everything back up could wait until the next day. They could grant their weary warriors that much.

Chandra still had not found Anake or Victor, but that suited her just fine then. She did not want to be the one to tell them, if they hadn't already heard, that their squad was now one member less.

She wasn't surprised, however, to find Roman waiting for her, outside of her tent and near the fire they had shared the last night before battle. It had only been a day ago, but it felt like months had gone by.

The prince looked haggard in the fading light, the skin drawn tightly over his sharp cheekbones, his hands thin and gnarled on the handle of his cane. He looked like he had aged years, not merely the months she herself felt.

They looked at each other for a long moment, as though unsure what to say or where to begin. It seemed foolish to point out the obvious, that both of them had survived, and Chandra was glad that neither of them did.

"Gideon's dead," she said, her voice flat. Better to get it over with, the news that would have to be imparted sooner or later. The timing did nothing to change the facts.

Roman paled. "I'm sorry."

Those simple, helpless words.

Chandra sank down onto the grass, though part of her wanted nothing more than to stand. She'd been in the saddle all day, and her rear end wouldn't let her forget it, even for only a moment, but she was suddenly so *tired*.

"I watched it happen," she said. "Right there in front of me, and I couldn't stop it."

Her voice was so devoid of emotion, it sounded like she was speaking about someone other than herself, an unrelated third party. It was safer that way, and her rage would do her no good here.

Roman sighed and, with an effort, lowered himself down beside her. "I've spoken to the officers."

Something about the way he said it made her think he hadn't wanted to, but he had no choice.

"We suffered heavy losses due to the siege weaponry. Dragons, valuable dragons, lost. But we won. Anarsha is still free."

Chandra looked at him. "Do you think the Empire will try again?"

"I think the fact that they tried a second time at all indicates that they don't intend to give up. The first battle was such a rout, it should have discouraged any further attempts. Yet here they were today, far sooner than they had any right to be. They lost today, too, but not as badly. They will take that as a good sign."

They're making progress. Chandra heard the unspoken words as loudly as if he'd gone ahead and said them.

"How many times do we have to beat them before they get the hint?"

His jaw hardened. "As many times as it takes."

And how many more will we lose each time? Will it be Anake next? Victor? Me? How many times can this be asked of us? How many times will we get lucky before that luck runs out?

"I'm sorry about Gideon," he said again. "I'm sorry I have to ask you to fight this war."

Chandra drew one leg up, wrapping her arms around it. She ran a hand along her calf, flinching at the pain that lanced through it from where Sheboleth had fallen on her. There was a nasty bruise blooming beneath her trouser leg, she was certain.

"It's not your fault."

"Still."

Roman planted his cane in the ground and, wincing, got to his feet. "I need to return to the palace and speak with my father. But I'll be back."

"We'll probably have returned to the keep by then."

"I hope so. It'll seem like a palace itself after this."

He gestured around at the camp, hastily assembled and just as easily torn down. In a few days, it would be gone, along with any sign that it had ever been there at all.

But the place was tainted now, with the blood that had been spilled, and the ground would not forget.

Roman's reprieve had run its course. He'd known better than to think of it as a pardon, but enjoying a few good days made returning to the bad all the harder. The return trip to the palace exhausted him, despite Koal's assistance, and by the time he finally arrived, he could no longer support himself, even with the aid of a cane, and had to be wheeled about by an attendant, the geared wheels of his chair clicking rhythmically through the corridors.

It had been invented by an Akkadian who had fled the Empire of Engines. Not all of their technology was bad, Roman reflected, lulled slightly by the chair's motion. What mattered was intent, the motivations of the people utilizing such technology. Unfortunately, it seemed that most could not be trusted when it came to such ethics.

As lulling as the chair's clicking was, he wanted nothing more than to collapse into his own bed, impossibly soft and welcoming after the war camp. But he needed to speak with his father first. His own rest could wait.

Roman had watched the battle from the camp, listening to the sounds of the ballistae firing, watching as too many of them struck true. It had been horrible, every second of it, but if he could not fight beside them, he owed it to them to bear witness to whatever happened.

He kept hearing Chandra's voice, seeing the flat look in her eyes as she stared into the fire and told him that Gideon was dead. He hadn't known Gideon all that well, but Chandra had—and anyway, that didn't matter. Gideon had been someone, with dreams and desires, fears and failures, little quirks of personality, that had been living one moment and gone the next, never to return.

He was but one of many such people who had fallen that day—and for what?

The least Roman could do was tell his father what he had seen and discuss their next steps so that it hopefully never happened again.

When he'd instructed the attendant to take him to his father, he was surprised to be wheeled in the direction of the library. His father had never been much of a reader, unlike Roman, who had taken to it because it was one of the few things he could do. The library had been his mother's sanctum. She had valued learning above nearly all else, though it hadn't saved her in the end.

Inside, the room was relatively dark, the heavy curtains drawn over the windows. The only light stemmed from candles, barely illuminating the tall shelves with their dark wood, the glass panels that protected the books beneath. Ulric was hunched over the central table, perusing a thick tome, and Roman wondered how long he had been there.

He looked up at the sound of their entry, scrambling to his feet at once. "Roman."

Roman waved at the attendant to leave them. His father looked haggard, deep shadows beneath his eyes, and was there more gray in his hair than there had been before?

"I bring news from the front," Roman said, and told his father what he had seen firsthand, grateful, for once, that he was already sitting down.

Ulric's expression progressively fell as he listened to his son, until he sank back into his seat.

"The battle was vicious," Roman finished, "and there were heavier losses than we would have liked—" He grimaced. "Any loss is too high."

The king ran a hand over his gaunt face. "I have a council meeting. You should come, if you feel up to it. Your testimony will be valuable."

Roman blinked in surprise. Things must be dire, indeed, for his father to suggest he attend a council meeting—

which were always overlong and dull at the best of times—instead of resting and recovering his strength.

"Of course," he agreed. "If you think it will be of use."

Ulric rose to his feet. "We shouldn't keep them waiting, much as I'd like to."

Roman followed, accompanying his father to the council chamber. He would have preferred to walk in, under his own power, even if he'd needed his cane, but willpower alone was no match for a body that didn't wish to cooperate.

The sound of the door opening echoed throughout the chamber as they entered, all eyes immediately turning their way. The council members who were already seated rose to their feet in a show of respect, whether they truly meant the gesture or not.

The chairs were high-backed, hard-looking things, and Roman eyed them with distaste, strangely grateful for his wheeled chair. Of course, one of those chairs was meant for him, should he wish it, and he was certainly strong enough to transfer himself from one chair to another, but he suddenly had no desire to.

His father's chair was the tallest, dominating the room. The other chairs were occupied by the various councilors and advisors. Some of them were empty, as they always seemed to be, which did not surprise Roman. He could feel their eyes on him like snakes and knew, for the most part, what each of them thought of him. The crippled prince.

"My apologies for the delay," Ulric said, taking his seat. Roman hoped the councilors wouldn't think the delay was because of him. "Let us begin with news of the battle."

Roman listened as his father recounted the battle, silently studying those present.

"Any losses suffered in the battle are regrettable, but far from our greatest concern," Lord Silva said, once Ulric had fallen silent.

Silva had long silver hair that reached his shoulders and there was something of a regal bearing to him. Of the council members, Roman had always respected him the most. He seemed fair, overall, in his judgements and at least participated in the meetings, which was more than could be said for some. Silva, for his part, tried to get things done. No one could accuse him of inaction.

"It is the rising food shortages we must discuss," Silva added.

Roman looked up sharply. *Food shortages?* When had this happened? He'd heard no word of any food shortages. But then again, it had been some time since he'd last been able to attend a council meeting, with the bad days outnumbering the good. Shuffled around from one healer to the next, his visit to the barracks and later the war camp had been his only connection to the world outside, and he'd heard nothing there.

Lord Vaughan tapped one meaty finger on the stone table. The motion made barely a sound, but the large green ring he wore flashed as it caught the light. "Yes, what's this I hear about shortages?"

He sneered the last word as if it were particularly repellent.

Lord Daladier glanced between the two councilors who had spoken, his face etched with concern, but he did not speak. Roman hadn't expected him to. The man rarely said anything much at all.

"We are cut off," Silva said simply. "Our allies have fallen under the control of the Empire. The very Empire who is hellbent on destroying us, so it stands to reason that these former allies are unable to trade with us, as they once did."

"To put it simply," Lord Salerno said, shooting Vaughan a pointed look, "we have no trade coming into Anarsha anymore. We can only trade within our own walls. And that is not enough."

Salerno reached up, fingertips brushing the ends of his mustache, which Roman suspected he waxed. The man was obviously quite proud of it; he could never seem to stop touching it. But Roman was grateful for the display of vanity; without the mustache, he had trouble keeping Salerno and Silva apart.

Vaughan's face darkened further. "Then we will have to turn away the Shemaran refugees and halt aid to the ones already here."

"But you can't—" Roman protested.

He had seen the forlorn lines of refugees, pouring toward the city gates from Shemar. Those people had braved the path through the Valderan forest to get there. They had nothing left, but what they had been able to carry, leaving their home behind. Anarsha could not turn them away now.

"It's bad enough that we did not help them while they still stood a chance," he added. "But now we are to abandon them, in their greatest hour of need?"

Silva shot him a pitying look. "Lord Vaughan is right. Harsh as it may be, we must look to our own people now."

"Perhaps if we had looked to the Shemarans, we would not now be standing alone against the Empire."

Or dealing with food shortages because there is no one left to trade with.

Vaughan snorted. "We are more than a match for the Empire."

"Are we?"

"I would think our victories would suggest so. No other enemy of Akkadia has sent them fleeing, twice over, back to their precious Capitol."

"For how long?" Roman challenged. "They lost men, but so did we. And each time they return, we will lose more, until we have no more weapons with which to fight."

"To that end," Salerno said, fingering his mustache, "we will have to recruit more soldiers."

"We've already increased recruitment efforts," Ulric said. "What more do you want?"

"Younger. And from the same households. We cannot afford sentimentality—not if we are to remain free. If a household has young men or women who are able to fight, they must all be given to the cause."

Sacrificed, you mean, Roman thought. *Sacrificed to the cause.*

"No," Ulric said. "I will not ask a family to part with all of their children, no matter how capable."

He glanced across at Roman and the prince knew what his father must be thinking. He was his father's only son. How would he feel, being asked to part with his only child—or all of his children?

"We don't have a choice," Silva said, lending Salerno his support. "The prince is right. The Empire will return and we cannot find ourselves without weapons when they do."

"What choice do we have?" Salerno pressed. "One battle can be the difference between victory and defeat. If we lose, Anarsha falls, and the lives of everyone within this city's walls are forfeit. Better to sacrifice the few to save the many."

Ulric sighed. "Yes...I fear you are right. We cannot afford sentimentality—none of us."

No, Roman thought.

"We will increase recruitment efforts. As for the food shortages, we will turn away any additional refugees and stop current aid. Let us hope that proves enough. If not, I fear additional steps will need to be taken."

"A problem for another time," Vaughan muttered.

The council came to an end shortly thereafter, but not nearly soon enough for Roman's liking. A few of the councilors lingered, speaking of inane things that he was no longer bothering to pay attention to. He caught his father's eye, trying to convey that he wished to speak to him.

He sent a silent thanks to the saints when the last few men rose to their feet, dithering even as they made for the door. At last, the great door shut behind them, the sound reverberating throughout the chamber, and Roman was alone with his father.

"Father, you cannot ask any more of the recruitment efforts. It's too harsh. How much are you going to ask one family to give?"

"I don't like it any more than you do. But you heard what was said. How many lives is freedom worth? What are a few sacrifices compared to the death of an entire kingdom?"

How many lives is freedom worth? There were some who would say that freedom was worth any price, but Roman wasn't so sure.

"This is hard on all of us, son," Ulric said kindly. "These are dark times and only likely to grow darker still. We did not ask for such troubles to be thrust upon us…and yet they were."

Roman took a deep breath. "Very well. But what about the rationing? What about the refugees?"

"What about our army?" Ulric countered. "You were just there, walking among them. Do you think such a force is fed by air alone? The Empire is still out there, and if both our fears are correct, it's only a matter of time before they strike again. We cannot afford to weaken our army. They must continue to be fed, and if that means taking food away from people who are not even our citizens, then so be it."

"I understand that, but this is our chance to make up, in some small way, for turning our back on Shemar when they were the focus of the Empire's assault. We cannot abandon them entirely."

Even if they continued to aid the Shemaran refugees, Roman knew it in no way made up for neglecting them when they were under fire from the Empire. He didn't understand, fully, why his father had ultimately refused to help Shemar or Elath, and if he were honest with himself, it wasn't something he cared to examine too closely, for fear of what he might find.

Far easier to blame the other members of the council. His father was a king, yes, but he could do nothing without the council's approval. Whatever the reason, there was just enough truth in that to placate him.

Ulric shook his head. "Your compassion does you credit, son, but Shemar has fallen. So has Elath. They belong to the Empire now. There's nothing more that can be done. If we truly wish to help them, defeating the Empire would be a good start. It's the only way any of them can be free again."

Roman frowned. His father made a convincing argument. No doubt Ulric was aware of the soundness of his own position and that was why he had played that final card.

And yet, it wasn't enough. It still did not excuse their own inaction. They had abandoned their supposed allies. The reason mattered less than the result.

Suddenly, he wanted to push, to peel back the edge of the envelope and see what truly lay within. To challenge his father on the one issue he had never dared.

"Yes, we must look to our own," he said, bitterness twisting his tone, "like we did when Elath and Shemar were under attack. We left them to fight alone."

Did his father truly feel no shame at all for what Anarsha had done—or failed to do?

"They would not have come to our aid, had we been the Empire's first target."

"We can't know that."

"Yes," Ulric snapped, rising to his feet. "We can. When the walls start closing in, everyone looks to their own. It's just the way of the world."

XVI

The return trip to the Capitol was just as arduous as the one before. The Empire had lost as many men, though not as quickly. They stopped in Shemar, briefly, to rest before continuing on, much to Desmond's relief. He would have happily stayed in Shemar, rather than face the city he loathed—not for itself, but for what it represented.

He would have to face his family again, as something of a failure. The Empire still had not conquered all the kingdoms, and that would be seen as a failure in his parents' eyes, no matter that he had managed, once again, not to get himself killed.

Desmond learned, through listening to various gossip around the barracks, that his was not the only mech to fail on the battlefield. It seemed there were still kinks that needed ironed out of the new models. Increased power was of no use if the thing couldn't be trusted not to die on you.

He sighed. That was his brother's problem to figure out, along with his precious Minister. Perhaps if he pointed out the new mechs' flaws within earshot of his parents, it might bring Alaric down a few pegs, in their estimation, at least. If the only way he could make himself look better in their eyes was to bring his brother down, well, he wasn't above the idea.

By the time he arrived in the city, word of the battle and its outcome had far outpaced him, and his father, who never lifted a finger from the pulse of the Empire, had no need to ask.

He arrived at his family's manor tired from the road, but thankfully not dirty. His father was seated at the writing desk in the sitting room, letters spread out before him, and he looked up as Desmond was shown in by the butler.

"I wasn't expecting you back," his father said.

The remark could have meant many things. Perhaps he'd merely assumed that Desmond would have rather stayed at the barracks instead of coming home. Desmond would have preferred that, but he knew better than to ignore his father's expectations. The moment it was learned that Desmond had returned to the city—and had been granted leave—questions would be raised as to why he hadn't come home.

The more ominous meaning behind his father's remark, of course, was that perhaps he had been expected to fall on the battlefield, in which case, he would never be coming back.

Desmond could never be sure and he didn't much care anymore, after everything.

"I've been given a few weeks' leave," he explained.

He felt his father's eyes rake over him, taking in the uniform that probably could have done with a bit more ironing, and the hair that had grown out. It would need trimming again, back to regulation length, and Desmond resisted the urge to run his hands through it, his scalp prickling beneath his father's gaze.

His father grunted. "Your mother is upstairs with a headache," he said, as if to explain, or excuse, her absence.

"Is it serious?" Desmond asked, feeling like a response was expected of him, but unsure what to say. Nothing felt adequate.

His mother had long suffered from headaches. As Desmond grew older, he'd begun to suspect such maladies were feigned, or exaggerated, more often than not, to offer a reprieve when his mother could no longer stand to be around her husband.

"I shouldn't think so. We're hosting a dinner party tonight. I asked if we should cancel, but she assures me that she'll feel up to it."

Damn it. He really should have stayed at the barracks, at least for one more day.

"Ah," he said, an entire world of meaning contained within a single syllable. *Feigned malady it is, then.*

His father gave him a sharp look, but before he could speak, Desmond carried on. "It's been a long journey, and I'd hate to intrude unexpectedly—"

He knew, all too well, how these things went. A certain number of guests were invited, so that no one was left without a partner to be paired with. His presence, unaccounted for, would throw that delicate balance off. To say nothing of the number of place settings at the table or meals that needed to be prepared.

"Nonsense," his father said, interrupting before Desmond could suggest that he spent the evening in his room. "It will be good for you to be seen."

You mean, it will do you good, Desmond thought bitterly, recalling the way his father had previously monopolized his return from the front.

He may not have been the favorite son, but he was still a soldier, and his presence so soon after the latest battle would be of instant interest to his father's guests. They would speak of him, but not to him. They would all but trip over themselves in their haste to ask questions, but never to him, putting such queries to his father, making him all the more interesting as a host and ensuring he was never without attention for the evening.

But Desmond knew better than to refuse. He was not in the position to do so. If he displeased his father, he could always cut him out of the inheritance or throw him out of the house altogether. Desmond would have nowhere to go aside from the army, and that couldn't last forever, could it?

He doubted such drastic measures would ever be taken, but the threat was there, hovering over him, and both men knew it. Desmond hated his father for it. He might have more respect for the man if he were to just come out and say it, brandishing the power he held over his son.

Until Desmond found himself in the position to refuse, he would have to go along with whatever he was told, with other people's plans for his life, the same as always.

Saints, he couldn't wait to return to the front. At least in war, things were simple. There was a clear objective in mind, you knew who the enemy was, and the only thing you needed to concern yourself with was their destruction.

Here, in the Capitol, in his own home, he was the conquered one, the one who had been subjugated.

All of that raced through Desmond's mind, but he felt no visible sign of his true thoughts other than a tightening of his jaw.

"As you wish, Father." He inclined his head with more grace than he felt. "I'll go prepare."

He took his time about it, too. If he must return home, the least he could do is indulge in the luxuries that were otherwise denied to him. He took a long bath, refilling it whenever the water became too cold, savoring the smell of the various perfumes and soaps. He lingered over his choice of attire for the night, trying on and then discarding one ensemble after another. There wasn't much that could be done for his hair, in terms of styling, but he was determined to enjoy its longer length while he could, slicking it back with gel until it gleamed. He could hang upside down if he wished and not a strand would be out of place.

Desmond had always enjoyed having longer hair and it pained him to think of cutting it again. He paused in front of the gilded mirror, staring at his reflection, a memory stirring to the surface of when he had been a child. His mother had spoiled him in the beginning, before his father forbade it. She had let his hair grow long, like a girl's. She had enjoyed brushing it out at the end of each day, saying what lovely hair he had, so rich and full.

That had all come to a swift end, of course. He had to be a man, his father said. And that meant things like no more long hair. No more shrieking, as he'd done when Alaric had come up to him and instructed him to hold out his hand. The moment Desmond did, wondering with a mixture of awe and excitement what gift his older brother was about to bestow upon him, Alaric put his closed hand over Desmond's and relaxed his grip, allowing the spider to scurry over Desmond's palm.

Later, Desmond wondered which had hurt more: the shame of his reaction, shrieking in fear at a creature so much smaller than him, who posed not the slightest risk of harm; or the sting of his father's hand across his face.

No, it had been many years since Desmond had worn his hair long or shrieked at the sight of a spider, though he still hated the creatures with their many legs.

There had been a time when Desmond had believed that being a man would finally please his father and earn his approval.

He was still waiting, but he no longer believed.

As he came down the stairs, wearing the first evening suit he'd initially tried on, he resigned himself to an unpleasant evening, telling himself that time still moved forward at the same steady rate, and that even this night could not last forever.

His mother was already downstairs, ready to greet their guests, having miraculously recovered from her headache. She was the picture of poise and elegance, as always, and no one who looked at her would think she had been indisposed but a handful of hours ago.

Desmond took his place and greeted each of the guests as they arrived, slightly late—if they were wise. It wouldn't do to arrive on time, or saints forbid early, and appear too eager.

At some point, he found a glass of something pressed into his hand. What it was, he couldn't tell by looking, but he didn't much care. He sipped it, wishing he could down the whole thing instead. Anything to distract from the slow, painful death that was a dinner party.

He hovered near his father, in case the man should wish to call him over at a moment's notice. But for the most part, his father seemed content to complain to the other wealthy, self-important men in his life.

Desmond couldn't help but listen, whatever he had drank not enough to dull his focus.

"It's such a waste," his father griped. "You'd think the emperor could come up with a better strategy than simply throwing resources at the Anarshans."

Desmond's eyebrows rose slightly. Risky talk, to criticize the emperor like that. Alaric might report it back to the Minister, who might feel obliged to inform the emperor. People had, supposedly, been punished for less.

He glanced around for any sign of his brother, but Alaric seemed to be absent that evening. He hadn't caught a glimpse of his brother all night, which meant that his plan to disparage the new mechs in front of him would have to wait.

How vexing.

"This campaign is quickly becoming too costly," his father went on. "To say nothing of how long it's taking."

One of the other men grunted his agreement—a habit that never failed to irritate Desmond; did people not know how to use words anymore? —and mentioned how one minor noble's iron mine in Elath had already dried up, or such was the rumor.

"Not that he had much of anything to begin with, mind you," the man added. "But it's still worrying. The mechs take an immense amount of raw material to produce, especially these newer models, and the Empire just keeps demanding more. *More!* And I'm not the only one who feels that way."

"The Empire is in a fractious position," Desmond's father remarked, frowning down at his glass as he swirled the contents. "It could splinter and fall apart before it ever truly begins. The first emperor may well be the last."

The Empire, fall apart?

One of the other men nodded. "Akkadia, Anarsha, Elath and Shemar have never been united under one banner. We knew going in that this would not be an easy task."

But it's never been this hard, either.

"They have fewer dragons now," the man continued. "The key is to press our advantage."

The Anarshans, for all the losses they may have suffered, had held out rather remarkably so far. If the

Empire had an advantage, as that man claimed, Desmond couldn't see it.

The dinner party came to an end, as all unpleasant things eventually do. Desmond spent not one more moment in the house than was expected of him, relieved, when the time came, to return to the barracks. It was hardly a place of luxury and his fellow soldiers could be uncouth, unhygienic creatures, but at least they seemed honest enough.

There were no social pretentions to be found among them.

Never one to waste time or opportunity, the engineers and mechanics began work at once on improving the mech models. Desmond's days were occupied with putting the new machines through their paces, both at the warehouses and the barracks themselves. He didn't mind the work, particularly if it ensured that the mech wouldn't die on him when next he entered the battlefield.

Not having to interact with other people much didn't hurt either.

One late afternoon, he climbed out of the cockpit, blinking in the sudden sun, and frowned at the sight of a familiar figure. His brother's back was to him, but there was no doubt that it was Alaric, dressed in his annoyingly pristine uniform.

He turned at the sound of the mech's panels sliding back, beckoning for Desmond to join him, a look of satisfaction on his face.

"What do you think?" he asked.

What do I think about what? Desmond wondered, irritated that his brother didn't just come out and say it. But he found out for himself soon enough.

The ground sloped downward from where they stood and Desmond walked to the edge, peering down at the district below. Groups of people were lined up, a regimented order to their ranks as they ran through drills.

They were not the usual infantry, Desmond could see that at once, though that was hardly surprising. Their infantry ranks had suffered the most casualties in the last skirmish. Their numbers would have to be built back up, no easy task—until it suddenly was.

Desmond didn't need Alaric to explain to him what he was looking at. He already knew.

"Genius, isn't it?" Alaric asked. Desmond wanted to wipe the smug, self-satisfied grin off his face.

"A good use of resources," Desmond replied and Alaric barked out a laugh.

Desmond hadn't meant to be funny; he'd merely spoken the truth. What else were the slaves good for if they weren't put to work in some fashion? The men and women—mostly men—arranged below him were from Elath and, more recently, Shemar.

They, like all the resources the Empire claimed wherever it went, were now Akkadia's to do with as she saw fit.

"They won't fight in mechs, obviously," Alaric said, "but on foot. They can't be trusted with such powerful weaponry—they might turn it on us—but they can still serve a purpose nonetheless. Beautiful, isn't it? Finding their proper place beneath the Empire."

Desmond merely nodded his assent.

It was canny, offering them as fodder without risking any of their own. But his thoughts strayed back to the night of the dinner party—the party his brother hadn't deigned to attend—and what had been said.

Was this simply wise strategy, or was it a silent admission that perhaps things weren't going as smoothly as the Empire publicly claimed? Proof that perhaps Akkadia was finally feeling the effects of failed campaigns?

He could have asked Alaric if there was anything in that, but he doubted his brother would have answered truthfully.

Anake and Victor had both come through the battle just fine, Chandra learned. Their squad was once again a member short, though if Gideon's loss troubled either of them, they didn't show it—not that Chandra expected Victor to lose any sleep over it.

No one seemed to want to talk about it, and if she were honest, Chandra was grateful. It felt like a sheet of ice had encircled her heart, to the point she felt nothing much at all—not that she tried too hard. She told herself that it was better that way.

They had work to do, after all. The threat of Akkadia had not disappeared with their second victory and so training resumed. Sometimes, it felt like the battle hadn't happened at all and she had merely imagined the whole thing. But then the sight of Gideon's empty bunk in the barracks would remind her, until even that was taken away, occupied by one of the new recruits. More of them seemed to pour in all the time.

She waited for Roman to return, but he didn't. If he'd been delayed, she thought he might send word, but no word came. She wondered if he was ashamed now to face her and the other soldiers after witnessing the battle. Maybe he felt as though he'd be unwelcome.

He's a prince. He has more important things to do than humor you.

In light of the increased siege weaponry and the newer, improved mechs the Empire had brought during the last encounter, a new training exercise was added for the dragons. They were divided into pairs and ordered to spar with each other, in the unfortunate event they found themselves downed and targeted by one of the mechs.

Chandra thought it a lost cause. A downed dragon was no match for the immense weight of the mechs, or their iron plating. But as she stood to the side, watching the beasts go at it, she marveled at their sheer power, the fierce savagery on display, and began to think that perhaps they might stand a chance after all.

The lots were drawn at random, pairing dragons of various skills, abilities, and techniques against one another. It was only a matter of time before Sheboleth's name was called and Chandra waited, beside her dragon, to see whom she would face.

"Bane!" Khan called out.

Chandra just managed to suppress a wince. Of course, it would be Victor's dragon. She glanced across at him, something curdling in her stomach at the sight of his self-satisfied smirk.

So, he was pleased with this arrangement, was he?

Make him regret it, she silently pleaded. *Tear him to pieces.*

But that would be easier said than done. She observed the two dragons' physiques as they stalked out into the open field. Sheboleth was wiry, the muscles visibly flexing beneath her black scales. But Bane was brawn itself, his limbs thick and muscular. He looked slow and clumsy compared to lithe Sheboleth, but if one dragon got ahold of the other, there was no doubt who would win in a contest of brute strength.

Bane curled his lip, his expression not unlike that of his rider. Sheboleth's lips peeled back in response, baring her teeth, as if picking up on the animosity between the two riders.

At the signal, both dragons rushed forward, colliding in a tangle of claws and snapping teeth. They fought with more effort than any of the other pairings had displayed, going at each other as if the fight were real.

Maybe it is.

Sheboleth's eyes blazed a furious green and she fought like a demon. She wanted to win, Chandra realized, as much as she herself wanted her to win.

But in the end, Bane was simply too strong. All it took was for Sheboleth to overextend herself and he was on her, pinning her, forcing her to the ground.

Instead of letting her go, now that the fight was at its end, as the other pairings had done, Bane hovered over Sheboleth, refusing to release her, his jaws hovering over her exposed neck.

Sheboleth squirmed, but Bane was too heavy, and she let out a frustrated huff. Fear seized hold of Chandra, sudden and irrational, that Bane would kill her dragon.

Her dragon. She wasn't sure when she came to think of Sheboleth that way, well aware that she didn't belong to her, after all. And yet, it was the truth.

Khan shouted something and Bane, reluctantly, relented. Sheboleth scrambled to her feet in an instant, hissing her displeasure. For a breathless moment, it looked like the two dragons might have a go at each other again, but Khan wasn't finished.

"I trust, in future," he said, a deep scowl etched into his expression, "you'll remember who the real enemy is."

As if Chandra could forget.

Reminders of the Empire were everywhere, her constant companion, the entire reason she was at the keep at all. And she could no more forget the enemy than she could the reason she was fighting in the first place. Now she had Gideon's death to avenge, not just Callum's. Who else was there to do it? She didn't know if Anake or Victor even cared and she wasn't going to ask.

It was hard not to think of either of them in the long, dark nights when she was supposed to be resting. When there was nothing for her to do, when she could no longer push her body to its limits, her mind came to life, refusing to still.

She didn't want to think such thoughts. She didn't want to think about how Gideon had told her that he was an only child, that he'd worked in his father's bakery. What was that father feeling now? Had he received the letter yet, the small box that represented all that remained of his son's life?

She couldn't imagine a father's grief at losing an only child. At least she and Callum had only their grandmother. Both of their parents were already gone, having been spared such sorrow.

And Gideon was just the one she knew about. How many more parents across Anarsha had lost their only son or daughter? How many had sent their child away to fight for their kingdom, knowing they might not return, and having that fear realized?

Chandra rolled over in her bunk, feeling sick. The thoughts were particularly repellent tonight. If she dwelled on it for much longer, the despair would threaten to overwhelm her.

Grief was not something with which she was familiar. It wasn't something she was allowed to feel. It was a useless emotion. It made it impossible to focus on the things that needed to be done, or so Chandra assumed from what she'd seen of it so far.

Anger, she knew, and it was far more useful. It made her want to take action. To *do* something other than drown in self-pity.

She swung her legs over the side of the bunk and stood. Her body ached, muscles crying out in protest. She had pushed herself hard that day, but they should have been used to it by now. She pushed herself hard every day.

Chandra could walk, if sleep wouldn't come to silence the thoughts. She could do that much. The movement would help and then, once she was fully exhausted, she could return and wait for sleep again.

She wouldn't have thought it possible to be more physically tired than she was already, but obviously, she wasn't nearly tired enough.

The night air was cool on her face, instantly calming some of her nerves. She would make a lap around the perimeter—the guards wouldn't mind. She had thought that one of them would stop her, confront her about being out after curfew, but none of them had. Perhaps they understood all too well.

She hadn't taken more than a few steps when she felt the air stir around her, a presence settling just behind her, and she knew who it was without turning to look. As if they had been drawn to one another.

"This is the third time this week."

Chandra turned to face Sheboleth. She didn't have to ask what the dragon meant—this was her third time that week that sleep had refused to come. And so she'd wandered the grounds, exhausting her body still further until her mind caught up and blessedly left her in peace.

"What do you think you're doing?" Sheboleth pressed.

Chandra turned and began walking away. "What do you mean?"

"I mean, running yourself ragged. Don't think I haven't noticed. What good will it do? Will working yourself to the bone somehow bring the Empire down?"

Chandra felt a flash of irritation. She had wanted to be alone, not have a nagging companion trailing behind her, keeping alive the thoughts she most wanted to kill.

"I wasn't ready," she snapped. "I won't make that kind of mistake again."

"You're just one person," Sheboleth said, not unkindly, her claws clacking on the stone walkway. "What difference can one person make?"

Chandra said nothing, though she knew the dragon was right.

She took a deep breath, turning back to her. "I just need to be alone for a little bit, all right? I need…some time."

Sheboleth gave her a long, hard look. Chandra had no doubt the dragon could see through the excuse, flimsy as it was, but at last, she nodded and turned away, leaving Chandra alone.

She sighed and continued on her way, hands balled into fists.

Why couldn't she make more of a difference? The familiar anger, that horrible beast, rose up. It felt powerful enough to wipe out the entire invading Akkadian force. But she knew it wasn't.

Her anger, strong as it was, was powerless in the face of something so vast. Something that seemed, she admitted to herself in the lonely hours of the night, to be unstoppable.

XVII

Chandra stared down at her tray, trying to keep her eyes open. She'd gone out again last night, making her rounds around the complex until she felt tired enough to finally sleep. Each time, it seemed to take her longer and the paltry amount of food on her tray wasn't helping her energy. She'd barely taken more than a bite and already it looked as though there was nothing left.

"Saints."

Chandra jumped as Victor slammed his tray down on their table, taking a seat next to Anake, who was across from her.

"I thought they were joking when I heard the portions had been reduced," he added, glaring from his own tray to Anake's and Chandra's and back.

"No joke," Anake said mildly.

The rationing program had been announced that morning, though no one had known exactly what such a plan would look like…until now. Peering glumly down at her tray, Chandra knew by sight alone that she would still be left hungry at the end. Or she would have, if she'd had any appetite to speak of.

Meals, once looked forward to, were now a chore. She didn't have to decide what to cook for herself, at least, but she still had to go through the laborious task of chewing it all, when everything tasted like ash in her mouth. Each time the thought sprang up anew—Callum's cooking was so much better.

And once the thought had taken root, it refused to go away, linking mealtimes forever with Callum's cooking, one inevitably paling in comparison to the other.

"How are we expected to survive on such meager rations?" Victor demanded. "How are we supposed to be in any shape to fight?"

Chandra did her best to ignore him, his whining grating on her nerves. No doubt he believed he should have been exempt, as the son of one of the officers. How frustrating to find out you were just like everyone else…

But Victor hadn't finished, glaring down at his food as he pushed it around with a fork. "Almost makes me glad the losses were so heavy."

The muttered words were so low, Chandra almost didn't catch them, and even then, nearly convinced herself she must have heard wrong until Anake snapped.

"You didn't just say that."

To Chandra's satisfaction, Victor seemed genuinely ashamed of his comment, glancing abashedly toward Anake. "All right, all right. Of course I don't mean it, I'm just saying…"

"Here," Chandra said, sliding her tray across to him. "You can have mine if it'll make you shut up."

"You don't want it?"

She cocked an eyebrow. "Do you think I'd be offering if I did?" *To you, of all people.*

Victor offered up no further hesitation and added her tray's contents to his own. He could have her lunch but she wasn't going to stay and watch him eat it. Chandra shoved to her feet and made her way out of the mess hall.

Roman blinked in the afternoon sunlight, his gaze drawn toward the entrance to the mess hall, as someone stepped out. The sun caught on her fiery hair and he knew he'd been right. She stopped as she spotted him and he raised one hand in greeting, the other leaning heavily on his cane.

Chandra changed direction, heading over to him so that he didn't have to cross the distance, a gesture for which he was grateful. He'd meant to return sooner, but he'd felt too weak, forced to wait. He hoped she didn't resent him for it, but he supposed he would find out soon enough.

"You came back," she said simply, once she'd reached him.

"I told you I would. My apologies, though. I meant to come sooner."

"Do you know anything about these new rations? Word just came down today and some people aren't taking it so well."

Roman winced. The rationing that he'd fought so hard against had only grown worse, now spreading to the soldiers that some of the councilors had championed so staunchly.

"I'm sorry for that, too. I tried to argue against it, in the council meetings, but I'm only one voice." He smiled ruefully.

"I wasn't blaming you."

"I know. But you're one of the few who wouldn't. Some people see royalty and are more than happy to lay all ills at our feet." He sighed. "In truth, the general populace has been on reduced rations ever since the last battle."

Her green eyes widened.

"The other councilors tried to hold out on the army as long as they could, but…" Roman hesitated, knowing he shouldn't say his next words, but neither could he bring himself to lie to her. "Things aren't looking good, Chandra."

She visibly swallowed, but when she spoke, she tried for levity. "Aside from the obvious, you mean?" A valiant, but vain attempt.

"We're cut off from Elath and Shemar now and neither of them are willing to trade with us—so long as they're under the Empire's control and we're actively opposing them."

"So it's a war of attrition now, is it? They can just wait and starve us out."

"I don't think it's that drastic," Roman tried to assure her. *Not yet, anyway.*

"Mechs don't need food," Chandra pointed out.

"No, but the people who pilot them do."

In spite of the confident front Roman tried to present, he was worried that Chandra was more correct than she realized. This could easily turn into a war of attrition, which only ended one way.

Elath and Shemar would remain cut off from Anarsha unless they found a way to change that—and that would require defeating the Empire, a task made increasingly harder with a lack of food. Anarsha was left to trade within itself, and with only so many options to choose from, that would neither last, nor solve the problem.

"What can we do?" she asked softly, as if sensing his thoughts.

"There's not much we can do. We need to trade with the other kingdoms, and we can't so long as the Empire controls them. We'd have to defeat the Empire first and we need food and supplies for that."

He'd already told her too much. What was a little more?

She frowned. "If we can't trade for it, could we steal what we needed?"

"From where?"

She shrugged. "Elath. Shemar. We could rob trains. That's how they transport supplies from the Capitol to the other kingdoms, isn't it?"

"Yes, trains carry materials between both. How would we do it though?"

"We have dragons that can fly—and they don't. It shouldn't be too hard to organize a raid. Get in, snatch what we need, and get out."

"It isn't a bad idea," Roman admitted. "And since we're already at war with Akkadia, we don't have to worry if they find out we're behind it."

"What would that do?" Chandra asked with a grin. "Escalate tensions further?"

Roman smiled in response and then frowned. "We'd need to recruit people for it though. And the level of risk involved makes me think it won't be a popular suggestion."

Chandra shrugged again. "Like you said, we're already at war. How much more dangerous can it get?"

"I know, but after the first few raids, the Empire will get wise to what we're doing, and things will only get riskier from there. And the amount of supplies we need will determine the number of raids…"

He didn't need to say it to know she understood. The more you did something dangerous, the better the odds that something would eventually go wrong. Each time, the odds would worsen slightly, as the Empire would hardly stand by and let them steal from them without a fight. Not every raid would be successful—and not everyone would come back.

Such a task was a hard ask and not one Roman took lightly.

"I'll speak to my father," Roman said, "and see what he thinks of the idea. I don't like the idea of forcing anyone to go on raids—not unless there's no other choice. But asking for volunteers seems too much to hope for."

"I'll volunteer." She said it with no hesitation, as casually as if she were agreeing to a stroll.

"Chandra, you don't have to do that—"

"I don't mind. I *want* to. It's important."

Roman couldn't deny that. As he'd already pointed out, the food shortage wasn't likely to improve on its own, and better that they addressed the problem before it became a full-blown crisis.

He nodded. "I'll speak to my father and let you know what he says. We'll have to discuss it with the council, of course, but it's a good idea."

Better than nothing. And certainly better than what the council had so far suggested—cutting off aid from refugees and forced to ration even their own army.

"That reminds me," he said. "There's something I need to do, and I'd like you to come with me, if you don't mind."

"Where are we going?" she asked, but she took a step forward as though to follow him.

"It's not far."

At the entrance to the compound, Koal, the blue dragon, stood waiting for him. Roman would have liked to walk all the way to the refugee camps on his own, but the streets were always crowded with people and there was no way to know how long the trip, short as it was, would take on foot.

Wordlessly, Koal knelt down, allowing Roman to climb up onto his back. He offered Chandra a hand, not wanting her to feel left out, but she hesitated, shaking her head.

"I don't mind walking."

Accompanying the prince was one thing, but Roman suspected that riding a dragon with one was a step too far. He withdrew his hand, slightly stung, and Koal rose back to his full height.

Outside the streets were just as crowded as he'd feared, people pressing close, hurrying on their way, or lining up at the various market stalls, ducking into stores. Roman glimpsed more than one unhappy expression, including a young woman who exited one of the stores looking disappointed.

His stomach clenched. Were these people trying to buy food for their families, only to be met with the bitter realization that there wasn't enough to go around?

The sight of a dragon, outside the complex, walking the streets, drew more attention than he would have liked and he felt his face heat beneath the weight of so many stares. It was unlikely any of them knew who he was. His presence at the keep was hardly common knowledge, and it had been some years since he'd made any public appearances.

But still, they took notice of him. They must have wondered who he was, of such importance that he commanded a dragon convey him around the city. Or perhaps their eyes lingered on the cane in his hand and suspected he was being carried for an entirely different reason. Roman wished he could make the cane disappear. He both hated and needed it, and hated it all the more for that.

At least none of the people they passed looked hungry or desperate yet. If Roman had his way, they never would. It wouldn't come to that.

The refugee camps had been set up on the outskirts of town, pressed as close to the Great Wall as possible. At least their backs were protected; no one could sneak up behind them, intent on harassing them.

But the tents, for that was all they were, were practically on top of one another, too many people crammed into too small a space.

Koal stopped at the edge of the camp and Roman slid to the ground, trying to hide his wince as his knee nearly buckled beneath him.

Chandra came to join him and together, they watched the mass of humanity that had been invited within Anarsha's walls and then found themselves forgotten.

He watched groups of children, bored with nothing to do and unable to venture beyond the limits of the camp. They darted around the tents, chasing each other, getting under foot. More than one woman sent them a glare, including one who stood over a large tub, up to her elbows in the water, as she did the laundry.

Other women, and a few men, made trips back and forth to the well at the end of the road, fetching the water to be used in everything from laundry to cooking, bathing and drinking. The refugees had to fetch all the water they needed and then bring it back to the camp, an exhausting task that could take all day, depending on how much was needed.

These people had an air of desperation about them. It wasn't enough to lose their home, but now they received no food. Roman had overheard a few complaints, petitions. They had little money, only what they had been able to bring with them—and even then, it was Elathan or Shemaran money, not Anarshan. One would think that coin was coin, but there were those who refused to accept such payment. Very few people would hire them, since they were foreigners, not native Anarshans, so they had no money to buy food or clothing or afford better shelter.

At least they had been able to rely on aid from the crown, until that, too, had vanished.

"They've been cut off from aid entirely," Roman muttered to Chandra. "The city gates are barred to any more refugees that may arrive and my father's council isn't opposed to the idea of tossing them back outside the city limits."

"That's barbaric!"

Roman ducked his head. "There's fear of unrest." As if that explained it all away or made it all right.

The refugees' discontent would only grow. How could it not, with the precarious position they had been placed in? How could they afford food if they had no money? How could they get money if no one would hire them for honest work?

The answer to that, of course, was that they would be forced to turn to dishonest work. They would steal what they needed to survive and were otherwise denied. Angry, they would lash out. There would be clashes with city guards and possibly with other citizens. Some Anarshans, resentful of the refugees' presence when so many were struggling, would target them and that would only lead to more conflict.

And then, once the refugees had set one foot out of line, it would give the council the perfect excuse, that they had just been waiting for, to have them removed from the city.

Roman sighed. "They're being set up to fail. I don't agree with any of it, but I'm not the king."

"Not yet," Chandra remarked.

"Not likely to ever be," Roman said with a sad smile.

He could feel her eyes on him, questioning, but she said nothing.

"Come on," he said softly, turning away. "There's nothing we can do for them at the moment."

Koal began to kneel down again, but Roman waved him off. He would walk back to the keep if it killed him. What was a little discomfort compared to what these people had to suffer?

"You should think about my idea," Chandra said, falling into step beside him, slowing her pace to match his. "If we want to help them, we need to first help the Anarshan people. Once food is no longer a concern, the crown will be free to resume aid."

"Do you think it's possible?" Roman asked. "Do you really think that raids can bring in enough food?"

Once, Anarsha had had two entire kingdoms to trade with. It was asking a lot for raids to make up the difference.

Anarsha's stores had bought them time, but it wouldn't last forever. Roman feared that even if Chandra's plan did work, it would be too late. This was something that should have been done two years ago, when the conflict was new, before the shortages got so bad.

She shrugged. "It's worth a try."

And that was logic Roman could find no fault with. It was better than nothing.

They walked in silence for a few steps and then he asked, "Do you think those refugees regret leaving?"

"Leaving where? Elath and Shemar?"

He nodded.

"How could they? They're under the Empire's control now. If they'd stayed, they could have lost everything."

"They've nearly lost everything as it is. At least under the Empire's control, they would be fed."

And their money would be accepted, Roman thought. United under the Empire, there was but a single currency.

Chandra scowled. "But they're free. That's worth any price."

Roman hoped that they felt the same.

Somehow, by sheer force of will, he managed to make it back to the compound on his own, but he knew his defiance had been foolish. His legs shook with the effort of remaining upright and he was visibly flagging.

The stairs were what did him in. He managed the first few, but no sooner had he placed his foot upon the first than he knew it was an impossible task. He was making demands of his body that were not realistic, and no amount of stubbornness would change that.

His body did not care that he was a prince. It was no respecter of pride or person.

Roman gasped as his right leg went out from under him. Before Koal could move, Chandra darted forward to catch him, halting his collapse onto the hard stone.

Briefly, Roman was reminded of moments when he had fallen in the palace, sometimes when he had pushed himself too far, and others without provocation. Some of the servants had watched it happen. He could see them so clearly in his mind's eye. The outstretched hands, the quick dart forward, only to freeze. Hesitate. Unsure of what to do and balking at the idea of laying hands on the crown prince, even to aid him.

But there was Chandra, touching him without second thought. Her hands were at once gentle enough not to hurt, but firm enough to be secure. He hung limply from her grasp for a moment and then she helped him up, Roman silently marveling at her strength, belied by her size.

She was neither tall nor broad, but her muscles had been finely honed during her time in the army. Roman was at once grateful to her and embarrassed at his own weakness.

"Easy there," she murmured. "I've got you."

Rather than release him, she kept ahold of one of his arms, tucked neatly into her own, as though they were simply two friends out for a stroll, not a soldier whose support was the only thing keeping the prince from sinking to the ground.

"Are you all right?" she asked.

For a moment, Roman considered denying it, but what was the point? She had seen his cane from the moment they had met. And now, supporting him as she was, the two of them pressed close, she might even be able to feel how frail his frame was, the evidence of which was usually concealed by his clothes.

"No," he replied heavily. "I'm not."

"Can you make it up the stairs or do you want to rest here for a moment?" She cracked a smile, made another attempt at lightness. "Personally, I'm in no hurry to get back to Khan's drills."

Roman smirked in spite of himself. "Then let's just stay here for now."

The two of them sank down onto the stair and Roman tried to catch his breath. Koal sat a few steps above them, peering out at the city as if he had nothing better to do. Roman hoped the dragon wouldn't report the incident to his father, but there was nothing he could do about it now.

"That was stupid of me," he said after a moment. "I should have known better."

He was certain Chandra must have been bursting with curiosity, wanting to know what had happened, but she kept silent, giving him time.

"I'm sure you've noticed I'm not exactly the image most people have when they think of a prince." He gestured to his cane. "I've had this illness for years now, but it's gotten progressively worse, and no one seems to know why. My father has called in the best healers from across the kingdom. And some who are far from the best," he added with a snort. "None of it has made the slightest bit of difference."

"I'm sorry."

He shrugged, trying to imitate her signature nonchalance. "I can't really complain. I've had a good life. I'm still here. And I'll continue to be here—until I'm not."

Chandra bit her lip. "So…that's it, then? There's nothing that can be done?"

"I'm sure if there was, my father would have found it by now." Roman sighed. "He's so determined not to accept what's right in front of him. I think he believes that I'm giving up, when, really, I'm just facing facts."

"That doesn't bother you?"

He turned to her. "You mean, am I angry that I probably won't live very long? Of course I am. But if there's nothing to be done about it, I'm certainly not going to waste what little time I do have by sitting around feeling sorry for myself. I want to live. I want to make the most of what I still have, while I still can."

She looked down at her hands, clasped in her lap.

From their vantage point, Roman stared out over the city spread below them.

"Sometimes, I think it must be harder for those who don't know that death is coming for them. They think they still have their whole lives ahead of them and so they don't cherish what time they do have. They don't strive to make the most of it, don't understand its worth. Anything in life only has value because there's a limited amount of it. Some just have more of it than others. You don't realize what you have until it's gone." Roman waited until she faced him again before offering her a smile. "So don't pity me. I know the value of what I have and I don't take it for granted. That is a precious gift."

Sometimes, when he was tempted to feel sorry for himself, he thought of people like the refugees they had both seen earlier and was reminded that he was very fortunate, in spite of everything.

"But that is why I was gone so long. I meant to come back sooner, but my father took some convincing. He didn't want to let me leave, but I insisted. I try to hide it from him, but it's getting worse."

"You don't have to explain," she said quietly. "You don't owe me anything."

"I want to," he said simply. "It's nice to tell someone. To feel seen. And—maybe it's stupid—but when you look at me, I feel like you really see me. Not just this—" He gestured to the cane in his hand. "—but all of me."

He felt himself flush at the admission, but he held her gaze, refusing to look away. He wanted to memorize the splash of freckles across her face, the way the sun lit her hair, turning it to flame.

"I just want to live," he murmured. "And I can't do that if I'm kept locked away. There's nothing out in the world that is more of a threat to me than whatever lurks within my own body—and that stays with me no matter where I go."

He turned his head to face the compound, looming over them. "And right now, I'd really like to make it up these stairs."

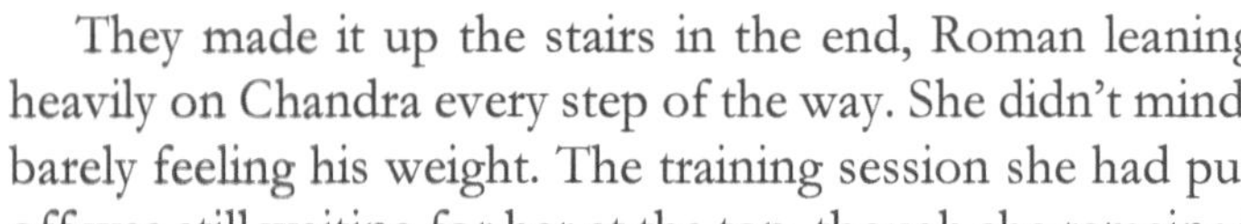

They made it up the stairs in the end, Roman leaning heavily on Chandra every step of the way. She didn't mind, barely feeling his weight. The training session she had put off was still waiting for her at the top, though she remained distracted throughout the day, his words haunting her.

She didn't have a chronic illness as he did, but his words applied to her own life just as much as they did to his. She was a soldier, fighting in a war that may not end in victory.

Or even if it did, she might not live to see it. The Empire could, however unlikely, strike tomorrow. She could die the very next day, out there on the battlefield.

Would she have been satisfied with her life, looking back, if that were to happen? Would she be content, knowing she had made the most of it?

Had Gideon felt the same way? Had Callum? She suspected the answer was no. She suspected the human answer would always be to yearn, to grasp for one day more. And so that was what she would do, until at last, there was nothing left to grasp for, when she would reach out, only for her hand to close on empty air.

How much longer until that fate was Roman's?

XVIII

With those thoughts still fresh in her mind, Chandra sought Roman out again after training had ended for the day. The sun was beginning to set, sinking below the walled perimeter, the compound taking on a relaxed air as the recruits found themselves free to go about their own tasks.

Roman smiled as she approached. "No letter writing tonight?"

"No." Chandra shook her head. Under other circumstances, she might have played a game of cards with Gideon, but those days would forever be nothing more than a memory now.

She'd known it couldn't last. Nothing ever did. But to acknowledge that she should enjoy the moment, because one day it would be gone, and then finding it suddenly taken from her…it was too soon. It would always have been too soon.

"No," she said again, sitting down to join him beneath one of the large trees. "Too many thoughts tonight. I've been thinking about what you said, about it being harder for those who don't realize that death is coming."

"Gideon?" he guessed.

"Yes. But also my cousin." She had never brought Callum up in conversation, never mentioned his death to Roman. But suddenly, it felt like she needed to.

"I lost a cousin, in the first battle. His name was Callum. He's the reason I'm here now."

"I'm sorry."

"I'm sure he knew it was a possibility, but he couldn't have known it would happen the way it did. We might not be able to truly make the most of every moment we have, but you're right—it's important to try. To live. And then I got to thinking about those refugees. Have you ever been to Elath or Shemar?"

"Once, a long time ago. I barely remember it. I'll bet it's changed since then."

"Yes," Chandra replied. "And not for the better."

Roman shifted beside her. "Why do you ask?"

"I want to go there. Either one, I don't really have a preference, but I've never been, and I want to see it at least once, while I still have a chance. And I think it would be good to see it. We're fighting for both of them, not just ourselves."

He shook his head. "It's too far."

"Well, that brings me to my second point. You want to experience a moment of freedom, there's nothing like flying. Everyone should do that at least once in their life, regardless."

Roman raised one eyebrow. "You want to leave the barracks and fly out to Elath or Shemar on a dragon?"

"Not just me. You're coming, too." She gave him a smile. "What harm could it do?"

"I don't think it's allowed, for one thing."

"You're the prince, aren't you? Surely the same rules don't apply. Come on, live a little."

His lips twisted, as though in indecision, but she knew she had him. "I am curious, I must admit. I've ridden a dragon several times now, but I've never flown."

She leapt to her feet. "Let's go now."

"Now?"

"Why not?" she challenged. "You want to wait around until it's too late or you manage to talk yourself out of it?"

Roman had no counterargument and he stood, more slowly than she had. "All right. I swear, you're going to be the death of me."

Chandra instructed him to wait there until she fetched the dragons. She wouldn't presume to think that they would ride on the same one and there was no need since he had come with his own.

"So," she asked, once the two of them were finally mounted. "Where are we going?"

She thought it only fair to let him pick which city they would fly to. Much as she wanted to see it for her own reasons, she thought the experience would mean more to him. He'd gone from being confined to the palace to visiting the barracks and reclaiming some freedom for himself. Tonight, he would experience flight for the first time.

Chandra's heart quickened at the prospect, recalling the way she had felt the very first time.

"Elath," Roman answered. "It should be the safer of the two. Shemar will still be crawling with the Empire's soldiers."

Chandra nodded at the wisdom of that statement. "Lead on, then."

She and Sheboleth would follow closely behind, keeping a careful eye on prince and dragon alike, and make sure they didn't run into any trouble—though she wasn't anticipating any.

Roman took a deep breath as Koal gathered himself, the blue dragon launching into the air with ease. Sheboleth followed a moment behind.

And then they were rising higher and higher, the city falling away below them, its winking lights aglow, soon replaced by treetops as they moved over the forest.

At first, Roman sat hunched rigidly in the saddle, clinging to Koal's mane. But once he realized he wasn't going to plummet to his death, he straightened up, looking around in wonder. Chandra heard him laugh aloud, the sound nearly stolen by the wind, and he turned back to grin at her, pure wonder on his face.

Chandra smiled back and urged Sheboleth forward so that they flew side by side, the moonlight silver on the dragons' scales.

The night air was cool against her skin. Chandra sat back, her arms slack at her sides, nothing but the strength of her legs and the straps of her uniform keeping her in place. She wasn't the least bit afraid, Sheboleth's broad wings keeping them steady and even.

How nice it was to fly just for its own sake, instead of into battle. A sense of peace washed over her. Up among the clouds, the familiar anger was absent. It couldn't follow her once she left the ground.

Eventually, the trees thinned below them, revealing the city, nestled at the foot of a mountain range. Chandra sucked in a breath as they soared over Elath, lit below with golden light. If there were people—or mechs—down there, she was too high up to see them.

Ahead of her, Koal beat his wings, rising higher as they approached the mountainside. The blue dragon settled onto a ledge, barely large enough for both dragons, and almost entirely hidden in the darkness. It wasn't as close as

Chandra would have liked, but they would be able to observe the city safely, with no risk of discovery.

She dismounted and walked to the edge, a sensation of vertigo threatening to overtake her, not unlike the feeling she got right before Sheboleth folded her wings and dove.

In the darkness, it was hard to make out the finer details, but Chandra's gaze roamed greedily over what she could see. The city backed up directly to the edge of the mountains, half of the buildings stretching out into the massive lake, propped up on stilts.

Everywhere lanterns were lit, both on the buildings and along balconies, and outlining the docks, marking out safe passages across the lake. Chandra could just see the dim outlines of boats bobbing in the water, slightly blacker than the rest of the darkness around them.

The moonlight shimmered on the lake's surface. Looking down at the city, Chandra could imagine what it had been like to live there before the Empire's occupation. There was something slightly cozy about its appearance, welcoming, inviting, that Anarsha lacked with all its stone. Her own kingdom was a bastion, a fortress, meant to keep people out. Elath had no such defenses. The Empire would have been able to walk right into the city.

Chandra frowned. It was too quiet. Perhaps they were simply too high up to hear anything, but she didn't think it was her imagination. Though the city still blazed with warm light, there were no familiar sounds to accompany it. No laughter, no chatter as people walked home from a pub. Elath gave every sign of a city not yet turned in for the night, and yet, there was no one to be seen.

"Where is everyone?" she murmured, stepping back from the edge. The height was starting to make her dizzy, her balance suddenly unsure.

She couldn't help but wonder what would happen if she fell. Would Sheboleth swoop down to catch her? Would she even be able to, before the ground rose up to meet her?

Roman frowned. "Probably inside, away from the guards. I've heard the Empire imposes a curfew—no one without permission allowed out after nightfall."

"A shame. It seems like a beautiful place."

"It was, from what I remember of it. But you don't have to change the landscape or the buildings to change the heart of a place. Sad what's been done to it."

Taking the heart out of its people is enough.

The hard knot of anger returned, so forceful after its absence that Chandra nearly gasped. It felt like a weight, always sitting on her chest, pressing down on her, preventing her from drawing a full breath.

This was Anake's home. Where she came from, what she had been forced to leave behind, and now what she fought against, so that this did not become Anarsha's fate. Chandra wondered what Anake could have told them about the place. Her eyes would have seen the small changes.

And with the anger's return came the source of it: Callum—and Gideon, too—fresher in her mind. Both yet unavenged.

It was as though their ghosts haunted her, when they should have been haunting the Empire. But what good would that do? Both of their killers never saw their faces, never heard them laugh, never knew a damn thing about either of them. They wouldn't feel an ounce of guilt.

Chandra recalled how, in the last battle, the Empire ruthlessly sent their ground troops in, to absorb the first blow, condemning them to be slaughtered.

No, the Empire wouldn't care. They didn't even value the lives of their own soldiers, much less their enemies.

Chandra clung to her anger, shoving away the grief that threatened, like a wolf lurking outside the threshold. Best to keep that door closed. The slightest opening and it would rush in and devour her.

She didn't want to think about Callum or Gideon—especially Gideon. Memories of him were tied up not just in grief, but guilt, the two entwined so tightly they were impossible to separate.

She had been *right there*, for all the good it had done. She had been worse than useless that day, unable to do anything but watch as he vanished beneath the flames. It was one of the images that hounded her at night, spurring her to climb out of bed and walk. *And walk and walk and walk…*

If she couldn't banish her demons, she would outrun them.

Looking down at Elath now, she no longer saw the beauty, and she began to wonder if she had ever noticed it at all. It was like a warning, an image of what Anarsha could become. Stripped of all identity, consumed by an ever-hungry, never satisfied Empire.

When they stepped out onto the battlefield, they weren't just fighting for Anarsha. They were fighting to free this place, to return what had been taken from them.

Chandra clenched her jaw, the beginnings of an idea coming to her, so tempting it refused to be ignored.

"Roman. You have a better idea of how bad the food shortage is. How long do you think we can afford to wait around for the Empire to strike again?"

He frowned. "Impossible to say, but we can't wait forever."

"Exactly. Instead of waiting around for the Empire to attack again, and fighting any such battle on their terms, why not take the fight to them?"

The Empire had dictated the last battle far more than Chandra would have liked and the Anarshans had paid the price for it. They couldn't allow that to happen again.

"What do you mean?"

"There aren't as many soldiers in Elath as there would be in the Capitol. And such an attack is the last thing they would be expecting. You wouldn't need much." She shrugged. "You could wreak untold damage with just a handful of dragon riders. And while we're at it, we could steal some supplies, like the raids I mentioned."

Roman shook his head. "That might be trying to do too much at once. Better to focus on one or the other. Sneak in and grab what we can, or an all-out assault."

"All right," Chandra conceded, trying to tamp down her rising disappointment. "Well, which one do you think would be more useful?"

"The supplies. But I'd still like to speak to my father about that first."

"So until we get approval for that, it sounds like an assault is our only option."

"The commanders will never go for it."

"Why not?"

"All kinds of reasons. We're trying to defend, not provoke the Empire further. We can't risk any potential losses. And even if we were to somehow wrest control of Elath from the Empire, we'd never be able to hold it. We'd be stretched too thin."

"I'm not trying to take back control," Chandra argued. Even she wasn't that ambitious. "Just weaken the Empire a little bit. And as far as provoking the Empire further, we're already at war, like I said earlier. I think tensions are already about as high as they can go. We'd have the element of surprise on our side. I really do think it's worth the risk.

If we can weaken the Empire, even in small ways, it might give us a better chance when they come back."

"You make a convincing argument," Roman replied. "It's bold. So bold that they would never think it of us."

"See?" Chandra encouraged. "We can't keep sitting around, waiting. We need to do something. We need to take the fight to them."

Roman held up his hands. "I agree. But the commanders will never approve it. We'd be acting on our own."

Chandra raised her chin. "I'm willing to take the risk." *I believe in this plan.*

"I don't doubt it," he said, shooting her a grin. "But you can't do it alone and we can't exactly recruit people to go with us."

"Us?"

He scowled at her. "What, you're allowed to go rogue and risk your life and I'm not?"

Chandra bit her lip, choking back the arguments that she knew would only wound his pride. "But you're the prince."

"And, what? I might die? I think that's pretty much a given, whether I do this or not."

"But…you're important."

"And you're not?"

Chandra stared at him. "Not as important as you!"

He scoffed. "My life is *not* more important than yours. You know as well as I do that there are those who would say my life is worth very little, despite my title. I don't know how much time I have left. At least give me the dignity of choosing what to do with the time that remains to me. And if I fall, at least my death will have meant something."

Chandra looked away, suitably chastised. "You're right. It's your life, not mine, and it's your decision to make."

Roman let out a breath. "Thank you. But that still only makes two of us, and while I don't doubt that we could cause some chaos..."

Chandra grinned. "I have someone I could ask."

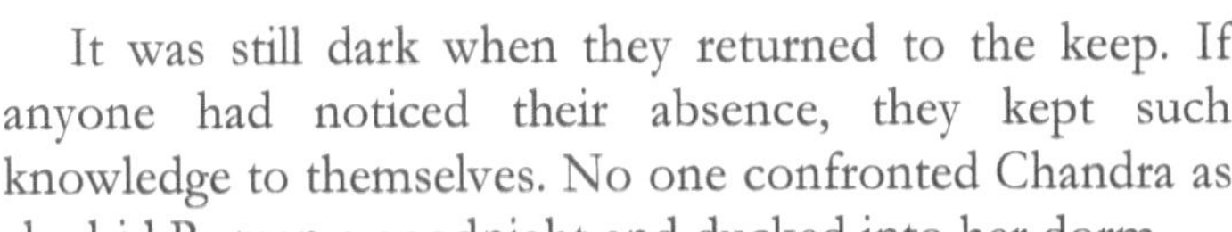

It was still dark when they returned to the keep. If anyone had noticed their absence, they kept such knowledge to themselves. No one confronted Chandra as she bid Roman a goodnight and ducked into her dorm.

She tried, unsuccessfully, to snatch a few hours' sleep, but the plan that she had planted in Roman's mind kept going round and round inside her own. Chandra was groggy and irritable by the time they were summoned the next morning.

Training was a chore, her body slow to respond. Chandra knew it was more than her night out that was affecting her. Her sleepless nights spent walking around the perimeter of the compound were finally catching up with her.

That evening, she wanted nothing more than to skip dinner in the mess hall and call it an early night. But she had told Roman that she knew someone who could help them, and the sooner she could bring Anake on board, the sooner they could put their plan into action.

She watched Anake throughout dinner, keeping her distance, not wanting to be anywhere near Victor. Her brittle mood wouldn't be able to take his presence. She picked at her food, wishing Gideon was there, sitting across from her, to keep her company.

The moment Anake rose, Chandra followed her out, keeping a few paces behind until they were clear of the mess hall. Only then did she call out to her squad mate.

Anake turned, brow furrowed.

"There's something I wanted to talk to you about. To see if you're interested," Chandra explained, coming close and keeping her voice down.

"Interested in what?"

Chandra took a deep breath. This was it. Hopefully, her instincts were right. "Roman and I were discussing what our next steps should be. And we both agree that we can't just sit around and wait for the Empire to make the next move. We need to act. We're going to start by attacking the Empire's forces stationed in Elath. If we can weaken them, it might give us a fighting chance."

Anake looked at her for a long moment, her expression inscrutable. "You…are going to attack Elath?"

"Roman and I, yes. And our dragons, obviously." Chandra bit her lip. Saying the plan aloud now didn't sound nearly as impressive as it had last night, shrouded in darkness.

She thought Anake might point out the obvious flaw in their plan. That they planned to carry out the assault with only two people—three, if she joined.

Instead, she said, "You are going to liberate my people?"

Chandra winced. "I don't think we can liberate all of Elath, but yes. That's the ultimate goal."

"Then I will come with you."

"Really?" Chandra blinked, hardly daring to believe her luck.

"Of course."

"Thank you." Chandra let out a breath.

Anake's dark eyes glanced around. "I take it this is not an official mission."

"No," Chandra admitted. "But Roman knows what he's doing and he's not without some influence of his own. But that does mean it will probably only be the three of us."

Anake shrugged. "It matters not to me. Any chance to strike back at the Akkadians, I will take. Let me know when you're ready to put this plan of yours into action and I'll be there."

"Thank you, Anake," Chandra said sincerely.

Anake gave her a nod and then turned and went on her way. Chandra turned, intending to find Roman and tell him that they wouldn't be alone—only to collide with something large and solid.

She let out a muffled grunt and stumbled back, narrowly managing to keep her footing. She looked up to see who she had run into and her heart plummeted.

Victor.

How much had he heard?

He cocked his head to one side. "What were you two gossiping about?"

Chandra took a step back. "Not you, if that's what you're wondering."

Before he could ask any more questions, she hurried away, pulse thrumming in her ears, glad to be rid of him.

Had he heard anything important, or did he merely want her to think that he had, to trick her into revealing more than she should?

If he had overheard their plans, would he turn them in? They hadn't really discussed anything certain, Chandra reminded herself. There had been no mention of a time or place, or even a day.

Roman didn't seem overly concerned when Chandra warned him about Victor, but just to be on the safe side, he thought they should plan their assault sooner rather than later.

Chandra agreed. The following day, the three of them gathered, Anake sketching out a rudimentary map of the city, as she remembered it. She pointed out key strategic targets, mostly along the docks. Warehouses and barracks.

"They housed Elathan soldiers when I lived there," Anake explained. "But I expect they've been commandeered by the Empire now."

Short of sending a scouting party, which was too risky, it was the best they could hope for.

And so, that night, the three of them met beneath the cover of darkness, under the tree that had somehow become their unofficial meeting place.

Koal and Sheboleth were already there and Anake brought Vitanni with her, saddled and ready to go.

"Good thing it's just us," Roman remarked. "Any more dragons and someone's bound to notice."

"Stealth will serve us better," Anake said, climbing up into the saddle.

The former Elathan was armed to the teeth, a quiver of arrows slung on her back, her longbow gripped in one hand. Chandra could just make out the daggers sheathed along her hips, more blades strapped around her thighs.

Chandra herself had a quiver and her longbow, a short sword at her side, though she didn't intend to have to use it. It was only for the worst-case scenario, if everything went wrong. Should its use become necessary, they were likely all dead anyway. Still, its presence gave her comfort.

Roman carried no weapons, not strong enough to physically wield them. Koal would be his weapon, far more deadly and effective than any blade.

"Are we ready?" Anake asked.

"One moment," Sheboleth spoke up, her green eyes luminous in the dark, fixed on Chandra. "I'd like a word."

She jerked her head to the side and Chandra followed her, out of earshot of the others.

"I don't think this is a good idea," the dragon hissed.

"Not now," Chandra replied.

"When, then?"

She suppressed a sigh. She had brushed off Sheboleth's concerns earlier, not wanting to admit that the dragon had a good point.

They needed to do this now, while they had a chance. The sky was overcast, the moon's light only bleeding through whenever the clouds parted. She was tired of waiting, of always being on the defensive. She wanted to *act*.

"You've seen Elath once," Sheboleth had argued earlier, "in the dark, viewed from a great height. Don't you think you should at least scout the place once? Properly?"

"That's what we have Anake for," Chandra had shot back. "She'll show us the way, what targets to aim for."

"And what if the city has changed? What if it's no longer the way she remembers?"

Elath had been conquered years ago. It was entirely possible. Likely, even.

But Chandra had waved away Sheboleth's concerns, saying they would talk later. On the cusp of putting their plan into action, she didn't want to revisit the conversation now. *Or ever, really.*

"I'm going," she said now, meeting Sheboleth's gaze, unblinking. "I need to know if you're with me."

The dragon let out a low growl, lashing her tail, but she gave a curt nod. "Someone needs to make sure you don't get yourself killed."

Chandra felt her shoulders slump, relief washing over her. She didn't know what she would have done if the dragon refused. "Thank you."

Sheboleth snorted. "Don't thank me yet. I'm going, but that doesn't mean I'm happy about it."

"Is there a problem?" Roman asked when they rejoined the others. He had mounted Koal and leaned forward in the saddle as he peered down at Chandra.

"Nope. No problem. Let's go."

She swung up onto Sheboleth's back, the dragon barely letting her get settled before launching into the air, retracing their recent path to Elath, Anake in the lead.

Anarsha fell away behind them, Elath not yet visible. Below, the Valderan rainforest sprawled out, far as the eye could see. Above, only the sky, vast and unknowable.

Chandra swallowed, trying to force down the doubt that had begun to creep up on her. Suspended between earth and sky, she felt small, vulnerable. Insignificant. She certainly did not feel powerful or invincible enough to take on the Empire.

How quickly confidence faltered, there one moment, swallowed up by doubt the next. It irritated her and she withdrew inside herself, searching for her anger.

"There it is," Sheboleth murmured, drawing Chandra out of her thoughts.

Her heart surged in her chest for a moment, fear threatening to undo her. How had they come upon it so fast? It felt like they had only left a minute ago.

I can't do this. In that moment, it was not yet too late. They could all turn back and forget the idea ever existed.

Then an unsettling calm came over her, her anger burning cold for once instead of hot. It frightened her, how calm she felt, how in control.

The Akkadians had no idea they were coming. They would strike hard and strike fast and be gone before the Empire realized what hit them.

"Stay close!" Anake called. Vitanni folded her wings and began to dive, Koal and Sheboleth doing the same on either side of her.

It would be difficult enough to communicate with each other, all the more so the further apart they drifted. Chandra was relying on Sheboleth's hearing more than she cared to admit.

Chandra thought back to the map Anake had drawn, its lines overlaying in her mind's eye with the buildings stretching out before her. She sucked in a breath as it came to life, the city lit up below her, the structures along the docks clearly visible.

Here we go.

Vitanni dove, the buildings growing larger until they loomed before them. Chandra gripped her bow with one hand, an arrow already nocked, the other wrapped around one of Sheboleth's frills. It was unlikely, in the dark, that she would have a clear shot at a target, but she had wanted to be prepared, just in case.

Anake's viper-green dragon parted her jaws and shot forth a torrent of flame, the night suddenly lit orange. Moving at such speed, the flames struck the warehouse with enough force to crack the wood, panels sent flying, as they sideswiped the building.

Following close behind, Sheboleth and Koal did the same. Sheboleth swung her head back and forth, scorching anything that lay in her path. Chandra could do nothing but sit back and watch, a fierce sense of satisfaction building in her chest, as the destruction grew.

The wooden buildings caught, the fire spreading, the night lit red. Chandra felt the heat roll over her.

They hadn't intended to target any homes, but the map had disappeared from her vision. With the flames spreading and smoke rising into the air, the buildings rushing by at a dizzying speed, she could no longer tell what part of the city they now flew over, the three dragons mercilessly raking their surroundings with fire.

Somewhere, a bell rang out, alerting the people of Elath that they were under attack. Cries rang out dimly, their words lost to the hot wind that brushed against Chandra's cheeks and stung her eyes.

She glanced over at Roman, Koal's scales lit a brilliant blue in the firelight. His profile was illuminated, the sharp cheekbones and proud nose, his expression stoic. In that moment, he looked every bit a prince, riding into battle on the back of a dragon, and Chandra wondered if he felt as alive as he looked.

She turned away, letting Sheboleth focus on flying, peering over the side and behind her shoulder. Behind them, their path was marked by clear trails of fire, their crackling roar drowning out the cries.

Along some of the walkways, guards were assembling, scrambling to get into position. Some wore uniforms, others armor, and still more looked as though they didn't have time to get dressed, rushing out still wearing their nightclothes. But they all carried weapons, iron-tipped arrows, swords and spears, the orange light glinting off the steel.

Vitanni had seen them, too, and without being instructed, she angled her wings, turning in a wide circle until she faced the way they'd come. Chandra leaned in the saddle as Sheboleth followed, the gesture instinctive, so attuned was she to her dragon's movements.

Sheboleth raked the walkways that crisscrossed the lake, the water glowing a fiery orange, cutting off the soldiers. A few of them leapt into the water rather than face the wrath of the flames. Some thrashed, their frenzied limbs disturbing the water, as they were dragged down by their armor.

Chandra twisted in the saddle as Sheboleth flew past, bowstring pulled taut. The light from the fires was more than enough to see by and she let the string go, watching as her arrow struck true. A kinder end than they likely deserved.

In a flash, she had drawn another, picking off the guards one by one, as they scrambled along the walkways, seeking cover.

Sheboleth let out a roar, her wings stilling as they swooped low over the walkways, claws outstretched. She plucked one of the guards off his feet, lifting him up only to drop him.

Chandra fought down the urge to laugh at their disorganization, the panic caused by an attack they hadn't seen coming, descending from the sky.

She flinched as an explosion sounded behind her. The bowstring slipped from her fingers and she grunted as it slapped the side of her arm, the shot going wide. Gritting her teeth, she turned.

A ball of flame rose into the air, around the area where the warehouses had been. Chunks of wood and other debris slowly rained back down to earth. *Must have housed something combustible. All it took was a spark.*

Chandra smirked, the expression falling from her lips as quickly as it had come. As the sound from the explosion faded, another took its place, familiar and chilling.

"Ballistae!" she screamed, hoping Anake and Roman could hear.

She cried out, losing her grip on Sheboleth as the dragon jerked beneath her, tilting her wings, rolling her lithe body midair. The straps connecting Chandra to the saddle snapped taut, the only thing keeping her in place. She heard the ballista bolt whistle as it passed through the air, too close for comfort, though she hadn't seen it.

Chandra let out a shaky breath, secure in the saddle once more, as Sheboleth righted herself, the tension going out of the straps. She could see the large siege weapons now, assembled on raised platforms and roofs around the city. Perhaps realizing that there were only three of them—and not a full assault, as they'd probably suspected in the initial confusion—the soldiers had rallied enough to man their positions.

Chandra gritted her teeth, the noise of the firing ballistae setting her nerves on edge, the massive bolts sent launching through the air at an alarming speed.

"I think it's time to go," Sheboleth murmured.

Chandra could barely hear her over the noise. Deep down, some part of her knew the dragon was right. They needed to know when to get out, before the chance was lost—and they along with it.

But she couldn't seem to drag her gaze away from the ballistae. Those weapons were the reason they had suffered such losses in the last battle. And with so many already stationed in Elath, it would be easy enough to deploy them the next time the Empire came marching.

She gripped her bow hard enough she feared the wood might crack. "Those ballistae have to be destroyed!"

Sheboleth growled. "We need to get out of here—"

With her other hand, Chandra tugged on Sheboleth's frills, desperate to make her understand. Without the dragon's agreement, she was powerless to do anything.

"Sheboleth, please!"

A ballistae was likely responsible for forcing Mael to the ground, where she and Gideon had both met their ends.

Was that how Callum had died too? Both dragon and rider plummeting to the ground? She could picture it too clearly, her mind crafting an image she had never seen—yet was all too real.

She saw it now as she stared at the nearest siege weapon, her vision bathed in red from the fire. Callum, strapped into the saddle, helpless to do anything as the ground rushed up to meet him. Had it been a quick end? Or had he lingered in agony, his body broken?

Her anger surged to the surface, so strong it nearly stole her breath away, blotting out every other thought and emotion, until she thought it would consume her too.

Perhaps Sheboleth heard something in her voice and knew what she must be thinking. Maybe the dragon's own thoughts strayed back to the moment they had both witnessed, when Gideon vanished beneath a wall of fire.

Chandra didn't care for the reason. Her heart sang with savage glee as Sheboleth dove forward, directly for the nearest ballista.

Behind her, she thought she heard Anake cry out as they swept past, but she didn't care, bowstring taut, arrow poised.

Chandra released it, aiming for the guards manning the siege weapon, and for a moment, it outpaced even the dragon. Then Sheboleth's jaws parted and the ballista vanished in a torrent of flame.

The flames were limitless, raking the tower, Chandra's rage given physical form through Sheboleth. The fire stung her skin, but she refused to look away, her war cry lost beneath the flame's roar.

And then they were on to the next one, and the one after that. The ballistae continued firing, their mechanical clanking filling the air, bolts whistling past but never striking true.

Just one more, Chandra prayed, the mantra becoming a chant in her head. Just a little further.

Finally, a chance to strike back at the Empire and deal a meaningful blow. It felt *good,* her anger singing in her blood, sated like a living, tangible thing.

Chandra flinched, struck from her revelry, as an arrow flew just wide of her head, its fletching slashing her cheek. Stunned, she reached up to touch her stinging flesh, her fingers coming away wet and red.

She stared at the blood, blinking in confusion. She was death, destruction, rage incarnate. She was untouchable on the back of her dragon. How could they have made her *bleed?*

"Chandra!"

She turned as Koal came alongside Sheboleth, wings beating furiously. "We need to go!"

Beyond him, she could see Vitanni hovering some distance away, Anake eager to leave. She was far enough away that Chandra doubted Anake would be able to reach them in time, should things go badly.

I've gone too far, she thought suddenly. Her rage was gone, fear threatening to take its place, the previous sense of power vanishing. *Just like Gideon.*

Chandra reached down to touch the side of Sheboleth's neck, mouth open to agree, when Roman jerked in the saddle, his face contorting in pain.

For too long a moment, Chandra's mind reeled, struggling to make sense of what had happened. Then she saw the shaft of an arrow, protruding from the back of his shoulder.

Koal shuddered, letting out a roar, as Roman was struck again, this time in the side. His hands instinctively went to his ribs, fingers splayed around the arrow embedded there.

Koal dove, trying to get out of range and Sheboleth followed without being told. The blue dragon alighted on the cobblestone path along the docks. Warehouses stood at their backs, still ablaze, timbers cracking and collapsing, sending plumes of smoke and embers into the air. The lake and its remaining walkways stretched out before them.

Sheboleth landed beside Koal, Chandra already fumbling with her straps. She slid out of the saddle and reached Koal's side in an instant, the blue dragon kneeling down so that she could get to Roman.

The injured prince slumped sideways in the saddle, teeth bared in a grimace. He'd been hit again, on the way down, the third arrow protruding from his left leg, though it didn't look too deep, shielded by the leather he wore.

It was the one in his ribs that worried Chandra the most. Already she could see blood seeping, bright red reflected in the fiery light.

"You're all right," she murmured, trying to tear off a piece of her tunic to staunch the blood, but her hands shook too badly. "I've got you."

She thought Roman tried to flash her a smile through the pain, and she wondered who she was trying to reassure more—him or herself.

"We can't stay here," Sheboleth warned.

Her stance was wide, ready to leap into action at a moment's notice, her eyes scanning the streets as soldiers converged on their location.

"Oh, damn it all!" Chandra cried, yanking her short sword free and slicing off a strip of her tunic.

It was unevenly cut and far larger than she'd intended, but it would do. She pressed it against Roman's side, moving his hand to cover it and keep it in place. He looked too pale in the harsh, flickering light.

"Shit," Chandra muttered. *Shit. This is my fault. I got too greedy. I went too far and Roman paid the price.*

"We need to go," Sheboleth said, an edge of impatience in her voice now.

"He'll have to ride with me," Chandra said. "In case..."

She wanted to say, *In case he needs support* or, *In case he might not be able to ride on his own.* But the words died in her throat. The straps would keep him secured to the saddle and if he lost too much blood, there was nothing she could do for him, regardless of which dragon he rode.

But it helped her feel not so helpless, the idea that she might be able to do something. To offer some comfort from her very presence.

"Fine," Sheboleth snapped. "Just hurry up."

Chandra slipped her arm around his shoulder, careful not to jostle the arrow buried there. He made a small sound of pain and something twisted in her chest, knowing she was hurting him. But they needed to hurry and she couldn't afford to think of such things now.

She gasped from the effort of helping keep him upright. His body seemed suddenly far heavier than it had that day on the stairs. But they hadn't been wearing leathers and weapons then and the adrenaline coursing through her veins made her movements jerky and uneven.

"Hurry!" Anake called, Vitanni swooping over them, blasting flame to keep the guards, now dangerously close, at bay.

But Chandra knew it wouldn't be enough. There were too many of them, swarming ever closer. They would be overrun in a matter of moments and it was *all her fault*.

She put her head down and focused solely on getting Roman into the saddle, climbing up after him, supporting him in front of her, using half the straps to secure him and snapping the others to her own harness.

She didn't know how well it would hold up and she wasn't too keen to test it, but it was better than nothing.

Across the walkway in front of them, more guards charged, emboldened. Sheboleth bared her teeth and let out a growl.

Her growl was answered by a roar, the walkway engulfed in flame. Chandra craned her neck, met with the sight of familiar black and orange scales. Her heart soared, never so pleased to see Bane in her life.

The large dragon passed overhead, the air stirring in his wake. One of the towers, that Chandra hadn't been able to reach, collapsed beneath the force of the dragon's flame, the ballista tumbling to the lake below.

Sheboleth unfurled her wings and sprang into the air, Koal following, as Vitanni and Bane provided cover. Chandra hunched low in the saddle, shielding Roman with her body, bracing to feel the sharp sting of an arrow piercing her flesh. But it never came.

Some arrows clattered as they collided harmlessly with Sheboleth's scales, lacking the force to puncture through. They rose higher, the heat and smoke of the burning city falling away behind them. Only once she was sure they were clear did Chandra dare relax, turning to glance back.

Koal flew at Sheboleth's side, Anake and Vitanni right behind. And on their other side…Victor astride Bane, his face streaked with soot, but appearing otherwise unharmed.

Chandra let out a breath of relief, turning her attention back to Roman, suddenly afraid he might have stopped breathing. But he was still alive, the labored sound of his breath just audible over the wind brushing past her ears.

"Hang on, Roman," she whispered, silently urging Sheboleth to go faster. "We're nearly there."

I'm sorry, she added, words she couldn't bring herself to say out loud.

Her vision blurred and she blinked, trying to clear it, to no avail, the wind stinging her eyes. But she knew she couldn't blame it all on the wind.

She tried to push the guilt away and reach for her anger, but she was met with only emptiness. It was gone.

In that moment, it too had abandoned her.

XIX

What happened the rest of that night became blurred, the images running together in Chandra's mind whenever she tried to think back to it—not that she wanted to.

Somehow, by sheer force of will, Roman managed to hang on until they arrived back at the barracks. Unsurprisingly, Anake and Victor went their own ways, likely not wanting to be caught up in whatever repercussions awaited. Chandra couldn't blame them. She would take any punishment, endure any hardship, if it meant that Roman would be all right.

When Sheboleth landed, Chandra handed Roman off to the keep's healers. And then he was out of her hands and she had no idea what happened to him after that.

"You did what you could," Sheboleth said, waiting for her outside of the healer's wing. "Get some sleep."

Too tired to argue, Chandra trudged back to her quarters and collapsed onto her bunk. Never had she felt so tired, her sleepless nights pressing down upon her. The fear and adrenaline had faded, leaving her scoured out. Empty.

She expected one of the officers to come for her, but she was alone when next she opened her eyes, having no memory of falling asleep. Bright sunlight streamed through the narrow windows along the top of the walls. She sat up.

She was late, having missed some of that day's training. But rather than rush to attend the rest of it, Chandra couldn't bring herself to care. She sank back down onto her thin mattress, dread and guilt curdling in her stomach, fear for Roman overpowering them all.

Still, no one came for her. Surely someone would, if Roman had died. She'd be punished for that. And the fact that she hadn't been was a good sign, or so she tried to tell herself.

She could simply venture outside and find out for herself what had happened. Put an end to her fretting. But some cowardly part of her didn't want to know, couldn't bear it. Easier to stay put.

It was late evening by the time anyone arrived and Chandra sat back up, bracing herself for whatever awaited.

But rather than an officer, it was Anake who appeared between the rows of bunks. Outwardly, she gave no sign of last night's activities. There were no dark circles beneath her eyes, no obvious injury.

Belatedly, Chandra realized she hadn't even asked Anake or Victor if they were all right—not that they'd given her a chance, scurrying off to the dorm while she saw to Roman.

So we're all cowards, in our own way.

"How is he?" Chandra asked as Anake came to stand in front of her, her voice scratchy from disuse. "Roman?"

Anake crossed her arms. "The healers managed to stabilize him enough to be transported back to the palace."

Chandra let out a breath, bowing her head. *Thank the saints.* "I thought someone would come for me."

"I made your excuses," Anake grunted. "Said you were ill. And I imagine Roman pulled a few strings of his own."

Chandra felt a rush of warmth toward the other woman, but it vanished in a flash at her next words.

"What were you thinking?" Anake hissed. "That was madness. You nearly got all of us killed. Hell, if not for Victor, you would have gotten the prince killed!"

Chandra winced. Roman had wanted to keep his identity a secret, as much as possible, and last night's outcome likely hadn't done him any favors in that regard.

She knew it was her fault. She knew she should feel guilty—and she did!—but that didn't mean she wanted to.

Instead, the anger that had abandoned her last night made itself known. Chandra raised her head, meeting Anake's defiant gaze with one of her own.

"You agreed to come." She rose to her feet. "In fact, if I remember correctly, you were all for it."

Anake's jaw tensed. "That was before. When I still thought you had a plan. Before you ran headlong into a cluster of siege weapons. Are you mad? Do you want to die? To throw away your life so easily?"

Chandra stamped down the urge to walk away. To end the conversation. She didn't owe Anake an explanation. But there was one thing that still nagged at her—and likely always would.

"You never did tell me how Callum died," she murmured. Whatever Anake had meant to say that day, they had been interrupted by Victor. Chandra thought she already knew, but she wanted to hear it all the same. "It was one of those ballistae, wasn't it?"

Anake looked at her and for a long moment, Chandra thought she would refuse to answer.

Then she sighed. "Yes."

A single word. A confirmation and nothing more.

Chandra nodded and stepped past Anake, making for the door. She had her answer and now what she wanted most was to be left alone.

Her heart sank at the image of Sheboleth, seated on her haunches, waiting for her in the waning light.

The dragon's tail flicked. "She has a point."

Chandra's jaw tightened. "What did you hear?"

"In there?" Sheboleth jerked her head at the doorway behind Chandra. "Only raised voices. But she told me she was going to talk to you."

"And did she ask you to try and talk some sense into me on her behalf?"

"She didn't have to. I'm here on my own."

Chandra made to move past her. "Well, I don't want to hear it."

No destination in mind, Chandra found herself heading for the entrance to the compound, stepping out onto the street. The guards said nothing as she passed, made no move to stop her. They barely acknowledged her presence and she wondered just what strings Roman had pulled.

She didn't care where she was going, she simply had to *get away*. She couldn't bear to be inside those stone walls a single moment more.

She slowed to a stop, blinking. In her haste and frustration, she had gone further, faster, than she'd realized, her steps bringing her to the refugee camp she had visited with Roman.

Roman... Her heart twisted at the thought of him, wondering if he was truly all right. If he blamed her for what had happened.

Chandra whirled, shaken from her own thoughts, as shouts rang through the air. Ahead, a group of refugees were being herded by soldiers, dressed in armor, spears brandished.

She watched as a family was torn from their tent, pushed up along the Great Wall. The refugees pushed back against the soldiers, tempers rising along with their voices.

One soldier raised his sword, bringing the pommel down across a man's face, the refugee buckling beneath the blow. It was all the spark they needed, both sides rushing forward, until the street became a writhing mass of bodies, shoving and pushing at each other.

"Stop!" Chandra cried, but her voice was only one of many among the din. There was nothing to make it stand out and she had no authority here.

What were they doing to the refugees? Another soldier reached up, tearing down one of the tents, and Chandra suspected she knew, dread coiling around her middle.

Roman had told her no further refugees were being allowed into the city and the ones that were already inside had been cut off from aid. Now the other shoe had finally dropped and these refugees were being forced from their camps, their makeshift homes, to be escorted out of the city walls.

Did Roman know what they were doing?

They had lost so much and were about to lose still more.

How much could one person be asked to give up and still keep going?

"No!" Chandra cried, pushing against the people in front of her, trying to make way, to just get to the guards…

But the crowd surged against her. Chandra gasped, bracing herself for a fall against the hard cobblestones, only to collide with something else instead, just as hard and unmoving.

She twisted her head around. Sheboleth had followed her and she had bumped up against one of the dragon's forelegs, halting her fall.

"We have to do something," she said, looking up at the dragon helplessly.

A dragon would be able to part the crowd. A dragon would be able to stop the soldiers.

But Sheboleth glowered down at *her.* With one large hand, she pushed Chandra down the street—in the opposite direction from where she wanted to go.

"What are you doing?" she cried.

"*I'm* getting you out of here."

Chandra pushed against the dragon, but she might as well have attempted to budge the Great Wall. "We need to help!"

Sheboleth stopped, planting her feet. "Like you helped in Elath?"

Chandra gaped at her. "That's not fair!"

The dragon lowered her head until they were nearly eye to eye. "When are you going to stop running?"

"I'm not running," Chandra forced the words out through clenched teeth.

Sheboleth scoffed. "Yes, you are. You've been running from the first and you haven't stopped since."

Chandra stared at her, throat tight, not trusting herself to speak.

Sheboleth's tail lashed, nearly toppling a few passersby. "I never should have indulged you," she hissed, half to herself.

"I knew the risks," Chandra said, drawing herself up. "We all did."

"Knowing the risks and believing them are two different things." Sheboleth sighed. "Anake's right. You've got to stop at some point. How long is all of this going to last?"

"All of what?" Chandra demanded.

Sheboleth shot her a look. "Don't think I haven't noticed the way you run yourself ragged. You've been trying to win this war all on your own."

"Not on my own," Chandra protested, her voice suddenly small. "I have you."

But the dragon's gaze didn't soften. "Even with me at your side, it cannot be done. This is not simply your war. You don't have to fight it alone. You're not the only one who has lost someone."

"I hate you," Chandra muttered.

"No, you hate that I'm right," Sheboleth returned. Only then did her glare soften. "You are a young woman who has lost her cousin, one of the few family members you have left. But that isn't all you are. You are so much more than what you have lost. I wish you could see that. I can."

Chandra's gaze flicked past the dragon to where the soldiers were still rounding up the refugees. The brief protest had been quelled, the soldiers' ranks bolstered by new arrivals. With barely enough time to gather their meager belongings, the refugees began to march toward the city gates.

Her shoulders slumped, the fight going out of her. Yes, she had lost something, but she could lose still more. And she hadn't lost nearly as much as these people had. She didn't have much to complain about, in comparison.

As she watched, one of the refugees halted at the gate, refusing to pass through. One of the guards prodded him with a spear, which only seemed to incite him further. He rushed the guard, moving with surprising speed, a dagger suddenly appearing in his hand, drawn from within his cloak.

Chaos erupted once again, the fragile peace shattered. A soldier raised his spear, the blade glinting in the fading light, as it stabbed into the man's side. Blood spattered the cobblestones.

Chandra let out a horrified gasp, but it wasn't the man's blood she was seeing. She shut her eyes, trying to blot out the image, but it was too late, seared into her memory.

The blurred moments from the night before bled back to her, those minutes after she had handed Roman over to the healers and trudged back to her dorm, still wearing her flight leathers. They had been stained with blood— Roman's blood, not her own.

She raised her hands in front of her, staring at them, seeing the blood that had covered them last night, a sense of horror crashing over her. Horror at what she had done, at what her rage had led her to, and what it had almost cost her.

In her desire for revenge, she would sacrifice them all on the alter of her fury. It would burn and consume every one of them.

And for what?

Suddenly, fear slithered around her chest, squeezing tight, severing her breath. If the refugees were being forced out of Anarsha, the food shortage must be getting worse, just as Roman feared.

In the end, what had her ill-conceived assault on Elath accomplished? She had nearly gotten Roman killed. Had they weakened the Empire at all? Or was their attempt merely akin to a mosquito, buzzing around a horse's ear? Annoying, but hardly likely to make a difference.

"Sheboleth," she whispered, lowering her hands. "What if we can't win this war?"

What if this only ends one way?

She knew it was a possibility, of course. They all did. But for the first time, she allowed herself to truly imagine it: Anarsha falling beneath the Empire's yoke. What that future meant for her, she didn't know. Would she be alive to witness it, or just another of the fallen, lost in a pointless struggle?

Much like Callum's death, she had never really allowed herself to consider the prospect. If such a fate came to pass, it would mean that his death, Gideon's death, possibly her own, and that of everyone else involved, would all be for nothing.

"We don't have a choice," Sheboleth replied. "We must fight on, to whatever end. But we'll do it together."

"Together," she echoed, the word coming out a sigh.

To whatever end.

An endless trail of healers passed through Roman's room. When he awoke, he was initially disoriented, not remembering where he was or how he had come to be there. Then it all came rushing back to him: the assault on Elath, the arrows piercing his flesh, the panic in Chandra's voice, at odds with the words she spoke.

The healers hovered over him, anxious and annoying. Roman wanted to drift back to sleep, away from the pain and his new reality, but their presence made that a difficult task, constantly drawing him back.

Still, when his father came, he shut his eyes, pretending to be asleep, measuring his breathing.

"How is he?" he heard his father demand.

"Resting, my lord. But he will make a full recovery."

Ulric grunted and Roman wondered if they were sharing the same thought. The arrows might not kill him, but he still wasn't cured of the mysterious affliction that plagued him.

Roman shifted position once his father had gone, his body sore from lying in one place too long. He winced, the wounds in his shoulder, side and leg throbbing. None of them were good places to be hit, in terms of comfort. He could hardly lay in any position without one or more of them giving him grief.

It's your own fault. You're not a soldier.

But he had wanted to live, to make the most of whatever time remained.

And how does it feel, having lived?

The next time his father checked on him, Roman was sitting upright in bed, not even attempting to feign sleep. Though the linen shirt he wore was loose and comfortable enough, he could still feel the bandages pull against his skin whenever he moved.

He tensed, bracing himself, unsure of what his father's reaction would be.

Roman wouldn't have thought it possible, but Ulric appeared to have aged even further since they'd seen each other last. His hair was now almost entirely gray, his eyes tired and sunken, his skin sallow. Roman's stomach twisted with guilt. Had he done this?

Ulric crossed his arms, his hands folded underneath, as though unsure what to do with them. "Care to explain?"

"Explain what?" Roman asked, more to find out what his father already knew.

His father let out an incredulous scoff. "I'm told that you went to Elath as part of a breakaway group of soldiers. Rogues. Who were they?"

Roman looked at his father and said nothing. He would never betray Chandra.

Ulric leveled a harsh stare at him. "I will find out. I have ways. I will have their names and see them punished."

"That doesn't give me much incentive to tell you, then, does it?"

"Saints, Roman! A soldier can't abandon their post and attack another kingdom! There will be—"

"What?" Roman demanded. "Repercussions? Consequences? We're already at war with the Empire, Father. And in any case, the attack was my idea. I ordered those soldiers to accompany me. You cannot punish them for following my orders."

Ulric let out a long sigh, his shoulders slumping, as if he weren't angry with Roman, merely dismayed. Somehow, that stung worse.

"Why?" he asked quietly. "Why would you do such a thing?"

In this, Roman could be honest with him. He could explain Chandra's reasoning, which he agreed with, without fear that it would lead his father back to her.

"Because we can't sit here, waiting for them to attack again. They've been calling all the shots from the start."

That seemed to give Ulric pause. "No," he murmured. "We cannot. Perhaps you have a point..." Then some of the previous fire returned to his eyes and he gave his son a stern look. "All the same, you are banned from returning to the barracks."

He swept from the room before Roman could argue, leaving him to seethe.

He cursed his weak body, so slow to heal, making unreasonable demands of it. He wanted to be up and about, doing something—anything—but lying there, helpless.

But even once the arrow wounds healed, his body would be no stronger than before. Roman closed his eyes, a single tear slipping free, trailing down the side of his face.

If his father had his way, he would not see Chandra again. Only now that the choice had been taken away from him did he realize how much her company meant to him.

She made him feel alive, more than the attack on Elath, more than flying on the back of a dragon, ever had. Perhaps that was why he had agreed to the idea in the first place, even more than the logic behind it.

She had such life, such *fire* in her. She had been the sun, and now he was to be locked away in darkness once more. But he had felt the warmth on his skin and he would never be able to go back.

He could see her, clear as day, in his mind's eye. Her back to him, peering over her shoulder. The freckles across her cheeks, the fire in her green eyes. The red of her hair.

Roman held the image there until sleep rose to claim him once more.

Ulric stalked down the corridor, away from his son's room, hands fisted at his sides. His son had done a reckless thing and despite what he thought, there would be consequences. *A reckoning.*

He had credited Roman with having more sense than that. Everyone made mistakes, but he feared his son's latest blunder would come at a great cost indeed.

Ulric paused outside the heavy door to the council chamber. He knew the councilors waited within. He had wanted to speak to Roman first, to try and get some sense out of him, some explanation for what had occurred. He doubted the answers his son had provided would satisfy any of them.

Squaring his shoulders, he pushed the door open and stepped within. Every head in the room turned in his direction, but to their credit, none of them spoke. Instead, Ulric was left to cross the room in silence, his footsteps echoing ominously.

Perhaps their silence had been calculated, meant to unnerve him, rather than a show of restraint.

Ulric remained standing when he reached his chair and turned to address the room. "I know you have all heard rumors of what occurred in Elath. I am here to assure you that my son is well and such an incident will not happen again."

"I wonder," Vaughan said, drumming his thick fingers on the table, "how it was allowed to happen at all. We know the prince didn't act alone—it would have been impossible. So, who helped him?"

Ulric's jaw clenched. "He refuses to give up any names."

"We must find out," Silva said, leaning forward, his long hair falling over his shoulder. "We can't have rogue soldiers in our army. Their numbers are already thin. We can't have them be undisciplined as well."

"Roman claims that the attack was his idea and that he ordered those soldiers to accompany him."

"And do you believe him?" This from Vaughan again.

Ulric met and held his gaze for several moments, but he had no answer to give.

Silva cleared his throat. "Still, we should be able to find out their names easily enough. Word spreads, after all."

"I will look into it," Ulric promised, grateful for the interruption.

Lord Salerno stirred in his chair. "I agree that the situation warrants investigation, but we cannot undo what's already been done. My spies in Elath reported that the damage to the city was extensive, if unorganized. Fire, once set, is difficult to control. But the attackers did manage to destroy several strategic warehouses along the docks, one of which contained a unit of mechs. I fear the Empire, rather than being weakened or discouraged, will see this act of aggression as an escalation, demanding of a response. Their wrath will be terrible. They will retaliate."

Vaughan nodded, his jowly face trembling, cheeks red. "This foolish act will only provoke the Empire further. They will come down on us, harder than ever, intent, this time, on crushing us for good."

"And if I may speak so frankly," Silva added, "I am not confident that we can survive another assault."

Saints preserve us, Ulric thought, his dismay growing. It was a dire situation, indeed, when the most vocal councilors were in agreement.

"The food shortages are only worsening, as we feared," Silva went on.

"The refugees have been removed from the city," Ulric said, grateful, for more than one reason, that his son wasn't present for this meeting.

"A step in the right direction," Silva nodded. "But perhaps too little too late."

"The refugees did not go quietly," Salerno said. "A confrontation which was witnessed by some of our own people. They're on rations themselves, and if we have to increase those rations, as I suspect we will, their own discontentment will grow. I worry that such displays of defiance will soon spread to the general population."

"People are angry," Lord Daladier murmured, his voice quiet from disuse. "They know we are not winning this war."

"We are not losing," Ulric protested.

"But nor are we winning," Silva said softly. "Such stress takes its toll. The people wonder how long they will have to wait. For the war to conclude. For things to return to normal. How long will things be this way?"

It will be this way, Ulric thought, *until someone wins.*

And as things stood at that moment, it wasn't likely to be Anarsha.

The Akkadian Empire was like the ocean waves, battering themselves over and over against a cliff. The cliff may seem unmovable, unyielding, but sooner or later, it would be worn down and collapse, to be absorbed by the sea.

The thought chilled Ulric.

Was he, in this moment, staring down the future fall of his kingdom? Was there truly nothing he could do? He could not save his kingdom. He couldn't even save his own son.

The horror chased all other thought from his mind throughout the rest of the meeting. He sat, silent and withdrawn, as the lords argued among themselves, unable to agree on the best course of action.

But Ulric had seen what the rest of them had not: there was no best course of action. No help was coming. Anarsha stood alone, cut off from all allies, a situation of her own making. Perhaps she deserved the fate that awaited her, the fate she had condemned her allies to suffer.

But no. Not if Ulric could help it. Not unless there truly was no other way.

He ducked out of the council chamber the moment the meeting came to an end, relieved to be free of the stuffy, airless room. Ulric hurried down the hallway, ignoring one of the lords who called after him, pretending not to hear.

His swift steps brought him to Roman's room. He hesitated, standing outside the door, fear clutching his heart, the certainty that his son had already died, while he was trapped in a council meeting.

Drawing air into his constricted lungs, Ulric eased the door open. Roman lay in bed, his chest rising and falling slowly in sleep. He looked so much younger, some of his worn expression eased in repose.

So fragile.

Ulric let out a breath. His son hadn't slipped away, as he'd feared. *Not yet.* But that fate still awaited him, awaited all of them, and Ulric was powerless to save them. There was no one left he could call upon.

Unless…

Shutting the door behind him with barely a sound, Ulric turned and left the palace. He told no one where he was going, didn't bother to look and see if any guards accompanied him—though they must have—hardly understanding the urgency that had come over him.

His steps took him to the temple at the end of the road, nestled in the heart of the city, an equal distance for all members of society, regardless of class, and therefore easily accessed.

It had been years since he'd last set foot in such a place. Not since the death of his wife and second child. Perhaps that had been the beginning of his loss of faith. But there was nothing like desperation to drive a man back.

The stone building was cold as he entered, shivering, his footsteps echoing in the empty space. The overcast sky filtered poorly through the stained-glass windows, lending the place a shadowed feel.

Ulric was grateful for the chance to be alone with his thoughts, something he seemed to be granted so little of these days. There was always someone wanting his advice, his attention, his judgement. But not here. Here, he was alone, surrounded only by long-dead saints.

Ulric made a slow circuit of the room, peering up at the stained-glass motifs. Each one depicted a saint and their dragon. The saint had sealed a demon in a soul stone. The dragon had destroyed the stone, completing the banishment.

How brave must one be, Ulric wondered, to face down a demon? He wished he could possess some of that courage for himself, but he didn't feel brave. He only felt frightened, that fear driving him to the temple.

Gazing up at the saints' faces, he felt no braver, no more encouraged, and his heart sank. There was something beatific about the way the saints had been portrayed. Something inhuman, that could not be touched or reached.

His steps slowed, coming to a stop before the only saint depicted without their dragon.

This saint did not look like the others. There was no sense of serenity about her. Her eyes instead were cast upward, beseeching, her hands clasped before her, a single tear tracing its way down her face.

Her dragon was nowhere to be seen, but the saint did not stand alone in the mural. Behind her stood a shadowy figure, its features indistinct. At first glance, it would easily be mistaken for a dragon, such was its form, but Ulric knew better.

It was the demon she had sealed. It hovered at her shoulder, bending close as though to whisper in her ear. And whisper it had.

This demon, whose name was long lost—if indeed it ever had one—was said to be the most powerful and dangerous of all the demons that were sealed away. It was also rumored that his whispers drove the saint who sealed him insane—to the point that she took her own life.

Ulric stared at the mural, the demon leering close, the saint's expression the picture of despair. He'd always wondered, as he did now, what it was, exactly, that the demon had whispered.

Ulric knew that despair well. It seemed to have descended over his kingdom like a black cloud, heavy and oppressive. Like the saint, searching for hope and finding none, he could see no way out of it.

Unless…

He turned, gaze landing on the altar, and the blue soul stone that rested there, glimmering in the light. His eyes were drawn to it like a moth to flame, hellbent on its own destruction.

Unless…

But it wasn't destruction that drew him, but salvation.

He stared at the soul stone and its implications, frozen. The idea that had taken root horrified and excited him in equal measure. It was so forbidden it made his breath catch and his heart race.

But once conceived, it was not so easily dismissed.

The Empire would come for Anarsha. That much he knew for certain. And his kingdom would suffer the same fate as Elath and Shemar.

Unless Anarsha has an ally that not even the Akkadian Empire can defeat.

PART III:
THE
FOLLY OF
MAN

XX

Chandra waited for the repercussions of Elath to reach her, but if anyone knew of her involvement, it seemed they intended to keep such knowledge to themselves. No one came to punish her. Nothing more was said.

It was almost as though the attack had never happened. But it had, Chandra knew. She questioned just how far Roman's influence would extend—and for how long. His very absence was proof enough that the attack had been real and she wondered when he would return, afraid that the image of him in her arms, limp and bleeding, would be the last she would ever have of him.

He's fine, she reminded herself sharply, for what felt like the millionth time. If the prince had died, not even the palace would be able to prevent word from spreading.

Roman was fine and so was she and Anake. And, much as Chandra hated to admit it, she knew the reason. On the second full day since the assault, she sought him out after training had ended.

Having recovered from her "illness", Chandra had returned to training that morning. No one had given her lingering looks. No one had reacted to her at all, though she could feel Victor's eyes on her throughout the day.

As she approached, he slowed, as though sensing her behind him, and turned.

Chandra was aware of the others, passing around them like water around a river stone. For a long moment, waiting until most of the others had gone, Chandra could only study her nemesis, as though she could find the answers to her questions written upon his face.

"Why did you do it?" she asked at last. "Why did you come?"

Why did you save us?

"I heard you talking earlier that day and knew something was up. And then I saw you leaving and thought I'd better follow you. Good thing, too."

"But *why?*" Chandra demanded. "I didn't think you liked me." And yet, he had risked his life for her. For all of them.

One corner of his mouth tilted up. "I don't. But you're still Anarshan. Still one of us. You're my squad mate. I'd hate to see you cut down by those filthy Akkadians."

Chandra looked away and when she glanced back, his expression was hard.

"What you did was reckless," he said harshly. Then his features softened in a way she had never seen before. "But it was also brave."

Her breath caught, unsure if she was really hearing correctly.

Now it was his turn to look away. "I admire the fire in you. Lifelong soldier or candle maker, that's not something that can be taught. And we'll need more of it in the days to come."

He turned and walked away, perhaps having said more than he intended. But Chandra found herself strangely warmed by his praise. It didn't erase the lingering guilt, but it helped ease its sting.

News of the attack on Elath spread through the Capitol like wildfire. Desmond had already heard more than he cared to before he was given leave to return home, for the sole purpose of attending a ball with his family.

Hosted by the emperor himself, it was to be held at the palace, and all noble families were invited to attend. Desmond was surprised his family bothered to remember his existence at all. He rather wished they hadn't.

Spending an evening with people who were as insufferable as his parents was not his idea of a fun time. But he suspected the ball had an ulterior motive—a boost of morale, to reassure the elite, in the wake of such troubling news.

Desmond wore his best suit and slicked his dark hair back, though it was so short he needn't have bothered, newly shorn back to regulation length.

Still, as he stared at his reflection in the mirror, judging his appearance, it wasn't a bad face that looked back at him. He could find little flaw in it. He had high cheekbones and a sharp, defined jaw in an otherwise narrow face. His dark eyes revealed nothing he did not wish them to, framed by long lashes that most women would kill to possess.

He would have thought himself more handsome had his hair been allowed to grow out, but he was certainly better looking than his brother, Alaric, and that alone pleased him more than he cared to admit. His shoulders were broad from his time in the army, something his brother would never experience—or benefit from.

The palace, at the height of District X, was lit up like a beacon, brighter than every other district in the Capitol put together. Every candle in the place seemed to be lit as Desmond entered, trailing along after his parents and brother. But rather than the stench of tallow, the candles gave off a pleasant, almost sweet, scent.

The guests, each more finely dressed than the last, made their way down the marble corridors, led by the herald who would announce each of them and their respective houses, until they came to the grand ball room, the doors thrust wide.

The ball room was connected to an adjoining hall where dinner would be served. Other than a few ornate, plush chairs for when the revelers wished to rest, there was little in the way of furniture. The walls were lined with tall, narrow windows on nearly all sides. The floors were polished to a mirror sheen and Desmond glanced down at his reflection as he crossed the room.

On one side, on a raised dais, sat the emperor himself, dressed in a resplendent uniform, medals pinned upon his breast. Desmond stared at him, never having been so close to the ruler of Akkadia. The man who had built an empire.

He might have been tempted to think the medals were fake, but he knew that the emperor had been a military man himself once, leading his men on the battlefield.

A true leader, Desmond thought with a sardonic twist of his lips as he raised his eyes to the emperor's mask. It covered his face from hairline to chin, completely obscuring his features. He could have been looking anywhere, at anyone. Or he could have been asleep behind the mask. But Desmond felt the painted eyes on him all the same and he couldn't shake the certainty that the emperor was watching him at that very moment, assessing him, taking notes.

Desmond wondered what the man saw and what he thought.

He tore his gaze away, attention directed elsewhere by the arrival of a young woman. She was so thin she appeared fragile, as though he could take her wrist in his fingers and snap it in an instant. She looked up at him with large, doe-like eyes, the neckline of her dress plunging.

When she asked if he would dance with her, Desmond accepted. A quick glance across the room revealed Alaric glaring at him with naked envy. Desmond couldn't help but smirk. So he was the one ladies wished to dance with now, not his brother.

As always, Desmond kept one ear open for bits of gossip, to distract himself throughout the evening. The news on the tip of everyone's tongue was still the assault on Elath and each time he heard it, it seemed worse than before.

"I heard it was the Anarshans."

"I thought it was a rogue group."

"They rode dragons. Either way, they came from Anarsha."

"They're growing bolder."

"They need to be stopped."

On that, Desmond could agree, as he listened to the number of buildings destroyed grow with each retelling, the number of deaths rising to an astronomical amount.

"I have a friend whose nephew was stationed there when it happened. The burns he suffered…he'll never be seen in public again, I fear."

Desmond gave an involuntary shudder at the thought of being burned alive. Dragons swooping down, under the cover of darkness, raining hellfire and devastation upon everything.

Anger kindled to life in the pit of his stomach. The audacity. Who did these Anarshans think they were to resist the might of the Akkadian Empire? He glanced back up to the emperor.

When he returned to his family's side, it wasn't Elath that his father complained about, but Shemar, griping about the mines he had taken possession of following the kingdom's fall.

"Worthless," he muttered, staring morosely into the glass in his hand. "Bloody worthless, the lot of them."

"Are they empty, then?" the man standing beside him asked, his face pale at the thought.

"Not empty, no. There are some iron mines there, of course, though nothing like Elath. No, most of them contain only these red crystals. And while they're pretty enough to look at, I grant you, they're unbreakable. You can't cut them, you can't shape them, you can't make anything out of them. And there's so many of them, it would be enough to satisfy any demand."

"Red crystals?"

Desmond's father reached into the pocket of his suit jacket, withdrawing a brilliant red gem, about the size of his palm.

He handed it to the other man with a shrug. "That's what they're pulling out of my mines these days. Never seen the like before, myself. No one seems to know what they are."

"Well, surely they can be used for something," the man said, turning the gem in his hands.

Desmond's father shook his head. "I'm telling you, they're damned near indestructible. They can't be chipped, cut, shaped, forged, nothing. Useless." He knocked back his drink, draining what remained, and stalked off.

The man held the gem out to return it, but Desmond's father brushed right past. If he'd even noticed the gesture, he'd chosen to ignore it. No doubt he didn't even want the thing anyway. He had more than he knew what to do with, from the sound of things.

"May I?" Desmond asked, holding out one hand.

The man dropped the gem into his palm, looking glad to be rid of it.

Desmond stared down at the stone in fascination, turning it in his fingers as the other man had done. A stone that could not be broken. What was it made of, to be so strong? And what purpose did it have—or could it have?

He slipped it into his own pocket, a puzzle to be worked out later, as the emperor rose to his feet and the room quieted to a hush.

"No doubt you all know why I invited you here," he said, his voice deep and rich, ringing out across the room without being muffled by the mask. "I know that the news out of Elath weighs heavily on your minds. But tonight is for you. Tonight, we share a toast to Akkadia's future victory. These careless actions of Anarsha demand a response, and Akkadia will answer."

A few brief cheers rang out across the room.

"Anarsha is stubborn," the emperor went on, "and their resistance persists. But they will soon learn, as Elath and Shemar before them, that it is futile to resist. The pull of the future cannot be denied. All four kingdoms will be united under the banner of one glorious, eternal Empire."

This time, when the cheers rang out, they were loud, fierce, deafening. And Desmond's voice was among them.

⚙⚙

While the festivities were taking place in the ball room, the real emperor waited in the throne room, empty aside from a few guards, posted at regular intervals, and so still they could have been carved from stone.

There, Hadrian waited. He'd been there the entire time, never having been present in the ball room. He'd sent one of his Masks, more than up to the task, having been drilled on exactly what he should say.

Hadrian sat up straighter upon the throne, his gaze sharpening behind his own mask, as the doors swung open and his general and Minister of Defense strode in.

"I'm glad you were able to extricate yourselves," Hadrian said dryly.

Both men bowed, acknowledging him with a quick, "My lord."

Hadrian frowned, his thoughts turning inward. The ball might be enough to satisfy and reassure the elite, but he wasn't so relieved himself. The attack on Elath was on everyone's lips and weighed on him more heavily than anyone.

"We have work that must be done," he said, wasting no time. "Anarsha's continued defiance has gone from a mildly irritating, but futile, exercise to an offense that must be answered. No longer am I content to merely conquer Anarsha, as I did with Shemar and Elath. I am no longer interested in anything the southern kingdom may have to offer, other than as an example. Anarsha must be destroyed. Let its resistance be a lesson to the others."

The general hesitated. "But…what about any natural resources Anarsha may possess?"

"We'll strip it bare," Hadrian assured him. "Don't doubt that. No use letting it go to waste. But the kingdom itself? I don't care if there's nothing left but ruins."

He wasn't interested in stationing troops there, in absorbing its citizens as his own. Some, perhaps, he conceded. The Empire could always use more slave labor. But that was all the Anarshans would ever be, if they were spared. They would never become citizens, as some of the Elathans and Shemarans had.

Hadrian tapped one finger on the arm of his throne, the movement making no sound. "To that end, I want preparations to begin at once. March out with everything you have. Begin gathering our forces at both Shemar and Elath. We will strike from both flanks."

A joint assault.

Shortly after the night of the ball, Desmond knew something was up. The barracks were a flurry of activity, soldiers rushing around, transporting weapons and taking inventory of supplies, mechs being gathered and prepared.

He soon found out the reason, as orders were passed down the line. His unit was being shipped out to Shemar, where they would remain until they received the final order to move out.

To march on Anarsha once more.

The news both ignited Desmond's blood and sat ill with him at the same time.

He frowned, scrambling to organize the needed supplies as he was ordered, watching his fellow soldiers do the same. It hadn't been all that long ago since the last attack on Anarsha and while it had been more of a success than the first time, it hadn't exactly gone their way.

They'd had losses of their own, and yet the Empire seemed to have absorbed the blow, shaken it off, and pressed on. He marveled at the efficiency of such a massive machine, though he knew the reason why. The price of such efficiency, the cost it consumed.

The Empire devoured soldiers like him, moving on in search of ever more. Already there were some vacant positions within his own unit, men who had not returned from the last assault.

The Empire would find more to fill the void, demanding more and more, until this conquest finally ended. And it would only end once Anarsha was defeated. The sooner Desmond could help bring that about, the sooner the insatiable machine would finally be sated.

And he… He could what? Go home? He didn't want that for himself. Desmond's only life now was as a cog in that machine, and an effective one. Whatever lay beyond that, he didn't know, and he didn't like to dwell on it. It frightened him.

Would he be expected to marry an attractive young woman, like the one who had approached him the night of the ball? Somehow, settling into a role of domesticity didn't appeal to him.

There was little point in thinking about it. He could fall on the battlefield during this next assault and then it would hardly matter. It would be *his* vacancy in the squad that the Empire would have to fill. The future didn't much matter when tomorrow was shrouded in uncertainty.

And yet, Desmond couldn't help but feel the small thrill of excitement coursing through his blood at the thought of stepping back into one of the mechs and marching upon the city of stone once more.

This would be Anarsha's last stand. He could almost feel it.

Even so, he could not completely shake a flicker of uncertainty. It followed him all the way to Shemar, nagging at him whenever he looked at the mechs, his father's words from the night of the ball ringing through his mind.

Was all of this happening too fast? Were they asking for trouble, pushing too hard, too quickly?

They were pushing the plundered mines of Shemar and Elath to the limit, demanding more raw materials for the construction of the new mechs. Desmond had heard his brother talk about the factories where the metal monstrosities were made. They were churned out at a breathtaking pace, the workers pushed to the limit, sometimes forced to go without sleep. Slaves and captured prisoners from the conquered kingdoms had been brought in to help shore up their ranks, forced to build the very machines that had subjugated them.

Desmond couldn't help but feel a twinge of unease whenever he looked at them. How sound were these new mechs? Were they being pushed out too soon, the engineers, in their haste, missing something?

He'd already heard rumors that the armor plating on the newest batch wasn't as thick as on previous runs, the Empire wanting to conserve the metal and stretch it as far as it would go.

Desmond shook his head. There was nothing he could do about any of it. He wasn't in charge, nor was he ever likely to be.

All he had to worry about was following orders and letting the pieces fall where they may.

Still, his father's words came back to him as he wandered the streets of Shemar, its many spires rising into the air. His father had warned that some of the mines were emptying and that his own mines here in Shemar were worse than useless.

Glancing around, Desmond didn't have to look too hard to see where all the materials had gone. He'd never seen so many soldiers stationed in one place before, mechs patrolling the streets, on high alert ever since the Anarshan attack and with the next assault coming—presumably— any day now.

He imagined Elath was in a similar state, though he wondered what it looked like after the raid.

The clanking of the mechs faded behind him as he left the city walls, venturing to the mines beyond. Some of those mines must belong to his father, though he didn't know which.

They were massive, open pits in the ground, sprawling before the gates of the city. Desmond's lip curled in distaste as he looked at them. They were hideous, scars upon the earth.

Massive pits opened up before him, concentric rings making up the various levels, spiraling ever downward, further into the earth. Peering over the edge, he could see workers along some of the rings, made to look small by the distance.

Already the conquered kingdom of Shemar was being plundered for all it was worth. Anarsha would soon follow.

For a moment, Desmond allowed himself to imagine the harsh terrain stretching out between the Valderan rainforest and the city, its gorse stripped bare, scarred by the yawning pits before him.

He reached a hand into his pocket, feeling the hard gem there, the same one his father had displayed the night of the ball. It was slightly cool to the touch, the hardest thing Desmond had ever felt, as he turned it with his fingers.

Gripping the stone, he squeezed it with all his strength, until his knuckles ached, the skin on his fingers splitting where the edges of the gem had bit into it.

He didn't need to look at the stone to know he hadn't managed to do a thing to it. His father was right. It would not break. Not even under the most intense pressure.

And neither would the Empire that had procured it.

Ulric strode down the corridor, his footsteps ringing off the stone in time with his frantic heartbeat, pealing like warning bells, foretelling of Anarsha's impending doom.

He shook the thought away, chastising himself for such fanciful notions, but the fear remained. Word from various spies, posted in both Shemar and Elath, had arrived, warning of Akkadian soldiers mustering in both cities. Their numbers were already on a large enough scale to reveal their intentions, with more arriving each day.

This was it, then. All or nothing. One way or another, there would not be another council meeting after this.

He'd been in the library when the news had come, forcing him to abandon his work, though he thought he'd found the information he sought. It would have to be enough. Leaving his books behind, Ulric had convened a war council at once, dispatching messengers to summon the members of the council.

When Ulric had stopped to check in on Roman earlier, his son had wanted to attend the meeting, insisting that his wounds had sufficiently healed.

But Ulric had refused, not wanting his son to know of the plan he intended to propose. It would shame him, if his son knew. Roman would not understand. He would not understand that he himself was a part of what drove Ulric to even consider such a thing.

But he would not lose his son. No matter the consequences.

Ulric could hear raised voices coming from the council chamber before he even arrived, the lords arguing among themselves as to the best course of action to take now that the one thing they had already feared, but never *truly* believed, had arrived on their doorstep, demanding an answer.

He pushed the heavy door open and the room fell silent, every head swiveling in his direction. Most of the councilors were standing, some with hands raised, frozen mid-gesture.

"So this is it, then," Vaughan spoke, breaking the stillness. "The Akkadians have returned—and so soon! We have no more soldiers to throw at them than we did last time—less, even! —and the food shortages are nowhere close to being addressed."

"Perhaps we should consider surrender," Lord Daladier murmured, his fear spurring him to speak. "They may yet show us mercy."

Silva snorted at that. "The time for negotiations has long since passed. If the Akkadians would have accepted such an arrangement before, they certainly won't now. Not after the attack on Elath."

"I don't suppose you ever found out who was responsible," Vaughan sneered, directing the question at Ulric. "We could always offer them up to the Empire, say that they acted alone."

"They won't believe such an explanation," Silva retorted, saving Ulric from having to respond.

The truth was, Ulric had not yet discovered the identities of the rogue soldiers. Roman still refused to tell him and Ulric knew his son well enough to know he wouldn't be getting the information out of him.

Truth be told, he'd been a bit preoccupied of late, the rogue offenders completely slipping from his mind ever since that day in the temple. A different thought had taken root, crowding out all others, no matter how Ulric tried to shake it free.

"But it's the truth!" Vaughan sputtered, his face turning an ugly shade of puce.

"The Empire doesn't care about the truth. They're interested in one thing only now—retribution. They will make an example of us."

"So what?" Vaughan cried. "We just sit here, waiting to be slaughtered? Or do you intend to take matters into your own hands and decide the manner of your death for yourself?"

"Nothing so dramatic," Ulric called out, raising his voice over the din. "No one need die. But I do intend to take matters into my own hands, providing you're willing to help me."

Some of the men exchanged confused glances, perhaps unsettled by Ulric's calm.

The calm feeling had come over him that day in the temple, when the idea first came to him, and only grew the more he thought about it, considered the possibility, and at last found what he was looking for in the library.

He couldn't remember the last time he had felt so unburdened.

"What are you talking about?" Vaughan demanded. "Help with what?"

"I know things seem bleak, but there may be something we can do," Ulric explained. "We may not be as helpless as we think."

Lord Salerno frowned, his thick mustache drooping. "I'm afraid I don't follow. Unless you can manufacture an army out of thin air, we don't have the kind of force needed to match the Empire's."

"We don't need an army. We simply need an ally the Empire cannot defeat."

"And where do you suggest we find such an ally?" Silva asked.

"No such ally exists!" Vaughan shouted, waving a single fist through the air.

"Not in this world," Ulric acknowledged. "Not anymore."

He reached into the pocket of his robes, his fingers closing around the soul stone he had taken from the temple. It was cold against his skin and harder than a diamond.

Withdrawing it, Ulric held it by its silver chain, letting the stone dangle, its blue facets catching the light. "Not anymore, but they could again."

A long heartbeat passed, the councilors staring at the stone, absorbing its implication.

"You can't mean…" someone whispered.

"Surely not…"

"Are you mad?" Salerno hissed, his hands slightly raised as if to ward off a blow. "What you are suggesting is unthinkable!"

"Look around you!" Ulric snapped, angered by their fear. "We are witnessing the unthinkable. We are watching our kingdom fall around us. The kingdom our forefathers fought and bled for. Would you not exhaust every possibility? Is it not worth sacrificing everything for?"

"But what you are suggesting…" Silva said uncertainly. "You would summon one of Anarsha's—no, humanity's—greatest enemies."

"It is an enemy not even Akkadia can destroy," Ulric said, clenching the soul stone in his fist. "Their war machines will be powerless before such a foe."

"Is such a thing even possible?" Daladier asked. "Has it ever been attempted before?"

Ulric suppressed a frown. The records had been vague, at best, when it came to such an answer. It was more theory than anything. To the best of Ulric's knowledge, no one had endeavored to prove the theory, one way or another.

There was no record of anyone ever attempting to summon a demon back into the world, only the banishment itself. What he *had* found were records of mortals making bargains with such creatures, before they had all been sealed by the saints.

In fact, there had been one would-be saint, whose name was so reviled it had been all but struck from history, who had bargained with a demon, coming to some sort of agreement in exchange for the demon's continued freedom.

"If something can be banished, surely it can be resummoned," he reasoned. "I will gladly take on the responsibility, the consequences, for any such action. I will pay any price that is asked."

Demons were treacherous creatures and only to be bargained with in the most extreme circumstances. But Ulric had found no record of a demon breaking their word once any such bargain was struck. There would be a price, he knew. There was always a price—and likely a terrible one. But he would pay it. He would sacrifice anything to keep his kingdom safe and his son along with it.

"I am the king," he added. "The responsibility to defend this kingdom and its people falls to me. I have found records of people making deals with these demons. The demon would be bound to me. He will do my bidding, so long as the terms of the bargain stand, and I will pay the price. This is not a price I am prepared for anyone else to pay—nor would I ask it."

"So..." Salerno said hesitantly. "What is it you need from us?"

"Simply to help with the summoning, nothing more."

"This is madness," Daladier murmured.

"If we do nothing, our kingdom falls and all is lost. Our way of life will be destroyed, our lives likely forfeit along with it. What choice do we have?" Ulric fixed each of the men with a glare, holding the soul stone aloft as he turned about the room. "No help is coming. Except that which we take for ourselves."

"Risk certain destruction or deal with a devil," Silva sighed. "How did it ever come to this?"

"Are you with me?" Ulric demanded. "Or not?"

The councilors looked at each other, as though searching for permission to speak, wanting someone else to make the decision.

Somehow, Ulric knew it would be Lord Silva who broke the spell.

He shrugged. "As long as *you* are the one who strikes the bargain."

Hesitantly, the others nodded, murmuring assent. None of their responses could be considered enthusiastic or confident, but neither had any of them refused.

Ulric would take that.

He lowered the soul stone, still gripped in his hand.

"Then let us begin."

XXI

The cool air of the dungeons enveloped Ulric as he made his way down the steep stairs, descending ever deeper beneath the palace, the councilors trailing nervously behind. He could sense their anxiety, so thick it seemed to rise up, choking the air. He had their acquiescence, but only just. It was a flighty, skittish thing that would flee at the slightest provocation.

"In any case," he spoke up, feeling the need to reassure them still further, "once this bargain is fulfilled, we need not keep the demon around. We can simply seal him again."

It was a great source of comfort to Ulric, knowing that the demon would not be free to roam the earth as such creatures once had, and he was counting on his advisors to feel the same.

"Can we?" Vaughan huffed. "None of us are saints."

"Neither were they," Silva retorted. "Until they'd done it."

In his arms, Ulric carried a longsword, its weight beginning to wear on him. Behind, Lord Silva, Salerno, Daladier and Vaughan all carried similar blades, each one belonging to an Anarshan king of old. It was upon that legacy that they acted now, for it would all come to nothing if they did not try.

"Here," Ulric said, reaching the bottom of the steps, and stepping into an empty, rectangular room. "We'll do it here."

His voice echoed slightly against the cold stone walls as he spoke, confident that no one would disturb them here. No one would see.

The floor in this room was dirt, lit only by a scant few torches. The atmosphere was one of chill and malice, which seemed to suit what they were about to do. Nothing good ever happened in dungeons.

Hefting his sword, Ulric drew a circle on the floor, the soul stone secure in his pocket, should he need it.

Once the circle was complete, the other councilors stepped up, laying the remaining four swords around the edges of the circle. Vaughan, the last to place his blade, retreated, and Ulric stepped forward, raising his sword high. He plunged it into the dirt floor, right in the center of the circle, and then quickly stepped back over the border.

Taking the soul stone from his pocket, he held it outward.

Now or never. This was it, the moment to put his theory to the test and find out whether it was even possible to summon such a being back into the realm of the living.

Taking a deep breath, he began to chant, invoking the names of the kings who had owned the swords, and then the name of the saint who had sealed the demon he had chosen—the one who had been pictured with the demon in the mural, rather than her dragon.

For a moment, Ulric thought it merely his imagination that the room seemed to grow colder still, the lights flickering, darkness drawing near. But the gasps and worried murmurs of his fellow men told him that it was real enough.

With the incantation finished, Ulric stood motionless, hands clasping the soul stone, as he watched, terrified, as a presence built in the room.

In appearance, it was little more than shadow, a whisp of living smoke, but he could feel eyes, yet unseen, piercing him, pinning him in place with their intensity.

A voice, deep but sinuous, brushed against his ear. It made him think of oil, of silk.

"How curious," it—*he*—whispered. "I haven't been in this realm since being sealed by one of your saints. And yet who but the king of Anarsha should stand before me now." The presence leered closer, but did not cross the boundary on the floor. "What would you ask of me?"

Ulric let out a shaky breath, the plume clouding in the air before him. The temperature in the room had plunged considerably, but he knew his trembling couldn't be blamed solely on the cold.

He needed to remember the correct words. He needed to be precise, leaving no room for the demon to misconstrue his intentions.

"I conjure, charge and command you to destroy Anarsha's enemies," he said, speaking clearly, pleased that his voice betrayed no hint of nerves. "The Akkadian Empire prepares to march upon us. I command you to destroy the Akkadian forces."

A rumbling growl rang out, sounding pleased to Ulric's ears. "I can do that," the voice purred. "But do you understand, king, that there is always a price to be paid for such bargains?"

"I understand. I will pay it, willingly."

The creature laughed then. Ulric thought, for a brief moment, he caught a flash of teeth, but it was gone in an instant, if it had ever been there at all.

"So eager! Are you so willing to part with your immortal soul?"

Ulric winced. He'd suspected that he would be asked to pay such a price, or something similar, but hearing it confirmed was another matter entirely.

Destroyed or damned. Not much of a choice. Not much of a difference between the two. At least, not for him. But he could buy safety for the rest of his kingdom.

For Roman.

"If it means keeping my people, my kingdom safe—" *My son.* "—then yes."

Though Ulric had not mentioned Roman aloud, it seemed the demon had somehow sensed the thought.

"Your son? You cannot protect him, king, any more than you can protect your little kingdom."

Ulric's heart sank. "So you won't destroy the Akkadians?"

What had he done? What had he sacrificed—and for what? It would all be for nothing if the demon refused to help them. They had nowhere else to turn. It had been one final act of desperation. Ulric supposed it was always going to be nothing more than a fool's hope—

"Oh, I never said that," the demon replied. "Fear not, mortal. When the time comes, it shall be done. And our bargain will be complete."

As soon as word came of the scouts' report, the barracks descended into a flurry of chaos, less organized than before. Chandra had heard the news from Anake, and an official announcement came not long after, in an attempt to quell any rising panic, but she wasn't sure how effective it was. In the mess hall, all anyone could talk about were the forces amassing in Shemar and Elath.

The morning after they'd received the news, orders were given. In preparation for what they believed was an impending assault, soldiers and dragons were once more ordered to leave the city behind and set up camp in the Badlands.

But before they could begin to gather supplies and head out, the order was rescinded. Chandra asked Victor, but no one seemed to know who had given the order—only that it had come from the palace.

There would be no war camp. No confronting the Empire before they could reach Anarsha. The army would remain behind the city walls.

It made no sense to Chandra and she said as much to Sheboleth, pacing restlessly. Waiting until the enemy was already on the stoop of your house—or worse still, inside—seemed like a terrible idea.

But she had disobeyed enough orders, even ones that had been implied rather than explicitly stated, and she knew better than to risk drawing attention to herself again. It still surprised her that there were no consequences from her assault on Elath.

No one had come for her. She hadn't been court-martialed, marched in front of her fellow soldiers and whipped or strung up for all to see.

Silently, she thanked Roman for his intercession on her behalf. There was simply no other explanation for it. She hoped he had recovered and was all right. She still hadn't seen him since that night and he hadn't sent word, perhaps in an attempt to help shield her from possible reprisal.

But still, the silence stung. Chandra longed to hear from him, if only to reassure herself that he was well—and that he didn't hate or blame her for the injuries he had suffered. Injuries that had nearly cost him his life.

He knew what he was doing, she tried to remind herself. Even so, she suspected that no one truly expected to suffer such injuries. If they did, it might all prove too much and they would never summon the courage to do what needed to be done.

Perhaps Roman's silence was to be her punishment. Every day she woke, stepping out of the dormitory expecting to see him standing beneath that tree, waiting for her. With each morning that passed by without his return, her hope faded a little more. She still looked—she would always look—but she no longer believed.

And now, they were facing down what might be the Empire's largest assault yet. Instead of riding out to meet them, they cowered behind the Great Wall, as if, despite its magnificence, it would truly save them.

If the battle went poorly, she might never get the chance to speak to Roman again. To hear his voice. Chandra missed him, more than she cared to admit. It felt as though there was a lot left unsaid between the two of them, though she wasn't quite sure what, and she would never find out if she fell, robbed of the chance to see him again.

He'd had a long time to make whatever peace he could with his approaching death, but Chandra hadn't. She didn't want to die and more than that, she wasn't ready—if anyone ever was.

That night, she wandered up to the aerie, where the dragons often roosted. The wind was stronger at such a height, bringing a chill with it. But Sheboleth's side was warm, pressed against Chandra's back.

She didn't want to talk to anyone, necessarily, but she also didn't want to be alone, on what very well might be the eve of battle. Sheboleth, saints bless her, seemed to understand that.

Chandra looked up from the letter she was attempting to write and frowned. How long would the Akkadians make them wait this time?

The Empire held all the cards. No help was coming for Anarsha. They couldn't produce more dragon-rider pairs as quickly as the Empire could mass-produce more mechs. The food shortage hadn't gone away. If anything, it only seemed worse.

Chandra wondered if Roman had had a chance to mention her idea about the raids to the king. Perhaps the king had refused after the disastrous attack on Elath.

She sighed, leaning her head back against Sheboleth's side, closing her eyes for a moment. She felt trapped, unable to do anything that would make a difference, unable to change even her own life, never mind thousands of Anarshans.

Chandra forced herself to turn her attention back to the letter. She'd fallen behind on her promised missives to her grandmother and this, once again, might be her last chance to put her thoughts and feelings to paper.

But it was difficult, when all she felt was frustration and fear. And anger. Ever-present, simmering beneath all else, was the anger—though much good it had done her.

"This is it, isn't it?" she whispered. "We won't be able to beat this one."

She'd secured her red hair into a bun, but a few unruly strands tore free, the wind whipping them around her face.

"You don't know that," Sheboleth answered gruffly.

Chandra swallowed. "It's my fault. I shouldn't have provoked them."

The admission settled into her gut like a stone. The only reason the Empire had retaliated so quickly was because of her insistence that they attack Elath. In the end, her actions hadn't made the blindest bit of difference. Instead, she'd brought destruction down upon the very kingdom she sought to save.

I'm such a fool.

"Don't give yourself so much credit," Sheboleth murmured. "Akkadia was already angry with Anarsha's defiance, not just your own."

Chandra's chest twinged. She wished Roman was there with her. If she could see him again, just once more, that would be enough.

But she was starting to suspect she would never see him again. And that, too, was her fault.

XXII

After the council meeting, Roman waited, expecting his father to return with news of how the meeting had gone. But when the minutes slipped by and his father failed to appear, Roman heaved himself out of bed, grasping his cane from where it stood, propped up against the nightstand, and made his way down the corridors, searching.

A passing servant informed him that Ulric had returned to the library. Roman's heart sank. The meeting must have gone poorly indeed for his father to seek sanctuary amongst his books, rather than coming to him as he'd promised.

Mentally, he braced himself for whatever disappointment was to come. Had the food shortages worsened? Were the Akkadians already on the move? Roman had heard of the Empire's forces amassing in the two neighboring kingdoms and knew it was only a matter of time.

It didn't bode well.

Confined to bed more often than not, Roman's mind drifted back to the barracks, to Chandra. He had steadfastly refused to give her name up to his father and eventually, Ulric had let the matter rest—though Roman wasn't sure if he was merely giving up or trying a different approach.

Whatever the case, Ulric would not learn of Chandra's involvement from Roman. He hoped she was all right, that her part in the raid had remained undiscovered. He desperately wanted to send word to her, but he dared not, in case the missive was intercepted. The very fact that he was writing to her at all would single her out and his father was cunning. It wouldn't take much for Ulric to put two and two together.

For her own safety, Roman stayed away, refraining from writing no matter how much he might want to. He dared not even draft mock letters to her, putting words to page that he wished he could say, getting them out of his head. That, too, was denied to him, in case someone should see.

And as far as returning physically to the barracks, Ulric hadn't budged on his position. He'd forbidden Roman from returning and no matter how much Roman might plead, his father would not be moved—not that there were many opportunities to try and change Ulric's mind.

Roman saw little of him. He stayed just long enough to check in on his son, inquire as to how he was feeling, how his injuries were progressing, and then he departed as quickly as he'd arrived, making some excuse. While Roman knew how busy his father was, he couldn't help but cynically suspect that his father couldn't bear to be around him for very long.

His condition was not improving and each time Ulric laid eyes on him, he was no doubt reminded of that fact. Taken into consideration with any lingering resentment over Roman's stubborn silence, it really was no surprise that the king found any reason to be elsewhere.

At least Roman's wounds had healed sufficiently that he could be up and about for short periods of time. Lying in bed with nothing to do but dwell wasn't good for anyone's psyche. And if they truly were facing down the end of their kingdom, as he'd heard some servants whisper, then Roman wanted to meet it standing on his own two feet.

Reaching the library door, Roman leaned against it for a moment, catching his breath and gathering his strength. He'd need it, to face what he feared awaited him on the other side.

Pushing the door open, he stepped inside, expecting to find his father seated at one of the tables, engrossed in whatever old tome he'd taken a fancy to. Instead, Ulric stood beside one of the shelves, a stack of books braced in the crook of one arm as he filed them away.

Ulric turned as Roman entered. Gone was the dim lighting of before. Now, the curtains had been thrown back, allowing the waning sunlight to stream in. The fire was blazing, suffusing the room with so much heat, it was almost stifling.

"Roman," Ulric said. "I'm sorry. I was…sidetracked."

"I can see that," Roman replied, frowning.

The sense of dread that had followed him down the corridor seemed to have retreated, now that he had arrived. Where was the bad news he had been anticipating? His father didn't appear the least bit worried—quite the opposite, in fact.

Roman couldn't recall the last time his father had looked so at ease. Certainly, it had been before the Empire had turned its gaze toward Anarsha.

"Has something happened?" he asked. "You seem…brighter."

What Roman really wanted to say was that his father seemed like a completely changed man. The lines that had etched themselves into his face had retreated somewhat, the furrow of his brow no longer quite so pronounced, his eyes no longer so shadowed. As though a burden had been lifted from his shoulders.

Yet, as far as Roman could tell, nothing had changed.

Anarsha still lacked enough food to feed all its people. And he somehow doubted that the Akkadians had called off their attack. They were still out there, waiting, like a reaper at the gates.

"How did the council meeting go?" Roman asked, when his father did not immediately reply.

What was it that he had so obviously missed?

"Oh, fine," Ulric answered, returning his attention to the bookshelf, hunting for the proper place for each tome. "Don't worry yourself about it."

"Father—"

"The only thing you need concern yourself with is getting better," Ulric interrupted, some of the old rigidity returning to his tone, brooking no argument.

Roman sighed. They both knew that was impossible, beyond a certain point. Why did his father insist on maintaining the charade?

Fine. If his father wouldn't tell him, he'd seek out someone who would.

Hefting his cane, he turned and set off down the corridor once more. It took him longer to find one of the councilors than he liked and he suppressed a groan at the sight of the first lord he came across.

Vaughan.

They'd never been overly fond of each other. Roman knew what Vaughan whispered behind his back, when he thought it wouldn't reach the prince's ears. Or perhaps cruelty was his intention all along.

Either way, he thought Roman a cripple, an invalid, a creature that was to be pitied, not one fit to ascend to the throne one day. For his part, Roman thought Vaughan a hedonist, too fond of both drink and women, the kind of pompous ass that liked the sound of his own voice far too much.

But even so, he wasn't the worst councilor for Roman to have crossed paths with. That would have been Lord Daladier, who wouldn't have told Roman a thing—not out of malice, but because the man never seemed to have much to say.

Vaughan, on the other hand, could never be accused of such a thing. If there was something to tell, he would tell it, and gladly, pleased to possess knowledge if it meant he could lord it over other people.

"Lord Vaughan!" Roman called.

Vaughan frowned, coming to a halt, unable to pretend he hadn't heard Roman call out to him. He waited for Roman to reach him, making no attempt to meet him halfway, the tapping of Roman's cane ringing on the hard floor.

Roman summoned a smile. "I was just on my way to find my father. I wanted to ask him what transpired during the council meeting, but I can't seem to find him. Perhaps you could tell me the news?"

The small lie didn't bother him at all.

Vaughan's frown turned into a scowl. "What happened is that your fool of a father has doomed us all, boy."

Roman resisted the urge to take a step back, not at all pleased by such a characterization of his father. "What are you talking about?"

Vaughan shook his head. "I knew it was a bad idea the moment he suggested it. I should have listened. I shouldn't have let him sway me, but now it's too late."

"Too late for what, Lord Vaughan?" Roman demanded with a flash of irritation. "Speak plainly!"

"He summoned a demon, for saints' sake!" Vaughan exploded. "May they have mercy on us all... Never thought I'd see the day. Demons brought back to our world…"

Roman stared at him. A demon?

"You're lying," he hissed.

"I wish I were. If you don't believe me, ask your father." With a final sneer, Vaughan stalked away, apparently having said all he cared to.

Roman stood there, watching him go, reeling. Then his shock faded, replaced by a steely resolve. His father couldn't have summoned a demon. Was such a thing even possible? And for what purpose?

On the eve of yet another assault, Vaughan must have abandoned all hope and decided to besmirch Ulric's leadership by accusing him of the most heinous thing he could think of. Something so opposed to everything Anarsha stood for, its very history.

Pivoting, Roman made his way back toward the library, his legs trembling with the effort by the time he arrived. But he didn't hesitate, didn't pause to rest. He flung the door open and strode in, not bothering to close it behind him.

"I've just spoken to Lord Vaughan," he said, his tone light, trying to turn such a hideous accusation into the joke it was. "He had some very interesting things to say."

Was it just Roman's imagination or did his father stiffen at his words? Slowly, Ulric turned from the bookshelf, only a single book left in his hands now.

"He claimed you summoned a demon. I called him a liar."

Ulric lowered the book. Some of the brightness Roman had glimpsed earlier was gone now as he stared at his father.

"It is no lie," Ulric whispered.

Roman stared at him, dimly aware of the shallowness of his own breathing. It felt like he had wandered into a dream—or a nightmare. Nothing had been quite right since the moment he'd left his room behind.

Perhaps that's all this was: a dream. He'd never left at all. He was still lying in bed, asleep.

A strangled sort of exhale escaped him. "A demon?"

"It was the only way!" Ulric snapped, defensiveness rising to the surface to meet Roman's challenge. "Don't you see? Our salvation is at hand. We don't have to fear the Akkadians anymore. This is one foe even they cannot defeat. We are saved."

"Saved?" Roman cried. "You summoned a demon! The *world* is not safe."

Wordlessly, Ulric reached into his pocket and withdrew the soul stone. Roman sucked in a breath, recognizing it from a long ago visit to the temple. When had his father taken it?

"I have a plan," Ulric said softly, running his fingers over the stone. "If it should be needed. After all, if the saints sealed the demons away all those years ago, why can't I? They were not named saints because they possessed some mystical power, but because they had soul stones. Nothing more. And so do I."

Roman shook his head, feeling like he was gazing upon a total stranger. What madness had overcome his father? Perhaps it was not Lord Vaughan who had abandoned all hope, but the king.

"Father…what have you done?"

"I've saved us all!"

"And damned yourself!" Roman cried. "What did you promise him? What did he ask for?"

"It doesn't matter," Ulric bit out. "You're safe now. We all are."

"But not you," Roman whispered.

Even if everything played out the way his father intended, even if the Empire was destroyed and Anarsha saved, his life would still be forfeit. Roman would lose the only family he had left. He would be thrust onto the throne, in charge of a kingdom that would still be reeling. The food shortages wouldn't magically go away, even once the Empire was defeated. It would take time.

And Roman had never felt more ill-prepared in his life.

Perhaps he would end up taking the throne after all, something he had never allowed himself to imagine, knowing it was impossible.

But a demon returning to the world was supposed to be impossible, too.

Roman wasn't ready. He was supposed to die before his father, not the other way around.

Ulric's jaw clenched, as though steeling himself against the pain Roman felt. Surely, he felt it, too.

"What's done is done," he said brusquely. "It's none of your concern."

A thousand words seemed to dance on the tip of Roman's tongue, each battling for dominance, yet none emerged. What could he say that would make any difference? The time for that was long past. His father had summoned a demon and whatever terrible bargain he had made, it could not now be undone.

I should have been there, at the meeting. I could have stopped him.

But could he? His father was a king, desperate to save his kingdom, and saints knew Roman couldn't do it for him. He was just as helpless, if not more so.

In a daze, Roman turned and left, returning to his room. Each step seemed leaden, the corridor stretching out before him without end. But at last, he arrived, slumping against the door as he shut it behind him.

Then he pushed himself up and crossed the room to his writing desk, caution be damned. Without pausing to compose his thoughts, to make the sentences perfect, Roman began to dash off a letter to Chandra, knowing it was still risky to write to her directly, but needed to warn her. The threat of her being discovered as the instigator of the Elath raid paled in comparison to the reality that a demon had been summoned back into the world.

But as he went to put those thoughts to paper, to tell her exactly what his father had done, his hand stilled, his quill hovering motionless above the parchment, a few drops of ink falling to mar its surface.

He shook himself and continued writing, making no mention of the demon. He simply warned Chandra that he was concerned his father had done something rash, hoping that it would be enough, knowing that he couldn't commit his father's crime to paper.

Chandra looked up as the messenger stopped at her table in the mess hall, her gaze quickly falling from his face to the letter he held out to her. Her heart seized. Could it be?

There was only her name scrawled on the envelope and she took it with shaking fingers, turning it over slowly. It took everything in her not to tear the envelope open right there and then. But if it *was* from Roman, she didn't want to open it where just anyone might see.

Weeks had gone by with no word. What did it mean if he was writing to her now? Her chest constricted at the thought. Had something bad happened?

She left early, abandoning the remnants of her dinner, glad to be rid of the oppressive atmosphere in the hall. It had been subdued ever since they'd received word of the impending attack, everyone all too aware of what it might mean.

Chandra returned to the aerie, where she had met with Sheboleth. Few recruits seemed to go up there in the evenings and they were unlikely to be disturbed.

"A letter," Chandra greeted Sheboleth, holding up the envelope. "I think it's from Roman."

Eagerly, she tore through the envelope and extracted the paper. Her heart soared as she scanned the first few lines. She'd been right.

Her eyes greedily roamed over the parchment, consuming his words, but her elation faded almost at once. Only a third of the paper had been filled out. He had written so little…and what he had said left her more confused than ever.

"What does he say?" Sheboleth asked.

"It—it makes no sense," Chandra sputtered.

He had written next to nothing about his condition, how he was healing from his injuries, whether he was all right, or letting her know about any news from the palace regarding the Elath raid. Disappointingly, there was also no news about whether he'd spoken to his father about her idea, as he'd promised.

He did include a quick line hoping that she was all right. But there was no news about him at all, which was what Chandra really wanted.

"He says he must warn me that his father has done something terrible," she added. "But he doesn't say what." Chandra lowered the letter, exasperated. "What could his father have done? Made a deal with the Akkadians? Is that why we were told to stay behind the city walls? We've surrendered?"

Sheboleth dismissed the idea. "It's too late for that. At this point, the Empire would probably reject such an offer, even if it was made."

"What, then?" Chandra exclaimed.

She almost wished Roman hadn't written to her at all. She didn't doubt that he meant well, but how was she supposed to know what she was meant to be wary of when his warning was so vague?

"I guess we'll find out when the Akkadians make their move."

Chandra sighed. "I don't think we'll have long to wait."

XXIII

The morning dawned gray and overcast. A heavy cover of clouds had rolled in overnight, concealing the light of even the moon and stars, making it difficult to judge what time it was. But Chandra knew dawn hadn't yet arrived when she sat up in bed, listening hard, for a moment unsure.

The belltowers had begun to toll. The Akkadians were here.

She was up in an instant, hurriedly slipping into her flight leathers, strapping blades to her belt and slinging her quiver over one shoulder, longbow in hand. With the others, she raced to find her dragon and get into position.

This was it, what could very well be Anarsha's last stand.

Before the sun had fully appeared, she had strapped herself to Sheboleth's saddle and taken her position along the Great Wall, awaiting orders. On one side of her, Anake sat astride Vitanni, the viper-green dragon shifting impatiently. On the other, Victor sat atop Bane, the large dragon's baleful gaze fixated on the forest, waiting for the army of the Empire to emerge.

And emerge they did, first ground troops, the same as last time. It was hard to tell from such a distance, but Chandra squinted anyway, trying to make out details. It looked like some of them wore no armor.

Beside her, Anake let out a hiss. "Some of them are Elathan!"

Chandra didn't bother asking how she could be sure, taking her at her word. *Elathans.* Dread settled in the pit of her stomach. That meant they were slaves or prisoners, conscripted into the army, forced to fight.

How many of them were taken from Shemar?

Chandra didn't relish the idea of strafing lines of slaves with dragonfire. But whether they were given a chance or not, they were still marching upon her kingdom. Her home.

And there were so many of them. There seemed to be even more infantry than the last time. They were many rows deep before the first mech arrived, stepping clear of the tree line, its bronze hide dull in the gray light.

Chandra leaned forward in the saddle, her eyes scanning the ranks of Akkadians and what little she could see past the tree line, searching for the ballistae. There was no mist to hide them this time, and she saw none, but knew they were out there somewhere, waiting.

She watched the approaching army advance and still no orders were given. The line of dragon riders stood along the wall, motionless.

"What are we waiting for?" she hissed to Victor. "Why haven't any orders been given?"

He shook his head, brow furrowed, looking just as frustrated as she. "We're to stay behind the wall for now."

"And what, just let them walk right up to us?"

"Look," Anake said, pointing.

Chandra followed the line of her finger. The city gates had opened, their own infantry spilling forth. The stone in Chandra's stomach sank further. They were going to let their foot soldiers meet Akkadia's, holding the dragon riders back to face the mechs.

The infantry would be slaughtered without aid.

"What are we doing?" Chandra whispered, her words intended for Sheboleth alone.

Down the line she could see a couple of officers, who appeared to be arguing, judging from their exaggerated gestures. Confused murmurs rose from her fellow riders, concerned glances exchanged. Was Anarsha's leadership truly so disorganized? Why did no one seem to know what they were doing?

Helpless to act without orders, Chandra waited, watching as the two lines of infantry drew ever nearer. They finally clashed in the middle of the Badlands, nearly too far away to make out any details. But the cacophony that rang out reached the riders along the wall.

The screech of steel on steel. Twanging of released bowstrings. Cries of pain as a blow found its mark.

For a moment, it seemed as though neither side were winning, that neither had yet lost any men. Until the sparse ground disappeared beneath fallen bodies.

The Empire's forces absorbed the first blow Anarsha had thrown at them and continued implacably forward. The belltowers rang out again, a series of chords giving the riders the order they had been waiting for.

Without hesitation, Sheboleth leapt off the wall, letting gravity drag her downward, the speed hurtling her toward the approaching Akkadians like an arrow.

Chandra's surroundings blurred, only the enemy in focus. She searched for ballistae, but still could see none. It didn't matter; if the Empire reached the wall, they were lost.

Sheboleth unleashed a torrent of flame upon the first infantry they encountered, who made it past their own foot soldiers, her flames carving a path. Chandra rained arrows down upon them, sending up a silent prayer to the saints for forgiveness. The Elathans and Shemarans were vulnerable, without the protection of the armor that their Akkadian oppressors wore. But that was exactly why she fired upon them, her arrows useless against a mech.

Better a quick death, she tried to tell herself, than being burned alive.

Suddenly, they reached the mechs, strafing a line through them, before circling around and doing it again. But with each pass, more came, stepping free of the forest to take their place.

With each sweep, Chandra expected to be greeted with the sight of fewer Akkadians. Instead, there seemed to be *more*. And fewer Anarshans, their remaining ground troops easy targets.

Chandra reached back for her quiver, her fingers meeting only empty air. She glanced over her shoulder, met with the sight of an empty quiver, devoid of arrows. She'd fired them all.

As Sheboleth dove to rake the mechs again, Chandra shrugged the bow over her shoulder, no easy task with the wind and heat from the flames buffeting her. Her lips would be chapped by the end of this run, her cheeks windburned.

If we survive.

It wasn't looking likely. From the start, the Anarshans had been heavily outnumbered. The Akkadians had thrown everything they had into this conflict, in a desperate all or nothing gambit. So far, it seemed to be paying off.

Chandra leaned low over Sheboleth's neck, using both hands to hold on. "There's too many!" she called.

"I hadn't noticed!" Sheboleth snapped back.

But Chandra didn't hear her reply, her chest tightening as a horrible, mechanical sound filled the air. *The ballistae.*

The strategy this time had been to hold the siege weaponry in the rear, waiting until the Anarshans had been lured out to face the mechs. And now that they were here, far beyond the safety of their wall, the ballistae would be brought to bear.

Without any arrows, Chandra could do little but trust Sheboleth's instincts. The dragon would have to be the weapon, for both of them. But that didn't mean Chandra was completely useless.

Clenching her jaw, blinking eyes that stung from the wind, she scanned the battlefield below them, searching for potential threats—or openings.

Beneath her, Sheboleth angled her wings, preparing to come around once more.

The foot soldiers fell beneath Desmond's mech like wheat before a scythe, the beast's iron claws making short work of them.

The strategy, if one could call it that, of Anarsha's leaders confounded him. What were they thinking, throwing their infantry at the Empire's forces? The act smacked of desperation, but he supposed that they had been deemed a worthy sacrifice, if their deaths somehow helped defeat the Empire.

Desmond didn't care either way. He knew his orders and the end goal—breach the city walls. If Anarsha was anything like Shemar, once that happened, everything would rapidly descend into chaos and it would be over in a matter of minutes.

But then again, Shemar hadn't had dragons. Desmond glanced up, raising his mech's head from the Anarshan soldier he had just torn asunder. The dragons still soared overhead, too high to make out through the grilles in the mech's chest. But he could see them through its eyes.

Desmond lowered the head again, returning his focus to the ground, and the wall he could make out in the distance, intent on reaching it.

A snarl rang out to his left and he turned the mech quickly, the beast fast to respond despite its size. Through the grilles, he made out a dragon, on the ground and charging straight for him.

It moved fast, eating up the ground. He could see no visible sign of injury. *Why was it on the ground?*

There was no time to wonder. Desmond planted his mech's legs, taking a wide stance, claws digging into the ground. With its far superior body weight, it would withstand the blow.

The dragon slammed into the mech. Desmond's eyes widened in surprise as he felt the mech shift beneath him, beginning to tip backward. His pulse galloped, blood surging to the surface of his skin, his body feeling suddenly hot and feverish.

It should have been impossible. The mech should have absorbed the blow. It should have been immovable.

He winced as the mech slammed into the ground, toppling over. His body jerked from the impact, the straps keeping him in place digging into him. At least he'd managed not to let go of the levers. He jerked them sharply, ordering the mech to rise before—

The dragon was on him. He could see little of it, his vision tilted sideways, but Desmond could hear its claws as they scraped against the metal, the only thing standing between him and certain death.

A horrific, tortured squeal rang out and Desmond watched in horror as part of the mech's side paneling began to peel away.

The mech got to its feet, at last responding to his frantic commands. It felt like he had lain there, helpless for an eternity. The mech rounded on the dragon, lunging forward. The dragon reared up on its hind legs to meet him.

For a long heartbeat, they tussled, one creature made of flesh and bone, the other metal and gears. Quick as a serpent, the dragon's head shot forward, its jaws clamping down on the mech's throat. Once again, the metal creaked in protest as it began to collapse in on itself.

Desmond yanked one of the levers to the side, as if by sheer force alone he could lend the mech the strength it needed to break free. With a shriek, the mech tore itself out of the dragon's grasp, the armor plating in its crumpled neck completely tearing away, leaving behind a gaping hole.

Desmond sucked in a sharp breath of the fresh air flowing through the gap, much cooler than the heat of the mech's interior. His finger hovered over the button that would summon the mech's flames, but he discarded the idea quickly. With the mech's throat crushed, the flames may not come.

The dragon lunged at him again. Desmond urged the mech forward to meet it, raising one leg. He watched the mech's claws swoop downward. The mech shuddered as the blow struck and a moment later, he felt something give.

He waited, every muscle tensed, for the next blow to come. When it didn't, he unbuckled himself, fingers still shaky from adrenaline. The undamaged panels on the other side of the mech slid away easily enough and he hopped down to the ground.

The dragon lay beneath his mech, eyes glassy. The mech's claws had punctured its neck.

Desmond let out a breath, turning to survey the damage to his machine. If it had seemed bad from within, the full extent was horrific to behold.

The mech's skeleton was shredded, rent, crumpled, and torn. Staring at it, Desmond imagined he could inflict similar damage if he took a knife to a tin can.

He reached out, trailing his fingers lightly over where the metal side had been peeled back. How was this possible? He tried not to engage the dragons directly, but even so, he'd never heard of any of them being able to inflict *this* kind of damage.

His thoughts turned back to the misgivings he'd had in the Capitol, and later Shemar, before they'd marched on Anarsha. The mines drying up. A shortage of material, combined with the urgent need to produce as many mechs as fast as possible.

Was the Empire's most powerful machine truly so fragile now? The thought unnerved him. He stared at the rent metal, the gaping holes, all that stood between him and the dragon's claws, and shuddered.

That was close. Too close.

As weak as the mech's armor had been, it was still better than nothing. He supposed it *had* done its job and shielded him from harm. But it was useless now, too badly damaged to continue fighting.

Will I ever finish a battle with a mech still intact?

That hadn't been such a problem before the Anarshans and Desmond realized how spoiled he had been on previous campaigns. In Shemar and Elath before that, the only time he'd ever had to worry about abandoning a mech had been due to running out of fuel.

Now he had to contend with fire raining down from the sky and the real, living counterparts to the Empire's machines. And he had to do it now without a mech of his own.

Resigned, he drew his sword. He'd finished the last battle on foot. He could do it again.

It shouldn't take long. The Anarshans were badly outnumbered and would soon be overwhelmed. In an hour or two, Desmond would be sitting around a warm fire, celebrating Akkadia's victory. Hell, he might even share a toast with his fellow soldiers.

And then, with the last free kingdom defeated, the last jewel in Akkadia's crown finally secured, he could return home showered in glory that not even his father could find fault with.

That victory was closer now than it had ever been, so close he could nearly taste it. With every Anarshan he cut down, he was one step closer.

One man at a time.

Hefting his sword, Desmond strode forward, his gaze fixed on the wall in the distance.

Chandra barely heard the belltowers as they tolled again, the bells low and sonorous, rolling over the battlefield, rising above the clamor. The roar of dragons, the burning fire, cries of pain, the clanking of the mechs, and above it all, the horrid ballistae.

She turned back to face the wall, head tilted, listening to the new orders. *Fall back to the city.*

No, she thought, even as her fellow riders were already turning. *No, we can't.*

But they had no choice. They must obey orders. Sheboleth turned, following after the others. If they remained, they would be cut down.

Sheboleth alighted nimbly on the wall, where they had begun their vigil that morning, turning to face the encroaching army. There were still so many of them.

If not for the small fires that burned along the Badlands and the unspeakable number of bodies—both human and dragon—that littered the ground, Chandra could have believed that Anarsha had declined to engage the Empire at all. Akkadia's numbers certainly hadn't seemed to suffer for it.

She blinked back frustrated tears, helpless to do anything but watch as the Empire drew near. *This can't be how it ends.* After everything, the Akkadians couldn't win, just like that. Everything they had lost, everything they had sacrificed—it couldn't all be for naught.

Callum and Gideon couldn't mean nothing.

She glanced over her shoulder, up the hill, but couldn't make out the palace from that distance. Still, she knew it was there and that Roman must be within.

What was he doing at that moment? Was he watching? Was he afraid? What had he meant about his father doing something rash and terrible?

Was his father even still at the palace? Or had he abandoned all hope and fled? Were the Anarshan soldiers only meant to bide the royals time to escape? Was that why their leadership had seemed so disorganized?

Turning away from the palace, Chandra faced forward again. There was no point in running now. They were Anarsha's last hope. However this day ended, she would face it, with her fellow riders at her side. With Sheboleth.

To whatever end.

From his room at the palace, Roman watched the battle below, though he could see little of it. Only the dragons as they took to the air. He could hear plenty, though, through the open window. And what he heard chilled his blood, particularly those hateful ballistae firing. There seemed to be no end to them.

Was Chandra down there somewhere? Was she still alive? Or had she fallen? A sense of dread churned his stomach as he wondered if she'd even had time to receive his letter. Perhaps he should have been more specific, but it was too late for that now.

What was his father playing at? Where was the great demon he had promised? Perhaps there was no such thing and his father only thought he had struck a bargain. Maybe no help, of any kind, was coming.

Would that be for the best? Roman wasn't sure.

He leaned forward, gripping the windowsill, knuckles turning white, as the belltowers rang out. He could make out the signal perfectly, calling the soldiers back within the city walls.

There were only so many reasons for such an order that Roman could think of. He felt the hair on his arms rise, hoping he was wrong.

From his own tower, Ulric watched as well, an odd sense of calm having come over him. Never had he felt so unconcerned, so detached from the threat of the Empire on his doorstep. Seeing the Akkadians crossing the Badlands, drawing ever nearer to the Great Wall, should have filled him with terror.

Moments before, he had felt nothing but unease. The threat that he had feared, spent many a night fretting about, had finally come to pass.

For a moment, he imagined how the day might have ended, had he not made the bargain—and lamented that such actions were necessary. He pictured the Empire breaching the city walls, flooding the streets, cutting down Anarshans where they stood.

How was it possible to feel so many different emotions at once? He felt afraid, sorrowful, and furious all at once—a combination that choked his breath.

Then it had all faded away. And in its wake, he felt almost gleeful. *Yes, come closer,* he silently urged the Akkadians. They were precisely where he wanted them. He knew how this battle would end, even if no one else did.

He couldn't remember the last time he'd possessed such a feeling of certainty, but he rather liked the sensation. What a counterpoint to the fear he'd been living beneath for so long! At last, it felt like he could finally breathe.

After today, it would all be over. His kingdom would be free, his people safe. Whatever troubles remained, they could be resolved easily enough, without the threat of Akkadia breathing down the back of their necks.

Without turning, he addressed the presence he could feel, lurking in the room. "You know what to do. Do not fail."

The soul stone hung from its silver chain around his neck. Always, he was aware of its weight, the cold of it against his skin.

The voice hissed. "Your will be done."

He felt, rather than saw, the demon depart.

Moments later, a roar sounded below.

✦

"What the hell was that?" Chandra demanded.

It had sounded like a dragon roar, but louder than any she'd ever heard. The very earth seemed to tremble with the force of it.

Sheboleth stared over the edge of the wall, down at the battlefield below. "Hell," she muttered. "That's what it was."

"What?" Chandra started to approach the wall's edge, but she didn't have to, in order to see.

One moment, the Akkadian army was alone in the Badlands. The next, a massive presence had joined them, the largest dragon Chandra had ever seen.

He towered over the infantry and mechs alike, taller even, than the Great Wall. His scales were the gray of stone, with darker armored plating trailing from his neck to the tip of his tail. There were black horns protruding from his chin and jaw. Two long horns jutted out from the back of his head. Tattered frills ran from his forehead to his tail.

But it was the beast's eyes that snared her attention the most—a strange combination of amber and orange, seeming to flicker from within.

The Akkadian army had halted their advance, turning at the creature's appearance.

The dragon's jaws parted, revealing long, wicked, yellowed fangs. Chandra could see the fire building in the back of his throat, glowing like the embers of a furnace.

The beast let out a roar and Chandra didn't think she imagined the Great Wall shaking beneath her. She cried out, fearing her eardrums would burst.

A torrent of flames shot forth, the heat so powerful Chandra could feel it, even at such a distance. Scores of Akkadian soldiers and mechs vanished beneath the fire and she knew they had died instantly.

Below, the Akkadian forces scattered, their organized ranks descending into chaos. They fled, some of them crashing into each other, as they scrambled for the forest, desperate to get away.

The dragon reached out with one hand, slamming it down upon the fleeing soldiers, leaving broken bodies and crushed metal in his wake. The Empire did not possess a mech sturdy enough to withstand such a blow.

The beast's massive head swung down, jaws snapping. Already, huge swaths had been carved out of the Empire's ranks. The dent in their numbers that Chandra hadn't seen before was all too apparent now.

She watched, eyes wide and unblinking, unwilling to look away from the spectacle of it all, as her enemies were destroyed before her. The anger in her chest swelled, mingling with another emotion. Pride. A sense of satisfaction that was almost savage.

Destroy them, she urged silently. *Destroy them all.*

Sheboleth let out a hiss. "So that's it. He summoned a demon."

That tore Chandra's gaze away. "What?"

"The king summoned a demon. That's what Roman's letter meant."

She turned back to the gray dragon. Was that what she was looking at, this creature before her? A demon? All of the demons, of course, had been long gone, sealed away, by the time Chandra came along and she hadn't bothered to pay too much attention to the saints. They were all long gone, too, and beseeching them had done nothing to spare Callum or Gideon.

But if this creature were a demon, that meant that they had been real. It had all been real, including the saints. How was this possible, to summon one back into the world?

Sheboleth was a dragon. Her kind had fought alongside the saints. If she said the creature before them was a demon, Chandra believed her.

She tried to think back to the last time she'd visited the temple and suddenly, she could see it. The gray dragon in front of her and the mural he'd appeared in. His form was more indistinct and shadowy than the one before her now, but she could see him, in her mind's eye, leaning to whisper in a saint's ear.

"Saints," she breathed, as the demon rained hellfire upon the Akkadians.

The saints hadn't answered their prayers. A demon had. In that moment, Chandra didn't really care who they owed their salvation to, so long as the Empire breathed its last that day.

But Sheboleth didn't appear to share that sentiment.

"The fool," she hissed. "He has no idea what he's done."

Desmond tore his blade free of a corpse as the first roar rang out. He was still on foot, his mech long gone, with nothing standing between him and the creature that had appeared on the battlefield. He blinked rapidly, struggling to make sense of what he was seeing.

It was the largest dragon he had ever laid eyes on. Where had it come from? Why had the Anarshans held back such a weapon, if they'd had it in their possession? He hadn't known that dragons could ever reach such a size.

He was still frozen, rooted in place, when the first flames shot forth, covering a far greater distance than any of the other dragons.

He stared in horror at the sheer power on display. It was like nothing he had ever witnessed before. He had never seen the Empire's war machines made to look so small, so fragile, so *weak*.

A strange emotion clawed at his chest, trying to burst free. It wasn't fear; he'd felt that in battle before, though little enough. This went beyond fear. It was a primal sort of terror, the knowledge that he could not win this fight. There was no chance—not even the slightest.

As he watched, the beast strafed a whole line of mechs with fire, incinerating some instantly. Others lingered, on the edge of the flames, their forms melting, warping in the heat.

Without thinking, he ran forward, toward the nearest one, though every instinct *screamed* at him to flee. To not take one step closer to the beast. But all Desmond could think was how he would feel if he were trapped in the burning, melting mech. How the metal, turned to liquid, would sear the flesh from his bones.

Better to be crushed, as some of his fellow soldiers were, the beast's claws descending on them from above, grinding their bones into dust.

He skidded to a halt, panting, as he reached the mech. Even from the outside, the heat was blistering. Desmond could only imagine what the pilot inside was experiencing.

He put his hands to the hatch, swearing as his skin sizzled in the heat. With fumbling hands, he tore a strip off his uniform, wrapping the fabric around his palms.

The pain was still searing and he gritted his teeth as he pried the hatch open. A body lay motionless within. The man might be dead, but Desmond grasped the pilot anyway, dragging him free of the doomed mech. At least he'd been able to undo the straps before Desmond reached him.

Coughing, Desmond stepped back, sucking in a sharp breath as he realized who it was he'd rescued.

The medals on the breast of his uniform and the pips on his shoulders proclaimed him as the general of their army. Desmond searched his memory for the man's name, but failed to come up with it, keeping one eye on the beast, should it turn their way—though there was little either of them would be able to do about it.

The general stirred, his lined face grimacing in pain. His skin was an angry red and there was a nasty burn on his thigh. If he'd suffered any further injuries, they were hidden from Desmond's view.

He knelt down. "Are you all right, sir?"

The man coughed, taking stock of his surroundings—including the mech behind him—and then clapped Desmond on the shoulder. "Damned good thing you came along when you did. Help me up, lad. We need to get away from here."

Slinging one of the general's arms around his shoulder, Desmond heaved the man to his feet. After a few steps, he was steady enough to continue on his own, though he limped heavily. Together, the two of them paused for breath, the edge of the forest so close and yet still so far away.

Desmond turned, watching as the dragon continued to rake what remained of their army. A few of the ballistae fired, their bolts bouncing harmlessly off the creature's hide.

He frowned, something nagging at him. There was something about the beast—about its size and power—that had bothered him from the beginning and suddenly, Desmond grasped what it was.

He should have known. They were in Anarsha, after all. But he'd chalked it up to pagan superstition, as did most of the Empire. There was no evidence that such creatures had ever existed—and they certainly didn't now.

But there was no denying the evidence before his eyes.

Anarsha had unleashed a demon upon them.

"By the saints," Desmond muttered.

It was an oath he never would have dared utter within anyone else's hearing, much less a superior officer. But it wasn't blasphemy or superstition any longer. It was real.

"Indeed," the general replied. He tore his gaze away, turning to Desmond. "This foe is beyond us. If this battle is to be anything other than a total loss, we need to retreat *now*."

Desmond didn't bother to wait for the order to be given. It was all but too late anyway and he doubted anyone would hear. He turned and ran for the Valderan rainforest as what little remained of the Akkadian army fled around him.

His lungs cried out for air, his side screamed in pain, but he dared not stop. He dared not look back, even as the demon's roars shook the earth behind him.

XXIV

It felt like an eternity had passed, for the earth was not the same place it had been when Chandra woke that morning. And yet, it was over in a matter of minutes, the demon making short work of the Akkadians.

Chandra hadn't seen the exact moment the demon had disappeared. One moment he had towered over the battlefield. The next, he was gone, though he left plenty of evidence behind.

An eerie silence fell over the Badlands, truly worthy of the name now. As Sheboleth flew low over the ground, Chandra saw great swaths of blackened land, where it had been scorched beyond saving. In other places, there were wide trenches carved into the earth where the demon had raked his claws through it. The landscape had been forever altered by what had taken place that day, seared beyond recognition.

Bodies lay strewn, torn and scattered. Rent metal husks were all that remained of Akkadia's once-mighty war machines.

Chandra and a few others had been sent to scout the battlefield, looking for any survivors. She doubted any would be found. But if there were, her orders were to kill them. There was little point in taking them prisoner.

That seemed cruel to Chandra, despite her hatred of the Akkadians. To strike them down while they were injured and dying seemed like something the Empire would do and it didn't sit well with her.

Wordlessly, Sheboleth angled her wings, swooping downward, and Chandra knew the dragon had spied something. Her stomach clenched as they drew near and she could see for herself.

A survivor. He'd nearly made it to the tree line, but the arrow protruding from his chest had felled him before he could reach it.

Sheboleth landed, keeping a wary eye on the Akkadian, while Chandra dismounted. She could hear his raspy breaths, each more labored than the one before. He wouldn't last much longer.

She feared he was one of the foot soldiers she had seen, from Elath or Shemar, forcefully conscripted into the army. She didn't want to have to kill him. It wasn't their fault that they were here. They'd had no choice.

But as she drew closer, she saw that this soldier wore at least some armor, the metal black with gold highlights. The colors of Akkadia. The enemy.

He looked so young—like a teenager. Barely more than a boy, who was dying and knew it. It seemed like only yesterday that she'd been his age, before all of this. Before everything had changed.

He tensed at her approach and drew himself up slightly, as though to retreat. But there was nowhere for him to go.

Chandra looked into his brown eyes, expecting to see the hatred she'd come to expect. The hate she imagined she would project at an Anarshan soldier, should their roles have been reversed. Instead, all she saw was pain, and beneath that, fear.

She reached for the sword at her side, but her fingers stilled as they wrapped around the handle. Behind her, she could feel Sheboleth's eyes on her, silent yet questioning.

Finish him!

For all she knew, this boy could have been the one operating the ballistae that brought Callum down that fateful day. Chandra tried to reach for her anger, but found only a hollow emptiness where it should have been.

Who was this boy? What was his name? How old was he? Did he have family back in the Capitol who were waiting for him? Did they know he would never return? They would find out soon enough…

Would there be tears? Would there be questions? Would they feel the same anger that threatened to consume Chandra?

What are you waiting for? Put him out of his misery, if nothing else.

Chandra let out a slow breath. It took more effort than it should have; the heavy weight that had settled on her chest didn't want to budge.

She couldn't do it.

"Chandra!" a voice called. "Are you all right?"

Anake.

Chandra tried to call back to her, but her throat wouldn't work. It seemed to have sealed itself shut.

Grass crunched beneath Anake's feet as she joined her. "Oh, you found one." She nodded at the dying boy. "Go on."

Chandra couldn't bring herself to admit that she could not, for whatever reason, kill the boy. "You can have this one," she murmured.

Anake gave her a funny look, but Chandra turned away. She'd only made it a few paces before she heard Anake's sword slide free. She flinched at the sound of it meeting flesh, the rattling sigh that followed.

And then silence. Horrible, absolute silence.

Ulric felt the exact moment the presence returned to him. He faced the window still, staring out over the battlefield. Though the Badlands had long since fallen silent, the sound still rang in his ears.

The Empire's forces were gone. Routed. Destroyed. He almost didn't dare to believe it.

"You did it," he murmured. "They're really gone."

"Did you doubt me?" the demon rumbled. There was no judgement in his tone, only a mild curiosity.

"No," Ulric replied. "I just didn't know what to expect."

"And are you satisfied?"

"Yes," he whispered. "Very much."

It had gone better than he could have imagined. He'd hardly allowed himself to even consider such a future, so impossible had it seemed. The Empire was destroyed. His kingdom was free. The threat that had hung over them for so long had been vanquished.

"Was it worth it," the demon hissed, "this bargain that you made?"

"Yes." *A thousand times, yes.*

"So you say, in this moment. You'll change your tune soon enough."

Something about the demon's tone, darkly amused, set Ulric's nerves on edge.

"Leave me," he snapped, some of his satisfaction leaching away. He didn't want the demon's foul presence to spoil his mood, his victory, further.

"As you wish."

He felt the presence leave him again. Where the demon went, he knew not, and didn't much care. He had what he wanted. The bill would come due, but for now, he had won.

Chandra expected to forget the nameless Akkadian soldier quickly enough, but she had seen his face. The fear in his eyes was forever burned into her memory. The sound—and the lack of it that had followed—kept replaying in her mind.

She avoided Anake that evening, not wanting to face her questions. She knew she'd made herself look weak in front of the Elathan. She *was* weak.

"Thought I might find you here," Sheboleth remarked, mounting the stairs to the top of the aerie.

Chandra looked up. She'd half hoped for another letter from Roman, providing further explanation now that his father's secret had been revealed. But none had come.

Sheboleth cocked her head. "I thought you'd stay in the mess hall. Enjoy the celebrations."

The mess hall had been riotous when she'd left. Despite the rationing, which was still in place, her fellow soldiers hadn't let that dampen their spirits, many of them indulging in a rare bout of drinking. The officers hadn't seemed inclined to stop them, no doubt thinking they had earned the right to celebrate Anarsha's victory—no matter how it had come about.

The whole kingdom, it seemed, was celebrating. Lights shone in nearly every building and the sound of cheering, laughter and music could be heard faintly, drifting up from the streets below.

Chandra knew she should be down there with them. This was what she had wanted, after all. She'd wanted the

Empire destroyed, Anarsha safe. But not even all the noise of the mess hall had been loud enough to silence the sounds ringing in her own mind.

Why did victory have to feel so hollow, all because of one Akkadian soldier she did not know and who certainly was not her responsibility?

"This is about that boy, isn't it?" Sheboleth asked.

"No," Chandra said, too quickly. The dragon was too perceptive for her own good.

Sheboleth shot her a glare that let her know exactly how little she thought of the lie.

Chandra sighed. The regret that she had felt when killing the deer, that she had deemed weakness, had returned in full force. It turned out that there was a great deal of difference between slaughtering an animal and a human, no matter that both had been suffering.

"I couldn't kill him, Sheboleth." It felt good to admit the words, to say them out loud. It seemed to lessen some of the hold they had on her. And if she couldn't confide such things to the partner she rode into battle beside, then who?

"He was so young," she added. "So afraid. He didn't look like a mindless, soulless automaton to me." The kind of soldier she'd been led to believe they all were. "But I should have killed him."

That was what haunted her. She should have killed him, and it should have been easy. So why hadn't it been?

"Why?"

"Because he's the enemy!" Chandra cried. "What if he fired that ballistae? What if he killed Callum?"

"We both know the chances of that."

"But what if he did?"

"Would knowing that have made it any easier?"

Somehow, Chandra thought it would have, and that made her feel ashamed.

The dragon stepped closer, claws clacking on stone, and Chandra looked away.

"Your heart is not a weakness, Chandra, and you shouldn't be ashamed of it."

Saints, but she could read her too easily.

"It makes you human," Sheboleth went on. "If more people felt as you do, perhaps we wouldn't be in this mess now. But too many people care nothing for the lives of others. The god the Akkadians worship is not any of the saints or even their modern technology, but simple greed. And that's the altar that most people worship at, no matter what they might claim."

The demon returned to Ulric late that same evening, when the rest of the palace had begun to quiet for the night, and he was left alone with only his thoughts for company. He didn't feel like trying to sleep, still mulling over the day's events and its outcome.

"Are you satisfied?" the demon hissed.

"Yes," Ulric snapped. "I already told you that I was. Why do you keep asking?"

"You summoned me," the demon pointed out. "If you do not want my company, perhaps you should not have."

Saints, was the creature really going to hang around, harassing him?

Ulric sighed. "You named your price and I said I would happily pay it. Is it truly so hard to believe that I am satisfied? The kingdom is safe. I can ask for no more than that."

The demon scoffed at that. "Safe? Your kingdom will never be safe."

"The Empire—"

"I'm not talking about the Empire. Mark my words, king, your kingdom will still fall. It will rot, crumbling from within. You have given up that which is most precious and saved nothing."

There was a savage glee to the demon's tone. He was enjoying this.

"You're wrong," Ulric growled, but the creature's words had rattled him.

On the one hand, it was true that he did not regret what he had done. If he hadn't summoned the beast and made a pact, Anarsha would even now be conquered. The Akkadians would have stormed through the city streets, plundering and slaughtering any in their path. The kingdom would have fallen by nightfall.

And yet, it was also true that Ulric found himself frightened after witnessing what he had unleashed. *A reaper. I set the reaper upon my enemies and then invited him within my walls.*

"You're trying to unnerve me," he added, drawing himself up. *Remember, he is a deceiver.* "It won't work. Anarsha's greatest threat is gone."

An image came to Ulric then of the saint, a single tear rolling down her face as she gazed upward, beseeching the heavens. Whatever the demon had whispered in her ear had been intended to torment. Given that she had taken her own life, Ulric would say the demon's gambit had been successful. But he was a king. He was made of sterner stuff than that.

"Gone, yes. And you, the hero that saved your kingdom through your action and the noble sacrifice that you agreed to. But the people will not see you that way for very long. They are fickle, their minds so quickly changed, their whims easily swayed. They will curse your name before the end. They will soon forget their fear of the Empire and hate you more than they ever hated the Akkadians."

"You're a liar!" Ulric cried.

The demon said no more, having blissfully left him for a time. But the creature—the reaper's—words circled around in Ulric's mind, keeping him awake long after he had gone to bed.

Now that the Empire was destroyed, no longer a threat, he would have to contend with what it was he had summoned. He had brought evil back into the world, for though the demon had done his bidding, there was no doubt that was what it was.

He began to think of the creature as Reaper, no longer simply the demon. That was what he was, what he did. He reaped death and sowed destruction. Ulric's kingdom was safe from the Empire, but was it safe from what he had unleashed?

Ulric knew what he ought to do, as he lay there in the darkness, long having given up on rest. He ought to seal the beast away and be done with it. It had served its purpose and he need not call upon it again.

But while the image of the destruction Reaper had rained down on the Akkadians had horrified him, he was also awed by it. That kind of power was rare—certainly the Empire had nothing comparable—and he was loath to part with it.

Such devastation had been wrought at Ulric's orders. So long as the demon remained under his command, there was no one more powerful than he.

And what if he should need it again? Besides, vile though Reaper undoubtedly was, that didn't mean he couldn't also be useful.

An idea came to Ulric, the soul stone around his neck growing colder by the moment. He could wait until morning, but better that he did this now, while he would be undisturbed and before he could talk himself out of it.

Throwing back the covers, Ulric left his bedchamber, stalking down the long, darkened corridors. The palace seemed chilly that late at night, the torches and wall sconces not penetrating the gloom the way they should have.

As Ulric approached the entrance to the dungeons, a few guards detached themselves from the walls and made as though to follow him. He held up one hand to forestall them. There was nothing in the dungeons that posed a threat to him, and anyway, none of them stood a chance against the Reaper.

The stone floor was cold against his bare feet and Ulric wished he'd thought to don a pair of shoes before venturing down here, but it was too late for that now. He had already arrived.

He ducked into the spare room where he and his councilors had first summoned the beast. The circle was still drawn in the dirt, but the swords had been removed, returned to where they belonged.

That didn't matter. Ulric didn't need them for what he was about to do. It seemed fitting that he should do this, for he had set all of it into motion.

"Demon," he called, feeling slightly foolish. To any onlooker, it would appear as though he spoke to thin air.

But a moment later, the demon's presence filled the room. He could see it before him, a shadowy outline, a hint of the beast he could become.

"Yes?" Reaper jeered. "Is there something more you would have me do, another bargain you wish to strike?"

"Not exactly," Ulric answered, fiddling with the soul stone between his fingers. He had taken it from around his neck on the stairs.

"What, then?"

There had been no record of a mortal summoning a demon back into the world. To Ulric's knowledge, it hadn't been done since the last demon was sealed away—if it had ever been done at all.

But the process of sealing a demon—now that was far more well-documented. It hadn't taken him long to find the proper words to say. He knew what to do and he knew what would happen.

Anticipating that the demon might not take too kindly to his efforts, Ulric didn't bother wasting time trying to explain. He simply began the incantation.

The demon let out a snarl, his shadowy form lunging forward. Ulric caught a glimpse of snapping teeth and then Reaper halted a few feet from him, as though held by an invisible tether.

The demon had never made it out of the circle.

He writhed, jaws snapping, railing against Ulric and the force that held him. "Stop this! This was not part of our bargain!"

But Ulric didn't care. This had always been his failsafe, a way of undoing what he had done.

In a matter of moments, it was over. The demon's presence winked out of the room, as though it had never been. And yet, Ulric was not quite alone.

He looked down at the stone in his hand. No longer blue in color, but a golden amber. No longer did it chill his skin, but instead pulsed with a pleasant warmth.

He could sense the demon's presence, trapped within. Though no words rang in his mind, he could feel Reaper's wrath, a wordless howl of rage. But the demon was safely contained. He could not harm Ulric now.

And there the creature would remain, sealed away for a thousand years, unless the stone was destroyed by dragonfire, the only way to complete the banishment. There was no other substance that could harm a soul stone and any attempt to break it would be futile.

Ulric knew that's what he should do. He should seek out Koal, the dragon he had asked to accompany his son, and have him destroy the stone, returning the demon to whatever foul hell he had been summoned from.

But Ulric couldn't bring himself to part with it, despite fearing the power within. It was that very power, now safely contained, that could still prove useful. Now that the demon posed no threat, holding on to the power it gave could only be a good thing.

Besides, he told himself, he *would* destroy it. One day, when it was no longer needed. Or perhaps the task should fall to Roman. He never approved of such drastic action in the first place and would not fail to see it done.

And if neither of them destroyed it, it didn't really matter. The demon would remain safely contained for a millennium. A thousand years was a long time. Surely before such time had passed, someone would destroy the stone, if not he or Roman.

If not, the demon would eventually be freed again. Both father and son would be long dead by the time any such event came to pass. As strong as Anarsha was, and despite the pride Ulric felt toward his kingdom, he doubted even she would remain after a thousand years had passed.

The Empire certainly wouldn't. No empire lasted forever. And a thousand years was nearly longer than the human mind could fathom, in many ways. Life, and the world, would look completely different.

Ulric tightened his fingers around the stone. He would hold onto it for now, even knowing the risks it posed for some far-off future.

But it would never come to that.

XXV

By some miracle, Desmond and the general—Halsing, his name came back to him on the way to Shemar—managed to escape. The demon did not come after them. Desmond half expected that the creature would, not content to cease its rampage until every last vestige of Anarsha's enemies had been destroyed.

The journey back to Shemar was arduous and seemed to take three times as long without a mech to eat up the distance. Desmond was tired and hungry by the time they arrived, the burns on his hands aching horribly.

But they were not alone. Their paths crossed with other survivors, lost and desperate to get away as they were. Only when they reached Shemar and an official tally could be conducted did the full extent of the Empire's loss become clear.

They had set out from both Elath and Shemar with thousands of men. And while Desmond did not know how many had managed to make it back to Elath, the number that returned to Shemar was sobering. Where once there had been thousands, by their best estimates, less than a hundred remained.

Never had the Empire suffered such a devastating loss. Never had they faced such a foe.

Never had Desmond felt so relieved to return to the Capitol, even though he would likely have to face his family. He no longer cared if they were disappointed in him; he was simply glad to put as much distance between him and that beast as he possibly could.

Let them say what they wanted. They hadn't seen what he had.

To Desmond's surprise, General Halsing sent word to him at the barracks, requesting that he accompany the general when he went to give his report at the palace. Desmond could think of no reason why the general would wish him to tag along—he was still a lowly mech pilot—but he had saved his life. Perhaps that counted for something.

Perhaps Halsing would recommend him for a promotion. The thought made Desmond's chest swell with pride, his pulse quicken. He might make the rank of officer yet.

Regardless of the reason, Desmond went where he was sent and he presented himself at the entrance to the palace, dressed in his uniform—a new one, pressed that morning, neither torn nor scorched.

There was no hiding the bandaging on his hands. They had blistered and were still quite tender, but the physician had been of the opinion that there would be no scarring, no permanent damage. He knew he should be grateful to even still have hands, but he'd felt disproportionately relieved at the news.

Silently, he trailed after Halsing down the long corridors, until they arrived at the throne room. Trying to appear casual, Desmond glanced around, never having reason to set foot in such a chamber before.

No doubt Alaric had and now here Desmond was himself. The thought pleased him and he fought down a smirk. They were here to deliver dire news and such a smug countenance would not be appropriate.

The chamber was long, the floor marble, every sound echoing, amplified. Desmond copied Halsing, hanging back slightly, letting the general take the lead. When they reached the stairs that led up to the throne, Desmond knelt with the general.

Emperor Hadrian was seated on the throne, which looked as though it had been carved from marble. His mask was gone, much to Desmond's surprise. His silk robes were as elegant as ever, but in the mask's place was a face that was neither young nor old. If anything, it was rather plain-looking.

Desmond felt a quick stab of disappointment, that there was a face beneath the mask at all, and one so…ordinary. Without his mask and his robes, Hadrian looked like he could have been anyone. Like he could have passed Desmond on the street and he wouldn't have given the man a second glance.

It all made him seem less regal, less imposing, less worthy of being emperor, somehow.

Rising to his feet, Halsing wasted no time. "My lord, I have brought this soldier with me, as a witness to what occurred. I know what I am about to say will sound fanciful, but Your Highness is welcome to go to the Badlands yourself and see the proof of what happened there, if you so desire."

"What I desire," the emperor said, his words unhurried, "is to hear your account. I have heard much of rumor, but now I would have the truth."

Halsing dipped his head. "And you shall have it. I regret to report that the battle was a near total loss. It will take some time to rebuild our army, both human and mechanical."

Hadrian stroked one finger down the arm of his throne. "I thought the Anarshans were weakened. How, then, could they muster such a force?"

"They were weakened, my lord, and it would seem that weakness drove them to desperation. To seek aid from a foe that cannot be killed."

"And what foe might that be?"

Desmond couldn't understand why Halsing was prevaricating so much. Even he could sense the emperor's rising impatience and this was his first time meeting the man.

Then again, he supposed the return of a demon, something most Akkadians didn't even believe in, was no easy thing to explain. When he closed his eyes at night, he still saw the beast, towering over the battlefield, his tattered wings blotting out the sun.

Desmond suppressed a shiver. Was there anything more terrifying than an enemy who could not be killed? An enemy who was not supposed to exist and yet, the very fact that he did made Desmond question everything he thought he'd known.

Halsing swallowed and Desmond didn't envy the man. "A demon, my lord."

"A demon." The emperor's voice was dangerously flat.

"The Anarshans summoned it and set it upon our forces. I would not have believed it either, had I not witnessed it with my own eyes."

Hadrian turned his eyes on Desmond and he stiffened beneath the emperor's dark gaze. "And you, soldier. Did you see this demon?"

"I did, my lord." Desmond inclined his head. "Would that I had not."

"How is this possible?" the emperor asked, turning his focus back on his general. "How could the Anarshans have summoned a demon back into the world?"

Back? Desmond frowned. It was always possible he was simply reading too much into things, but from the emperor's choice of words, it almost sounded like he wasn't all that surprised to learn of the demon. As though it wasn't the demon's existence that gave him pause, but the fact that the Anarshans had managed to summon one.

Had the emperor believed in their existence all along? Had he known something that Desmond had not?

"I don't know," Halsing replied.

"It begs the question," Hadrian hissed, "if Anarsha possessed the ability to summon such power and bind it to their will, why they did not decide to go on campaign and build an empire of their own. They are weak—always have been. But, now that they have seen what this demon can do, the idea may yet strike their fancy."

"You think the Anarshans will come here?" Desmond asked, forgetting for a moment to whom he spoke. He ducked his head quickly. "Your Majesty."

The thought that the Anarshans would march on his home—his city—horrified him. If they brought the demon, there would be nothing the Akkadians could do to stop them. They could lay waste to the entirety of Akkadia—and given what the Empire had done to them, Desmond wasn't entirely sure he could blame them. At least not honestly.

"It is a possibility," Hadrian replied. "Even a coward may find some courage, if he believes he cannot lose."

"But we can't let that happen!"

"No," the emperor agreed. "We can't. But our army is decimated. It will take time to rebuild. The Anarshans have dealt us a severe blow, one that will not be so easily shaken off."

"If there's anything I can do, name it, and I will see it done, if I can." Desmond spoke impulsively, and yet he meant the words.

Not only for his city, but he recognized the significance of the person seated before him. He might not get another chance to appear before the emperor, and he intended for the man to remember him.

The emperor's eyes narrowed. "What is your name, soldier?"

Desmond told him and saw the moment recognition flared in the emperor's eyes.

"Ah, yes. The Renaults. A noble line. You do your house credit."

"He is a fine soldier," Halsing added. "When others fled in the face of the demon, he ran back, to pull me from the wreckage of a burning mech." He turned to face Desmond. "I don't like owing a debt to anyone, but I owe him my life."

The emperor grunted. "Very brave indeed. A pity the same could not be said of you, Halsing."

The general tensed, turning back to the emperor. "My lord?"

"Yours is not the only report I heard. I have many sources. I've found that one will often tell me what the others do not, a trait that has proven to be most helpful over the years."

"I—don't understand, my lord. Everything I told you was true."

"Oh, I don't doubt that. It's what you do not say that I find more interesting. The fact remains that you ran. You fled, leaving your men scattered, disorganized, left to fend for themselves. Had you gathered but a little courage, you might have rallied them, given them some direction, and fewer lives might have been lost."

"Forgive me, Your Highness. It was a situation none of us were prepared for. We'd never seen its like."

"No, I imagine no one has for quite some time. And yet, this isn't the first instance you've failed me, general. Even before the Anarshans summoned their foul beast, you failed to deliver a victory, time and time again. Your poor leadership and ill-advised tactics cost us men, valuable resources, and time. Had you secured a victory, the Anarshans never would have had time to call upon a supernatural ally. And now, your incompetence may well have doomed us all."

Halsing's jaw tightened. "I was hardly acting alone out there on the battlefield. You know how battles are, my lord. They're chaotic, unpredictable. Even the most well-planned, well-executed strategy can fall short in the face of such volatile factors."

Given that the man had been singing his praises mere moments ago, Desmond couldn't help but feel charitably disposed toward Halsing.

"Yes," the emperor agreed. "I do know. And I also know that when you assume a position of leadership, everything—down to the smallest detail—is your fault. I'm afraid examples have to be made, from time to time. The honorable thing would have been to die on the battlefield with the soldiers you abandoned, not return home in disgrace. A misjudgment I intend to rectify."

"No," Halsing cried. "My lord, please!"

Hadrian ignored him, signaling to one of the guards standing watch along the wall. The man had stood so motionless, Desmond would have believed him to be a statue, but at the emperor's gesture, he came to life, moving with shocking speed.

In one fluid motion, the guard had ripped his sword free of its scabbard, burying the blade in Halsing's chest. The general had no time to reach for a weapon of his own, if he'd even had one. But he and Desmond both were unarmed, relieved of their weapons before being allowed into the emperor's presence.

The guard tore his blade free and stepped back into position. With a wet gurgle, Halsing slumped to the floor, a puddle of crimson spreading across the marble beneath him.

Desmond forced himself to remain still, to not react or show any kind of emotion. Inside, his mind reeled, his pulse racing. But outwardly, he stared at Halsing's body with a cool detachment, as though the turn of events shocked him not at all.

In a way, it didn't. The emperor had tolerated neither fools nor failure during his time on the battlefield, leading his own men in the quest for glory and empire.

"You don't seem surprised," Hadrian remarked.

"Any empire that coddles failure will not reign for long," Desmond replied.

The emperor nodded, as if pleased with his answer. Desmond certainly hoped he was. "You have a brother, if I'm not mistaken. Remind me of his name."

At the mention of Alaric, Desmond's heart sank. Why was the emperor interested in him? On the other hand, the fact that the emperor could not remember his brother's name pleased Desmond. Alaric would not be happy to learn he'd made so little impression on Hadrian.

"Alaric, my lord."

"Ah, yes, I remember now. He's apprenticed under the Minister of Defense. I've heard things about both of you. Good things."

Desmond couldn't fathom who had been talking to the emperor about him, but he was grateful to them all the same.

Perhaps his father had mentioned a thing or two. Hadrian might have expressed an interest in the son he had heard next to nothing about and, forced to talk about his second son, Desmond's father had decided to play the opportunity for all it was worth. It was likely something as simple as that.

Of course, that would be the one time his father had anything positive to say about him, but Desmond would take what he was given.

Hadrian was still speaking and Desmond quickly banished all thoughts of his father.

"You've shown great promise on the battlefield, which is more than I can say for some." He cast a disdainful glance at Halsing's corpse. The rattling sound of the general's breath had mercifully stopped. "Alas, with our army destroyed, we have little use for good soldiers at present. It will take time, far more than I'd like, to rebuild our forces. Anarsha has won a reprieve, but it will be only that."

The emperor tilted his head to the side, the movement oddly reminding Desmond of one of the mechs. "I'd hate to see such potential wasted. It could be years before we're ready to march again. But I have a proposal for you, if you're interested."

A proposal, from the emperor, personally. Desmond tried to quell his excitement, not wanting to appear too eager. Alaric would be consumed with envy if he only knew!

"A proposal, my lord?"

"You could become one of my Masks," the emperor replied. "I've recently found myself in need of a new one.

You have heard of them, I presume?" Without waiting for Desmond to answer, he continued on. "Masks are my bodyguards—or perhaps body doubles would be more accurate. When in public, there is no visible difference between them or me. Behind the mask, they could be anyone, but outwardly, they are identical to me in every respect. It is a position of great honor, I assure you."

A bodyguard to the emperor. It certainly sounded more impressive than a mere mech pilot. And, despite the inherent danger that every ruler faced, a lot safer, too.

"You're the right height and build," Hadrian went on. "The choice is entirely yours, of course, but as I said, I think a man of your talents would be wasted in the army."

Desmond bowed his head, eager to take on any position that would bring him closer to the most powerful man in the Empire. "I would be honored, my lord."

Hadrian spread his hands. "Wonderful." He gestured to an attendant, stationed along the far wall. "Show this young man to his new quarters. I'm sure that you'll find it to your liking and that you will have all that you require, but let me know if there's anything more you need. Once you've been shown to your rooms, you'll be fitted with new clothes, and given a mask, of course."

Dazed, Desmond thanked the emperor again and followed after the attendant, careful not to step in the pool of blood that had spilled across the floor. As the throne room faded behind him, he thought he heard the emperor giving more instructions to some other servant that the mess should be cleaned up.

Through the winding halls of the palace, Desmond trailed behind his escort until he came to an ornate door. He suppressed a gasp as he stepped inside, not wanting to appear like an overawed peasant.

And yet, he felt like one. He was no stranger to wealth—or hadn't thought so. His life had been one of privilege, his family powerful and influential. But he'd never seen anything like this.

It was, he realized almost at once, a replica of the emperor's own chambers. Of course. Even in this, the façade was maintained. The Masks must stay in a room like this, if they were to be convincing. They would need to make any potential intruder or assassin think that they were the emperor and it naturally followed that he would stay in a place like this.

The large room was divided into multiple sections. The sitting room contained richly upholstered furniture, thick carpet underfoot. The bed was large and canopied, the curtains tied back. The bedroom section alone was larger than Desmond's own room back home. He'd thought he'd known wealth, but only now was he beginning to understand just how great the divide was between the emperor and his family. There was even a pool of water nestled up against one wall, flowing continuously like a fountain, the noise soothing. A faint suggestion of steam rose from the running water. He could indulge in a bath whenever he wished, with no need to summon servants to heat the water.

Desmond turned his attention back to the doorway as more attendants arrived, to take his measurements. He had been to a tailor before and he endured their ministrations, the way they fussed over him, insisting that every measurement be precise.

By the time they finally left him alone, it was late, the light fading beyond the tall, thin windows. The sudden silence in the wake of their absence was startling, the only sound the stream of water.

Desmond sighed, still feeling a bit dazed by all that had happened. If only Alaric could see him now! He'd been offered a position at the palace, one that required him to essentially pretend to be the emperor himself. Short of ascending to the rank, which was impossible, Desmond felt he had risen as high as it was possible to go.

He smirked and walked over to one of the windows. There was no balcony to step out onto—he supposed that would be a security risk—but he stared down at the city below regardless. Here he was, on the highest tier in the entire Capitol, gazing down at the districts sprawling below him.

Satisfied, Desmond turned away from the window. He wanted to see if the bed was as soft as it looked—but first, he wanted to try the heated bath for himself.

<hr>

The next morning, his robes arrived, and Desmond couldn't help but wonder if the seamstresses had stayed up all night working on the garments. If so, he could find no evidence of haste, no flaw in the design. The silk slid over his skin like liquid. Never had he worn something so fine.

Every aspect of the emperor's wardrobe was now his to wear, even down to replicas of the man's rings. Desmond had no doubt the jewels were fake, but they glittered prettily enough when they caught the light. No one would ever know the difference.

Some of his enthusiasm faded when he turned to the last piece of his ensemble—the mask. It was surprisingly light, the metal cool against his skin, but the very feel of it bothered him. He was shocked by how well he could see through the eyes—from the outside, they appeared solid.

But he instantly despised it, even knowing how important it was, hating the feel of it pressing against his skin. He felt trapped somehow beneath it, the feel of it closing all around him. Even though he could breathe just fine, his mind refused to believe it.

One of the attendants who had come to assist him was a Mask himself. "You get used to it," he remarked, having noticed Desmond's discomfort.

And how long does that take? Desmond wondered, not sure if he wanted to get used to it. But that was the price of his new position. He was a Mask, and therefore he needed to wear one.

"What's your name?" Desmond asked.

He didn't really care, but there was something so inhuman about the masks. There were no facial expressions to rely upon to gauge someone's mood—only the inflection of their voice. It made him uncomfortable and he thought knowing the man's name might help.

The other Mask cocked his head. "We are Masks. We do not have names."

Saints, the way the man talked, even in casual conversation, was eerily reminiscent of the emperor. The tone of voice, the pitch, the inflection.

"We exist to serve the emperor, so we must become the emperor, in all things. Come, I will take you to meet the others. It is imperative you learn all you can about the emperor. His likes and dislikes, the way he speaks, the way he moves, even the way he thinks."

A sinking feeling settled in Desmond's gut, but he followed after the senior Mask, until he finally stopped before another door.

He hesitated and turned back to face Desmond before opening it. "A word of advice, Mask? Forget your old life. Forget who you used to be and what you used to know. You must be the emperor at all times. You must think and react the way he would. You must come to know him even better than you ever knew yourself. Your old life is gone, your old identity dead. You are the emperor now. The sooner you make peace with that, the easier it will be for you."

Desmond clenched his teeth, resentment rising within him, as he followed the other Mask. He was the emperor in name only, possessing no more power or influence than the man in front of him.

But he was nothing if not a quick study. He was observant and good at taking orders and he fell into his new role quickly, trying to enjoy it for what it was.

When he next stepped into the real emperor's presence, it was as a Mask, and not as himself. There, he stood beside the other two Masks. He'd learned that Hadrian always liked to have three bodyguards at a time.

He also learned that the Masks were addressed by their numbers rather than their names. He was no longer Desmond Renault, but simply Three. He'd never felt overly sentimental about his name, neither liking or disliking it one way or another, but something about the loss of his name, a part of himself, stung.

Three was little different from One or Two, nothing to distinguish them.

Desmond was reminded further than he could not tell anyone of his new position, for security reasons. Not even his own family. To them, it must be as though he were dead, at least to his old life.

He had not returned home before accompanying General Halsing to the palace. For all his family knew, he really had fallen in battle this time, hardly surprising given the extent of their losses.

Would there be a falsified report of his death or would he simply fade from the record altogether?

Desmond tried to convince himself that it was better this way, better that his family think he perished. And yet, he couldn't help the flash of resentment. He expected it to fade overtime, but instead, it festered and grew.

His life had never been his own, and now it felt less so than ever. He wished his family could have seen him. He wished his father would finally recognize his worth, to see something more in him than a superfluous second son. He wanted Alaric to be jealous of him, rather than the other way around.

What would they think of him now? He had finally attained a position arguably more important than that of his minister brother.

But it didn't feel that way. As the initial excitement wore off, Desmond began to regret accepting the position. But it was too late to back out now. He doubted he would be able to. He likely knew too much, about the emperor, to say nothing of the elaborate system of Masks. They could not trust him to keep such information to himself, should he choose to walk away.

And so he spent his days following the emperor around, with the other Masks, silently observing how he moved, how he spoke. Trailing him in council meetings, dealings with advisors, and watching—always watching—how he behaved in each situation.

In one meeting, Desmond fought down surprise at seeing Alaric, his brother having accompanied the Minister of Defense. He so badly wanted to call out to his brother, once the meeting had concluded. To pull him aside and reveal to him who he really was.

To see the shock spread across Alaric's face, the envy that was sure to follow.

But he could not speak to him, could not call out, could not reveal himself. And when his brother's gaze passed over him, almost without seeing him at all, he knew that Alaric had no idea that it was him beneath the mask.

The desire to call out to Alaric faded. Beneath the resentment and frustration, a new emotion emerged.

Strangely, the idea pleased Desmond.

PART IV:

THE

FALL

XXVI

Chandra continued her training, along with what remained of Anarsha's army following the attack, but the sense of urgency that had overshadowed their every move since the beginning was gone. Now, it felt as though they were all going through the motions, but nothing more.

Everyone seemed to be holding their breath, waiting to see if the Akkadians would return or if they were truly gone. After witnessing the demon lay waste to their army, Chandra didn't think they would come again. Even knowing how vindictive the Akkadians were and their determination to claim Anarsha, the final jewel in their crown, she couldn't see them trying again. There was surely no recovering from the blow they had been dealt.

As for the demon, there had been no sighting of him since the battle and Chandra couldn't help but wonder what had become of him. Was it still out there? Was it a greater threat to them now than the Empire?

She wished she could write to Roman, but it wasn't possible. Once again, she regretted ever suggesting the raid on Elath. But at least now, the conquered kingdoms could finally be freed.

Sheboleth was more deeply unsettled by the appearance of the demon, a sentiment shared among the dragons.

More than a few had left the barracks and hadn't returned. The place seemed empty and even larger without the sight of them. So far, Vitanni and Bane weren't among the dragons who had departed. Chandra couldn't imagine how she would feel if Sheboleth were to leave, a soldier without a dragon, and she didn't envy those who now found themselves without.

When she asked where the others had gone and why, Sheboleth replied that the dragons had left because of what Ulric had done. Summoning a demon back into the world, the very beasts dragons had once risked their lives to banish, was a line never to be crossed.

"But isn't it a good thing?" Chandra asked, trying to convince the dragon to see events in the same light she did.

"Ulric is a fool," Sheboleth argued.

"But it saved us. We only won because of it." Otherwise, Anarsha would already be under the Empire's control and all of them would likely be dead.

"Maybe," Sheboleth acknowledged. "For now. But at what cost?"

There wasn't a cost—at least not that Chandra could see—unless one counted the loss of some of the dragons. That was a blow, to be sure, but she couldn't see a cost for the rest of them.

But rumors and news from the rest of the kingdom inevitably found their way inside the barracks, and letters from Chandra's grandmother painted a more uncertain future.

It wasn't clear how many people recognized the demon for what it was, but from her letters, Chandra gleaned that the people were uneasy, waiting to see if the Empire would return, wondering if they were really gone. She supposed such reservations were only natural, after living in fear for so long.

Chandra waited, impatiently, expecting orders to arrive any day, instructing them to ride out to Elath or Shemar. Now was their chance to strike, while the Empire was weakened and still reeling. Now was their chance to liberate the other kingdoms. But no such orders ever came.

"I don't know why the king doesn't press his advantage," she griped to Sheboleth. "If the Empire's forces are all but destroyed, why not take the fight to them before they can recover? Why sit around and wait, allowing them time to try again?"

She still wasn't convinced that they would try again, but she didn't want to give them the chance.

She was reminded of the conversation she'd had with Roman, about not wanting to sit around and let the Empire call all the shots. That impetuousness had led to the disastrous raid on Elath, which she couldn't help but regret. But now they had an opportunity to do something real, something that would make a difference.

"Don't forget," Sheboleth reminded her, "we need time to lick our wounds, too. The last battle was costly for us."

"I'm not saying it would be easy, but wouldn't it be worth it?" Chandra asked. "Especially while we still have the demon? We could use it somehow."

There still had been no sign of the creature, but she had no reason to think it had been banished. To do so, and lose the one weapon that would guarantee them victory, would be extremely foolish on the king's part. Even more foolish than summoning the beast in the first place.

"No, it wouldn't be worth it," Sheboleth growled. "Such things never are."

"But if we do nothing, we're right back to where we used to be," Chandra protested.

She knew the Empire may have been defeated, but it wasn't destroyed. The Capitol still stood and there were still Akkadians in that city who drew breath, as well as Shemar and Elath.

They were like rodents, and if you didn't quash the infestation completely, they would only multiply, their numbers growing until they were a problem yet again.

"Do you think Akkadia will give up?" Chandra asked.

Could they trust that the Empire had learned its lesson and would leave Anarsha in peace? It wasn't a risk Chandra was personally willing to take. She didn't think she would ever feel safe again until the Empire was well and truly crushed.

"I don't know," Sheboleth admitted, a tinge of uncertainty in her voice. "If what they saw out there that day doesn't convince them not to come back, nothing will. Hopefully, they're ignorant of how such bargains work and will assume that we still have access to the demon's power if they should return."

Chandra turned to look at the dragon, the sun glinting off her black scales. "Why wouldn't we?"

Sheboleth flicked her tail. "I don't know what Ulric promised that beast in exchange for what he did, but he'd have to promise something more if he wants the demon to fight on our behalf again. I already shudder to think what he sacrificed initially. I don't know what he would have to pledge a second time, and I hope we don't have to find out."

On that, Chandra could agree.

Training continued, her life locked into an ordered routine, but there was no sign of Akkadia's continued aggression.

Slowly, Anarsha began to breathe a sigh of relief. But the rationing continued and within the rest of the city, things were worse. Chandra's grandmother wrote of increased prices whenever she went to the market, with fewer goods on offer each time.

The news only grew worse.

Roman's letters to Chandra were few and far between, but she appreciated him trying to keep her aware of the greater picture—even if the picture was bleak.

Anarsha's actions cost the Empire greatly and in turn, Akkadia responded by cracking down on the other kingdoms, demanding more in taxes from Shemar and Elath, and more materials to fund the rebuilding of their army.

In response, more refugees fled the other kingdoms, only to still be turned away at Anarsha's Great Wall. They could not afford to feed their own people, much less the refugees.

Chandra's chest ached as she read Roman's latest letter. So it was true. The Empire was attempting to rebuild their army. They hadn't given up. And if given the chance, they would be right back on Anarsha's doorstep one day. Meanwhile, just what was Anarsha doing to prepare for such a day?

Her grip tightened on the letter, trying to resist the urge to crumple it and hurl it off the side of the aerie. What was the king waiting for? Why did he not order them to attack?

Or did he intend to hold the demon in reserve, content to wait for the Empire to return, only to annihilate them once more? Chandra couldn't deny that the idea was an appealing one, but if Sheboleth spoke truth, Ulric would have to make a deal with the devil again. Would he run out of bargaining chips before the Empire ran out of men?

The Empire's aggression had ceased, for the time being, but the food shortages had not. They had solved one problem, which seemed at the time the most pressing, but ironically, the second problem was not one so easily remedied.

Just because the Empire was no longer attacking did not mean that trade would begin again. The other kingdoms remained under the Empire's thrall and needed to be liberated first.

Chandra sighed. Why was the king not implementing her idea, of raids on the Empire's own supplies in order to feed their people? If, for some reason, they couldn't liberate Elath or Shemar, that was the next best option.

Had Ulric dismissed the idea when Roman mentioned it to him? Had Roman even suggested it at all?

At last, Roman had been cleared, by both his father and the physicians, to attend council meetings again. Cynically, he suspected his father had used his injuries as an excuse to bar him from attendance. Though he didn't approve, Roman couldn't say he blamed him.

If he had been there that fateful day, he would never have allowed his father to go through with it. Summoning a demon! The Empire might have been evil, but they had brought something far worse into the world. And once that door was opened, it couldn't easily be shut again.

The saints would have been turning over in their graves. His father had undone everything they had struggled and suffered so much for.

Roman couldn't deny the demon's effectiveness. He couldn't deny that he'd been pleased at seeing the Empire brought low. Nor could he refute that his father seemed to have suffered no ill effects thus far.

Roman hadn't seen the demon since the day of the battle. He didn't know where it had gone—though it was too much to hope it had truly vanished—and he knew better than to ask his father about it. Whenever he dared ask, Ulric simply snapped at him, saying he had everything under control and that Roman had no faith in him.

It was hard to have faith after such a betrayal, of everything the Anarshans believed in, but Roman knew better than to say that either.

He did notice, however, that his father had taken to wearing the soul stone around his neck. Usually, he kept it out of sight, but Roman had glimpsed it during one of their arguments. No longer was it blue, but amber. Roman knew what that color meant, if the records were to be believed, and he could guess what his father had done.

That was a relief, at least. The demon could pose no physical threat to them. But even sealed away, he still remained in their world.

He failed to understand why his father didn't simply get rid of the thing. Just how much use would the demon be, sealed away in the stone?

Roman took a deep breath, pausing outside the door to the council chambers, exhausted by the walk down the long corridor. He needed a moment to compose himself before he stepped inside and met the gazes of the men responsible for bringing such evil into the world.

He could hear muffled voices from within and frowned. Had they already started? He shoved the door open and strode in. Lord Silva was saying something, but he trailed off as Roman entered.

The room turned quiet, the silence oppressive. Roman flushed as every tap of his cane against the hard floor was amplified a hundredfold, feeling every eye on him. He'd thought himself immune to such things by now. He was used to being the center of attention, to being stared at, for all the wrong reasons. *The crippled prince.* People liked to stare, whether they realized it or not.

"How good of you to join us, Your Highness," Vaughan remarked.

"My apologies. Do continue," Roman huffed, hating how breathless he sounded. But he'd pushed himself hard to get there—and still hadn't been fast enough.

Had they not wanted to wait for him?

"We were discussing the rationing," Lord Daladier said.

Roman gave the quiet councilor a grateful nod.

"What can we do?" Salerno asked. "We can only hunt and produce so much food ourselves."

"As callous as it may be to point out, with no more soldiers being killed in the conflict with the Empire, those are just that many more mouths we need to feed," Vaughan remarked.

Roman shot the man an incredulous look, quickly schooling his features, but the man had seen. Was he serious? Those very soldiers had stood between him and the Empire and without them, they would be just another vassal state and Vaughan would likely be dead.

"With the threat of Akkadia gone, I would think it's no longer imperative that we maintain such a robust, healthy military force," Salerno agreed. "We should slash the rations again. It's the only way."

"It might also help if we reduce their ranks. After all, such numbers are no longer needed, and I understand many of the dragons have already departed," Vaughan added.

Roman began to wonder if the man's personal portion sizes were starting to feel the effect of the rationing. Was that why he protested so much?

"Before we do anything rash," he called out, leaning on his cane as he stood, "I have a proposal to make."

He sensed his father's gaze out of the corner of his eye. Chandra's idea about the raids had been a good one and he knew how much she believed in it. How much she'd meant it when she'd made the offer. And if the other councilors were seriously considering such drastic actions, they should consider her suggestion first.

"I think we should consider sanctioning raids upon both Elath and Shemar, as well as supply shipments coming to those kingdoms from the Capitol."

Salerno raised an eyebrow. "You would risk angering Akkadia further?"

Saints above, could these people not make up their minds? One minute, the Empire was still a threat, the other, none at all.

Roman exhaled slowly through his nose. "As you so astutely pointed out, councilor, the Empire is no longer a threat to us. But they do have what we need. If trade is not an option and we can't produce enough on our own, I say we take it. I have it on good authority that there are soldiers willing to take such risks. And that means we can't slash their ranks just yet. With their dragons, they are still invaluable to us and they can get the food our people need."

Roman could feel Ulric's gaze burning against his skin, no doubt wondering how he knew there were soldiers willing to go on such raids, and perhaps even wondering if there was any connection to the Elath raid.

Well, let him wonder. He's not the only one who can keep secrets.

Lord Silva raised his hands. "I say, why not? What do we have to lose? The Empire is hardly in a position to stop us. If they have what we need—and we know they do—why let them keep it? We must do something, and it's a better idea than any I've heard thus far."

"Very well," Vaughan said, surprising Roman. "You have my support. But I still think we should increase rationing in the meantime, until these raids can get underway and prove to be successful. Since the army is still so useful, as the prince pointed out, the rationing will be harsher for the civilians and slightly less for the soldiers."

To Roman's disappointment, there were no objections, but he had gotten what he wanted and he supposed he should be grateful for that much. It made sense that stricter rationing might be needed until the raids bore fruit.

Ulric nodded. "As for reducing the ranks, let's not go that far yet. If discontent continues to grow, I fear the dissenters may not stop at mere talk. We must keep in mind that we may need the army to corral our own populace soon enough, to maintain order."

Roman stared at his father. Surely he hadn't suggested that they would turn the army on their own people?

He heard things, of course, though not nearly as much as he would like. He knew that, even with the threat of the Empire gone, things were far from perfect beyond the palace walls. He hadn't thought they were so dire that the army would need to be called in.

"Surely you don't think it will come to that?" he asked.

"We need to be prepared, that's all I'm saying," Ulric replied, shaking his head. "Just in case."

The other councilors began to speak up, no doubt with thoughts of their own, but Roman no longer heard them. He was still stunned that his father had brought up the idea at all, his ears ringing. Had things really devolved so far?

Would Anarsha's people—his people—truly rise up against them, to the point of inciting violence?

Yes, they will.

The voice, deep and lulling, whispered across Roman's mind like silk. He froze, completely lost to the conversations around him.

He had never heard the creature speak, and yet he had no doubt who the voice belonged to. His gaze cut to his father, to where he knew the soul stone rested just beneath his robes.

It was not his own fears he heard, but the voice of the demon in his head.

XXVII

When news of the raids made its way through the barracks, speculation running rampant, Chandra knew Roman had come through, as he'd promised. He must have found some way of convincing his father and whether her name was brought up or not, she was one of the soldiers chosen by Khan to carry out the raids. As was Anake, though Chandra suspected the Elathan had volunteered so staunchly that no one dared tell her no.

"Just like old times, eh?" Anake joked, as they saddled up the day following the announcement.

Chandra nodded, tightening the straps on her leathers. Everything had felt like it was moving too slow and now, things were happening too quickly. This was really happening. They were going to strike back at the Empire and take what they needed to help their people.

Though some part of Chandra wanted the Empire to know exactly what they had done—and feel powerless to stop it—stealth was the favored approach. They were to get in, grab what they needed, and get out, preferably without engaging or being seen.

As Khan had put it during their briefing, "We do this right, and they won't know anyone has ever been there at all, at least until it's far too late to do anything about it."

Their first target was to be the docks of Elath and the warehouses along them. Chandra had impatiently waited all day for the sun to begin to set. By the time they reached the city, darkness would have completely fallen, providing the necessary cover.

Impatience warred within her, barely contained. She wanted to make the raid a success, to show Roman and the king that they had made the right decision in trusting her plan.

And, if they could pull it off, it would go a long way toward feeding starving Anarshans.

But Chandra knew, even as they set out, that they would need far more if they were to make a big enough difference that Anarsha could once again help the refugees. And if they wanted to liberate Elath and Shemar, they must first help themselves.

Chandra took a deep breath as Sheboleth launched herself into the air. She had to remember to take things one step at a time, rather than get ahead of herself. Rather than staring down the barrel of every single thing that needed to be done, every hurdle still in her way.

It felt good to be flying again, outside of merely training, rising high above the forest canopy, miles of verdant green stretching out before them, bathed by the dying sun. She closed her eyes and leaned back in the saddle, letting the wind play through her hair. If she didn't think too hard about what they were about to do, she could almost relax.

Almost.

Never far away, her thoughts strayed back to Callum— and naturally, Gideon followed. She wished the two of them could have seen such a day, to be flying beside her. A day where the Empire was all but defeated, the victory they had fought so hard for no longer a dream.

She shook the unwelcome memories away. She was feeling far too pensive tonight, when she needed to be sharp for the task ahead.

As night fell and visibility dropped, the lights of Elath came twinkling into view. Chandra swallowed, hoping this visit would go more smoothly than the last time she was here. If they were spotted—

We won't be. Best to not even allow herself to think it.

With Victor in the lead, the dragons folded their wings, plummeting downward, Chandra grateful for Sheboleth's black scales, indistinguishable against the night sky.

As they dropped, Chandra studied what she could see of the city, comparing it to her memory of what it had looked like when they'd left. There were obvious repairs still underway, particularly the walkways that spanned across the water. But the amount of progress the Empire had made in such a short time was impressive.

With barely a sound, the small group of dragons alighted on the wooden dock, the massive shadows of the warehouses to their backs.

"Ten minutes," Victor hissed, already keeping an eye out.

Anake set to work picking the lock of the nearest warehouse and within seconds they were in. Chandra's pulse thrummed as she unbuckled herself from the saddle and stepped through the door, trailing after the others.

It took longer to find what they were looking for. Through their various spy networks, they knew this stretch of warehouses held goods awaiting transport back to the Capitol. Everything from lumber and weapons to fish, coal and iron.

Chandra glared at the latter as she passed, the wheeled carts already filled with ore, waiting. Materials to produce more of the wretched mechs.

Finally, in another section further down, they found what they came for. Along with the others, she stuffed as many of the food supplies as her pack would hold, the rest being carried out to the dragons, who could lift far more.

In minutes, it was done, though it felt more like hours had passed. Chandra expected at any moment to hear shouting ring out, the alarm raised, to signify that they had been spotted. But all remained quiet.

Still, she didn't allow herself to truly breathe until they had taken once more to the air, Sheboleth letting out a grunt of effort as she struggled to lift the weight of the supplies.

For a moment, Chandra feared it was too heavy for her. That she had gotten greedy and asked the dragon to carry too much, when she should have had the good sense to leave some of it behind. But the dragons were strong creatures and Sheboleth more stubborn than most. Slowly, they rose, clearing the treetops, the others behind.

A giddiness replaced Chandra's nerves. They had done it and it had been *easy*. Almost too easy.

Returning to the barracks, their small party was met with cheers. Chandra felt slightly dazed as she slipped from the saddle. It had all happened so quickly, and without the slightest hitch, she could scarcely believe it. But was that not the idea she had proposed to Roman?

Be swift or be killed. Get in, get out, as fast as possible. Unlike her raid on Elath, which had been intent solely on destruction, on inflicting as much damage on the Empire as possible, these raids had a clear goal in mind.

The officers took possession of the supplies they had stolen—mostly fish—for distribution. Where any of it ultimately ended up, Chandra didn't know, but it wasn't on her plate. Their own rationing continued, as harsh as ever, but Chandra didn't mind that evening in the mess hall.

Their reduced portions had never seemed like such a feast as they had that night, savored with a sense of satisfaction. They had done it. They had pulled off their first raid and proven it could be done. And not only that—it could bear fruit, or in this case, fish.

Surely, now, they would do it again.

Her suspicions were quickly proven correct, when Khan announced they had been ordered to conduct another raid. Each time one was announced, Chandra was among the first to volunteer.

With the Empire gone, or at least far from the threat it had been, this was her purpose now. This was the means by which she would strike back, help her people, and avenge Gideon and Callum at the same time.

Each time, the target was slightly different, but Chandra tackled every challenge with the same zeal she had assigned to training.

They attacked train shipments, larger ones, heading from the Capitol. They struck the docks at Elath and the warehouses along them. They even burned some of the Empire's fields, destroying their crops. If there was something they could not take, they destroyed it, each blow weakening an already frail Akkadia.

And yet, it wasn't enough. Chandra wanted the Empire crushed beneath her boot. She wanted to watch them squirm.

The satisfaction the raids brought, however, was short-lived. Chandra had known better than to expect to see immediate results from the raids they went on, but she thought they would begin to see some improvement, at least, even if small.

Small, but steady, progress was better than no progress at all.

But for all their efforts, it didn't seem to make the slightest bit of difference. Roman still sent her letters, keeping her informed of the climate beyond the palace and complex walls. He praised her efforts and encouraged her to keep going, but his optimism was lost amidst the reality contained in his other reports.

Unrest still grew within Anarsha. The food shortage seemed no better than it had been before. Chandra's grandmother confirmed such news in her own letters. The people were increasingly frustrated. They were hungry, but there was no increase in food.

How could that be? Chandra had written to her grandmother in confusion after one such letter, telling her about the raids and the efforts they were making, trying to assure her that she would see improvement soon.

Her grandmother had simply replied that if the raids were working as intended, she saw no evidence of it thus far.

"I don't understand," Chandra said to Sheboleth. There had been no raid that day and the two of them were resting—or trying to.

Chandra felt too pent up to rest. She paced along the wall, despite Sheboleth's remark that she would wear a hole in it.

"Are we just not bringing in as much as we think we are?" she added. "Where are all the supplies going if not to the people who need them?"

"I don't know," Sheboleth murmured. "But something tells me we wouldn't like the answer…"

Chandra scowled. *That's it.* She was tired of being kept in the dark, tired of the lack of progress, of nothing being done or getting better.

"I'm writing to Roman," she announced. The risks be damned.

"Are you sure that's wise?"

"If they haven't figured out my involvement in the Elath raid and punished me for it yet, they're not going to," she said, with slightly more confidence than she felt.

But in exchange for answers, she would take any risk.

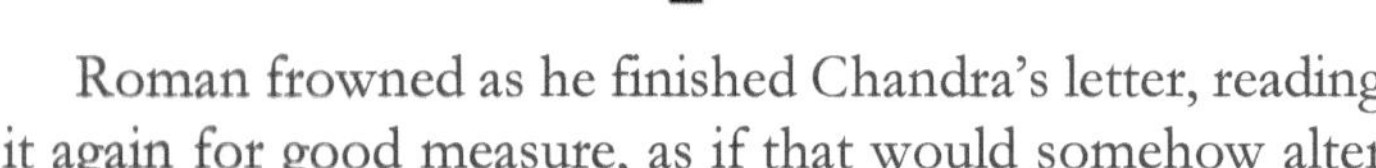

Roman frowned as he finished Chandra's letter, reading it again for good measure, as if that would somehow alter its contents.

Everything he had heard about the raids would indicate that they were a success. So why, then, was there nothing to show for it?

The weight that had settled on his chest seemed heavier. It had rested there ever since the day the demon had spoken to him in the council room. The creature hadn't whispered to him since, thank the saints, and Roman could almost convince himself he had imagined the whole thing.

But if the demon spoke to him, who else might it speak to? Did it whisper its poison to his father as well? What unspeakable things might it have told him?

He'd known, from the moment he heard the demon's voice in his head and recognized it for what it was, what must be done, but he'd yet to find the courage to do it. No more. Chandra's letter gave him the perfect reason to approach his father and then, he would find some way of broaching the subject.

It would be so much easier to mention once the conversation had already begun, than to try and bring it up first thing. He was under no illusions that his father would be pleased with the idea. But he had already waited long enough. This must be done. The sooner the better.

Roman needed to sever whatever hold the demon had on his father. He'd barely seen Ulric since that day in the council chamber, when he'd given permission for the raids to go forward. The king had retreated to his own chambers, rarely leaving them. But it wasn't his own company that he was enjoying, Roman feared, but that of the demon.

Even sealed away, the beast was a threat, perhaps a more insidious one. In his physical form, it was easy to be afraid, to see the demon for the danger he was. But sealed away in a soul stone, the demon gave every illusion of being harmless enough, when he was anything but.

No, the soul stone must be destroyed. Only then would Anarsha be safe, free of the creature's corrupting influence.

Before he could allow himself to hesitate and come up with all manner of excuses as to why the confrontation could wait, Roman pushed open the door to the library, the only place aside from his room where his father spent most of his time these days.

The heavy drapes were pulled across the windows, blocking the sunlight. The only light that suffused the room came from a handful of candles. For some reason, the sight of them made Roman think of Chandra and his chest tightened.

Between the thick, cloying scent of the candles and the dim lighting, the room felt constricting, far too small. It was also impossible to tell what time of day it was beyond the library's walls. How long had his father been in here like this?

Ulric sat at one of the tables, head bowed, furiously scribbling away on a piece of parchment. From his vantage point, Roman couldn't read the text, but whatever Ulric wrote there, it commanded his full attention. The king wrote like a man possessed, as though he might forget the words if he didn't get them out fast enough. In some places, the ink smeared or blotted, but Ulric hardly seemed to notice in his haste.

Roman closed the door behind him, not wishing for their conversation to be overheard, even though he would have been grateful for the fresh air and a bit more light.

He waited for his father to look up, but if Ulric noticed his son's interruption, he gave no sign.

Roman cleared his throat. "Father, I wanted to speak to you about the raids."

Ulric looked up, blinking in confusion. Then his expression cleared, his eyes brightening, the writing forgotten. "It was a good idea. I'm glad you suggested it. They've been a success."

It was Chandra's idea, not mine.

Roman took a deep breath. "That's why I wanted to talk to you. Where are the recovered supplies being distributed?"

Ulric made a dismissive gesture with one hand. "That's up to the officers. They handle it all."

Roman frowned. "But they answer to you, Father. You must know what they do with them."

"I believe they're sent all over." Ulric shrugged. "Why do you ask?"

"I've heard some interesting things. It would seem that none of the supplies are making their way to the people who need them most. I'd like to know where, in fact, they are going. *Who* they are going to."

His father did not answer. Slowly, Ulric rose to his feet and turned his back on Roman, walking over to the shuttered window.

And that was an answer, in and of itself.

Disappointment settled in Roman's stomach, adding to the weight he already carried.

"So my source was correct. The supplies aren't going to feed the people."

"They're not bringing in enough!" Ulric whirled to face him. "What would you have me do? I must think of the council. The nobles. If they are unsatisfied, they could see me deposed!"

"Do you care about clinging to power more than you care about our people?" Roman demanded.

Of course, the food was going to feed the wealthy, those who had never done without and couldn't bear to do so now.

Roman knew of the existence of corruption, of course, but it had always seemed like a vague, abstract notion. Not something that touched his life. He'd never seen it so blatantly alive and well within Anarsha. And by the hand of his own father, no less!

"I thought better of you," he added, not bothering to hide his disdain. Let his father know what he really thought of him, this man he had become. "Then again, these days I hardly recognize you."

"The only way I can help our people is by staying in power. Don't you see?" Ulric pleaded. "Would you really place such an important task in the hands of the council? You've seen for yourself how feckless they are!"

That much was true and Roman shuddered to think what would happen if a man like Lord Vaughan were to gain power. Then again, Vaughan was likely benefiting the most from the new arrangement with the raids. Roman knew the man had various appetites that he liked to cater to. And as a member of the council, he was perfectly placed to ensure that such bounty never ran out.

Roman's lip curled. The council had initially been put in place to curtail the king's individual power, ensuring he could do nothing without approval from a panel of advisors. The ultimate purpose behind the idea was to prevent the kind of rule that dictated the Empire.

But whether one man was corrupt or an entire council mattered little to Roman. He failed to see the difference between the two. Corruption was corruption. A festering rot.

"Fine," he sighed, willing to concede the point, knowing he had a far more important one to argue. "If you won't confront the council about this, there's something else you must do."

Ulric looked slightly hopeful at the prospect of being handed an out. "And that is?"

Roman hardened his features. There would be no compromise. Not for this.

"The soul stone. You must destroy it."

The king flinched as if Roman had physically struck him, recoiling. "Destroy it?"

"Yes—"

"You would destroy Anarsha's greatest weapon?"

"The demon is sealed, Father. He can no longer rise up and defend us again should the Empire return. He did what you summoned him for. Now is the time to dismiss him."

Ulric reached up, cradling the amber stone in his hands. "That's where you're wrong. To have such power at our disposal..."

He gazed down at the stone lovingly, with such naked adoration in his eyes that Roman felt disgusted for having witnessed it.

His anger surged. Who was this shell of a man, who looked like he hadn't bathed or changed his clothes in days? Who was this man who wore the guise of his father, but would sanction such blatant corruption, all in the name of saving his own neck, at least politically?

Roman had never thought of his father as a man who lusted after power. If anything, the crown had always seemed more like a burden to him, something he would have gladly set aside if he were able and he thought it the right thing to do.

He couldn't picture the man standing before him now ever doing such a thing.

"Can you not see that his words are poison?" Roman cried. "Whatever lies he's told you, don't listen! Don't you think the demon would say whatever he thinks you want to hear, in order to avoid being cast back into the abyss?"

Ulric opened his mouth to reply, but then froze. His head cocked to one side, as though he were listening to something only he could hear.

Roman's blood ran cold. The demon. He was certain of it. The demon was speaking to his father.

And his father was listening.

Irrationally, he wanted to shout, to stamp his feet, to demand the demon leave, to not interfere in their conversation. But he had neither the ability nor the authority to do that. If his father wanted to listen to the demon, he would, and there was nothing Roman could do to stop him.

"No," Ulric said at last. "The stone remains. When you are king, you can do as you see fit, and not a moment before. That is my final word on the matter."

"What's happened to you? Do you even hear yourself? Do you see what you've become?"

Rage erupted across Ulric's features, where only moments before there had been none. The suddenness of it all was as shocking as the outburst that followed.

"Get out!" Ulric roared, pointing to the door. "Leave me! I will not speak of it again!"

Roman winced, backing toward the door, grateful when he had shut it behind him, placing it between him and his father—and the beast within.

He hadn't gotten what he'd wanted, and yet, he was grateful for the conversation to be over. He leaned against the door, breathing hard.

He would try again later, when his father was in a better mood. Perhaps he could engineer some way to separate his father from the soul stone and then, he could convince him to see reason without the demon butting in.

Yes, he could fix this. There was still time. And if he could, he would use his influence to see that the supplies went where they ought.

He could step into the role of king, at least in so far as it was needed. Just until his father came back to himself. After all, he'd been training for this his whole life.

He would write to Chandra. He wouldn't tell her what he'd learned; it would be too damning if word got out. But he would assure her that he would do all he could.

If he were honest with himself, as disappointing as it was to see the change in his father, he was surprised that Ulric was even still alive. Roman didn't have much experience with how demon pacts worked, but when his father had first told him the news, Roman had feared for his life, thinking that the demon would claim it the moment the terms of the bargain were fulfilled.

Perhaps his soul remained damned, but for now, he still lived.

You thought I would kill him? The voice brushed against Roman's mind, slick and smooth like oil, laced with amusement. *Foolish boy. There is more than one way to die.*

XXVIII

Despite Roman's assurances that he would do everything in his power to see to it that the recovered supplies reached the right people, Chandra saw no improvement in the coming weeks. Her grandmother's letters were increasingly dour. Chandra volunteered for ever more raids, knowing that with every additional attempt, their chances of success decreased.

Eventually, the Empire would catch on and take whatever steps they must in order to stop the raids. Eventually, when they next left, they might not come back.

No longer were the raids confined to the dark, as they took on increasingly risky targets in their desperation. How much longer could the people afford to wait? How much longer until they started to see results?

They targeted a train during one raid, knowing the timetables through their spies—and the locations of the tracks, snaking through the forest, but always on the outskirts, as if afraid to venture further in.

But when the dragons dove down, tearing open the compartments with their claws, the shriek of metal rending the air, there were no supplies on board.

Furiously, Sheboleth and Vitanni scorched the train, wanting to leave nothing for the Empire to salvage.

That failure haunted Chandra for days afterward, keeping sleep at bay. She took to walking the grounds again, a habit she thought she'd left behind when the Empire fell.

She knew she should be trying to sleep. Another raid loomed before her, scheduled for the following day. Or was it today? Had midnight come and gone? If the bells had tolled, she hadn't heard them.

Few of the raids had yet targeted Shemar. The kingdom was the most recently conquered and it stood to reason that the Empire would have more troops stationed there than in Elath. But the time had finally come to try their hand and Chandra was more than willing to lead the effort personally.

So long as I don't screw up again…

She couldn't afford to get too greedy, to push too far, as she had in Elath. She was relying on the fact that she had learned her lesson the hard way—and the fact that Sheboleth would be there with her—to keep out of trouble.

Chandra paused along the parapet, snapped out of her musings by movement down below. She turned to get a better look, squinting against the darkness. An outbuilding stood just below the parapet she stood on and several uniformed men were gathered around the entrance, where crates and barrels had been loaded onto a wagon, pulled by a single horse.

As she watched, a few more men emerged from within the building, carrying more sacks and crates.

Without quite knowing why, she crouched down, peering along the wall. There were no guards within sight and she was between the lit braziers. There was no moon that night, helping to conceal her presence. Her nightly strolls didn't break any rules, but for some reason, she felt as though she were witnessing something she shouldn't see.

Cautiously, she peered over the edge of the parapet.

"Is that the last of it?" a male voice asked.

"Finally," a second voice grunted. "Saints' blood, this stuff is heavy."

"Come on, then."

There was a rustling sound as a tarpaulin was pulled over the wagon's contents. A moment later, the horse strode forward, the wagon's wheels creaking softly.

Chandra watched them pull away, standing slowly, her pulse thrumming. There was no chance of sleep now; she was wide awake, stunned by what she had just seen.

It was dark. She could have been mistaken. But Chandra discarded each excuse as quickly as it came, certain of what she had seen. These were the supplies from the last successful raid, before the train incident. She was sure of it.

What were these men doing, gathering them in the middle of the night? And where were they taking them?

Shaken from her reverie, Chandra bolted back the way she'd come, up the many stairs toward the aerie. She passed a few guards on her way, but none of them questioned her. They didn't ask what she might have seen or what she was doing out so late, no doubt used to her strange routine by now.

Her lungs burned by the time she reached the top. Never had she mounted so many stairs so quickly and for a long moment, all she could do was gasp, bent over, breath heaving.

A dark shape stirred, luminous green eyes taking her in. "Chandra?"

"They're moving the supplies," she panted. "We have to follow them—see where they go. Hurry, they'll have left by now!"

Sheboleth frowned, but to her credit, she didn't ask any questions. Chandra suspected, as she scrambled up onto the dragon's back, that those would come later. Clenching her thighs to Sheboleth's sides, her frills gripped in both hands, Chandra sucked in a sharp breath as the dragon leapt from the side of the aerie. She had no saddle, no straps, but there was no time.

"What am I looking for?" Sheboleth asked, her wings angled as she circled around the compound.

Briefly, Chandra described what she'd seen of the men and the covered wagon. She didn't think it would be that hard to find—how many horse-drawn wagons were on the streets at this time of night? And if the supplies weighed as much as the one man had claimed, they surely couldn't have gone far.

The wind tore at her unbound hair. Chandra cursed softly as she leaned to the side, trying to make out the street below, but all was darkness and she saw no sign of her quarry. Hopefully, though, the dark would help hide the two of them, should anyone glance up as they passed overhead.

"Are you sure of what you saw?" Sheboleth asked.

"As sure as I can be," Chandra replied. "What else could they have been doing?"

Sheboleth didn't answer, her eyes far better, picking out what Chandra could not. "There. Just ahead."

Silently, her wings stilled. They dared not sink any lower, but Chandra could make out the wagon now, trudging along. It was headed up the street toward the palace and the mansions that surrounded it.

Neither of them spoke, Sheboleth circling around as they observed the wagon's progress. Finally, it stopped outside one of the mansions, one of the men unloading a sack or crate and carrying it around to the servant's entrance. Someone must have known to expect them, because Chandra could glimpse a light on in the kitchen when the back door was opened, a maid or footman standing in the doorway to receive the delivery.

Then the wagon left the mansions behind, trundling the rest of the way up to the palace. The palace kitchens were larger, but functioned much the same way. Chandra wasn't the least bit surprised as she watched the rest of the supplies, the largest delivery by far, deposited to the kitchen entrance.

"Well," Sheboleth said flatly. "Now we know."

The men turned, leading the horse and the much-lighter wagon back the way they had come, no doubt intending to return to the barracks.

"Let's go," Chandra muttered. "Before they get back."

She slid to the ground the moment Sheboleth alighted nimbly atop the aerie. The sensation of solid ground beneath her feet should have come as a relief after being up in the air with no saddle, but the ground didn't feel solid at all. It felt like the earth had shifted beneath her, no longer reliable, not to be trusted.

Her body felt oddly weightless, as though she might float away or pitch over the edge at any moment.

"So," she ground out, "that's where all the supplies have been going. To feed the wealthy. *This*—" she flung out a hand in disgust— "is what we've been risking our lives for?"

"Are you really surprised?" Sheboleth asked.

And Chandra found she wasn't. That, perhaps, was the most disappointing of all.

"No," she sighed, her hand falling back to her side. She sank down, the stone floor hard against her knees. "What's even the point? Why go to Shemar tomorrow? And here I thought we could make a difference..."

"We *are* making a difference."

"For who?" Chandra shouted, not caring who might hear. "For some rich bastard who can't be bothered to give a damn?"

"Maybe some of the other supplies made it to where they were supposed to go," Sheboleth suggested.

"You don't really believe that." Chandra huffed. "That *is* where they're supposed to go."

"What's the alternative? Do nothing?"

"I don't know."

Sheboleth laid down, shuffling to get comfortable. Chandra joined her, the dragon's warmth against her back.

"Do you think Roman knew?" Chandra asked after a moment. She wasn't sure she wanted to know the answer.

"I don't know."

Chandra sighed. Even if Roman knew, he was likely as helpless to do anything as the two of them. He wasn't in charge—his father and the council were. The council, who had rooms at the palace and friends who lived in the mansions surrounding it. The king, who had summoned a demon back into the world.

Dawn broke over the city and Chandra hurried back to the barracks. For the first time since she'd suggested the idea, she no longer looked forward to the raids. It wasn't a chance to strike back at the Empire. It wasn't even a chance to help her people. It was performative, to make them feel like they were doing something, making a difference. Nothing more.

But she had volunteered for Shemar and so she would go. She would go where she was sent, do what she was told. But she would not volunteer again.

They saw the mines before they reached the city itself. Since the mission was already risky enough, they approached as dusk fell, the light fading from the sky. But not so much that they couldn't see the open pits yawning below, ugly scars upon the earth. Evidence of the Empire's insatiable appetite.

Chandra frowned down at the mines below, the wind tugging at her braid, wondering what they could all possibly be for. No doubt to satisfy the endless demand for raw materials to build their damnable mechs.

Then the mines were behind them, the city of spires ahead. Shemar sprawled out below them like a jagged mountain range, the tall towers stabbing toward the sky. It was beautiful in an austere sort of way.

As they flew over the streets, Chandra glimpsed a few mechs patrolling and hissed out a breath. The sight of the machines, that any of them had survived, boiled her blood.

Their target was a series of warehouses near the center of town, theoretically well protected—at least against anyone not on the back of a dragon. The buildings housed grain and corn from the farms outside of the Capitol.

Sheboleth had expressed concern before they'd left about how far in they would need to go, but Chandra shook the thoughts away for now. She already had more than enough to think about, after last night's revelation. Hard enough to venture into the city knowing that only the wealthy would see the fruits of this night's efforts.

She wished she had known before volunteering to lead the mission. To back down would be to invite uncomfortable questions—and it was too late now.

The warehouses were tall, with multiple levels, so at least they could land on one of the walkways and avoid the street. The mechs weren't likely to glance up and spot them. They wouldn't see what they weren't looking for.

Sheboleth's claws clanked against the metal as she alighted, Anake and Victor following.

"Look," the dragon hissed, jerking her snout.

Chandra followed the gesture. Two lookout towers were positioned on either side of the warehouses, standing even taller than the building they had landed on. And at the very top of each stood a ballista, its metal bolt shining dully in the watery moonlight.

Chandra's blood ran cold at the sight of the machines, her earlier anger leaching away.

"They're not manned," she whispered back. She could see no guards posted atop either tower. They had time to do this, if they were quick.

Sheboleth snorted. "Hurry, then."

Chandra slid from the saddle, dread coiling around her stomach. She couldn't shake off the warning, telling her that it wasn't worth the risk, knowing how little they would get out of it. She glanced at her companions, wondering if they would have come if they knew what she did now.

Anake was already attempting to pick the lock on the door, but from her muttered curses and the minutes ticking by, these particular locks were giving her trouble.

"We could always smash the door," Victor suggested helpfully.

"And draw every eye in the place," Sheboleth retorted.

At the moment, no one knew they were here, but that could change in a heartbeat.

"Got it!" Anake said, her voice breathy.

Silently, she slid the padlock free and Victor helped her push the door open. Chandra stepped forward, her gaze raised, taking in the contents of the room. There were shelves and racks, many times taller than her, stretching away into the darkness. She squinted. It was hard to tell in the blackened interior, but there didn't appear to be anything on them. Maybe further in?

She took another step. Her boot connected with something, meeting the slightest resistance, before it gave way suddenly.

"What the—" Her gaze snapped down just in time to see the wire she had dislodged.

A piercing wail rang out, the sound unlike anything she had ever heard, and she clapped her hands over her ears.

"What is that?"

"Time to go!" Sheboleth called, as the first ballista shot fired.

The three of them ran back out onto the walkway. A bolt from one of the ballistae embedded itself at Sheboleth's feet, puncturing through the metal. Chandra fumbled with the straps, but the adrenaline was on her now, rendering her fingers useless.

Sheboleth darted a quick glance at the room they had been forced to abandon. Chandra let out a cry as the dragon sprang forward, leaping off the walkway. Not yet strapped in, she clutched tightly to the dragon's frills.

She screamed as the warehouse exploded behind them, the force throwing her from the saddle. Sheboleth was already leaping toward the ground, wings slightly outstretched to slow their fall, but Chandra still struck the ground hard, a flash of white dancing across her vision.

For a moment, she lay there, dazed. Chunks of wood rained down around her, remnants of the destroyed warehouse. Dimly, she could still hear the ballistae firing over the ringing in her ears. She tensed, expecting one of the massive bolts to pierce through her body. If it could punch through a dragon's scales, she shuddered to think what it would do to a human.

A large black form hovered over her, materializing out of the smoke. Sheboleth, her bright green eyes fixed on Chandra as she nudged her.

"Come on. We need to move." The dragon hesitated, then added, "*Can* you move?" As though the thought had just occurred to her that Chandra might have been seriously injured in the fall.

Her ears still rang, an incessant whine that curdled her stomach, and the world seemed to spin around her. What happened next, Chandra scarcely remembered, but she managed somehow to stand and scrambled up onto Sheboleth's back.

Every movement felt like she was submerged, fighting against the current. She secured a single strap before Sheboleth took off, but it would have to be enough. She slumped forward in the saddle, resting against the dragon's neck.

One last glance behind revealed the warehouse on fire, orange flames licking up its side, smoke still billowing into the air.

We got nothing, she thought. Nothing at all to show for their efforts. She had felt such rage at the empty train they had raided, but after what she learned, she found she couldn't summon much feeling at all.

Chandra closed her eyes and the sight was lost.

She came to hours later, in the infirmary, safely back at the barracks, Sheboleth resting beside her. It was impossible to tell what time of day it was now, but Chandra was immensely grateful to not be alone.

She winced as she moved. Her ribs ached where she'd landed on them. So did her hip. Her left wrist hurt most of all and she glanced down at the brace that now supported it.

"Broken?" she asked, voice rasping.

"Badly sprained," Sheboleth answered, "according to the nurse."

Chandra flexed the fingers on her other hand. "At least it's not my writing hand."

The dragon grunted. "You also have a concussion, and there was a scrape along your hairline that needed stitching. You're lucky that's all it was. We all are."

Chandra looked up. "The others?"

She hadn't seen Anake or Victor after the explosion. What if they hadn't made it out? What if they'd been caught too close to the blast?

"They're fine. An archer on one of the towers grazed Victor with an arrow, but I'm sure it'll be just another scar to add to his collection. Anake suffered some minor burns from the explosion, but otherwise, they're both fine."

Chandra breathed out a sigh of relief. "You knew, didn't you?" she asked softly. "You knew the explosion was about to go off."

Sheboleth nodded. "That's why I jumped. I figured gravity would get us away faster." Her gaze darkened. "I'm sorry that I let you fall."

"No," Chandra protested. "You saved me. Both of us."

"Of course I did," Sheboleth said brusquely. "You're my human, foolish creature that you are."

Chandra smiled, reaching out with one hand. A moment later, Sheboleth shifted slightly, her scales brushing against Chandra's fingers.

Her smile faded. "Why did they rig the warehouse to explode? Were they really willing to destroy all those supplies in order to stop us?"

Sheboleth scowled. "Yes, although I suspect there may not have been any supplies at all."

Chandra thought back to the racks she'd glimpsed, appearing empty in the dark, but there hadn't been time to be sure. "A setup, then."

"We've not exactly been subtle lately. Our raids are ever-increasing in number. The Empire knows what we've done by now, and it was only a matter of time before they retaliate. And yes, I suspect the Empire would be willing to blow up an entire warehouse, full of food or not, in order to stop us. They knew we would be coming."

"How? Lucky guess or do you think we might have a spy in our midst?" Or was one of their own spies the traitor? Had they been fed false information to lure them out? Chandra swallowed. "Sheboleth…you don't think this was all because of what we saw the other night, do you?"

Had someone seen them and, fearful of what they might choose to do with such information, tried to have them silenced? Saints, she really didn't trust anyone anymore.

Chandra shuddered at the memory of the explosion erupting behind her. She could still feel the force of it slamming against her, the air rushing past her face as she hurtled toward the ground.

"I doubt it. There wasn't enough time and a trap like that requires careful planning. It was a guess, I'd say," Sheboleth said, finally answering her question. "Educated, though, rather than lucky."

"That was close," Chandra whispered. "*We* were lucky." She closed her eyes. "We should have left when we saw the siege weapons."

They hadn't been manned and she hadn't known to expect an ambush, but still, she knew the risks and just like in Elath, despite everything, she'd wanted to push forward anyway.

Because all they did was never enough. But what was the alternative? To do nothing?

Chandra was tired of feeling like she was running as fast as she could—not to catch up, but to avoid falling further behind. When would she ever feel like she could *breathe* again?

"You're doing it again," Sheboleth chided. "I can tell."

"Doing what?"

"Overthinking. Caught up in your own head."

Chandra gave a weak laugh. "Well, where else am I supposed to be?"

"Whatever it is, stop worrying about it. Get some rest. Anarsha will still be here. The world isn't going to end if you allow yourself a few moments to relax. This isn't all on you, you know."

Chandra felt tears prick the back of her eyes, her chest swelling with gratitude. "I know."

"Just making sure. Sometimes we need to be reminded every now and then."

XXIX

Chandra tried to take Sheboleth's advice and not think too much about what she couldn't control. After the disastrous raid, all other operations were temporarily halted. The outrage that she would have felt at such news only a short time ago was notably absent. The raids had been a farce from the beginning—what difference did it make now?

But while they waited to see if the temporary suspension would lift, no new supplies came in. She trusted that Roman was doing all he could on his end, but word continued to reach the barracks of the growing unrest beyond their walls.

Refugees, cast out from the city, railed at the gates, demanding to be let back in and given aid. Chandra heard rumors of refugees who had tried to force their way back in—only to meet with resistance.

Violence spilled outward, no longer contained to just the disgruntled refugees, Anarshan citizens perhaps inspired by their example. Roman wrote to her every other day, holding nothing back, for which she was grateful to him. He'd received increased reports of rising crime, refugees and Anarshans clashing.

The final straw came when a granary was targeted, the desperate, frustrated civilians attempting to raid the stores.

Orders came from the palace directly that the military was to respond and restore order, before any further damage was done.

Chandra's heart felt like a stone, lodged in her throat, as she mounted Sheboleth, longbow in hand. Her wrist had nearly healed, though there was some lingering pain. And still, there had been no news on the raids.

There were nights where she was half tempted to ask Anake and Victor if they wanted to go rogue, as they had in Elath, and try and make a difference on their own, if the army wasn't going to do anything.

"I don't like this," she murmured to Sheboleth.

"Keep calm," the dragon replied. "The slightest spark and this place is primed to blow."

Chandra shuddered, Sheboleth's words bringing to mind an image of the warehouse in Shemar exploding behind her.

Her sense of unease only grew as they reached the square, grateful that she wasn't the only dragon rider present. Powerful as dragons were, there was little they could do against their own people, and the crowd gathered before her looked angry enough to do something drastic.

Anger rid people of their inhibitions. It made them fearless, in the moment, and Chandra wasn't convinced they wouldn't be able to overpower a dragon, there were so many of them.

She gripped her longbow so hard she feared it would snap beneath the pressure. Spears flashed in the low light, carried by some of the other riders. In such close quarters, they were better suited than a bow.

Khan, atop a dragon of his own, called out, his voice carrying cold and clear over the crowd. "By decree of the king, you are ordered to disperse. Return to your homes."

"My son hasn't had anything to eat all week!" one woman cried. "I'm not leaving empty-handed. Not again!"

Another man nodded. "Where are all the supplies promised by your raids? We've yet to see anything from it!"

Chandra bit her lip, fighting down the sudden urge to tell them where the supplies had gone, to blurt out the truth, heedless of the consequences. They deserved to know the truth. Thankfully, she was saved from making such a decision.

"I'll tell you where it all went," someone else shouted. "Up there!" He pointed in the direction of the palace, unseen from here, but they all knew where it was. "Onto the tables of the wealthy, who couldn't give two shits about us!"

Chandra wondered whether the man had seen the proof for himself, as she had, or if he was merely guessing. It didn't make the words any less true.

"That's enough!" Khan barked. "Be on your way!"

"If the king really cared about the people, why hasn't he done anything? Now that the Empire is gone, he doesn't care about us anymore. There's nothing for the nobles to worry about now."

"We'd be better off under the Empire!" one woman shouted, the one whose son was going hungry.

Cold horror curled itself around Chandra's heart at the words. Only a short time ago, they would have been unthinkable. But from the nods and murmurs of assent traveling through the crowd, the woman wasn't the only one to think so.

"We'd be a vassal state!" one of the riders cried—Anake, Chandra thought.

"At least we'd be fed," the woman snapped. "The Empire treats the people it conquers better than our own king!"

"What does she know?" a man cried, pointing at Anake. "She's a saints-forsaken refugee. You need only look at her to see she's Elathan. But they've given her a dragon. She's one of their loyal dogs. I bet she never goes to bed hungry."

Vitanni let out a low snarl, lips peeling back from her teeth. That gave the crowd pause, a few taking nervous steps back.

But the hesitation lasted only a moment.

"See? Instead of helping, they've set their attack dogs on us."

"Damned dragons. They're no longer needed. Why do we keep them around?"

"That's where all the food is going! How much do you think it takes to feed just one of them?"

Chandra wanted to shout at them that most of the dragons had left after the demon appeared and hadn't come back. And without them, the Empire would have conquered Anarsha the first time they came marching.

"We don't need them anymore. We should be able to eat at least one."

More growls rang out at that.

"Enough!" Khan roared, spurring his dragon forward. With spears lowered, the riders advanced. If the crowd refused to disperse, they would be forced to move.

It happened in an instant. Chandra caught only a glimpse.

One of the men, refusing to move, pushed against a guard's spear. Chandra didn't see exactly what happened. Perhaps the man slipped, or the guard tried to prod him, but it ended with the man impaled on the end of the spear.

Screams rang out at the sight of blood, pooling on the cobblestones. And then, emboldened by a fresh wave of fury, the crowd seemed to surge forward.

Surrounded, pressed up against the crowd, one of the dragons lashed out, claws slashing through the air, a swath of the protestors cut down in an instant.

They could have been anyone. They could have been her neighbors. They could have lived along her street. They could have bought candles from her, once upon a time, in another life.

Tears pricked her vision. These were her people. The people they were supposed to be fighting so hard to save and protect, not strike down in the streets.

To think that things had grown so dire that people would wish for Akkadian rule over the freedom that had been so hard won. That so much blood had been spilled for.

What was it all for? What was *any* of it for, if they would now gladly throw it all away? What did Callum die for?

Chandra suspected that the answer, the horrible truth, was *nothing*.

Somehow, they managed to get the streets cleared. But blood had been spilled and there were those who would not be walking away from this day.

As Sheboleth turned to leave, Chandra heard Khan muttering something about implementing harsher curfews.

"Thank you," she whispered, laying a hand against Sheboleth's side. "For not firing on them."

She couldn't control what other dragons did—and if she were honest, she could no more control Sheboleth either—but she was pleased to see that her dragon was just as reluctant as she was to lift a hand against their own.

"The fools," Sheboleth muttered, but there was no rancor in her voice. "What do they think they're doing? The only thing they're going to accomplish is to make things more difficult for themselves."

"They're angry," Chandra said.

And if the fury simmering inside of them was anything like the rage she carried within herself, then what had happened today was no surprise. It had been inevitable.

Some of that anger, which had been so quiet lately, flared to life as she pondered some of what the protestors had said. She turned to look up, in the direction of the palace. They likely had no idea just how right they were.

"Saints damn them all."

Chandra turned, shaken from her musings. Anake had come up alongside her, atop Vitanni.

"Do they not understand what they're asking for?" she seethed. "Do they know what it means to become a vassal state of the Empire?" Her dark eyes blazed. "My kingdom fell to the Akkadians. To me, that's not some abstract idea. It's reality."

Chandra's heart sank. She could well imagine how hurtful it must have been for Anake, to see the people she fought for yearn for the fate that had befallen her native kingdom. Disrespectful didn't begin to describe it.

"I'm sorry, Anake," Chandra said, knowing how inadequate words were. They couldn't touch the pain.

Anake shook her head, her anger giving way to a kind of despair. "This keeps up, we might find ourselves a vassal state yet."

"No," Chandra said fiercely. "We won't allow it."

Anake let out a breath. "If the Empire ever does come back, I worry we won't have the strength left to resist at all."

And would the Anarshan people even want them to offer up any sort of resistance? Or would they welcome the Empire with open arms, viewing them as some sort of perverted savior?

The thought curdled Chandra's stomach, planting a seed of fear in her unlike any she had ever known.

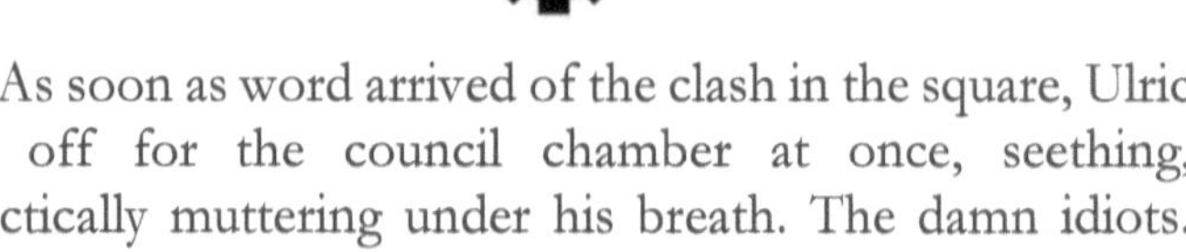

As soon as word arrived of the clash in the square, Ulric set off for the council chamber at once, seething, practically muttering under his breath. The damn idiots. They were supposed to quell the unrest in the square, not fan the flames.

And why couldn't the people be a little more patient? Did they not understand that such difficulties were not solved overnight? Could they not see that throwing a fit, assaulting his guards, would help nothing?

He was one of the first to arrive in the chamber. No meeting had been planned for the day and so it would take time for the others to assemble. Ulric slumped in his chair and then almost immediately rose, pacing around the table. He only stopped when the first councilor, Silva, arrived, and forced himself to sit still, every nerve in his body firing with unspent energy.

A muscle twitched in his cheek at the arrival of his son. He'd hoped Roman wouldn't hear of the summons, or that he'd feel too tired to attend. He wouldn't like what Ulric had to say and would no doubt have some sanctimonious suggestion to offer.

But whether his son liked it or not, these were the harsh realities of being king. Of leading a group of people. They may not like what you had to say, but neither did they possess the steel needed to assume such command. No one liked to be led, but few wished to step up and lead.

As soon as they were all gathered, Ulric wasted no time, launching at once into his explanation of how one of the dragons had lashed out during the clash and some of the protestors had been killed.

"I hesitate to put it quite like this, but this may have been a good thing," Vaughan offered.

The remark earned him a few sharp, incredulous looks—one from Roman, Ulric didn't fail to notice.

"Think about it," Vaughan went on. "It was bound to happen sooner or later. It's good for them to be reminded of who is in charge. Such violence will help no one. They'll think twice next time."

"Or it will only serve to further escalate the violence," Roman muttered.

Unfortunately, it was Roman, not Vaughan, who was correct. In the coming days, Ulric received more reports of clashes between civilians and riders. Not every encounter ended in death, but blood was almost always spilled, necessitating yet more council meetings.

"Why does this keep happening?" Lord Daladier asked, during one such occasion.

"Why do you think?" Roman snapped. "The people are hungry."

"I thought the raids were supposed to take care of that," Vaughan said. His tone conveyed that he couldn't care less, but there was something almost challenging in the lazy way he said it, as though daring Roman to accuse him—all of them—of hoarding the stolen supplies for themselves. "It was your idea, as I recall."

"Yes," Roman said flatly. "They were. And yet, no supplies are being distributed to those who need them most. But I suppose that would be news to you, Lord Vaughan, since you can barely tear yourself away from your parties. I heard you had another one just two days ago, was it? Quite the affair."

Vaughan shrugged the insinuation away. "You know you're always welcome to attend, my prince."

Ulric had to suppress a snort of derision, doubtful that a more blatant lie had ever been uttered within the chamber.

"That's very generous of you, my lord," Roman replied, his voice stiff, but still well within the bounds of civility. "I wasn't feeling up to it, unfortunately."

His eyes flicked across the room, finding his father's. Ulric shifted in his chair. Roman knew where the supplies were really going, even if Ulric had never said as much. He felt a stirring in his chest, an uncomfortable sensation, and it took him a moment to realize what it was—shame.

He was ashamed that the supplies were being redirected to people like Vaughan, all so he could throw his decadent parties. It was wrong, but Vaughan wouldn't stand for it any other way.

You need his support, the voice whispered. *You can't afford for the council to turn on you. Keep them happy, at least for now, and then, when you ask a favor, they'll fall over themselves in their haste to be the first to grant it.*

Yes, that was it. He just needed more time. He could afford to placate the council a little while longer. The demon was right, as always, so full of wisdom, guiding him when he felt more alone than ever.

But in the meantime, the food shortages were still a problem and aside from the nobles on the hill around the palace, the army was the greatest drain on their provisions.

In a previous meeting, the council had suggested slashing the army's numbers, no longer needed now that the threat of the Empire was gone. Ulric had shot down the idea then, but he thought the time had come.

The army's size was too large, unable to justify it any longer. Besides, a handful of soldiers and their dragons should be more than enough to suppress any unrest that might linger.

They would be able to hold the line for as long as it took.

I just need more time...

Roman shot from his seat, hurrying after his father once the council had been adjourned. Ulric had barely participated in the meeting, looking distracted and withdrawn, and Roman didn't have to wonder as to why. The demon was speaking to him again.

Ignoring the other councilors, Roman pushed forward, calling out to his father. Ulric ignored him, quickening his pace as he reached the corridor.

Roman clenched his teeth against the pain, trying to keep up, but it was no use. Even at his best, he couldn't maintain such a pace, and he quickly fell behind.

"Father!" he called.

Was it his imagination, or did Ulric flinch at the sound of his voice? But the king kept going, until he was out of sight.

Roman sighed, slowing his pace. He could guess where his father had gone, where he spent most of his days. In that accursed library. Roman had liked the room once, but as time went on, he began to suspect that the plot to summon the demon had been born there. Perhaps some old passage in some dusty tome had revealed its secrets and told Ulric, in theory at least, how a demon could be summoned.

No matter. Ulric wouldn't be able to avoid him forever. Roman would find him and then they would talk. Until then, Roman wasn't going to kill himself in his haste to chase after a father that clearly wanted nothing to do with him.

It wasn't the first time Roman had tried to speak to his father after one of the meetings. Chandra had written to him after the first clash between rider and civilian, describing to him how violence had erupted. He didn't need to speak with her face to face to know how shaken the incident had left her—and he felt anger stir on her behalf.

He was angry that she'd had to go through such a thing. Angry that it had even happened at all, when it so easily could have been avoided. All his father had to do was give the order and the supplies would be distributed as they should have.

Roman didn't understand the hold Vaughan seemed to have over his father. He hadn't thought Ulric liked the man overmuch.

But each time he attempted to speak with the king, Ulric evaded him. Not this time, Roman vowed. Not today. The time for hesitating, for waiting, for meekness had passed. Now, he needed to summon his courage and confront his father. To convict him and challenge him to do the right thing. He knew his father's morality was still in there somewhere, the noble and proud man he had once known.

Despite easing his pace, Roman's legs still trembled beneath him as he reached the door to the library. Sure enough, his father stood within, his back to the door. Roman didn't bother announcing himself, knowing that the particular tread of his gait gave him away.

"Father," he sighed. "I need to speak with you about the protestors."

"Oh?"

"I'm worried it will happen again and I—"

"Of course it will happen again."

"It doesn't have to. If you but gave the order, the supplies would be sent this very day. These people are starving, Father. Our people. But they don't have to."

"I'm afraid I can't do that."

Roman glared at his father's back, the man not yet having turned around. Did he not even have the courage to face Roman, to look him in the eye?

"You could order the raids continued again. If they bring in enough—"

"But they didn't. And with the army's ranks being reduced, I don't have the numbers to maintain order within the city and go off on raids. Besides, even when they were at their full strength, they still didn't bring in enough."

A sense of helplessness washed over Roman, each idea shot down almost before he could suggest it.

"Then at least instruct the soldiers not to fire upon the protestors. We don't need any more violence and they're only acting out because they're being ignored."

"I've ordered the soldiers not to instigate any violence, but if things get out of hand, they're to respond however necessary to restore order. If that means meeting violence in kind, so be it."

"Is that coming from you, or the demon?" Roman demanded. When his father didn't respond, he pressed forward, far bolder than he would ever have dared only a short time ago. "Or perhaps there isn't much of a difference anymore."

As much as the words stung, he couldn't deny their truth. The longer Ulric stayed under the demon's thrall, the man he once was faded further and further away.

"When you're in a position of leadership, Roman, you sometimes have to make difficult, unpleasant decisions. But I don't expect you to understand that."

"No, I don't understand. The father I thought I knew would never have sanctioned violence against the people he gave up everything to save."

Roman's voice cracked and he forced down the wave of emotion that threatened to choke him. His father had sacrificed his very soul for his people. How could he forget that? How could he turn away from them now?

"You have to destroy the stone, Father. Please. Just give it to me. I will see it done. You won't have to worry about it anymore." Roman held out one hand. Still, his father did not turn.

"Is this coming from you," Ulric asked, throwing Roman's earlier words back at him, "or someone else?"

"What do you mean?" Roman asked, the hair on his arms prickling in unease.

"I just wondered if perhaps Chandra had put you up to it." At last, Ulric turned and Roman saw what had ensnared his father's attention throughout their conversation.

His breath caught at the sight of the piece of paper in his father's hands. He would recognize his own handwriting anywhere. It was a letter that he had been in the middle of drafting to Chandra when the council meeting convened. Loath to leave his thoughts unfinished, but needing to hear the discussion even more, Roman had left it on his desk, with every intention of finishing it later.

It was a moment's carelessness, believing it safe enough. He took care to burn each of the missives she sent him, after he had read them. It pained him to part with the only contact he had with Chandra now, but he had wanted to avoid the very situation he now found himself in.

"Who is she?" Ulric pressed. "She's not anyone in the palace or else I would know of it. And the only other place you've been is the barracks, which means she's a soldier. Perhaps *the* soldier you were so intent on keeping from me."

Roman felt lightheaded and he leaned nearly all his weight on his cane, fearful that it would snap beneath the pressure.

"Father…"

Ulric held up one hand. "No matter. I'll forget I ever saw this letter. If you forget about the soul stone."

Roman closed his eyes. So this was what it had come to, resorting to threats. He didn't need to ask in order to know at whose feet he should lay the blame.

Damn you, he thought fiercely. *If you're listening, damn you.*

A rumble of laughter, resounding in his mind, was the only response.

So much for courage.

"As you wish, Father," Roman sighed. "Have it your way."

Unable to stand being in his father's presence a moment longer, he turned and left, his steps unsteady. But he hardly noticed, thinking of the time Chandra had caught him on the stairs leading up to the keep.

He hated himself for being a coward, for putting one person over the good of the whole. But most of all, he hated his father for placing him in such a position.

But he had tried, to appeal to what little reason his father had left, only to be refused, blocked, and denied at every turn. He couldn't force Ulric to do the right thing. He couldn't convince him. He couldn't compete with the demon that lurked within the king's mind at all times, whispering his poisonous, honeyed words.

XXX

Chandra sat on her bunk, staring at the discharge papers in her hand. She would have thought the raid on Elath had finally caught up to her, that she was being punished, told to pack up and go home, if so many others hadn't received similar notices. It had been the talk of the mess hall that morning, the letters handed out first thing. Two-thirds of the army were being slashed, their services no longer needed now that the Empire was gone.

But, of course, it wasn't gone, was it?

She clenched the paper in her fingers. The raids had never started back up again, for better or worse, and now they never would. A different kind of fury rose up within her, born of impotence—the worst kind of all, that she could do nothing about.

Chandra had already packed her meager belongings, only a handful more than she had arrived with—mostly letters from Roman. She knew she should destroy them, but they meant too much to her for that. Saints knew she had few enough people left in her life that she cared about; she wasn't going to lose the one piece of him she could still claim.

All that was left now was to officially check out and walk through the gates that she had passed beneath on her very first day. But Chandra wasn't ready yet.

She looked up, folding the discharge notice away, as Anake walked through the rows of bunks toward her. Anake hadn't received such a notice, and neither had Victor, neither of which surprised Chandra. They had both been in the army long before she had arrived. It seemed only right that they would stay.

"I heard the news," Anake said as she reached her.

Chandra nodded, unsure what to say. Nothing seemed adequate to convey or acknowledge all they had been through together.

"I'll be sorry to see you go," Anake added. "So will Victor, believe it or not. In his own way."

"I'd stay, if it were up to me." Chandra didn't want them to think she was eager to leave, to be rid of the responsibility, content to thrust it upon them. "It feels strange to go back to my old life."

As soon as she said the words, Chandra regretted them. Anake didn't have an old life to go back to. Not yet.

But there was no judgment in the Elathan's dark eyes. "Go," she said softly. "And good luck."

She offered a hand and Chandra clasped it wordlessly. Taking her small pack, she left the barracks behind, for the last time, and mounted the stairs to the aerie.

Sheboleth lifted her head. "You're early." Her eyes fell to the bag, questioning.

"I've been discharged. They're cutting the army's ranks. I can go home."

"Why do you not sound happy about that?"

Because I'm not.

Strangely, Chandra had always imagined she would have been happy on the day she was finally discharged. It would have meant the Empire was defeated and Anarsha had won. And while that might be true, as far as it went, it didn't feel that way.

The circumstances of her discharge were not the way Chandra had imagined.

"I didn't picture it would happen like this," she admitted. "In a way, I'm almost glad. I never imagined that I would be asked by my kingdom to turn my weapons on my own people—and now they'll never ask it of me again."

Sheboleth concurred.

"On the other hand, that means I can do nothing to try and make things better. We're right back where we started."

I'm *right back where I started.*

"Well, if you go, so do I. I'm not hanging around here, only to be assigned to someone else. I can return to the forest, go back to my old life, too." She shook her wings out slightly, gazing into the distance. "It's been too long…"

Chandra felt touched by Sheboleth's loyalty. "I'll miss you."

"Oh, I'll still be about. After all, you're my human—"

"Foolish creature that I am." Chandra smiled, ducking her head.

"Exactly." The dragon spread her wings. "Climb on. I can take you home. Faster than walking, and you can finally show me where you live."

Chandra's heart seized in her chest. One last flight. Sheboleth didn't have to say the words for her to know that's what the dragon was offering.

"No saddle," she remarked. They belonged to the army, even if the dragons didn't, and Chandra wouldn't be allowed to take it with her. She didn't even have her flight leathers anymore, with their straps and buckles.

Sheboleth snorted. "I think, by now, we don't need it. Do you trust me?"

With my life.

"Yes," Chandra answered and climbed onto the dragon's back before she could be prompted again. They had flown without such precautions before, after all.

The strange feeling in her chest, the bundle of emotions, swelled as they rose into the air. She tried to choke it back down; she could untangle it later. The keep fell away below them, the complex that had once seemed so large and intimidating made small and insignificant by the distance.

Sheboleth flew low over the rooftops so that Chandra could identify her street. She would never get used to how different everything looked from the air.

"There!" she called, pointing, as her house came into view. Her throat tightened at the sight of it, the small workshop across the lawn where it had always been.

All too soon, Sheboleth touched down, returned to the earth once more. Chandra hesitated to dismount, staring at the front door, expecting any moment that it would fly open and her grandmother would be there.

But she hadn't time to write to her grandmother about the discharges. She didn't know to expect Chandra, who had herself only found out that morning.

Slowly, she swung her leg over the side and slid to the ground, clutching her bag.

Sheboleth glanced at her. "Do you want me to stay?"

"No," Chandra murmured. "I'll be all right."

"Of course you will."

Suddenly, she wished there were some way for her to keep in touch with the dragon, but she could hardly write her letters the way she did with Roman.

Her steps leaden, Chandra approached the door. What if it was locked? She didn't have a key and would have to knock, asking to be granted entry like a stranger in her own home.

But the handle moved beneath her touch and the door swung open without a sound. Chandra glanced over her shoulder. Sheboleth still stood in the street, attracting attention, but the dragon seemed not to care at all.

Sheboleth nodded to her and Chandra, taking a deep breath, stepped fully into the house.

"Grandmother?" she called, voice echoing through the house.

The kitchen looked exactly as she remembered and suddenly, she could have been gone mere days instead of months—and the years they had turned into.

Saints, had it really been so long?

She could imagine Callum responding to her voice, hurrying into the kitchen. Or more likely, he would already have been there, a dish towel draped over one shoulder, the air filled with the scent of whatever dish he had concocted to celebrate her return.

The image was so real, she could see Callum standing there at the stove. Tears stung the back of her eyes and she blinked rapidly. Callum was gone. That simple, unalterable fact proved that not everything was the same, no matter how it might appear on the surface.

She could hear the faint sound of her grandmother shuffling through the house and a moment later, she appeared around the corner. Chandra sucked in a breath.

Had her grandmother always been so frail? Her skin, wrinkled and shrunken like old leather, seemed to cling to the bones beneath in a way Chandra didn't recall. But her gait was as steady as ever as she crossed the kitchen floor, wrapping her arms around her granddaughter.

Chandra stiffened slightly, taken aback by the gesture. Their family had never been one for physical affection, but she soon sagged against the other woman, returning the embrace. That, too, had changed.

She could well imagine what it had been like, living alone in the house during Chandra's absence, knowing one grandchild would never return, fearing constantly for the safety of the one who remained.

Her vision had blurred completely by the time her grandmother released her and stepped back, her hands moving to cup Chandra's face, staring up at her, as though afraid she wasn't real, merely an illusion that would dissolve beneath the slightest scrutiny.

"I've been discharged," Chandra murmured. "They've reduced the ranks."

Her grandmother nodded. "I can't say I'm sorry to have you back. The army's loss will happily be my gain." She let Chandra go and stepped back. "Do you need anything?"

Chandra shook her head. "I'll just take this stuff up to my room and then…I think I'll go out to my workshop for a while."

More than anything, she needed to think, to decompress. To make peace with her new circumstances and try to reclaim the life that had once seemed so familiar, the only thing she had ever known, but now felt utterly alien.

Her grandmother nodded again. "I'll be here. See if I can't whip up something special for dinner. Things are pretty limited with the rationing, but I'm nothing if not determined."

Chandra summoned a smile for her sake. The rationing and shortages were yet one more thing they would need to discuss and Chandra wasn't looking forward to explaining to her grandmother all the things she couldn't put in her letters.

How she had failed.

It's not all on you, you know, a voice whispered in her head—a voice that sounded suspiciously like Sheboleth. Chandra had been around the dragon too much; she'd begun to rub off on her. She wondered if Sheboleth heard her voice in moments of silence. The thought pleased her, to know she had left her mark on someone as much as they had on her.

Free to go on her way, Chandra ducked into her bedroom, intending to toss the bag onto the bed and leave. But she lingered in the doorway, taking in the small space that seemed massive after the barracks.

It was exactly as she had left it, though she hadn't expected anything else. Not a speck of dust could be seen. Her grandmother had kept it pristine, in anticipation of her return. Chandra was touched by the gesture.

Turning, she left, pausing outside the door to Callum's room. It was closed, its occupant never to return. Chandra imagined the dust had taken over in there and she was reminded of the night she had lain awake in her own room, fretting over Callum's departure to the army.

Once more, she was struck by the sense of injustice, the unfairness of it all. He should be there. He should have made it back.

"Damn you," she whispered, trailing her fingers along the door. "Why couldn't you have just listened to me?"

Abruptly, she turned her back to the door and rushed out of the house, feeling like she couldn't get in enough air. The workshop was dark inside and she drew back the shutters, motes glinting in the beams of sunlight that streamed through.

The place cried out for a good cleaning. It looked like no one had set foot in there since she'd left—and why would they? At least everything was where she had left it, her tools and supplies easily located beneath a layer of dust.

Chandra spent the rest of that first day back cleaning, trying to return the place to working order. The mindless work helped settle her restless thoughts and chase away unwanted memories and reminders of all that had happened and why she was there now.

But she knew it wouldn't last forever and Chandra dreaded the moment all of the work was done and there was nothing left to act as a buffer, a barrier, between her and the thoughts that were never very far away.

The life of a Mask was not so different from the life of a soldier, Desmond reflected, made up of orders, expectations, and most of all—routine.

He had settled comfortably into his new role. It had come easy to him—perhaps too easily. Even in the rare moments he had to himself, he found himself copying the emperor's movements, his mannerisms—even going so far as to think about things the way in which Hadrian would— until it felt as though little of the man behind the mask remained.

What the one Mask had told him on his first day proved true. They each became the emperor, at all times, the façade never allowed to slip.

Desmond didn't mind the loss of identity exactly. His old life wasn't anything special, nothing he yearned to return to, especially not if it meant giving up all the comforts of life at the palace—and life as the emperor.

What he despised instead, the resentment growing a little more each day, was that this new life condemned him to being nothing more than someone else's shadow. He'd known that when he'd agreed to the position and yet, he hadn't truly known.

He hadn't known how it would eat away at him. Some days, the discontentment would fade a little, and Desmond would chide himself for being unreasonable. This wasn't so bad. He could do this.

Only for it to rear its ugly head again, in the dark of the night, when he'd finally retreated to his opulent room. The trinkets, the bits and baubles that had so enraptured him at first now seemed dull and empty.

This was a life, though grand, that would never lead to anything more than what he currently had. He was the emperor—even coming to know the man better than he felt he knew himself—in all respects bar one.

The most important one.

It was all nothing more than an elaborate game of dress up—one that could cost Desmond his life, if a would-be assassin believed him the emperor. That was what he was for, what all of them were for.

What had seemed like such an honor quickly curdled, though Desmond could see no way out, aside from death. Much as he had faced it on the battlefield, Desmond did not want to die.

One morning, Hadrian summoned all three of his Masks into the throne room, informing them that they would all be departing shortly for Elath and then Shemar. The purpose of the visit was to check on the progress being made there.

They would need to move quickly if they were to rebuild their army and the emperor was eager to do so before the Anarshans had a chance to take advantage of the Empire's weakened state.

Desmond didn't know why the Anarshans hadn't already pressed their advantage. He was one of the few who had been there that day, seen the demon with his own eyes, and lived to tell the tale. He knew better than most what was at stake.

But he pushed the thought aside, grateful to be out of the palace. Its walls had begun to feel stifling, pressing in on him like the gilded bars of a cage.

Despite the reprieve Hadrian was offering, Desmond allowed himself to scowl behind his mask, letting some of his true feelings bleed through. No one could see, of course, but it gave him some small satisfaction just to be able to do it. To engage in his own private defiance.

A bad habit, he knew. All it would take was one unguarded moment, when he wasn't wearing the mask, but he found he didn't much care.

Once the trip was over, he would return to the bars of his gilded cage, still the canary trapped, forced to perform and satisfy the whims of his master.

Desmond still admired Hadrian—it was hard not to—but he also despised him, too. More than anything, he wanted to be him. To rule an Empire, to be answerable to no one, to take life by the throat and claim one's own destiny.

That was true power and how he yearned to know what it felt like! To taste it for himself. To get drunk on it, like the most intoxicating wine.

But he was trapped, playing his part. And he would play it well.

None of them needed to pack anything; the servants saw to that. They each boarded their own train car. Should they come under attack, with each of the Masks separated and dressed identically, there would be no way to tell which was the real emperor.

Desmond found himself seated across from a group of guards, maintaining the appearance that he was the real emperor. He sighed, keeping his posture rigid the way Hadrian did, when he would have liked nothing more than to lean back, close his eyes behind the mask, and enjoy the ride. But he couldn't risk falling asleep.

One of the guards in the compartment with him seemed to know who he really was, however. They had barely pulled out of the Capitol before the man leaned forward, an eager expression on his face.

"Is it true?" he asked. "You saw the demon?"

Desmond suppressed another sigh. Either news of the true purpose for their trip had gotten out or, he supposed, it didn't take a genius to put it all together.

Regardless, it was a fear that weighed heavily on most Akkadians' minds. Would they be able to rebuild their army in time or would the Anarshans press their advantage?

For the most part, the knowledge of the demon had been kept quiet. It would have been a hard concept for most Akkadians to grasp, having been taught all their lives that such creatures were pagan superstition, nothing more. All the people knew was that the last battle had gone poorly for the Empire. So poorly that they would be ill equipped to defend themselves, should Anarsha seek vengeance.

But within the walls of the palace, such secrets were not so easily kept.

"Yes," Desmond said. The words he spoke were his own, but the clipped tone was all Hadrian.

"What was it like?"

There was still nothing but eager curiosity in the guard's gaze. No hint of terror, not the slightest inkling of what had really transpired that day.

Desmond jerked forward in his seat and the guard slammed back into his own, startled by the sudden motion.

"It was like hell unleashed," Desmond hissed. "You cannot fathom. Pray you never have to find out."

The guard suitably cowed, Desmond leaned back, resuming his position. He was Hadrian once more, but for a moment, he had sounded just like his former self, and the thought brought an unexpected pain between his ribs.

Whether Desmond had frightened him into silence or his answer had satisfied the guard, the man said nothing more the rest of the journey to Elath, the only sound in the compartment the clacking of the train.

Desmond's relief at escaping the palace quickly faded as the train arrived in Elath and they disembarked. He had been here when the kingdom had been conquered and from the looks of things, it hadn't improved much.

If anything, it looked worse, not all of the buildings yet rebuilt following the Anarshans' raid. The air still stank of fish. It was hardly a kingdom at all, not worthy of the name, paling in comparison to the glory of the Capitol. A sprawling city-state of fishermen and miners.

Desmond accompanied the emperor dutifully to the warehouses and then the mines, wanting to check on how material production was progressing. But he was relieved when they finally left Elath behind them, departing for Shemar.

The city of spires was instantly more sophisticated, made of granite and polished stone. There was something breathtaking about the sight of the towers, piercing the sky. It made something swell within Desmond's chest, a sense of pride that this city belonged to the Empire now. And he had helped bring that about, in another life.

Curiously, the emperor wanted to see the mines located on the outskirts of the city and Desmond accompanied him, interest piqued. These were some of the mines that his father owned, though he still didn't know which.

Their party walked up to the edge of one of the giant pits, peering over. Desmond stood slightly behind the emperor, the other Masks on either side of him, each of them copying his stance unconsciously.

How easy it would be to push him.

The image of the emperor stumbling forward sprang into his mind unbidden, his arms wheeling for a moment before he toppled forward into the abyss. His body would lie broken at the very bottom.

Without moving, Desmond shook the thought away, though every muscle in his body yearned to physically recoil, as if that would somehow make the thought go away.

Where had that come from? And in any case, pushing the emperor would achieve nothing. Everyone here would see him do it. He would not risk so much in exchange for so little.

Desmond allowed himself a small shake of the head. It was merely the edge's proximity, his mind warning him of the inherent danger, what would happen if one was to fall. That was all it was, his subconscious trying to warn him, nothing more.

One of the foremen handed each of the Masks one of the red crystals retrieved from the mine, keeping up the façade, the real emperor's identity concealed. Desmond hardly glanced at his stone. He'd already seen one for himself and he thought it likely that Hadrian had as well.

Regardless, the emperor deemed the red crystals worthless and urged the mine operators to keep searching for more iron.

Returning to the city, Desmond pondered the quandary of the red crystals. There were very few things in the world that were of no use whatsoever. Could it be possible that the stones, though lovely, were one of them? He thought it unlikely. Surely, they had some purpose to them. They just hadn't discovered it yet.

So engrossed was he in his own thoughts, trailing after one of the other Masks, the emperor bringing up the rear, guards marching on all sides, that he failed to observe his surroundings.

He didn't realize anything was amiss until it was too late.

A shout rang out. Desmond's gaze, which had been focused on the cobblestones beneath his feet, shot up in time to see the Mask in front of him jerk. There was a brief spray of blood and then Desmond saw what the man was reaching for, hand hovering helplessly over the arrow shaft protruding from the side of his neck.

He toppled forward, collapsing onto the cobbles, blood pooling around the wound. With his mask still in place, it was impossible to tell if his eyes were widened in fear or already vacant and unseeing.

Heart galloping, Desmond whirled, searching desperately for the source of the shot. Following some of the guards' pointing fingers, he quickly spied a lone archer, having scaled one of the sentinel towers.

As he watched, one of the guards drew his own bow and fired at the assassin, but the arrow fell short, embedding itself in the wood near the man's feet. The archer turned away and began to duck out of sight.

The guard drew another arrow, but Desmond shouted at him, "After him!"

They needed to take him alive, in any case, if possible. They needed to know whether he had acted alone or if there were yet more threats to fear.

As some of the guards charged forward, in the direction the archer had disappeared, Desmond subtly stepped in front of the real emperor. The action was not so overt that it would alert any other assassins that might be waiting as to the identity of the real emperor, but his body would help shield Hadrian in case of another attack.

Moving as one, their remaining group stepped into the doorway of a nearby building, out of the open. Behind his mask, Desmond's breath came quick and shallow as he thought of the third Mask, still lying out there in the street where they had been forced to leave him. He hadn't moved again or made a sound and Desmond knew the man was dead.

He still didn't know his real name.

Desmond could feel sweat beading along his scalp, the mask sticking to his skin. He itched to rip it off.

His stomach churned even though he knew it shouldn't. This was their purpose, after all. This was why they were here, to sacrifice their lives in the place of the emperor's. Hadrian didn't have Masks for no reason. The threat of assassination was terrifyingly real, even now.

Elath and Shemar might have been conquered, but there would always be those who dissented, who would rise up against their rulers.

Crush them. Crush them all, until none would dare.

Through the blood furiously pounding in his ears, threatening to drown out all thought, Desmond fervently hoped that the guards tracked down the assassin. Once they had the answers they wanted, an example would have to be made of him.

The adrenaline slowly began to fade, leaving Desmond's hands trembling and his body cold. It had been so close. The dead Mask had been right in front of him. If the archer's aim had been slightly off, or if he had chosen a different target, it could have easily been Desmond lying in the street, bleeding out.

Any assassin would have four options to choose from and this one had guessed wrong, though his aim had been true enough.

Just like that, Desmond's life could have come to an end, right then and there. And he would have been powerless to stop it. It was one thing to know the risks and quite another to see the consequences play out before his very eyes.

For every battle he had fought, Desmond had never felt closer to death than he had in that moment, on the streets of a city that should have been safe. The realization chilled him.

It was terrifying how quickly it could all come to an end. How every dream and ambition could shatter in an instant, ended by someone else's whims.

He did not want to die. Not now, not ever. And he certainly did not want his death to be at the hands of another.

He vowed that no one would ever have that kind of power over him again. Not if he could help it. But what could he truly do when not even emperors were safe?

XXXI

The assassin did not get far. He was rounded up and brought in later that very day, much to Desmond's satisfaction. He yearned for punishment to be meted out at once. Let the people see the consequences for such actions and how quickly the Empire would respond.

But Hadrian postponed any such action until the next morning, saying that they would get it done and return to the Capitol. Though he'd longed to leave it, Desmond found himself relieved by the news. The emperor needed time to recover after the attempt on his life—and so did the remaining two Masks.

Desmond lingered in his room for the rest of the day, reluctant to leave it unless he was summoned. Here, at least, he was safe. The guard had been doubled, more out of an abundance of caution than fear of any real threat. Here, no assailant was going to leap out at him.

Here, in the privacy of his own quarters, he could do what was forbidden elsewhere. He reached up, hand no longer shaking, and removed his mask, inhaling deeply. He'd hated the feel of it against his skin at first, feeling every single point where it made contact with his flesh. But now he scarcely noticed it.

He took it off now as a matter of defiance, a reminder to himself of who he really was. The person he was fighting so hard not to lose entirely.

Desmond glanced up at the mirror in front of him, the circular glass reflecting his own image back at him. His eyes looked slightly sunken and haunted, the mask still held in one hand, only a short distance from his face, as though he couldn't decide whether to leave it off or put it back on.

In the end, he tossed it aside and collapsed onto the bed. Even now, his life was still being dictated for him. He let his thoughts drift back to the barracks, the battlefield. What would his life look like now if he had rejected the emperor's offer?

He would be one of the soldiers working hard to rebuild the army, testing out the newest model of mechs, that he had seen from behind his mask. He would have looked at the Masks, not knowing which was the true emperor, and then wouldn't have given them a second thought. He certainly never would have pictured himself being one.

The thought would never have crossed his mind. But if it had, would he have wanted to become a Mask? Would he have made the same choice?

Desmond sighed, running a hand along his face. He would need to shave soon. Hadrian didn't wear a beard and the mask needed to fit as smoothly against his skin as possible.

No, he reflected, the soldier he had been wouldn't have wanted to be a Mask, but that had been before the demon. In the privacy of his own quarters, he allowed his mind to drift back to that day. If he let his guard down, he could still hear the beast's roar shaking his bones, feel the earth tremble beneath him, feel the heat—the unbearable heat— of his flames.

That creature was likely still out there. He saw no reason why Anarsha would part with their most powerful weapon. A weapon Akkadia had no answer to. They could rebuild their army and mass produce more mechs all they wished, but Desmond couldn't see how the end result would ever be different. They would march upon the city of stone and be turned back, the same as before.

They were only fortunate that Anarsha seemed to have no interest in conquest, content to be left alone. They would use the demon to keep the Empire at bay, but nothing more. They wouldn't seek to turn it on the foe that had cost them so much.

Desmond curled his hand into a fist. And that was why Anarsha was weak, why they didn't deserve such power.

It's not your responsibility anymore, he reminded himself. *It's none of your concern.*

His only job now was to protect the emperor, to play his role so convincingly that any assassin would have to choose—one out of four—and choose wrong.

No, he reminded himself. It was one out of three now.

One of the Masks that day had played his role a little too well. Desmond knew that he and the Mask that remained were just as skilled actors. There were times when he himself hadn't known which was the real emperor behind the mask—and which was one of them.

Desmond sympathized with the Anarshans, whichever one of them had summoned the demon. There were times when he felt as though he, too, would be willing to strike such a bargain, if it meant he could finally have the life he wanted.

A life where he was finally enough. A life where he could be himself, where no one would tell him what to do. But the only person who gave orders and took none was the emperor himself, and that was a position that would always remain out of reach.

Or if there was a way, Desmond couldn't see it.

And he didn't know how to summon a demon to make it so.

He closed his eyes, trying to push the thoughts away, to bury the discontentment for a little longer. Tomorrow, he would watch an assassin's execution. What came after, he dared not think.

Chandra swore as the candle cracked beneath her fingers. None of the batches she had attempted had turned out that day, despite her every effort at coaxing them gently from the mold. She was almost out of bayberries and would have to halt her attempts until she could get more.

It would have been so much easier to ease back into things with simple tallow candles, but she hadn't wanted that. She'd wanted the nice, sweet bayberry wax.

It was a symbolic gesture, in many ways. She hadn't been away from her workshop all that long, in the grand scheme of things, and yet it felt like an eternity. If she could get the more complex candles to turn out, she could do anything. She could reassure herself that she wasn't out of practice.

But she was. Her movements were slow and uncertain where once they had been sure. Her hands were better suited to wielding a bow than candle wax these days.

This was the life she had returned to. That she had left behind, with the knowledge that it would wait for her, and with every intention of coming back.

A surge of anger spiked through her and Chandra lashed out, dashing the mold to the floor. Immediately, regret replaced her rage and she retrieved the mold, hoping she hadn't managed to break it.

She raked a hand through her hair. Why had she done that? She needed to get out of the workshop and stop wasting what little supplies she had left.

A glance out the windows revealed a darkening sky as Chandra untied her apron. She sighed. Another day gone and she had nothing to show for it.

Her grandmother didn't inquire as to how the candle making had gone, for which Chandra was grateful as she stepped back into the house, the smell of dinner suffusing the air. Perhaps her sullen silence was answer enough.

Sooner or later, though, she could afford failure no longer. Lurking in the back of her mind, its weight pressing down on her, was the knowledge that there would be no more money coming in from the army. The two of them would once again rely on the income from her shop and for that, she needed goods to sell.

Chandra stared down at the food on her plate, her thoughts far away, as she pushed the potatoes around. They would have tasted better with some herbs and butter, but they were lucky to have food at all.

Released from the army, Chandra saw now the kind of rationing that had been forced upon the civilians, and she instantly regretted every uncharitable thought she'd spared for the army's fare.

Her grandmother cleared her throat and Chandra glanced up. They'd never been chatty, exactly, in the past, but a silence had descended between them since Chandra's return. She could sense there was much that her grandmother wished to say, but something, an uncertainty, held her back.

She waited for her grandmother to speak now, but when no words came, she asked, "What is it?"

"You know I'm grateful to have you back," her grandmother said. "But I worry."

Chandra bit her lip. If this was about the candles—

"I know you have enough on your plate already. I don't want to burden you with any more, but…if things don't get better soon, I worry what will happen. Every day, it seems like things only grow more unsettled. I worry about the state of things out there—" She jerked her head toward the door. "I feel that you are less safe within the walls of your own kingdom than you ever were in the war."

Chandra didn't want to admit that she was beginning to feel the same way, though she tried not to leave the house if she could help it. But even on the few, essential trips she did make, she could see evidence of the people's desperation.

It was the only insight she got into the state of things. Roman could hardly write to her now, not knowing where she was. She wondered if he even knew that she had been discharged.

Her stomach twisted at the knowledge that she would likely never hear from him again. There had been gaps in communication before, but this…this was different. She missed his letters more than she cared to admit. Receiving one now, even if there was nothing he could say or do to fix the situation, would make everything seem so much better.

But that was part of her old life. Nothing ever stayed the same.

She summoned a smile for her grandmother's sake. "I don't think things are that dire. I'm more afraid of one of the Empire's mechs than I am of my neighbor."

Her grandmother's lips pursed as though she disagreed, but she let the matter drop.

The next morning, Chandra glanced across the lawn at her workshop, vowing that she wouldn't leave it until she'd managed to successfully make a batch of candles. But before that, she had to venture out to the markets and find what food she could. Their pantry was running low.

She braced herself, as she stepped out the door, to keep her expectations low. She hadn't yet seen evidence for herself of how sparse the pickings had become, but she'd heard plenty from her grandmother.

"Ah, you're back," Peter, the butcher, remarked as Chandra stepped beneath his door.

"Discharged," Chandra said, by way of explanation.

"You and everyone else. Here for more tallow?"

"Not this time. I came to see what you have."

Peter grimaced. "Not as much as I'd like, but you're welcome to look."

Chandra could tell at a glance that the shelves and racks were more depleted than she'd ever seen them—even on celebration days. But they weren't celebrating any saint today.

She swallowed down the urge to ask if this was truly all he had. She already knew the answer. She dithered, lingering over cuts of ham. There was little enough beef to choose from and no lamb. Lamb had been a delicacy even before the war, one that was reserved for special occasions.

Chandra pointed to one of the hams. "How much?"

The sum Peter gave her nearly made her choke. She could easily blow through her army salary at a price like that—and she was no longer receiving such sums.

I'll have to get back to candle making, soon as I get home.

There was no time for more errors, or for messing about. The price of food would only continue to rise.

In the end, she purchased a few slices of the ham. It wouldn't last more than a few meals, but it was better than nothing. Perhaps she could forage something from the forest when she went to collect more bayberries.

Clutching her small parcel, Chandra turned to make for home, but paused in the middle of the street, slowly turning. She had time enough for a little detour.

Her steps took her toward the temple, but it wasn't the saints' shrine that interested her. A different shrine had been erected not far from the temple, the stone statue a memorial to those who had fallen in the war. Chandra supposed they had lost too many to give each of them a marker, but it felt too impersonal.

She shook her head. Never mind. This stone was for Callum and Gideon. A few scattered bundles of flowers had been left, an extravagant gesture in such trying times, but the memorial currently had no other visitors.

Heedless of any prying eyes that might be watching, Chandra knelt in front of the memorial. A great weight had descended on her chest and she wanted to lift it off and lay it at the foot of the stone, an offering of her own. It was all she had left to give.

Her anger had all but burned itself out, a slow, lingering death, not the fierce rush of release that she had expected to feel. In its place there was now only a hollow restlessness, and she knew the cause, even if she didn't like to admit it.

Anarsha hadn't really won. They—she—hadn't destroyed the Empire. Or if they had, it was the demon's doing, not her own.

Briefly, she wondered where the demon was, what had become of it, and inevitably such thoughts led her back to Roman.

Despite her vows, she had not avenged Callum's death or Gideon's. Her plans, all her best intentions, felt unfinished.

And all for what? What had any of it been for? Chandra was ashamed of her own reaction, but she could understand now why those protestors in the square would have welcomed the Empire.

Her rations weren't stretching as far as they used to. Now that she was no longer a soldier, she received less. It wasn't enough. She went to bed hungry most nights and already she had begun to lose some of the muscle she had gained from her time in the army.

Muscle that had been hard and painfully won.

They had beaten back the Empire, yes, but was *this* to be her kingdom's fate? Slowly withering away, rotting from within, starving until there was nothing left?

The only thing crueler than having no hope at all was to have a reason for hope, only to watch it be snatched away.

Chandra reached up, rubbing a hand over her cheek, and her fingers came away wet. She hadn't even realized she'd begun to cry.

That, too, wasn't what she had imagined. She'd kept her grief locked behind an iron wall, fearful of what would happen the moment it broke free, the moment she allowed herself to feel. It would break her completely, acknowledging that he was really gone.

She had imagined wrenching sobs, a physical reaction to match the pain in her heart. But instead, the tears fell silently, spattering onto the cobblestones.

It didn't feel like grief so much as defeat.

But what did she know of grief? She barely remembered her parents; certainly not enough to feel more than a hollow sort of sadness, simply because she knew that was how she was supposed to feel. It was the knowledge of mourning something that she would never have, that most other people took for granted. It was an echo of loss, not something that touched her personally.

Not like this.

She was tempted to say something, but what words could breach such a void? It was pointless, anyway. Callum couldn't hear her. He was gone.

Brushing her tears away, Chandra stood, clutching her package to her chest and turned away, resolved to never come back.

The sky was overcast that morning and yet the world looked more gray, colorless, than it had before, every line too harsh and jagged. The sounds of the city bustling around her were muffled in her ears and yet too loud. Everything blurred and swam before her and she realized, with some annoyance, that her eyes hadn't stopped watering yet.

She swiped at them again, impatiently. *Damn it all.* She hadn't wanted to cry in the first place, but now that she had, why couldn't she stop? What good would more crying do?

Dimly, footsteps pattered behind her, drawing nearer. Chandra gasped as her arm was suddenly jerked and she blinked as she made out a young woman, yanking her arm away from her chest. Away from the package of sliced ham she had purchased.

Chandra's sorrow evaporated and she bared her teeth, pulling against the woman's grasp. "Let go of me!"

But the woman's grip held firm. She was stronger than Chandra, or perhaps Chandra had grown weaker.

More footsteps behind her. A young man this time, at her shoulder. With frantic, greedy fingers, he scrabbled for the parcel.

Anger speared through Chandra's veins, overtaking reason and she lashed out, hooking her foot behind the woman's leg. The woman yelped in surprise as she went down, her hand still latched around Chandra's arm, pulling her down with her.

Chandra rolled, preparing to rise, and caught a glimpse of the young man's boot as it hurtled toward her face. Pain exploded in her skull, bright light filling her vision.

She didn't know how long she lay there, stunned, fighting unconsciousness, hovering somewhere in between. It might have been only moments, but it felt like an eternity.

When she cracked one eye open, the two assailants were gone—and so was the package she had tried so hard to protect.

Letting out a growl, Chandra looked around for any sign of them, but they were gone, the ham along with them.

Gingerly, she brought one hand to her cheek, assessing the damage. The inside of her mouth tasted like blood. Her nose was bleeding, but it didn't feel broken. She prodded her teeth with her tongue, but none of them seemed loose.

Thank the saints for that. If the bastard had knocked out a tooth, she would have *really* been mad.

Wincing, Chandra picked herself up off the street. No one had come to help her, to stop the attack or inquire if she was all right. If any of them had noticed, they had turned their head and went about their business, not wanting to get involved or draw attention to themselves.

With nothing to show for her wasted trip, she made her way back home, keeping one eye out for any sign of the two attackers. But as she walked, the memory began to fade until she wasn't sure she would recognize either of them even if she saw them.

"Anything?" her grandmother called out as soon as she had shut the door behind her. "I thought perhaps Peter would cut you a deal since—"

Her grandmother broke off as she rounded the corner and took in Chandra's disheveled appearance. "What in the name of the saints!" She hurried forward as fast as her gnarled joints would let her. "What happened?"

"Someone wanted some sliced ham badly enough to fight me for it," Chandra replied. "I wish I could say they came out of it worse than I did."

Her grandmother glanced down, no doubt taking note of the lack of ham and drawing her own conclusions. "How many were there?"

"Just two." But it had been enough.

If she hadn't been so distracted…if she hadn't allowed herself to lose focus, to be consumed by the very grief she had tried so hard to keep at bay…

"It's my fault," she added. "I should have been paying better attention."

But even as she spoke the words, anger simmered low in her belly. How dare they attack her and take what was rightfully hers? She had paid good money for that and now she and her grandmother would have no meat for dinner.

They're desperate, the reasonable part of her mind whispered. But Chandra didn't care. That was no excuse to break the law, to steal something that wasn't theirs, that they had no right to.

She was a soldier. She had fought for this wretched kingdom, to keep people like them safe, and this was how they repaid her. By stealing from her and leaving her beaten in the street.

Her right hand clenched into a fist, the desire to lash out strong. But there was nothing to lash out at. They were gone and if they knew what was good for them, they would never cross paths with her again.

Her grandmother waved away her blame. "What did they look like? We could find one of the sentries and file a report."

Chandra sighed. "I don't know, Grandmother. It all happened so fast and one of them was behind me."

Her grandmother shook her head. "What have we come to, that this is the kind of behavior we engage in? We defeated the Empire and people are more miserable than ever!"

"I'll be more careful next time," Chandra promised, wanting to assuage the old woman.

"You most certainly will! I don't want you going anywhere unless that dragon of yours goes with you. Let's see them think twice about accosting you then!"

"Grandmother, Sheboleth isn't my dragon. She has a will of her own." *And what a will it is!* "She doesn't belong to me. And anyway, I'm not afraid to go out on my own."

Her grandmother gave her a look that was somehow pitying. "You should be. I wish I could say what happened to you is an exception, but…not from what I've heard."

That gave Chandra pause. She'd never been afraid to wander the streets of her kingdom, even before she'd gone off to the army and learned how to defend herself.

But this was no longer the Anarsha she knew, that much was clear. Should she be afraid?

Perhaps her grandmother's suggestion wasn't without merit. Certainly, those two thugs would never have accosted her if Sheboleth had been by her side. And if they had, they would have swiftly regretted it.

In any case, it would be nice to see Sheboleth again. Chandra would mention it to her when next the dragon visited. *If she visited…*

She didn't know where Sheboleth was these days, but she missed her terribly.

XXXII

Time passed slowly. It felt like the world was collectively holding its breath, as the Empire rebuilt their tattered army and Anarsha continued to struggle.

Winter could always be harsh in the best of times and Roman wondered whether he would still have a kingdom by the end of it.

The cold of the palace walls seeped into his bones, embedding itself so deeply, he felt he would never be warm again. His joints hurt. What progress he'd seemingly gained during his time at the barracks wore away, leaving him even more gaunt than before. He scarcely recognized himself whenever he dared glance in the mirror.

Yet another sudden change came over his father, as though he remembered something of the man he used to be now that his son's health was deteriorating once more. He hovered, fussing over Roman, but the prince sent him away, not wishing to see him.

Beneath his concern, he was still the same apathetic king he had become, the soul stone still around his neck. They hadn't spoken of it again, for Chandra's sake.

Roman had written to her, but all of his letters went unanswered. Part of him was relieved. His father would never have learned of Chandra's existence if he hadn't intercepted one of their letters. The other part of him was fearful.

He tried to tell himself that she had merely been discharged, along with most of their army. He didn't know where to send her letters now and so it made sense that she would not respond to what she never received.

The other part of him, though, couldn't help but eye his father with suspicion. Had he done something to her, despite his insistence that he would forget he'd ever seen the letter?

There was a time when such a thought never would have crossed Roman's mind. But his father was no longer the man he'd known.

So Roman spent that long winter penning other papers, ones he would never share. If he couldn't write to Chandra, he could at least chronicle what had happened in Anarsha to lead them all here. He hadn't forgotten the soul stone, though he'd never mentioned it again since his father had threatened her.

Still, if he couldn't convince his father to destroy the stone, someone would have to. It seemed unlikely that the task would ever fall to him. Roman would consider it a miracle if he lived to see another winter.

It seemed more important than ever to document the truth, for someone else to find and act upon in the future. That much he could do. He had his own father to thank, partially, for the idea. Ulric spent so much of his time sequestered in the library, reading old tomes or obsessively scratching away at his own parchment. Roman had no idea what he was writing down, but he wouldn't trust his father to be overly generous with the truth.

Regardless, he would write his own version of events. Confined to his room, it was all he could think to do.

When he could, he made an effort to go out, if only to keep apprised of the gossip making its rounds. From it, his fears were confirmed. His father mostly neglected his other duties, preferring to attend to his son or lock himself in his precious library, sometimes for days on end.

He no longer attended council meetings. Roman wished he could attend the meetings himself, but he knew his limitations. Some days, he felt too weak to even climb out of bed.

The meetings were full of nothing but bad news anyway—Roman gleaned that much. The latest being that the hunger crisis had worsened to the point where people were dropping dead in the street, succumbing to the deadly combination of cold and starvation.

Knowing it was bad for morale, and not wanting anyone to be tempted into the awfulness of cannibalism, Ulric had demanded that the bodies be gathered up and burned.

Roman ran a hand over his face, staring down at the paper before him. It was nearly full, marred by his erratic handwriting. He could see the runes scattering before him, no longer neat and orderly, made unsteady by the tremors in his hand.

Reluctantly, he set his quill aside and looked out the window. How had it all come to this?

He told himself that he just needed to hold on a little longer. Much as he still loved his father, in his own way, and hated the idea of parting from him, he just had to live long enough to outlast Ulric. Then, once Roman was king, he could destroy the soul stone and put an end to it.

It was the delusional hope of fools, but he clung to it, unwilling to give it up. Those were the thoughts he clung to, in the long, lonely hours, when his mind didn't drift back to Chandra. It gave him something to hope for. He just had to hold on a little longer and then the soul stone could finally be dealt with.

But just in case…it didn't hurt to have the papers.

Steeling himself against the discomfort, Roman picked up his quill again. He'd already lived longer than many healers had predicted. He'd been lucky, all things considered. But he didn't feel lucky.

He'd known such a fate was coming, waiting for him, for a long time. He had thought he was ready. Why else had he tried to make the most of every moment, in whatever way he could?

But as he lay there in the growing darkness, he yearned desperately for one day more.

While the rest of the palace quieted down for the night, and fires burned beyond its walls, the councilors assembled in the circular chamber. This was no official meeting and not every member was present, both the king's and prince's chairs conspicuously absent.

The latter was no longer surprising to Lord Vaughan, who had called the meeting. And the former's presence was not wanted. Not this time.

They had waited on Ulric long enough, trying to convince him to show himself, to do his duty, as a good king should. It had been months since he'd last graced the council chamber with his presence and Vaughan thought they had waited long enough.

"What's this all about, Vaughan?" Lord Silva asked, coming into the room.

The past months had taken a toll on him. His long gray hair, which once held a lusty sheen, was now dull and lifeless. His eyes were sunken and he looked thinner. They all did, Vaughan suspected. Even he, who had never been what one would consider thin.

"I think you know," Vaughan replied. "We've all known for some time. We need to discuss Ulric. I don't need to remind you how he shirks his duties. Things have only worsened, and yet he no longer so much as attempts to provide a solution."

"And what do you propose we do about it?" Salerno asked. His mustache seemed to droop. "We've tried to convince him, but he won't be moved."

"We, the council, are not without our own power," Vaughan replied, twisting the green ring on his finger. "It's time for us to ponder the question: would Anarsha be better off if Ulric were removed as leader?"

"That's unfair," Lord Daladier spoke up. Quiet Lord Daladier, but loyal to a fault. "He's a good king. He saved us all from the tyranny of the Empire, don't forget."

But enough time had gone by that people *had* forgotten. They had forgotten their primal fear of the Empire.

From the nods of the other councilors, Vaughan gathered he would win more support by praising Ulric than deriding him. Fine; he could play that angle, too.

Vaughan nodded vaguely. "He *was* a good king. But what has he done since then? He sold his soul to make a deal with a demon. It was a noble sacrifice, to be sure, but such bargains come at a price and we are seeing that cost for ourselves. He is not the same man. And what has the demon done for us since? We are no better off now than we were back then."

Lord Silva looked down at the table, unwilling to meet any of their eyes. "There are some who say that what Ulric did was the greatest mistake. If we had surrendered, we would be a vassal state of the Empire, yes, but at least we would be fed. I'm not saying that I agree, but that's what the people are saying in the streets."

Vaughan slammed a fist down upon the table, making a few of the others jump. "We did not sacrifice all that we have in order for this to be the end of our kingdom. We can still save it, but we must act now before it's too late. We must remove Ulric, and his son, while we still have a kingdom. Ulric has only the one heir and everyone knows he won't last. He will not be able to succeed his father and what then? What kind of turmoil will that create?"

Salerno examined his nails. "Are you sure you're not suggesting this simply because you've had to cease hosting those infamous parties of yours, Vaughan?"

Vaughan frowned at the reminder. It was true that he'd had to put a stop to the revelry, no longer able to procure enough food and refreshments. Despite the number of people succumbing to hunger, with no more raids the food shortage had only worsened, to the point where it now affected him.

Most vexing.

He supposed he'd been rather naïve to think that such hardships would never touch him, but he could hardly be the only one in the room to think so.

No, he knew his fellow politicians well enough. The only time they would ever be spurred to action was when they themselves were personally inconvenienced.

He tapped his fingers along the table. "Come now, Salerno, you of all people know this goes beyond such things. If Anarsha falls, there'll be no more lavish parties, no more council. No feasts, no more expensive silks. Every luxury that you enjoy will be gone—and all of us along with it." He shook his head. "Ulric has done his bit. It's time for someone else to step up now."

"Someone like you?"

Vaughan smiled. "I have no desire to be king."

And that was one of the few completely honest things he'd ever said. Why would he wish to be king when he could exert far more influence as a councilor than anyone gave him credit for?

The fact that they were all here, gathered at his behest, was proof enough of that.

"I doubt Ulric will step down," Silva warned.

"We can always hope that he'll see reason, but you're probably right. And if not, then we'll force his hand."

Daladier sucked in a sharp breath. "This is treason, what you speak of!"

Vaughan fixed him with a glower. "It's not treason if it's for the good of the kingdom. I take no more pleasure from this than you do, but even you cannot deny that Ulric needs to go."

"How do you suggest we force his hand?" Salerno asked.

"Nothing violent, if that's what you're worried about," Vaughan assured them. "All we would need to do is invoke the fact that he summoned one of our greatest enemies. In doing so, he went against everything the saints stood for, the values this kingdom was built upon. His reasons may have been noble, but the fact remains that the saints would hardly have approved."

"You seem to forget we all played a role in that," Silva pointed out quietly.

"A fact we need not mention," Vaughan said firmly. "After all...we were only following the orders of our king."

Ulric stood in his chambers, staring out the window at the fires that dotted the landscape below. The need for sleep had finally driven him from the library. The room was dark, only a few lit candles providing any light. The dark velvet curtains on the canopied bed stood out starkly, inky pools of darkness against the surrounding black.

He knew what the fires were, of course. Everyone did by now. But he would not have his people resort to such barbarous acts. He'd already heard reports of what happened when his sentries couldn't reach a body fast enough, and it sickened him.

Not all of the fires were fueled by the dead, however. Some of them were heaped high with wood, harvested from the Valderan rainforest, kept burning day and night to provide warmth.

A few snowflakes drifted lazily past the open windows, just beginning to fall. The smell of smoke coasted on the wind, faint, hardly reaching Ulric at such a height.

He felt a presence stir within the soul stone, becoming as attuned to the demon's habits as his own. He knew when he was no longer alone and he wondered where the demon went when he felt its presence fade, trapped as he was in the stone.

"Your enemies grow in number," the Reaper hissed. *"They close in, even now."*

"Who?" Ulric demanded, a jolt of fear disturbing what had been peaceful reflection only a moment ago. "The Empire?"

"No, not the Empire. This threat lurks within your own walls."

"Enough of your games," Ulric snapped. "Tell me!"

He sensed a shifting, as though the demon were drawing himself up, pleased somehow with Ulric's impatience.

"Your own council. They have decided they are better off without you—and your son. They think someone else should rule in your place, that they know better than you."

White-hot anger surged over Ulric. The audacity of it!

"Treacherous vipers," he hissed.

"So ungrateful, after everything you've done for them."

Yes, none of them would have dared do what he had. None of them would have bargained away their soul. They could bemoan Anarsha's current state all they liked, but if such a decision had been left up to any of them, their kingdom would now belong to the Empire.

They owed him their lives. The only reason they were still alive, still in power, was because of him.

Well, no matter. He could remedy that easily enough.

Ulric summoned some of his guards, those loyal only to him, who had nothing to do with the council, and ordered the councilors rounded up and thrown into the dungeons, where they could do no more harm.

They were traitors, every last one, and if they thought that they could depose him, he would strike first.

Only once the guards returned to him, reporting that it was done, did he leave his chambers, stealing through the castle on near-silent feet, retracing the steps that had led him to his now constant companion.

The cold leaching from the stones seemed to close in the deeper he went, down the stairs, past the room where he had summoned the Reaper. He slowed as he reached the cells, illuminated by the weak, sickly light of the torches.

There were his councilors, brought low. His detractors, his enemies, conspiring against him in the dark. From the torn collar of Vaughan's robes, Ulric surmised the man had put up a fight. Not all of them had gone quietly.

Salerno leaned close, gripping the bars that separated them. "My king, it was Vaughan's idea. I never agreed to anything. I would never—"

Ulric raised a hand, cutting him off. He slowly paced the hall, meeting the gazes of those who were not too ashamed to look him in the eye.

"You think me weak," he murmured. "Unfit to rule. What you fail to see is that I am stronger than ever."

The demon had alerted him to their treachery. He would keep Ulric safe from any other danger, within or without.

Ulric said nothing more to them, ignoring their pleas as he turned to leave. He had nothing more to say. To see them completely at his mercy, any threat they may have posed eliminated, was enough.

Tomorrow, they would be punished. For tonight, they could linger in the cold, with nothing but the stones for company, and reflect on what they had done.

Ulric felt a low humming, the demon's presence, and felt Reaper's approval of what he had done. The council had been a thorn in his side for too long, blocking whatever action he might take and dragging their feet, arguing amongst themselves.

No more. No longer would anyone tell him what to do.

As it should be. He was the king.

Roman met his father at the top of the stairs.

"What are you doing down there?" he asked, though he suspected he already knew.

He'd heard the commotion, the cries of protest as the councilors were dragged from the chamber, and he'd hurried from his room as fast as he were able, arriving just in time to see the last of them taken away.

It wasn't difficult to guess where they had gone—or what would become of them.

"The councilors have betrayed me," Ulric replied. "They've turned against us both. They were plotting to have me overthrown and replaced—and I don't think I need to tell you that they didn't have you in mind as a successor."

"Can you blame them?" Roman challenged. "You've neglected your duties. You don't attend council meetings anymore. I hardly need to point out what's going on in the rest of the kingdom. Things have only gotten worse! Why will you not act?"

But Roman knew. It was there, peeking out from beneath Ulric's robes. The soul stone.

"I have," Ulric protested. "By removing that traitorous council. I should have done it a long time ago."

"Does that mean the raids can begin again?"

If Ulric was no longer interested in pandering to the needs of his councilors and fellow nobles, perhaps some progress could finally be made. But supplies could still not be distributed to the proper recipients if there was nothing to hand out in the first place.

When his father didn't answer, acting as though he hadn't heard, Roman asked, "Father, what will happen to the councilors?"

He wasn't sure he truly wished to know.

"What always becomes of traitors."

"Father, they're not traitors. They were only acting in what they believed to be the kingdom's best interest. If you return to your duties, I'm sure they'll see reason. You can't afford to lose your advisors."

"I have an advisor," Ulric replied. "Far more valuable than any of them."

The stone. As if on cue, Ulric reached up to touch it. There was something to the movement, as if he were hardly aware that he was doing it.

Roman scoffed. "Of course this is the demon's doing. Making you see threats where there are none. Anything to distract from the fact that he is the greatest threat of all!"

"They are a threat!" Ulric roared, Roman taking a step back at the sudden outburst. "To me and to you! Why don't you see?"

"This isn't you, Father!" Roman cried, as Ulric began to walk away. "The demon is poisoning you against everyone, making you see threats lurking around every corner. Soon you'll be the only one left and what then? You must destroy the stone. Return to yourself before it's too late."

Perhaps it already was. Perhaps it had been too late from the moment Ulric struck the bargain. That didn't seem like the kind of path people found their way back from.

Ulric stopped, turning around. "You would have me throw away the one weapon we have. You would have me make myself vulnerable. Weak. Perhaps that would suit you just fine."

Roman froze, the accusation skirting a little too close to the truth. He did not wish to take his father's place, not for his own sake and certainly not for the power it would provide. He longed only to do what his father would not and free Anarsha from the demon's influence.

Would that he could do the same for his father.

Ulric stalked back toward Roman until he was standing before him, his head cocked to one side, as though listening. "He tells me that you are a threat, too. That you would see yourself in my place. I will not listen. I do not believe it."

Yet. The unspoken implication hung in the air between them and Roman swallowed hard.

This time, when his father turned away, he did not call to him.

The next morning, before the sun had even risen, the councilors' sentences were carried out, their bodies left to hang from the castle's parapets, swaying in the wind for all to see. A warning.

Roman stood out on one of the balconies, taking in the gruesome sight. He truly did not recognize his own father. His manic, paranoid father, who saw evil everywhere—but not where he should.

He'd gotten little sleep, his mind replaying their confrontation, and he mulled it over even now.

The demon recognized the threat Roman posed to him. As he stared at the bodies displayed before him, he knew that if the demon managed to convince Ulric that Roman was a threat to him as well, he would share the same fate.

Cold air stung Chandra's cheeks, making her eyes water even when she closed them—which she couldn't afford to do. She was supposed to be scanning the forest below, searching for any sign of deer. She'd settle for something smaller—rabbits or pheasants, if she could get them. If the creatures were smart, they were huddled up somewhere and wouldn't be found.

She shivered, chilled despite Sheboleth's heat, pressing against her legs. They had already been soaring for almost half an hour now and there'd been no sign of anything.

As if sensing her rider's discomfort, Sheboleth folded her wings, slipping below the forest canopy and alighting softly to the ground.

Chandra slid off, her fingers numb and painful within her gloves. She needed to walk, to warm her body back up.

She'd fashioned a bow for herself, spending nearly as much time on it as she did her candles, when she resigned herself to hunting. It was nothing like the one she'd wielded in the army, but it would do in a pinch.

And if not, if it missed, Sheboleth wouldn't.

The two of them had been hunting for the better part of two weeks as things worsened in Anarsha. At first, Sheboleth had been more than willing to accompany Chandra to the market, but now there was so little on offer that it wasn't worth venturing out.

At least this way, her grandmother no longer spared her rations, refusing to eat them, as she had been doing. Chandra tried to get the old woman to eat something, hating watching her waste away in front of her. But her grandmother was too stubborn and had refused, wanting her portion to go to Chandra.

Now, with Sheboleth helping, Chandra no longer had to worry that the woman would wither away to nothing. *If* they could find something to hunt.

Her breath pluming in front of her, Chandra walked along the forest floor, craning her head back to stare up at the trees, admiring their height. Here, her footsteps were softened by fallen leaves, where the frost could not reach.

She froze, whirling, at the sound of something crashing through the undergrowth. The white of a deer's tail waved goodbye as it fled. Chandra drew her bow, but even as she released, she knew the shot would fly wide.

At once, Sheboleth leaped forward, the muscles in her limbs rippling as she gave chase. Chandra waited, breathless in the cold air.

Before the dragon could vanish from sight, she pounced. A scream rang out, an animalistic cry of pain and terror, abruptly cut off.

Sheboleth turned, dragging the deer beside her.

Chandra smiled, warmed despite the chill. "Thanks."

She climbed onto the dragon's back and, gripping the deer in her claws, Sheboleth leapt into the air. Not wanting to parade their catch through the streets, they didn't land again until they had reached Chandra's door.

She could feel eyes on her, but she didn't bother to look. This wasn't the first time Sheboleth had helped her haul a catch back home and if things continued the way they were going, it wouldn't be the last.

Having such an advantage made the neighbors resentful. None of them were fortunate enough to have a dragon who helped them hunt and bring food back to put on their tables.

Chandra tried to spare what food she could and had even gone so far as to suggest she and Sheboleth help some of the others. But in such desperate times, compassion could be dangerous, and whatever happened, she couldn't afford to be seen as weak.

Grunting, Sheboleth dragged the deer over to Chandra's workshop, which doubled as a makeshift butcher shop some days.

Chandra ducked inside, preparing to skin the animal. Sheboleth stood near the doorway, her head turned away, staring toward the street.

Chandra knew even with the deer out of sight, some of them would continue staring. Sheboleth bared her teeth at them in a clear warning.

"I don't like it," she muttered.

"They won't do anything while you're here," Chandra assured her, gently brushing the blade of one of her knives against her thumb, testing its sharpness.

She hoped that would continue to hold true. But she wasn't so sure. She'd seen the look of desperation in some of their eyes and knew, when forced to choose between a slow, painful death and confronting a dragon, some might be tempted to choose the latter. After all, what did they have to lose?

"I know," Sheboleth growled. "But what about when I'm not here?"

Chandra had no answer to that.

Suddenly, the dragon swung back to face her. "I could stay permanently. I don't have to leave."

Chandra paused, startled by the offer. "Where would you stay? There's not much room in the house…"

"I don't care. I'm sure I could cram in somewhere. Or else, stay out here."

Chandra already knew that the cold, while unpleasant, didn't seem to bother the dragon much. It certainly didn't pose nearly the sort of danger to her that it did to a human, warmed from within by her own internal heat.

"If you want," she answered, touched by the dragon's loyalty, the bond that they had forged.

"I do, but is it what you want?"

By now, Chandra knew Sheboleth wanted an honest answer, for her to state what it was she wanted without fear of reprisal.

"Yes. I'd feel much better having you here."

"Then I'm staying."

Chandra let out a sigh of relief. Having the dragon close by would do much to relieve her anxiety. She needn't worry about anyone breaking into the house—or even the workshop—at night.

The cold helped keep the smell down as Chandra went about dressing and skinning the deer, steam escaping from its still-warm body. She wrinkled her nose as another unpleasant, familiar smell drifted to her, heavy in the air.

The smell of smoke. The smell of burning.

It seemed to be always present anymore, and she could tell when they were burning wood for warmth and when they burned bodies. The charred smell of flesh made her want to gag. It was all she could do some days to eat the meat they caught.

She did her best to ignore the smell, but it seemed particularly acrid that day, gathering in the back of her throat, choking her.

It hung like a pall over the kingdom, a cloud as dark as the smoke itself.

She sighed, staring down at the blood on her hands, her knife. "Sheboleth, how long can this go on? Where does it all end?"

For once, the dragon had no answer to give.

XXXIII

The palace held few balconies, but Desmond sought them out in his free time, wanting to stare out over the Capitol, the seat of the Empire. He could pretend, if only for a moment, that he was the emperor—in more than just a charade—surveying his domain.

It filled him with a sense of pride, even if he wasn't this great city's ruler, to look out across its districts. There was evidence of its industry everywhere, a triumph, a study in resilience after the blow they had suffered.

Its dull palette, of bronze and gold, steel and stone, was dulled by the sun's absence, its harsher edges softened in the moonlight. And yet, the city blazed with light, fires still burning even at such a late hour, lending it a golden glow.

But it was the glint of bronze that drew Desmond's eye. Silvered beneath the moon, the latest batch of mechs stood at attention. They were motionless, but something about their posture conveyed a willingness to strike at any moment—though they would need a pilot for that.

They stood several districts below him, but the veritable army that stretched out was impossible to ignore. He had toured the warehouses, foundries, factories, and barracks with Hadrian in the past few weeks.

Progress had seemed slow and yet now that the moment had arrived, it felt like he'd blinked and suddenly, the months and years vanished as though nothing had ever happened.

Akkadia was the Empire once more. Powerful, unflinching. None could stand against her. It was as though their disastrous defeat at the hands of Anarsha had simply never been.

That was the effect, certainly, that he knew Hadrian wanted. The effect portrayed to the public. But Desmond knew better.

"Beautiful, aren't they?"

Without turning, he knew who had come to join him. He heard the voice often enough. It came out of his mouth more than his own. It followed him into his dreams.

The emperor came to join him at the rail, gazing down proudly at his mechs, the way a father might survey his children.

Desmond glanced at him out of the corner of his eye, not wanting his interest to be obvious. They were dressed in similar robes, but neither man wore a mask. They were high enough here that there was no need.

Desmond had forgotten the emperor's true features, how plain they were. He wondered what the other man saw in him now, their differences laid bare.

"At last, our efforts are complete," Hadrian sighed. "We are ready once more to march upon the last free kingdom."

"Is that wise?" Desmond asked, giving voice to the concern that had plagued him since the last battle.

Hadrian turned away from the mechs, his eyes finding Desmond's in the dark and pinning him there. "Should we leave Anarsha alone? Do you think that they have somehow earned their freedom? Have you lost your hunger for conquest?"

"Not at all, my lord. I, too, wish to see the kingdom fall. But what about the demon they summoned? That was no myth; it was real enough. What if we should face it again? We could throw as many mechs at it as we like and never win. It cannot be defeated. It cannot be killed. It is a fight we cannot win."

Even as he spoke the words, he could see Hadrian's gaze dimming, losing interest, and knew he had failed to move the emperor.

No matter how detailed his reports or how impassioned his pleas, he had to remember that Hadrian had not been there that day. He hadn't seen what Desmond had.

And until one laid eyes on the demon and saw what he was capable of for oneself, they could not understand.

The emperor brushed away his concerns. "Whatever became of the creature, the Anarshans clearly do not have it anymore. Or else they would have brought it here. They would have struck while the advantage was theirs and destroyed us by now. The fact that they have not tells me that, for one reason or another, they *cannot*."

Desmond had to admit that Hadrian's argument made sense and he certainly wanted to believe it, but he wasn't so sure. The fact that he wanted to believe it made him wary. Wanting something to be true did not make it so.

"Perhaps that's just Anarsha's way," he argued. "They will not attack us, but they will defend, just as fiercely as ever."

"That is why," Hadrian replied, "they are weak and must be conquered. They need a strong hand to guide them. The demon, if nothing else, is evidence of that. The Anarshans slew their gods—or demons, or whatever you wish to call them—but instead of claiming their newfound freedom and autonomy, they replaced their fallen gods, venerating saints and putting them on pedestals in their place."

"Do you not believe in a higher power, my lord?" Desmond asked.

The emperor spread his arms, taking in the army arrayed below him. "These are my gods. Innovation, modernity, and the machines of war. They are what forged this Empire and they are what will allow it to endure. Anarsha, on the other hand, clings to the past, and it will be their undoing."

Desmond frowned. The demon certainly was Anarsha's past, but if it was to be their undoing, he could see no evidence of it yet. If anything, it seemed more likely their salvation. Were it not for the demon's interference, Anarsha would already belong to the Empire.

But he knew better than to argue with the emperor.

He glanced sidelong at Hadrian again, noting his proximity to the railing. How easy would it be to push him, to lift his body and tip him over the edge.

Desmond was stronger than the emperor—younger, too—and he was confident he could strike before Hadrian had time to react or call out for help.

There would be a moment's shock, but by the time his brain could comprehend what was happening, he would already be hurtling toward the ground.

He studied the emperor silently. No, he would not do such a thing, indulging in the fantasy only within his own mind. But he found it amusing that he could stand beside the emperor and yet the man had no idea what thoughts were lurking just below the surface.

***

The winter passed in Anarsha, but the return of spring brought no hope along with it. Very few people now ventured out into the streets, either having died from the cold and hunger, or they cowered inside, fearful of the violence.

Chandra went nowhere without Sheboleth at her side. Her grandmother's health was declining, continuing the slow decay that had begun during the winter. It was no longer from lack of food, and Chandra feared that her last remaining family member could slip away from her at any time.

They had never been close, not in the way that Chandra imagined other families were, but she spent every spare moment with her, reading to her or simply working nearby, wanting to be close.

She heard nothing more from Roman, not that she had expected to. It sobered her to think that his condition could have worsened, that he could have died, and she wouldn't know of it unless she heard the news making its rounds out on the street.

There were times when she was tempted to ask Sheboleth to fly her up to the palace, but she knew she would not be granted entrance—and it would be foolish to draw further attention to herself.

And so she waited, like everyone else. Waited for what, she wasn't sure. It felt like waiting for the end.

She felt as though she were barely living, going through the motions day to day. With less to trade, the value of most goods had plummeted. It was increasingly hard to make a living from something like candle making. She missed the days when she seemingly had nothing more to worry about than how to coax recalcitrant wax from its mold.

"Maybe we should leave."

Chandra turned to see Sheboleth had followed her. She'd stepped out onto the lawn for a moment, her grandmother having slipped into sleep, lulled by the sound of her reading.

"And go where?" Chandra asked. "There is nowhere to go."

"Anywhere is better than here."

Regardless, it wasn't an option.

Chandra sighed. "I won't leave my grandmother. She may not have much time left, but until then…"

She glanced down at her hands. They were still a young woman's hands, but she felt unspeakably old. When she glanced in the mirror, she thought she looked gaunt, old beyond her years.

She felt as though her youth had been wasted. Everything about the war, about the girl she used to be, seemed far away. Another life, as if it had all happened to someone else.

Chandra could have believed that, if she didn't still carry the grief around with her. And once her grandmother passed, she would be the last of her family. She would have no one left, no friends aside from Sheboleth—who was arguably the staunchest—and the climate in Anarsha made finding a lover unlikely.

She would eventually follow, fading away from the world, without ever knowing that part of life. She would never have children of her own. Chandra wasn't even sure she wanted that for herself, but not having the choice at all left a bitter taste in her mouth.

Her thoughts strayed back to Roman. He was the closest she had ever come to loving someone. She thought the two of them could have been happy together, if he felt the same way, and fate had been kinder.

"Are you lonely?" Sheboleth asked, breaking into her thoughts.

The dragon always seemed to sense whenever she drifted too close to self-pity.

"No," Chandra replied, making sure to pause, to give the question the appropriate consideration so she didn't answer too quickly.

"How could I be?" she added. "When I have a friend like you?"

Sheboleth was a rare kind of friend, indeed, always totally honest. Chandra never had to guess what she was thinking. Unwavering in her loyalty.

Perhaps the two of them could run away, after her grandmother was gone. She would climb onto the dragon's back and soar away. Perhaps they would fly over the Elathan mountains and find out what lay beyond.

The thought cheered her a little. It was a plan, when she otherwise had none.

A plan made her feel grounded, more in control, as if the world wasn't falling to pieces around her.

But before she could do anything with such plans, Anarsha's reprieve finally ran out.

Chandra was in the town square, perusing what the ever-dwindling stalls had to offer. Sheboleth stood beside her. Chandra was haggling with the merchant, about to give in and hand over her few remaining coins, when the dragon's head snapped up sharply and Chandra followed the movement.

"Victor," Chandra whispered.

Her old squad mate sat atop his dragon, Bane, as he stalked down the street. If Victor noticed her, he gave no sign, continuing to call out his news.

"Scouts report the Akkadian Empire is once again on the move!" he shouted. "They are on their way here!"

Something clenched in Chandra's chest. Dread. And beneath that, kindling back to life, was a spark of the anger she thought she had buried and forgotten.

But it wasn't dead yet—and neither was the Empire.

An old threat—nearly forgotten by most, it felt so long ago—had returned. Just as they all feared. And just as they knew it would.

Victor's eyes found hers, devoid of the old malice between them. Instead, Chandra saw only grim resignation and something else—something she would have missed if she hadn't fought beside him, risked her life alongside his.

Fear.

"Saints," Chandra breathed.

XXXIV

Chandra leapt onto Sheboleth's back, her earlier reservations gone. "To the palace! We have to find Roman!" *Before it's too late.*

Hardly knowing what she was doing, Chandra clung to the dragon's frills as she sprang into the air, the palace looming ever nearer. What would she say to Roman after all this time? Did he know about the threat drawing closer to their doors?

Not bothering with the entrance, Sheboleth surged upward toward the towers and balconies, searching for any sign of the prince. The dragon roared, hoping the call would bring someone to investigate, the sound thrumming through Chandra's bones.

"There!" Chandra cried suddenly, pointing, as she caught a glimpse of movement from within. A figure, distorted by the glass, approached the doors to one of the balconies.

The doors parted, revealing the prince. Sheboleth swooped down, alighting on the balcony, the wind from her descent buffeting Roman's hair and his too-loose clothing.

Chandra slid from her back and rushed forward, stopping before the prince as he leaned heavily on his cane. The weight of months of silence hovered between them.

"Is it really you?" Roman asked at last.

Chandra nodded. "I had to come, when I heard the news. The Akkadians are on the move again. They're on their way here."

If possible, Roman suddenly seemed even smaller than before, folding in on himself. "I hadn't heard," he murmured.

"There's still time," Chandra said, wanting to comfort him. To take some of the weight that bowed his back. "We need to find your father and convince him to summon the demon again."

Roman shook his head. "That won't be possible."

Chandra stilled, a chill snaking through her. "Why not?"

"My father sealed the demon away in a soul stone, but he refuses to destroy it. The demon is trapped inside; he cannot take physical form, but he can still whisper poison in my father's ears."

"The soul stone must be destroyed," Sheboleth said, knowing all too well, as a dragon, what would happen if the stone were never destroyed.

"I've tried to convince him, but he won't see reason. I'm sorry, Chandra," Roman said, turning his attention back to her. "No help is coming. Not this time."

The wild, desperate hope in Chandra's chest sputtered and died. "So this is it, then."

There was no one left to stand against the Empire now. Their kingdom had all but fallen, collapsing from within, ripe for the plucking.

All the times Chandra had feared this was it, that any given battle would be her last, that this would be the moment the Empire won, that Anarsha would not be able to withstand the assault…

She had been wrong. This was it. This was the moment there would be no coming back from.

"I will do what I can," Roman promised. "I must go find my father and try to convince him while there's still time." He hesitated, his gaze intent on Chandra, as though memorizing her. "Whatever happens, I am glad to have known you."

Chandra's throat tightened. She couldn't speak, couldn't breathe, couldn't find the words. She knew she should say something, but what? There were no words that were enough for all she longed to express.

In the end, she simply nodded, watching as he turned and walked away, knowing it was the last time they would ever see each other.

Sheboleth shifted her weight on the balcony. "Now what?"

"We go to the barracks," Chandra said, hoping her voice held more conviction than she felt.

If she were going to take up arms to defend her kingdom once more, she was going to do it with a proper bow in her hand.

"They are coming."

The demon didn't have to specify whom he meant for Ulric to understand. He had finally run out of time. The Empire, a threat long believed dead, had returned. He didn't need the demon to tell him what would happen once they arrived.

He left the seclusion of his chambers behind and stalked down the corridors, unsure where he was going. Only when his feet came to a stop outside the council chamber door did he recognize his instinctual urge to summon a meeting, to beseech wisdom from his advisors.

But the men he might have once turned to were all dead.

At his hand.

A wave of horror overcame Ulric and he snatched his hand back from the door. What had he done?

"Sire?"

Ulric turned to see a man standing in the corridor behind him, dressed in rich burgundy velvet, his robes so long they nearly trailed along the ground. A minor nobleman, though the man's name escaped Ulric's memory at the moment.

"The Empire approaches. Please, you must use the demon's power again. Summon it and set it upon our enemies."

The man's face was blanched with fear, but he looked at Ulric with such hope, such assurance that they would once again be saved, delivered from their fate. Ulric hated that such hope was to be in vain.

Within his mind, laughter resounded, loud and harsh. *"Oh, now they want you to use me? Now they encourage you!"*

Ulric did not share the demon's mirth. He looked at the man, his voice sounding flat even to his own ears. "I cannot. I sealed the demon away, years ago."

He watched as that hope faded, replaced by horror, and then rage. Rage was easier, burning hot in the moment, but Ulric knew which would win out in the end.

"You fool!" the man sputtered. "Then you have condemned us all! You did not save us, you merely bought us a reprieve, not a pardon."

Ulric suddenly felt not simply old, but ancient. He waved a languid hand. "Go, then. Seek out whatever you will in your final moments."

He turned his back on the man, the demon still laughing in his mind. Internally, though, despite the image he had just portrayed, Ulric felt anything but calm. His thoughts were jumbled, fear clawing its way up his throat like a trapped beast eager to be free.

"Did I not tell you, old man?" the demon taunted, no need for obsequiousness now. *"Did I not warn you?"*

Yes, he had warned Ulric and Ulric had ignored the signs. He had not wanted to listen, believing himself untouchable. The man who had summoned a demon back into the world and brought an Empire to its knees.

Now it was his kingdom on its knees, the executioner's blade arcing down.

I have been a fool. He had done a terrible thing and the entire world may yet pay for it.

As soon as he was out of sight of the nobleman, he broke into a run. He needed to find Roman.

The barracks were in a state of disarray when Chandra arrived, what few soldiers remained scrambling to take up their positions. If anyone took note of her presence or the fact that she wasn't supposed to be there, they kept such knowledge to themselves.

Chandra strode onto the training fields, where targets, bows and full quivers were laid out in preparation for that day's session, now abandoned.

She snatched one of the quivers and slipped it over her head, hesitated, then grabbed two more, attaching one at each hip. She wasn't used to securing her quivers in that position, but she couldn't afford to pass up the extra arrows.

Tentatively, she tested the longbow, drawing it back all the way to her lips. It had been a long time since she'd last taken one up. Her arms trembled, muscles remembering what to do—what little was left of them.

She climbed back onto Sheboleth. There would be no saddle this time, or leathers, but she didn't have time to waste searching for them. In any case, the lack of armor made little difference. It wouldn't be needed—not for this one.

"Let's go. I want to see if we can catch a glimpse of the army we're expecting."

Sheboleth launched into the air, the compound falling away behind them, wind lashing Chandra's skin. Her eyes stung, vision blurring, and not just from the air rushing past.

This would be the last time the two of them ever flew together. Chandra hunched lower, wanting to savor the moment of freedom, the feeling of flying. She wanted to slow time down, for Sheboleth to never crest the city wall.

But she did, all too soon, rising up and over, the Great Wall vanishing below them. The Badlands spread out before them and Chandra sucked in a breath of dismay.

Already, the army was nearly upon them. There were so many of them, the bronze hides of mechs glinting beneath the gray sky. It was as if the last battle had never happened.

And Chandra knew they could not win. They would need the demon again if they were to stand a chance, and that was no longer possible.

Despite the stone sinking ever lower in her stomach, Chandra was glad she had spoken to Roman. Aside from being able to see him one last time, if she hadn't, she would have still carried the false hope that the demon would return to save them again.

Now, at least, she could face her fate with a clear, unclouded gaze.

Chandra didn't know how many dragons they had left, but she knew it wouldn't be enough. She had seen remarkably few in the brief moments she had ducked back into the barracks to fetch her weapons, and she knew from Sheboleth that many of them had already left Anarsha, turning to their own affairs.

Even at the height of their strength, Chandra doubted it would have been enough to challenge the army arrayed before her. There were not enough people left in all of Anarsha now, and half of them were like her grandmother, in no state to fight.

Her heart twisted at the thought of her grandmother, thankful that she could not see what was coming.

Sheboleth said nothing, turning back to the city. But as soon as they landed and Chandra dismounted, she rounded on her.

"We should leave," the dragon insisted. "Now, while we still have a chance."

"I can't," Chandra refused. "I can't leave her."

"She can come with us."

"Take her, then. Get her to safety."

"Not without you," Sheboleth growled.

Chandra could have cursed her stubbornness. "I *can't.*"

Saints, how could she explain, in a way that made sense?

"This is my kingdom," she cried. "My home. I didn't give up all that I did only to turn my back on her now."

"Anarsha doesn't care about you, Chandra. It never did."

Chandra shook her head, the backs of her eyes beginning to sting, and she blinked fiercely. "Everything that I sacrificed—it can't have been for nothing."

"It will be, if you stay," Sheboleth argued. "Is it really worth sacrificing everything for?"

Chandra drew herself up. "This isn't just about Anarsha. Not anymore. It's about freedom. If the Empire wins, that's it. They own everything. There will be no place left that is free. Anarsha may not be worth sacrificing everything for. But freedom is."

Sheboleth stared at her and Chandra could see frustration and admiration both warring within her green eyes. Finally, she huffed out a breath.

"Fine," she bit out. "Then I am with you, to whatever end."

Chandra's heart swelled with gratitude even as it broke beneath the weight of sorrow. "To whatever end."

Roman hurried down the corridors, pushing his body as fast as it would go. More than once, his legs trembled, threatening to give out, but he gritted his teeth and ignored it. This would be the last demand he ever made of it. It wouldn't likely be needed after today.

He'd already ducked into the library and his father's personal quarters, but Ulric wasn't there. Frustration mounting, Roman began to wish he'd never left his own room. He could have savored a few more moments with Chandra.

He squeezed his eyes shut at the thought of her. He was glad to have seen her one final time, having long since given up hope of that ever happening.

He was half tempted to give it up and return there. Maybe Chandra hadn't left yet. Maybe they could wait out the end together. He thought he would like that, better than being alone, at any rate.

But no, he knew she had already gone. His knees crying out in protest, Roman mounted the stairs to one of the towers, leading neither to his quarters or his father's.

The room was as lushly appointed as either of their quarters, but Roman took no notice of that. The room was empty. His father was not here.

Where was he? The palace was large, a lot of room to cover for just one man, but even so. Perhaps he had already fled, one final attempt to save himself and the demon. It would have been unthinkable of the man Roman had once known, but the thought came as no surprise now.

Heaving a sigh, Roman trudged over to the windows, opening them, pushing the panes outward. It was a beautiful day, if overcast, the air warm on his skin. He leaned over the edge, staring down at the nearing doom.

"Roman."

He spun around, heart in his throat, to see his father standing in the doorway.

"Father—" Roman made to move away from the window and approach his father, but Ulric sank to his knees.

"I'm so sorry," he whispered. "So sorry, my son. I beg your forgiveness. I have sealed the demon away and cannot order it to defend us a second time."

Roman swallowed past the lump in his throat, pulse thundering in his ears. This was it. This was what he had wanted. "That's all right, Father. There's still time to make this right."

Ulric shook his head, inconsolable, tears streaking down his face, his beard. "I was a fool. I see that now. I should have listened to you."

Roman blinked. He couldn't remember if he'd ever seen his father cry. What a piteous figure he made, the man who had always seemed so strong, so much larger than life, reduced to weeping, begging for forgiveness.

For sentencing them all to this fate.

All of the anger, the frustration, Roman had felt toward his father faded away. He could not summon such feelings toward the man kneeling before him, though he deeply wished he had never summoned that wretched beast in the first place.

"It's still not too late," he murmured. "There's something you can do, Father."

Ulric looked up, blinking back tears. "Anything. I'll do anything."

Roman pursed his lips. "Destroy the stone. There are still dragons within the city. Send for one and have the stone destroyed before it's too late."

He wished now that he'd thought to ask Sheboleth to stay, for that very purpose.

Ulric recoiled from him. "Destroy it?"

Roman's stomach sank at the sudden change that had come over his father. Of course, the demon would not let him go so easily. He would rail against Roman and the fate that he would bestow.

"Yes," Roman urged. "You must. We don't want such a powerful weapon falling into the hands of the Empire."

But as soon as the words left his lips, Roman knew they were the wrong thing to say.

"Weapon..." Ulric hissed. "Yes, you're right. We have nothing to fear. The beast will protect me. He's promised me himself."

"He's a liar!" Roman shouted. "Why can't you see that?"

But Ulric's eyes had clouded over and he knew his father was lost to him. He was too far gone, lost to the demon's influence, and Roman could not reach him.

Desperately, Roman lunged, his fingers clawing for the stone around his father's neck. But Ulric pushed him aside, tossing him to the ground as easily as one might a child.

Roman cried out as he struck the floor, staring up at his father, who had moved to the window, watching the enemy approach.

Roman was not strong enough and so he, too, was helpless to do anything but watch.

Chandra watched as the remains of the reduced army scrambled to set up siege weaponry, to man the walls and towers. But they were unorganized and more than that, scared.

Together, she and Sheboleth turned to watch the Akkadians approach, waiting to see if they would reach the Great Wall or if they would be miraculously spared a second time.

Please, Chandra prayed to the saints, the only word that would come, unsure of what exactly she was asking for. *Please.*

Outside the city, the refugees that had remained abandoned their encampments, trying desperately to get into the city. Some of them succeeded, beating the gates open, and they fled inside. But where did they think they would go? There was nowhere to go.

As the line of mechs drew nearer, the siege weapons fired—ballistae, trebuchets, and catapults all brought to bear. But the Akkadian line didn't so much as flinch, continuing implacably onward.

Sheboleth sprang forward as they passed through the gates, the entrance creating a chokepoint. Dimly, Chandra was aware of other dragons and their riders moving around them, raking the advancing line with fire.

For a moment, the advance seemed to stall. But the Akkadians had brought ballistae of their own, forcing the dragons to retreat back into the city. The line kept coming, stepping over the fallen mechs, pressing the Anarshans ever further back, and countering with fire of their own.

Hissing, Sheboleth turned and retreated further into the city. Chandra glanced over her shoulder as the dragon ran. The mechs were splitting up, flooding the streets that the

Anarshans had given up. In their midst, she glimpsed a few foot soldiers and her fingers twitched on her bowstring, eager to lash out.

"Chandra!"

Sheboleth skidded to a halt. Victor raised one hand in acknowledgement, Bane striding over to meet them. They were, Chandra realized, in the same square where she'd last seen him, making his announcement, warning the people to be ready.

All those people...

Everyone in the homes and businesses along the streets that had been surrendered were at the mercy of the Empire now. Chandra shuddered to think of it, horror and fury warring within her. They were too powerful, too big to be contained in her body, leaving no room for fear—or anything else.

Chandra could still hear the sound of ballistae firing from the Great Wall, but those belonged to Anarsha. The sound, familiar and chilling, didn't raise the hair on her arms. But the hiss of steam and metallic clanking, drawing nearer, did.

"They're coming," Victor said grimly.

"They'll make it all the way to the palace," Chandra said.

"Yes. If someone doesn't stop them."

His dark eyes found hers and an understanding flashed between them. They couldn't keep running. There was nowhere to go. They had to make a stand somewhere.

Chandra turned, her eyes finding what she thought was the tower where she had found Roman, though it was hard to tell at such distance.

Her gaze lowered, drawn by a flash of viper green rushing past, down the street.

"Anake!" she cried out.

Vitanni jerked to a halt and Anake turned in the saddle to face them.

"You should get out, while you still can," she said. "You have minutes at the most before they're upon you."

"You're running?" Chandra asked, disappointment rising above her anger for a moment.

Anake's expression hardened. "I will not throw my life away for a kingdom that refused to fight for my own and refuses, even now, to fight for itself." Her eyes softened, looking at Chandra with something resembling pity. "I still believe we can fight back. But not here. Not like this."

She turned, urging Vitanni onward.

"Anake!" Chandra screamed after her, but the other woman didn't acknowledge her cry. Chandra watched them until the two were out of sight.

"Let her go," Victor muttered. "She's right; there's no winning this." He looked down at Chandra. "You can run, if you like. I won't think any less of you for it."

"But I would," Chandra said, raising her chin defiantly. "I'm staying."

Victor nodded. "I thought you might. And I'll be right here with you."

How strange, to be facing down the end with the man she had once so despised. But it was as Khan had implored them, long ago. She knew who the real enemy was.

She swung down from Sheboleth's back, feeling too exposed up there, too easy of a target. Nocking an arrow to her bow, she stood, muscles tensed, the four of them waiting as the Akkadians poured into the city.

<h1 style="text-align:center">XXXV</h1>

From a safe distance away, in the Badlands, Desmond watched as the Empire's forces flooded the city. The Anarshans had fought fiercely, managing to keep them out for a little while. But one by one, he watched as dragons plummeted out of the air, brought down by ballistae, until no more rose above the city walls. And where the mechs went, smoke sprouted along their route, making them easy to track. He could see a hint of fire, flickering behind the city's walls.

This was no longer about mere conquest. It was about revenge, making an example of the kingdom that had defied Akkadia for too long.

Desmond tore his gaze away from the city, studying the blackened earth around him, scorched forever by the demon that had walked here. They had passed the lifeless husks of crushed mechs and more than a few sets of armor, no trace left of the person who had once worn it.

Beside him, the emperor took a deep breath. "It's time."

Like Hadrian, Desmond wore full battle armor. It was heavier than he'd expected, even though it, of course, fit him like a glove. He'd only ever worn the barest smattering of armor and it was so different from the light uniform he was used to.

Within a mech, there was no need for such protection. The mech's iron hide would offer more armor than what they wore now could ever hope to provide. But they weren't in mechs now. Desmond felt like he *was* the mech, or at least wearing one.

The emperor turned to face him and the other remaining Mask. No replacement had yet been found for the one that had fallen victim to the Shemaran assassin.

They were dressed identically, the black armor both gleaming in the gray light and absorbing it, edged in gold. None of them wore a helm, though. Just the simple, familiar mask.

"The mechs will have advanced far enough by now," Hadrian stated. "And if we should encounter any opposition…"

He glanced meaningfully at the sword at Desmond's side. Desmond had no doubt the emperor knew how to wield one of his own. Part of him hoped he'd get to see Hadrian's prowess with his own eyes. The other part did not relish the idea of facing a foe without his mech.

He'd done it before and he could do it again. But he was a mech pilot, first and foremost. In the past, when he'd stepped onto the battlefield alone, it had been out of necessity.

"Come," Hadrian barked, his tone brooking no argument.

He strode forward, his armor clanking as the plates shifted against each other. Desmond suppressed a sigh. With no choice, he hurried to stand at the emperor's side, the other Mask doing the same.

The trudge across the Badlands seemed to take forever. Desmond kept holding his breath, expecting the demon to appear at any moment, looming over the Great Wall, to seal their doom.

He was surprised the beast hadn't already appeared. Perhaps the emperor was right and the Anarshans, for whatever reason, couldn't summon the creature again.

Suddenly, the Great Wall towered over them and the three men passed underneath. No demon waited for them.

This part of the city was eerily silent. Desmond glanced up as they passed beneath the wall. The siege engines that had fired upon the advancing Akkadians were silent, no soldiers left to man them, having all fled or been killed.

Passing through the gate, Desmond edged around fallen mechs, their hulls darkened and warped by fire. He shuddered at the sight, remembering all too well how close he had come on more than one occasion to burning alive. The Anarshans had at least some dragons left.

Better a hundred dragons than that demon.

No one came to meet them as they strolled through the city, their footsteps echoing on the cobbles. The further they advanced, Desmond began to hear signs of activity, though he saw no one. Cries carried over the lingering smoke and a roar rang out in the distance.

A few times, he thought perhaps he glimpsed a figure, fleeing into the smoke, but he couldn't be sure.

He kept one hand on his sword, ready to rip it free at a moment's notice. The only people he had seen for certain were bodies, lying in the street where they'd fallen. Most of them civilian, by the look of it.

Hadrian had given the order, when both armies had set out from Elath and Shemar, joining before the Badlands, that not every Anarshan was to be killed. The Empire could always use more slaves and lower-class citizens to add to its ranks.

But the soldiers, Desmond knew, were not going to discriminate in who they spared and who they did not.

He sucked in a deep, smoke-filled breath. This was it. He could scarcely believe he was really here, walking the streets of this city—beside the emperor, no less!

He had imagined Anarsha's fall countless times, but never like this. It was eerie, how quiet the city was in the mech's wake. If anyone had survived their initial rampage, they were either in hiding or had fled deeper into the city.

Onward they went, the ground rising beneath their feet, as the palace drew near.

Unable—or unwilling—to join his father at the window, Roman stood off to the side. He did not want to look. His imagination could conjure well enough what it was he would see.

He imagined his city on fire, the lines of mechs that he had glimpsed earlier racing through the streets, cutting down all in their path.

His thoughts strayed to Chandra. Was she still here, somewhere? Had she fled, realizing the hopelessness of the situation? He hoped she had escaped; he wouldn't think less of her for it. But if she hadn't…was she still fighting valiantly down there, or had she already fallen?

He wanted to weep, but for what, exactly, he wasn't sure. It wouldn't do any good anyway.

His back to the windows, Roman faced the door to the tower. He was still facing it when it burst open and three figures entered.

Ulric spun from the window, indignation burning in his eyes, as if that would be enough to stop them.

The three figures—men, Roman assumed, from their height and builds—wore black armor. They looked identical, no distinguishing features to separate one from the other. Their faces were blank, expressionless masks. And in each of their hands was a drawn blade.

Roman's instinct was to step in front of his father, to shield him from these men and whatever they intended to do. But he dared not move, frozen to the spot.

One of the men tilted his masked head to one side. "King Ulric, I presume?"

Ulric raised his chin. "What do you want with me? If it's surrender, I'll never grant it."

Fear clawed its way around Roman's throat. Everyone else in the palace must already be dead, for these men to make their way up to the tower.

He stared at his father, who displayed not a trace of fear. He doubted the Akkadians would honor a surrender even if it was granted, but for his father to be so defiant at the end, as though no harm would come to him…

He still thinks the demon will save him, Roman realized. *Even now.*

"No need," the Akkadian replied. "Your kingdom has fallen and now it's your turn."

He gestured to one of the other masked men, who stepped forward, the blade gleaming in his hand.

"No!" Roman cried, darting forward.

He saw the blade draw back. He didn't see the moment it pierced his stomach, but he felt it, mouth opening in a silent scream, the air stolen from his lungs.

"Roman!" Ulric roared.

The prince barely felt it as the sword was yanked back and he collapsed to the floor. He peered up at the scene before him, tilted sideways, one hand pressed to his stomach. He could feel the blood spilling through his fingers, pooling around him, seeping into his clothes, and he suddenly felt cold.

The Akkadian who had spoken stepped forward, his own blade drawn back, primed for the kill. Roman tried to warn his father, but no words would come. Not even a sound.

He watched as the blade took his father in the chest, sprouting clean through the other side. Roman whimpered, a fresh wave of pain rolling through him, as if he were the one being stabbed, a second time.

The tip of the sword had punctured through Ulric's robes cleanly, no armor to shield him. There, having fallen free of his clothes, resting just to the side of the blade, lay the soul stone, unharmed.

Freeing his sword, the Akkadian let Ulric sink down onto the floor beside his son. Roman tried to reach out to him, to say something, but his father's eyes were already glassy. He was gone, his suffering ended, while Roman lingered.

The Akkadian paused, standing over Ulric, his gaze snared by the soul stone.

"What's this?" he murmured, lifting the chain with the tip of his sword. Leaning down, he freed it from around Ulric's neck.

No, Roman cried, the word reverberating only within his own mind. His voice was gone. *No...*

The soul stone could not fall into the hands of the Empire. They did not realize what they were dealing with. Or even if they did, he doubted they would destroy it. If everything were to end like this, at least let the stone be destroyed...

He reached out one hand feebly, as if he could either reach the stone or wrest control of it away. His fingers unfurled languidly, far too slow, and then his hand dropped back to the floor.

He was too weak. He was out of time, like Anarsha itself. Roman let his eyes drift closed. He was no longer cold, no longer in pain. His body felt strangely weightless, almost the way it had when he'd had a particularly bad fever as a child.

Was this what death felt like? Yes, he could sense it now, hovering. It had come to claim him at last, though not in the way he'd always thought.

No matter. He was ready, to be free of the body that had too often failed him, to leave all the suffering and sorrow of this day behind.

And perhaps, he mused, his last conscious thought, if the Empire took the soul stone and never destroyed it—perhaps it was only just if the Empire reaped the consequences.

Desmond stared at the stone in Hadrian's palm. The emperor's sword gleamed red, having claimed the Anarshan king. Desmond's own blade was similarly stained, having cut down the prince, laying at his feet.

With the two monarchs deposed, there was only one thing of interest in the room now: the stone.

Desmond wondered at the significance of it. It looked strangely familiar and it hadn't escaped his notice that the prince, in his last desperate moments, had tried to reach for it.

What was so important about this stone that the prince would reach for it instead of his own father?

Then again, perhaps their relationship had been a poor one, not unlike his own relationship with his father.

The memory of his father triggered something in Desmond and suddenly, he realized why the stone looked so familiar. The color was wrong—a rich amber instead of red—but it looked exactly like the indestructible stones that had been harvested from his father's mine.

And he knew then, more certain than he'd ever been, that he had to have it. Desmond couldn't have explained why, if asked. But the powerful, overwhelming urge to take it, to possess it, would not be ignored.

He recognized power when he saw it and he could sense power emanating from the stone, drawn to it, a lure impossible to resist. As he stared at it, the amber surface rippled and a great, fiery eye looked back at him. It was both yellow and orange, the color of flame itself, the slitted pupil fixed on him.

Desmond's breath hitched. Somehow, this was the demon, the beast that Ulric had summoned, now safely contained within the amulet. For that was what the stone was. He could sense it.

He had seen the power on display that day. The one who could wield that kind of power could do anything. No one would be able to criticize him. He would cease to never be good enough, never measuring up. His life would cease to be meaningless in the eyes of others.

With that amulet, he could ascend to the position of emperor himself. He could be powerful. He could be all that his family had hoped, wanted for him, and more.

Desmond's actions felt not entirely his own, and yet, he'd never felt so in control. Finally, he was choosing for himself, seizing what was rightfully his.

He drew back his bloodied sword, punching it through Hadrian's neck, in the gap between armor and mask. He'd noted the vulnerability in his own armor and knew exactly where a strike would hit.

The emperor let out a choked, gurgling sound, as he staggered away, one hand reaching up to staunch an undammable river. Desmond imagined his eyes wide beneath the mask, horror dawning in his last moments.

"What are you doing?" the other Mask cried.

They were trained not to think, but to act. But Desmond's actions were so unexpected, so unthinkable, that the Mask hesitated. And it cost him.

Desmond whirled, his blade already flashing toward that weak spot. The blade bit into the Mask's neck, severing his head from his shoulders.

With one shaking hand, Desmond pulled his own mask away from his face as he took in what he'd done. The Masks were created to protect the emperor. No one would ever think such devoted servants would be the one to turn on him.

Desmond stood at the pinnacle of a tower, the highest vantage point overlooking a decimated, fallen kingdom. He stood in a room full of dead men. Where once there had been five, only one would walk out again.

Blood soaked the rich carpets. It was spattered on the wall from when he'd swung his sword. The air was thick with its copper tang, but Desmond was no stranger to the sight or smell of death.

Letting out a breath, he reached down, retrieving the amulet from where it had fallen out of Hadrian's grasp.

Once more, certainty filled his mind, a plan already forming. He was not out of danger yet, but he knew how he could use this. How he would spin it.

He would assume Hadrian's identity. After giving up his own, it would be easy. He had lived as the emperor, *been* the emperor, for some time now. He knew everything about Hadrian, his habits, his desires, his every little quirk. There was no one better suited to assume his identity and take his place.

Desmond would claim that the final confrontation with the Anarshan heathens had been fierce. The king and his son had put up fierce resistance and would not go quietly. He might even go so far as to say that the pagan Anarshans summoned a wicked power to attack him—but it had all been in vain.

He had proven triumphant—though barely. Victory had come at the cost of his two remaining Masks and he himself had been left terribly scarred by the incident. He would wear the mask from then onward to hide his wounds—and no one would ever guess at his true identity, the face beneath the mask.

Desmond smirked. Yes, that would suit him just fine.

The eye he had glimpsed was gone, no longer visible in the amulet's surface, but he felt a presence stir. He was no longer alone in the room. *The demon.*

And then, a voice, *"A kingdom fallen. A throne deposed. Just as I warned, but he would not listen."*

Desmond sensed the beast's disdain for Ulric, almost as though he could feel the baleful eye glaring down at the corpse.

"Ulric was a fool. He risked much, and gave up even more, to bring me into this world. He was frightened of the power he had summoned. And so, rather than use such power, he chained me within this stone."

The man was a fool, Desmond agreed. That was why the demon had not attacked, had not reappeared to stop them. He was unable to take physical form.

Ulric had been too afraid of the demon's power to use it. He could have marched upon the Capitol. He could have brought Akkadia to its knees, finished what had begun in the Badlands that day, and destroyed the Empire entirely.

Instead, he had cowered in fear. And now, he lay dead at Desmond's feet.

"Ulric's mind was weak and failed him in the end. But you," the demon purred. *"You are different. I sense something more in you. Not only do you desire power, you recognize it, and you're not afraid to reach out and take it. Together, emperor, we will do great things."*

Chandra felt no satisfaction as her arrow slipped through the gap between mechs and found one of the foot soldiers. There were too many of them. She'd known that before they'd even arrived, coming in waves.

Sheboleth lashed out at another mech, her claws rending through metal. On her other side, Bane kept the rest at bay with a torrent of flame. But it wouldn't be enough. Eventually, they would be overrun.

Much of the city was already on fire. There was nothing left to fight for, nothing left to save—other than pride. Chandra didn't regret her decision not to accompany Anake, but she did regret that everything had come to this.

With a savage swipe, Sheboleth struck down another mech. She bared her teeth at the advancing enemy lines, roaring out a challenge, daring any to come within reach of her claws.

Chandra drew her bowstring back and let another arrow fly. A sense of desperation rose within her, battling with her fury. Fury that raged all the hotter for its own impotence.

She could scream and curse. She could rage at the world and damn the saints, but it would change nothing. If her fury were enough to burn the Akkadians from the face of the earth, they would already be gone. But it wasn't.

It wasn't enough.

This story only ended one way, but not everyone's had to come to an end. Perhaps Anake was right. Perhaps there was more that could yet be written. But not if they stayed.

"Sheboleth," she called, hoping that the saints would grant her this one prayer. "You need to go."

The dragon turned to her. "What?"

"You need to go," Chandra repeated. "Get out of here."

"Not without you," Sheboleth growled.

"I'm not going."

"Then neither am I."

Chandra blinked back tears, both touched and frustrated by the dragon's loyalty. "Please, Sheboleth. I don't want all of this to be in vain, and it will be if there's no one left to keep fighting."

"I'm not leaving you!"

Chandra shook her head, her vision completely blurred, all but useless. "Please, go. Remember what happened today. Someone should. Maybe one day what happened here will be avenged. But not if there's no one left to remember." She swallowed back the sob that threatened to rise in her throat. "Please, if you've ever cared about me, do this one last thing. For me."

Amidst her tears, she met Sheboleth's gaze, the brilliant green bright and blazing.

"Is this really what you want?" Sheboleth asked heavily.

No, Chandra thought. *I want Callum and Gideon back. I want to see Roman again. I want my grandmother to be well. I want to be in my workshop, making bayberry candles. I want this war to be over. I want the Empire gone.*

The one thing, however, that she could not wish was that the war had never happened. Horrible and selfish as that may have been, if the war had never happened, Chandra would never have met the dragon standing beside her now.

Their friendship was one she wouldn't have traded for anything. And that was why she wanted Sheboleth to go.

To live.

That was what she wanted.

"Yes."

She could see the pain in Sheboleth's eyes, the effort it took to tear herself away. For a moment, she pressed her muzzle to Chandra's forehead.

No words passed between them. There was no need and nothing that would have been enough to convey all that needed to be said.

Maybe Sheboleth would find Anake and they would keep fighting against the Empire in whatever way they could. Maybe, one day, Sheboleth would finish what they had begun, do what Chandra could not, and see the Empire fallen at last.

But none of that would be possible if Sheboleth did not go. It hurt to lose her, but it would hurt even more to lose her in a different way.

Wordlessly, Sheboleth pulled away, severing the connection. Chandra felt cold in the dragon's sudden absence. She watched as Sheboleth turned away, her wings spread wide, and launched herself into the air, taking a piece of Chandra with her.

Chandra wanted to watch until she was out of sight, but there was no time. With only Bane left to defend both her and Victor, the Akkadians closed in.

An inhuman cry rang out as one of the mechs brought the remaining dragon down, its metallic jaws clamped around Bane's neck. With Victor, of all people, by her side, Chandra raised her bow.

Finished with Bane, the mech turned on Victor next. Claws raised, it struck him down in front of Chandra, his body shredded to ribbons.

Chandra swallowed. Her turn had come. Strangely, she was not afraid. The rage still burned, hot as ever, crowding out all other emotions.

Fiercely defiant until the end.

"Anarsha will rise again!" she screamed.

The mech turned toward her. Briefly, she wondered if it would incinerate her, if she would die the way Gideon had, or if it would slash her, the way it had Victor.

In the end, it was neither. Its massive foot pushed her to the ground, cutting off her war cry. One of its claws pierced straight through her. And then it was gone.

Chandra stared up at the sky, what she could see of it through the smoke. The gray clouds were beginning to clear, revealing a strip of blue. Sheboleth was gone, nowhere in sight, and that brought a smile to Chandra's lips. Her body might be lying on the ground, but her soul was up there, flying free.

Anarsha will rise again.

She no longer had the breath to shout the words, but she could still hear the echo. Her spirit carried on the cry. Even as sound faded around her, those words continued to ring in her ears.

They were the words that followed her into the dark.

Thank you for reading!

When I was twelve, I decided that my dream was to become a published author. I have since achieved that dream, but an author is nothing without their readers. So thank you, reader, for giving this book a chance.

If you enjoyed this book, it would mean the world to me if you would consider leaving a review on Amazon/Goodreads. Reviews are essential for authors. They help our books get seen, they help our books get promoted, and they can be the difference between whether or not another reader decides to take a chance on a book.

Thank you again for your support and happy reading!

ABOUT THE AUTHOR

Rachel Terry grew up in a small town where nothing much ever happened, dreaming of grand adventures and far-away places, which she found between the pages of books. When not writing, she can be found reading, making YouTube videos, gaming with friends, or indulging in her love of history. She currently resides in the Midwest with her family and a cat named Crinkles.

Visit her online at: rachel-terry.com

YouTube: RachelTerryAuthor

Instagram: rterrywriter

TikTok: rterrywriter

Facebook: rachelterryauthor

BEYOND THE THRONE

BEYOND THE THRONE
Empire of Engines Book 1

Once there were four kingdoms.
Now there is only the Empire.

But every empire must fall…

THE PHOENIX AND THE CROWN

THE PHOENIX AND THE CROWN
Atlas Sea Book 1

A pirate with a deadly secret.
A princess desperate to save her dying kingdom.